The HARLOT COUNTESS

JOANNA SHUPE

ZEBRA BOOKS
KENSINGTON PUBLISHING CORP.

http://www.kensingtonbooks.com

ZEBRA BOOKS are published by

Kensington Publishing Corp.
119 West 40th Street
New York, NY 10018

All Kensington titles, imprints and distributed lines are
available at special quantity discounts for bulk purchases
for sales promotion, premiums, fund-raising, educational
or institutional use.

Special book excerpts or customized printings can also be
created to fit specific needs. For details, write or phone
the office of the Kensington Sales Manager. Attn.: Sales
Department. Kensington Publishing Corp., 119 West 40th
Street, New York, NY 10018. Phone: 1-800-221-2647.

Zebra and the Z logo Reg. U.S. Pat. & TM Off.

First Printing: May 2015
ISBN-13: 978-1-4201-3554-1
ISBN-10: 1-4201-3554-6

First Electronic Edition: May 2015
eISBN-13: 978-1-4201-3555-8
eISBN-10: 1-4201-3555-4

10 9 8 7 6 5 4 3 2 1

Printed in the United States of America

Chapter One

Spring, 1809
London

Silence rippled throughout the ballroom the moment her slipper hit the top step.

Before Lady Margaret Neeley had a chance to comment on this odd reaction, her mother began tugging her down the stairs. Only then did the impending doom become apparent: the way each person avoided her gaze, the hushed tones sallied around the room, dancers paused mid-turn.

And she realized at once that they knew.

They *knew.*

Somehow, despite her best efforts, stories of what happened the night before had circulated through the streets of London this afternoon. On morning calls, rides in Hyde Park, and promenades down Rotten Row, the *ton* had spread the tale hither and yon.

With Maggie's younger sister ill today, Mama hadn't wanted to go on calls. Relieved, Maggie had spent the time drawing, grateful that they hadn't received any callers. Now it was clear why.

She hadn't done anything wrong, she wanted to shout. In fact, she had tried very hard during her debut to appear a proper English girl. With the black hair and fiery temper of her Irish father, it had been a constant battle. She neither looked nor acted like all the other girls, and the *ton* seemed to enjoy casting her in the role of outsider despite that she'd spent most of her life in London.

"Why has everyone gone quiet?" Mama hissed in her ear. "What have you done, Margaret?"

Of course Mama would pick up on the disquiet. Also unsurprising she would place the blame for the uneasiness squarely at Maggie's feet. Even still, Maggie couldn't answer. A lump had lodged in her throat and even breathing was a challenge.

Escape, her mind cried. Just run away and pretend this whole evening never happened. But she'd done nothing wrong. Surely someone would believe her. All she had to do was explain what had occurred in the Lockheed gardens.

Lifting her chin, she continued down toward the glittering candlelight. Stubbornness had forever been a defect in her character, so everyone said. Mama lamented that Maggie would argue long after the point had been made. So she would not turn tail and run, though her stomach had tied itself into knots. No, she would face them, if only to prove she could do it.

When they reached the bottom of the steps, the quiet was deafening. Their hosts did not bustle forth to greet them. Not one of her few friends rushed over to share gossip or compliment her dress. No young buck approached to request a spot on her dance card.

Instead, the crowd swelled backward as if an untamed beast had wandered inside and might run amok at any moment.

"Come," her mother ordered, taking Maggie's elbow. "Let us return home."

"No," Maggie whispered emphatically. What had happened was not her fault, and she would not allow anyone to bully her. Someone would believe—

A blur of blue silk sharpened into the flushed features of Lady Amelia. "I cannot believe you are so foolish as to show your face," the girl hissed.

Maggie straightened her shoulders and focused on her friend. "Whatever you have heard—"

"He told me. Did you think he would not? My betrothed confided in me of your . . . your *wickedness*, Margaret. You tried to steal him from me, but you failed."

The entire room was now avidly watching and listening to this conversation. Even the orchestra had quieted. "Amelia, why would I—"

"You were always jealous. I've had three offers this Season and you haven't had a one. It comes as no surprise that you would try to steal Mr. Davenport for yourself." As the heir to Viscount Cranford, Mr. Davenport was widely considered the most eligible man in London. He had proposed to Amelia more than a month ago and Maggie had been nothing but pleased for the other girl.

So Maggie ignored her mother's gasp and kept her eyes trained on Amelia. "You are wrong."

"Amelia." Lady Rockland appeared and tugged on her daughter's arm. "Come away this instant. You will ruin yourself by even speaking to that . . ." She did not finish, did not add the hateful word before spinning away in a flurry of obvious revulsion. Maggie could well imagine what Lady Rockland had been about to say, however.

Whore. Harlot. Strumpet.

Is that what she'd become in their eyes? It seemed incomprehensible, especially since Mr. Davenport had lied. Maggie had agreed to meet him to, as he'd said, discuss Amelia. Yet once on the edge of the gardens, it had become apparent the young man had something else in mind. He'd grabbed her, tried to pull her close and put his mouth on her. He'd ripped her dress. Maggie had struck back in the one place it counted on a man and he'd released her. When she'd hurried back to the house, the couple arriving on the terrace must have drawn their own conclusions about her dishabille.

Mr. Davenport had tricked her. Attacked her. Then he'd compounded the sin by lying about it to Amelia, one of the few girls Maggie had befriended. The need to make everyone understand tore at her insides. Did no one care for the truth?

As she swept the room with her gaze, the hatred staring back at her made it undeniably clear that the truth did not matter. The *ton* had passed judgment. She wanted to scream with the unfairness of it. Would no one come to her aid? Surely one of the other unmarried young girls or the man she thought—

More than a little desperately, she searched the room, this time for a tall, blond-haired man. He had been her safe harbor this Season, the one person who truly knew her, who would believe she'd never do anything so reckless. Likely he'd heard what happened by now. So why had Simon not stepped forward to defend her?

There, in the back of the ballroom. Her eyes locked with the brilliant blue gaze she knew so well, a gaze that had sparkled down at her for more nights than she could count. His eyes were not sparkling now, however; they were flat, completely devoid of any emotion whatsoever. A flush slowly spread over his cheeks, almost as if he was . . . angry or perhaps embarrassed—which made no sense at all.

She clasped her gloved hands together tightly, silently imploring him to rescue her. Yet he made no move to come closer. Holding her gaze, he raised his champagne glass and drained it.

Hope bloomed when Simon shifted—only to be quashed when she realized what had happened. He'd presented her with his back.

Simon had turned away.

No one stirred. No one spoke. It seemed as if they were all waiting to see what she would do. Hysteria bubbled up in Maggie's chest, a portentous weight crushing her lungs.

Dear God. What was to become of her?

Chapter Two

December 1819
London

A man's past could easily be forgotten—unless it hung in a shop window on the busiest stretch of St. James, of course.

Simon Barrett, the eighth Earl of Winchester, stood frozen in the cold winter air, staring at yet another shining reminder of his illustrious, drunken youth. Despite the frigid temperature, an uncomfortable heat crawled up his neck. Hell, he hadn't blushed since boyhood.

Still, he couldn't drag his eyes away from the drawing in the print shop window, a depiction of a man too soused to stand while a lady nearby was robbed of her jewels. There could be no doubt of the man's identity. As if the tall frame, blond hair, and bright blue eyes weren't enough, the artist had provided the character with a name: Lord Winejester.

Bloody hell.

"I'd almost forgotten that side of you, the rogue from our youth."

Simon glanced at his good friend Damien Beecham, Viscount Quint. "Rather the artist's point, I believe."

Simon wondered again why this artist, Lemarc, had fixated on him. Was one of his opponents accountable for the cartoons? One did not rise to the upper ranks of Parliament without stepping on some toes.

"What number is this? I daresay it's the fourth or fifth caricature of you in the last year. Lord Winejester is becoming quite popular. Mayhap you'll get a commemorative spoon or plate, like Rowlandson's Dr. Syntax," Quint said, referring to the artist's popular fictitious character.

"Oh, to dream," Simon drawled.

Quint chuckled and nudged Simon's shoulder. "Come now. You have laughed off the others. Why so grim now?"

Not entirely true. Simon may have laughed publicly, but privately these cartoons worried him. He'd worked too hard building his reputation to allow it to be tarnished. His influence and prestige amongst his peers would suffer if he continued to be portrayed as a buffoon. Mayhap it was time to suggest a certain artist apply his skills elsewhere.

And if said suggestion was perceived as a threat, well then, so be it.

"Shall we go inside?"

A bell tinkled over the door as Simon entered, Quint on his heels. A spacious room, the shop had rows of windows set high, right up to the ceiling, allowing light to bounce off every available surface, even on a gray winter day such as this. Framed art crowded the walls—landscapes, portraits, fashion plates, and life scenes in all different shapes and sizes—while racks of unframed canvases rested in the far corner. Simon strode to the long counter along the back wall, where an older woman stood patiently waiting. From behind small, rounded spectacles, her eyes widened and darted to the front window before settling back on his face. *Well, at least I won't need to introduce myself.*

She dropped a curtsy. "Good afternoon, my lords."

Simon removed his hat and placed it on the counter. "Good afternoon. I should like to speak with the owner."

"I am Mrs. McGinnis, the owner. Would your lordship be interested in purchasing a print?"

"Not today. I am more interested in information." He gestured to the front window. "Can you tell me how I might find the artist Lemarc? I find his work . . . interesting." Quint snickered, but Simon ignored him.

"I am afraid the artist wishes to remain anonymous, my lord."

This unsurprising response didn't deter him in the least. Over the past few weeks, he'd made some casual inquiries regarding the artist and learned Lemarc was a sobriquet. "What if I offer to pay you for the information? Say, ten pounds."

Her lips twitched and he got the distinct impression Mrs. McGinnis held back a smile. "My lord, I've had an offer as high as fifty pounds."

"What about one hundred pounds?"

"I must apologize, my lord, but my loyalties remain with the artist. It would not be proper for me to disregard his wishes."

Inwardly, he cursed the woman's stubbornness,

though one had to admire her devotion to Lemarc. "I'd like to purchase his cartoon in the window, then."

Mrs. McGinnis shook her head. "I must apologize again to your lordship. That particular drawing is not for sale."

His jaw nearly dropped. "Not for sale? No matter the offer?"

"No matter what your lordship offers. The artist would prefer to keep the piece in his own private collection."

Damnation. Simon drummed his fingers on the counter, his mind spinning. He couldn't even buy the cartoons to get rid of them.

Quint leaned forward. "Are there any other Lemarc pieces for sale?"

"Why, yes, my lord," the shopkeeper quickly answered. "I have a collection of bird paintings done in watercolors by that particular artist, if your lordships would be interested to see them."

"He'll buy all of them." Quint pushed a thumb in Simon's direction. "Whatever you have."

"Birds?" Simon gave Quint a hard glare. "*Birds*, Quint?"

"Buy them, Winchester. Trust me."

Simon turned back to the shopkeeper. "How many?"

"Almost twenty, my lord. They're quite nice, all done within the last few years. Would your lordships care to see them?"

Quint answered, "No, that won't be—"

Simon gripped his friend's shoulder and began towing him toward the front door. "Excuse us a moment, won't you, Mrs. McGinnis?"

"Of course. Take all the time your lordship requires.

I'll just be in the back." She disappeared into the recesses of the shop, leaving the two men alone.

Simon frowned at Quint. "Why the deuce am I purchasing almost twenty bird paintings? I loathe birds."

"Because some are regional, you oaf," Quint whispered. "We might be able to find a common thread in the types of birds drawn and narrow down a county where Lemarc resides. At least that will give you a location in which to begin your search."

Simon blinked. "Quint, that's . . ."

"I know. Now buy the blasted pictures so we can get to the club. I'm starving."

He'd momentarily forgotten Quint's love of puzzles. "Fine. Consider this your project, then. Give me one of your cards." Quint produced a card, and Simon called for Mrs. McGinnis. "I'll take all the bird paintings," he told the shopkeeper when she returned, withdrawing a card from his breast pocket. "Send the bill to me, but deliver the pictures to this address." He handed over Quint's card.

"With pleasure, my lord. Would your lordship care to have them framed?"

Might as well, he thought. He'd find somewhere to use them. Shooting practice, perhaps. "Indeed. I bow to your expertise, Mrs. McGinnis. Choose whatever frames you deem appropriate. How long before they're ready?"

"I'll get my boy on it straightaway. I should have them to your lordship day after tomorrow."

At that moment the bell over the door clanged, and he turned to see a small figure burst into the shop. A lady, by the look of her fashionable bonnet and black pelisse. She seemed to freeze upon seeing them but then inclined her head. There was something oddly familiar—

"Lord Quint," he heard her say.

Quint bowed. "Lady Hawkins. How nice to see you again."

The room suddenly lost all its air. Or perhaps Simon's lungs refused to cooperate because a burn had sparked in his chest, a pressing heat as if the ceiling had collapsed on him. God's teeth, he hadn't expected to see her here. To see her anywhere, really. Ten years. It had been ten years since they'd last faced one another. He'd heard all about her, of course. From all accounts, the woman thrived on spectacle and notoriety—which struck him as odd, considering he remembered her as thoughtful and, well, shy.

But he'd never really known her at all, had he? The scandal when she was still Lady Margaret, along with the behavior she'd exhibited since the end of her mourning period, had certainly proven that.

Shock rendered him frozen, and the only thing he could do was stare. The years had certainly been kind to Lady Hawkins, if her appearance was any indication. Wisps of black hair fell out of her bonnet, her delicate features fairly glowing from the cold. She had creamy skin without a hint of imperfection, and green eyes that whispered of the Irish meadows of her ancestors. As he watched, her generous mouth twisted into a small smile. He remembered the simple beauty of that smile, the lengths he'd gone to in order to see it.

There had been a time he would have done anything to make her happy. Such a foolish, foolish boy he'd been. Anger simmered in his gut at her faithlessness—anger he forced away for its sheer ridiculousness. It had been a decade, after all.

"Lord Winchester, it has been a long time," he heard her say, her tone cool and quiet.

He bowed stiffly. "Lady Hawkins. How wonderful to see you." Even to his own ears, it sounded flat.

She didn't respond and an awkward silence fell. Devil take it, but he had no *idea* of what to say to her. Both his feet and tongue felt rooted to the floor.

Finally, Quint asked, "Are you purchasing a print?"

She stepped toward the counter, the top of her head barely reaching Simon's shoulder. "I did, last week. Now it's been framed and I've come to collect it. You?"

"Winchester's the one buying today," Quint said.

Lady Hawkins turned, her questioning gaze colliding with his. Hard to miss the intelligence—at once both familiar and mysterious—lurking there. He cleared his throat. "I'm purchasing a collection of bird paintings."

"Are you?"

"Indeed, my lady," the shopkeeper confirmed. "All nineteen pictures by Lemarc. His lordship bought every one."

"Ah. Have you discovered an interest in ornithology, sir?"

The sound of her voice, teasing him in that unique, husky way, prickled over his skin. He didn't intend the visceral response but found himself helpless to stop it. She'd teased him quite often over the months they'd spent together. She'd made him laugh, more than he'd ever thought possible, and it had not gone unnoticed when it had stopped.

Had she made the late Lord Hawkins laugh? And what of the other men in her past?

"That means *birds*," she said, drawing his attention

back to the conversation. "I asked if you are interested in birds."

"More like ladybirds," Quint muttered, and Lady Hawkins chuckled.

"Yes, I'm aware what ornithology is," Simon answered. "While I do not claim to be an expert on birds, I find myself suddenly fascinated by them. And you, madam?"

She turned away in order to stare at some bric-a-brac in the glass case. "Oh, no. I wouldn't know a partridge from a nuthatch, I'm afraid."

"Have you been to any of the other recent art exhibitions?" Quint asked her.

Other exhibitions? Simon wondered over that. Quint had definitely failed to mention bumping into Lady Hawkins. Odd, since Quint knew the history between her and Simon. Not that Simon cared, of course. He most definitely did not.

"I haven't had the time," she was saying. "Did you purchase that painting you were admiring at the Waterfield exhibit?"

"No. I had no interest in buying it," Quint admitted. "I was trying to deduce how the artist achieved that particular shade of yellow. I've not seen one so bright before."

"It's produced from a metal called cadmium. I'd only read about the technique before that exhibit."

"Extraordinary. They must use an acid solution. . . ." Mumbling under his breath, Quint pulled a small notebook and lead pencil from his pocket, then began making furious notes as he strode directly out the door.

"Nice to see some things never change," Lady

Hawkins said. "It appears Lord Quint still becomes utterly absorbed in whatever he's doing."

"I had no idea you and Quint were so friendly."

She searched his face. "Yes, well. Not everyone turned their back on me, I suppose."

Murmured under her breath, the comment struck Simon as odd. She had made her choices all those years ago, deciding on Davenport, who was now Lord Cranford. That it hadn't worked out with Cranford had been unfortunate for her, assuredly; her reputation had suffered a heavy blow. But she must have known the potential consequences when she'd risked it all to dally with Cranford. So how was any of what had happened a surprise?

"Would your lordship care for a receipt?"

Startled, Simon turned to Mrs. McGinnis, whose presence he'd completely forgotten. The older woman waited patiently for his answer, but then Lady Hawkins shifted, unintentionally gaining his attention as she drifted off to investigate a painting on the far wall. He shouldn't want to stay, should take this opportunity to put as much distance as possible between the two of them . . . but he couldn't do it. He needed to trail after her, talk to her. *To what end?* he berated himself. To make polite chitchat? God, he was an imbecile. "Yes, I would," he heard himself tell the shopkeeper.

Mrs. McGinnis hurried to the back of the store, and Simon strolled to Lady Hawkins's side. "You seem to know a bit about art."

"A bit. I've studied here and there over the last few years." She shrugged and then gave him a bold appraisal, the pale green flicker raking him from head to toe. "You seem well. Not that I would have expected otherwise."

Something in her tone had him frowning. "Meaning?"

"Meaning it has been a long time and you appear more . . . I don't know, more earlish than I recollect."

"Earlish?" Despite himself, he chuckled. "I am the earl, Lady Hawkins. I was also the earl back when—"

He couldn't finish it, the words sticking in his throat. Had she known? Had she any notion of what he'd felt for her? Hell, there was a time when just a glimpse of the curve of her neck would give him fits.

He had dreamt of seducing her but intended to wait until they could be married. The more fool he, believing she felt the same.

"How is your mother? I have such fond memories of her," Lady Hawkins asked.

Simon shifted on his feet, restlessness nearly overcoming him. He wanted both to bolt and never move in equal measure. "She is quite well, thank you. And yours?"

"Her health is rather poor, I regret to say. But we're managing."

"I'm sorry, Maggie." The familiar name slipped out before he could take it back.

She swallowed, but her expression gave nothing away, her gaze still trained on the paintings. "No apologies necessary, Simon," she said, returning the familiarity. "One thing I've learned about myself in all these years is that I'm very good at managing."

"Yes, that's what I hear."

Her head swung to face him. "Do you?"

"You are all anyone talks about."

Her brow lifted. "And here all I find is constant commentary on your feats in Parliament, Lord Winejester."

His shoulders stiffened, an instinctual reaction to the character name. Of course she had seen the cartoon in the window. Resisting the urge to stalk to the front and rip it down, he gritted out, "I am afraid they exaggerate."

"Yes, but that is what the *ton* does so well."

He couldn't very well argue with that.

"I thought you would have attended one of my parties by now," she continued.

"I do not recall being invited," he countered.

"Hmm. Is that what keeps you away? An invitation?"

She was laughing at him, he realized. Mocking him. But something else . . . Her rigid shoulders and the flat line of her mouth suggested anger. Simon turned that knowledge around in his mind and tried to make sense of it.

"Pardon me, but here is a receipt, my lord," Mrs. McGinnis called from over by the counter.

Maggie moved to the other side of the store, dismissing him, and Simon had no choice but to retrieve the receipt from the shopkeeper. He tucked the small piece of paper in his pocket.

"Good afternoon, Lady Hawkins," he said to Maggie's back.

She didn't turn, merely waved her hand. "And good afternoon to you, Lord Winchester."

Once outside, he found Quint still scribbling away. While Simon waited for his friend, he couldn't resist turning toward the shop, telling himself it was to study the embarrassing drawing once more . . . yet found his eyes drawn to Lady Hawkins instead.

"You saw her and did not tell me," he mentioned as casually as possible.

Quint's head snapped up. "I didn't think you would care either way."

"I don't. I was merely surprised."

"Indeed," Quint drawled, then returned his attention to his notebook. "And people say I am a terrible liar."

"May I stop smiling?" Maggie felt foolish, with a fake grin nearly sewn on as she stood at the counter.

"Not yet, my lady. The gentlemen are still in front of the window, looking at the shop."

"Any suggestions? I feel like a half-wit standing here and gawking at you."

"Why don't you stroll about, and I'll go in the back as if I'm retrieving your frame." Mrs. McGinnis gave her an apologetic glance before escaping into the depths of the store. Taking the woman's advice, Maggie strolled to the stack of prints resting against the wall and tried to calmly flip through them, though her heart raced faster than a sparrow's wings. Simon had actually been here, staring at the cartoon. What had he experienced when he looked at it? Humiliation? Anger?

Satisfaction roared through her.

He didn't know, of course. How could he possibly realize who was responsible for the caricatures of Lord Winejester? Only three people knew of her hidden talents: her sister, her mentor, Lucien, and Mrs. McGinnis. None would ever reveal her secret.

Heavens, when Simon had turned that intimate, boyish smile on her she'd felt the warmth all the way down to her toes. He must have every woman in London falling at his feet, just as she had done once.

Never again.

Yes, she'd been foolish enough to trust him. Love him, even. But she was no longer foolish or naïve. She was smarter now. Stronger. An entirely different person.

Worse than the flirting had been Simon's effort to engage her in friendly conversation, as if he hadn't a thing to apologize for. As if he hadn't turned his back on her at the precise moment she'd needed him most.

Out of all that had happened since the scandal, Simon's betrayal had hurt the most. Which was why she took such delight in his very public humiliation at her hand. She knew of his reputation now—a respected and powerful young leader in Parliament. Never on the losing side. Reputed to be fair and intelligent, the rakehell ways of his youth long forgotten.

Maggie had not forgotten. How could she, when the whispers of her downfall followed her wherever she went?

The Half-Irish Harlot.

The name used to upset her, especially when the ladies did not bother lowering their voices before saying it. But over the years she'd learned to embrace the name, to use it to her advantage. If one is a fallen woman, one learns to pick herself up or stay down— and Maggie had no intention of letting the *ton* crush her. No, it would be quite the other way around.

Well, perhaps not *crush*—but definitely suffer. Fortunately Lemarc's popularity gave her the forum to expose the hypocrisy and ridiculousness that comprised London Society. Lucien, her friend, frequently said artists should use art to expunge any pain and suffering, and she'd held on to her anger for far too long.

"They've left, my lady." Mrs. McGinnis returned, a brown parcel in her hands.

"Thank heavens." Nearly collapsing with relief, Maggie placed a hand over heart. "I nearly expired when I came in and found him here. What did he want?"

"The cartoon, of course. Tried to bribe me in order to get Lemarc's real name. When that failed, his lordship offered to buy the picture, whatever the cost."

"Whatever the cost? Well, I'm sorry to have prevented a sale. Just think of all the money you would make if we could reveal Lemarc's identity."

Mrs. McGinnis shook her head. "If we did, I'd certainly lose in the long run, my lady. It's the mystery that brings 'em in the door, if you don't mind my saying so, and your ladyship's talent has them buying up everything as quick as you draw it. Those bird watercolors were the last I had." She reached out and patted Maggie's hand. "And there's nothing I wouldn't do for your ladyship. Indeed, no one could offer me enough money to give up our secret."

Maggie squeezed the other woman's fingers. "Thank you. Your loyalty means everything to me."

"It's me who'll be giving thanks. If not for your ladyship, I'd still be in Little Walsingham, suffering beatings from that devil I married. I owe everything to you for giving me a bit of money and artwork to set up my shop. And I shan't be forgetting it."

"We saved each other, then. Without your friendship, I wouldn't have survived." The other women in the village had only wanted to gawk at the scandalous woman who'd married their old, wealthy baron. Friends had not come easily.

Mrs. McGinnis chuckled and pulled back to wipe her eyes. "Aren't we a pair, then? Well, those days are behind us now. And look at you—the talk of London!"

Simon's words came back to her. *You are all anyone talks about these days.* She wondered what stories he'd heard. No doubt whatever he'd been told only confirmed the intelligence of his actions ten years ago. "Well, I'm proud of the work all the same. Speaking of work, why did Lord Winchester buy the birds, do you suppose?"

The shopkeeper shrugged. "Could not say, my lady. His lordship's friend, Lord Quint, talked him into it. They retreated to the corner for a private conversation. After that, Lord Winchester agreed to buy the pictures without even seeing them, and the lot's being shipped to Lord Quint's address."

Maggie frowned. Bought them without looking at them? Sending them on to Lord Quint? The whole business struck her as odd, plus she hated not knowing *why* someone did something. An annoying quality but one that made her a keen observer of human nature, which in turn produced sharper and more provocative drawings. Her sister had told her time and time again to let things be, despite her stubbornness to reason things out. But Maggie simply *couldn't.*

"Care to tell me what the earl did to your ladyship to be featured in so many of Lemarc's drawings?"

Maggie waved her hand. "He hasn't been in that many. Prinny's been in far more, and I've never even met the Regent."

"You cannot fool me. I know your ladyship only too

well. You've made a mockery of Lord Winchester, and there's a good reason why."

Oh, yes. She had a good reason.

Mrs. McGinnis studied her carefully, so Maggie said, "I remember him from my debut, and those are days I'd much rather forget. I trust you are charging him a handsome sum for the watercolors."

"I will, indeed. Your ladyship will earn a small fortune off the Earl of Winchester. Now, to what do I owe the honor of this visit today?"

"I wanted to let you know I finished the architectural drawings as well as a new cartoon for the window. We'll use the usual delivery procedure. How's the day after next?"

"Excellent!" The shopkeeper clapped her hands. "The tourists will love the architectural prints. There is another matter we should discuss as well. I've received a letter from Ackermann. He's compiling a travel book on Scotland and Wales and wishes to hire your ladyship—er, Lemarc—for the illustrations."

Rudolph Ackermann, owner of The Repository of the Arts, produced highly successful books on travel, architecture, and gardening. Mrs. McGinnis had been showing him Maggie's work for months now, begging him to allow Lemarc to illustrate an upcoming book. The work would be tedious, but it would pay well and provide excellent exposure. More importantly, Ackermann's approval would go a long way; the man never worked with fly-by-night or avant-garde artists. This would put her work alongside notable current artists such as Rowlandson and Gillray.

"He requires almost one hundred aquatints," Mrs. McGinnis continued into Maggie's stunned silence. "Shall I tell him yes?"

"Yes! By all means, what wonderful news," she

blurted and reached forward to squeeze Mrs. McGinnis's hands. "Thank you for working so hard on my behalf."

"The arrangement will do us both good, my lady. Between Ackermann's job and your friend from Paris, we'll soon have all of London buzzing. Perhaps by summer, we'll be able to afford a larger shop over on the Strand."

"Oh, excellent. You've heard from Lucien."

Lucien Barreau was one of Maggie's dearest friends. She met him while studying in Paris a few years before Hawkins passed on. He'd served as her mentor, teaching her about the business of being an artist as well as helping her hone her craft. His talent was limitless, but he refused to show his work in Paris, the fear of rejection keeping him from acclaim. After a long battle, however, Maggie had finally convinced him to sell his work in London with Mrs. McGinnis.

"Indeed. He wrote earlier in the week, saying he's got upwards of two hundred etchings to send us. The sample he sent, it was remarkable. Would your ladyship care to see it?"

"No need. I know his work well. The public will lap up his elegant style of drawing like sweet cream."

"I certainly hope so. Shall the new cartoon go up immediately, or did your ladyship want to keep this one up a bit longer?"

"Keep this one up another week. No use giving Lord Winchester the impression his visit swayed you into taking it down. No, let him stew a few more days."

The bell above the door tinkled as three young ladies entered the shop. They were young, apple-cheeked English blossoms, dressed in clothing that bespoke wealth, their maids dutifully waiting outside.

Clutching each other's arms, the girls laughed and smiled gaily. Maggie felt a hundred years old merely observing them. Had she ever been so carefree, even before the scandal?

"Pardon me, my lady," Mrs. McGinnis said before hurrying over to assist the newcomers.

Maggie wandered to study a group of paintings on the near wall. She encouraged Mrs. McGinnis to stock all the *au courant* artists; after all, Lemarc alone could not sustain the shop. In addition to garnering sales, this practice offered Maggie a chance to measure up the competition. These were a series of new pretty Irish landscapes by Mulready. Quite nice, actually.

"Do you know who that is?" she heard one of the girls whisper behind her a few minutes later, the comment purposely loud enough to reach Maggie's ears. Maggie stifled a sigh, kept her back turned.

"Shhh," another girl said.

"No, who is it?" the third one asked.

Maggie resisted the urge to spin and hiss at them like a snake-headed Gorgon. While it would be supremely satisfying, Mrs. McGinnis wouldn't appreciate Maggie scaring the customers, not to mention a thwarted sale would deprive the owner her livelihood. Maggie did stand her ground, however; under no circumstances would she give the girls the satisfaction of chasing her away. Let them say what they would. She'd heard it all anyway.

". . . Irish harlot."

A gasp. "Are you sure?"

"Positive. I saw her at the Reynolds exhibit a few months ago. Mama wouldn't even let me look at her."

Lest you be turned to stone, Maggie thought.

"Wait, I have no idea who you're talking about. Who is she?"

There was some murmuring and then, "I heard all about her from Lady Mary, who is friends with Lady Cranford."

Amelia. Maggie should have known.

The girl continued in a quieter tone, so Maggie only caught pieces of the conversation. ". . . debut she . . . half the men of the *ton.* Lady Cranford caught her . . . her betrothed at the time . . . scandal . . . marry Lord Hawkins."

Maggie could guess at what she'd missed, and she was surprised that the words still stung after all these years. The twisting of facts, the gross injustice of the lies spread about her. Only the last portion, about the scandal and her subsequent marriage to Charles, happened to be true. She swallowed the lump of resentment in her throat.

"And you're certain that's . . ."

Maggie could feel the weight of their stares on her back.

"Most definitely."

"Mama told me not to wander off at parties or people might think I am like her."

"No one would ever think that, silly. I vow, it's in the blood. What else could one expect from a piece of filthy Irish—"

Maggie spun on her heel to face them. The girls shrank back, startled, and Maggie made certain to look each one in the eye. No one spoke, and unsurprisingly the girls did not hold her gaze. Each one turned to the counter, silent as a painting. At that precise moment, Mrs. McGinnis stepped out from the back room of the shop, a canvas in her hands. When she saw Maggie's face, she raised an eyebrow.

Maggie shook her head but stepped up to the counter. "Mrs. McGinnis, thank you for your assistance today. I believe I shall return later when your shop isn't quite so . . . overrun."

Concern evident behind her spectacles, Mrs. McGinnis returned, "Very well, my lady. It has been my pleasure. I am always happy to help your ladyship."

Chin high, Maggie swept out of the shop. The frigid air slapped her skin, though she hardly felt it with all the anger coursing through her veins. Not about to scurry away like vermin, she stepped over to examine the front window. Mrs. McGinnis was a genius with arranging paintings and engravings to best draw the customer's eye. The woman hadn't known much about art in Little Walsingham, but some people had a gift for discerning beauty. Mrs. McGinnis liked what she liked and, as it turned out, customers agreed.

She sighed. Really, it had been absurd to let those three vipers-in-training get under her skin. Provoking a reaction was precisely what the gossips wished for, and Maggie tried, in a perverse sort of revenge, to never give them the satisfaction. Today's failure had likely been a result of Simon's unexpected presence. She'd never thought to run into him here, for heaven's sake. Perhaps at one of her gatherings or an exhibition—a place where she'd have a bit of warning, some time to prepare herself.

The Winejester cartoon caught her eye. Right in front, it held a place of prominence in the display. The image made Maggie smile, her first real smile of the day.

Perhaps it was time for another party.

Chapter Three

Simon rapped on the door of a large town house on Charles Street. "We might very well be turned away."

The Duke of Colton snorted. "I've never been refused entrance at a dissolute party in my life."

The revelry from inside reached the front steps, a steady hum of noise. In addition to the voices, notes from a string quartet played. Simon could only wonder what the neighbors thought.

"Your illustrious reputation notwithstanding," the Duchess of Colton noted dryly, "we also received an invitation. So I would say there's very little chance we'll be refused."

"An invite?" Simon glanced at her. "You never mentioned that."

Julia shrugged. "We receive invitations to almost everything, Simon, no matter the event. As do you, I'm certain. Of course, I never had reason to attend one of Lady Hawkins's parties before."

"As if I'd let you come without me," Colt told her.

"As if you could stop me," she shot back. "Besides, tonight we're here for Simon."

Simon stifled a groan. He hadn't wanted company for this errand; but Julia had been insistent after learning his plans. The entire outing might very well be a waste of time if Maggie refused to speak to him. He'd sent her four notes over the past week, asking for an audience, and she'd refused him each time. Therefore, when news of her party reached his ears, he'd decided to approach her here. She couldn't very well avoid him then.

All he needed was to ask a favor of her, though even he had trouble accepting such a paper-thin excuse. The desire to see her again, to talk to her, had been an uncomfortable itch under his skin since their meeting at McGinnis's Print Shop. Curiosity, he told himself, nothing more. He'd satisfy that particular need tonight and then be done with her. Of course, there was a slim chance she could help him after all, which would be an additional boon to this venture.

The wood door swung open to reveal an older, plump woman. She gave them a quick appraisal and held the door to allow them in. After accepting their personal effects, she led them up the marble staircase. Simon followed, keeping pace. The interior was far from ostentatious, but well appointed, he noticed. Tasteful art on the walls. Plush carpets. Gold accents. Nothing the least offensive. He hadn't known what to expect, but he'd hoped for clues on how to reconcile the girl he'd once known with the woman she was now. And while he hadn't imagined her lodgings a brothel, perfectly bland decor didn't suit her either.

"My mistress don't stand on ceremony," the house-keeper said over her shoulder. "She don't like her guests announced. Party's under way through here."

She threw wide two double doors, and Simon crossed into the ballroom—then stopped.

It was like nothing he'd ever seen. The room had been transformed into a lush haven of nautical life and greenery. Garlands of flowers looped with golden rope hung along the ceiling and the columns, while fat wooden casks were grouped in the corners, some with empty flutes on them. Hemp netting covered one wall, with replicas of various sea creatures tied into the webbing. The dance floor, however, took up most of the space and she'd decorated it appropriately. Intricate chalk drawings of naked mermaids and lusty sailors swirled in brilliant hues on the floor in a blatantly risqué depiction.

A few guests talked and sipped champagne at the edges of the room, but most were gathered near the back. Simon couldn't tell what they were looking at.

"I'm impressed," Colt murmured. "I recall a party like this during *Carnevale di Venezia* one year. We all ended up in the lagoon in the wee hours of the morning."

"Couldn't be worse than the time we were caught in the fountain at Cambridge," Simon noted.

"What wastrels we were," Colt said fondly before strolling away, Julia on his arm, toward a table stacked with glasses of champagne.

When Maggie's mourning had ended eight months ago, stories of the unconventional parties at the Hawkins town house had begun circulating. They were infrequent and small, yet quite popular with the male half of the nobility. Hell, White's fairly tittered the day after one of her events. The respectable Society matrons and unmarried ladies never attended, of course, but that still left the faster set of widows and wives.

Listening to the men recount the previous evening's debauchery at Maggie's home never failed to set Simon's teeth on edge. Was the woman so determined to turn herself into a spectacle? She'd quickly and quietly married Hawkins—no surprise there considering the scandal—and all but disappeared until his death, upon which the she-devil had wasted no time in returning to London and causing a stir.

Simon noted the faces of the men nearby, recognized nearly all of them. These were men he drank and gambled with. Men he debated in Lords. Which one was her lover? He tossed back the glass of champagne, reached for another. Perhaps coming tonight was an enormous mistake.

"What do you suppose is happening back there?" Colt asked, gesturing to the crowd in the corner.

"No idea, but I'd like to find our hostess." Second champagne in hand, he started toward the swarm of bodies on the far side of the room but was soon waylaid by a few young Whigs. It took upward of twenty minutes to break off from the conversation, which covered the unrest after Peterloo to speculation whether the Regent would successfully bring divorce proceedings against the Princess of Wales.

Simon spotted Julia and Colton in the crowd and came alongside to see what had everyone so enraptured. In a small pool of water, three young ladies were dressed as mermaids and perched on rocks. Each wore a long, colored wig to match the bright hue of her tail—either blue, red, or yellow—and strings of pearls around her neck. Transparent material with a silver shimmer clung to their arms, shoulders, and bellies, with only a scrap of material across the breasts. Simon's first thought was that they must have been freezing.

He leaned down to ask, "What's this?"

"A performance of some kind, I'm told," Julia whispered. "We are waiting for it to begin."

A raven-haired woman in a blue feather mask stepped forward and clapped her hands for attention. A jolt of unexpected awareness washed through Simon, tightening in his groin. He would recognize her anywhere. Layers of gauzy blue silk comprised her dress, the skirt falling to the floor in waves. The fabric stretched across her small breasts to push the plump mounds up. More enticing was the dazzling smile she wore, the radiance she exuded merely by breathing.

Not that he would ever allow himself down that path again, but one couldn't help but notice.

At Maggie's command, the orchestra struck up a jaunty tune. Three men dressed in rough sailor clothing appeared and began to sing a popular sea tale. The words had been slightly altered to make them more ribald, commenting on the mermaids' breasts and loose morals.

The guests roared their approval as the song reached a conclusion, with the sailors expiring when the mermaids rejected them. Everyone clapped enthusiastically while the actors bowed—as much as one could bow while encased in a fabric tail. Once the adulation died down, one of the sailors rushed over to Lady Hawkins, then lifted her up and shuffled to the pool. Laughing, she clutched his shoulders as he pretended to drop her into the water. Everyone in the room gasped—save Simon, who was too busy gritting his teeth.

The sailor finally set her down on the ground, and

she kicked off her slippers and stepped into the shallow pool. The crowd began hooting and cheering as she performed a few dramatic dance steps, a playful, masked water nymph showing off for the crowd. The idiocy of attending tonight hit Simon with all the subtlety of a wooden mallet. Why the hell was he here?

"I *like* her," Julia murmured at his side.

"You would."

"You liked her once as well," she continued, her eyes fixed on Maggie. "Or need I remind you?"

No. He could remember only too clearly. But those days had long passed. "I forget the two of you never met. She debuted the year you married Colton."

Maggie climbed onto a rock recently vacated by a mermaid and bowed. The room broke out into riotous applause. Simon clapped as well, though he'd shown more enthusiasm during a political opponent's speech.

No one seemed to notice, however. Maggie held the room enthralled, so damn beautiful no one dared look away. Holding her hands up for quiet, she called, "You are too kind. My thanks to our mermaids and sailors. Now we dance!"

The crowd dispersed, with most headed toward the champagne while the orchestra struck up a waltz. A few guests circled around Maggie, but Simon stayed close. Colton fetched fresh glasses of champagne and chatted with his wife while Simon waited.

After what seemed an eternity, Simon saw his opening. The group around Maggie thinned so he moved in to hover at her elbow. She glanced up, the green gaze sharpening behind the mask, and he saw her shoulders stiffen. Blue peacock feathers twitched and bounced as she turned to excuse herself. When her companions departed, she said, "Lord Winchester. This is a surprise."

"Good evening, Lady Hawkins." He quickly made the introductions and, despite her apparent displeasure at Simon's presence, Maggie fussed over the legendary Duke and Duchess of Colton.

"I am so pleased you both came," Maggie said with an elegant curtsy. "I've longed to meet you both for ages."

"Likewise," Julia returned. "The performance was inspiring, and I adore your costume. Are you Amphitrite?"

"No. I am the humble Naiad Daphne."

"Ah, but she gives Apollo a merry chase," Colton noted. "A formidable woman if there ever was one."

"All women are formidable, Your Grace—or haven't you realized yet?"

"He is well aware of that fact. I taught him never to underestimate a woman." Julia raised her brows at Colton as if daring him to contradict her.

"Quite true, Duchess," the duke responded with a smirk.

"Who designed your chalk drawings?" Julia motioned toward the dance floor. "They are simply breathtaking."

"Thank you. They were done by an artist of my acquaintance."

The group turned to study the drawings now being trampled underfoot by the dancers. "Magnificent," Julia said. "It's almost a pity to ruin them."

Simon shot Colton a look over Julia's head. Knowing each other since boyhood meant no words were necessary, and Colton instantly offered his arm to his wife. "Well, lovely or not, shall we dance?"

Maggie's lips curved when the duke and duchess departed. "That was nicely orchestrated, Lord Winchester. Dukes at your command. Parliament at your feet. I am anxious for your next triumph. Shall I call back the crowd?"

"Not very subtle of me, but I did wish to speak with you. If you had not refused to see me this week . . ."

"Yes, I have no doubt this is the last place you wish to find yourself this evening."

Absolutely correct, though he would never admit it. "You would be wrong. I've been quite entertained, in fact."

"Then I shall consider tonight a success."

"From what I'm told, all your parties are successful. Is it true you once had actual tigers?"

Her green irises sparkled like emeralds. "A bit of an exaggeration. One tiger and he was quite tame. Most of the guests were disappointed, I think."

The uniqueness of her beauty struck him, as it always had. Pitch-colored, glossy hair. Creamy skin without a blemish or mark. Full, pink lips. There was no woman on earth like Maggie. He'd known it the first time he clapped eyes on her—as had any number of other men, if the rumors of her numerous *affaires* were true. "The duchess was correct. You are quite beautiful this evening." His tone was sharper than it ought to be when paying a compliment, and he nearly winced.

Her look turned measuring. "Thank you, though I might catch my death if I do not change out of my wet clothes." She picked up the skirts of her dress, showed him the soaked fabric. Instantly, he was transfixed by the vision of her shapely leg covered in damp, transparent silk. His blood began to simmer. He wanted to feel her, to hold her . . . to run his tongue over the smooth knob of her ankle. A monumental mistake, if he allowed it, though desire was hardly ever logical.

Nevertheless, what came out of his mouth surprised even him. "Reminds me of the time I taught you to ice skate. Do you recall, at the Serpentine? The hem of your dress became damp and you nearly froze."

She blinked up at him. "I haven't thought of that outing in quite some time. That was a . . . nice day."

"Yes, it was." The urge to touch her worsened, a strange ache at the fond memories. "Will you dance with me?"

"Oh, I never dance."

"Why not? You like to dance. At least, you did."

She lifted a shoulder. "Dancing bores me to tears. Besides, it's the sort of thing done at respectable parties."

"Oh, the horror," Simon drawled.

Her lips thinned. "Mock if you must, but I am no longer the girl you once knew—and I have no desire to become her ever again."

The moment stretched and Maggie realized with humiliating alacrity she'd said far more than she'd intended. Simon's eighth-generation, noble brow furrowed as he considered her words. Blast. Well, too late to take it back now. Unfortunately, she had her father's temper as well as his creativity, and Simon had angered her over dancing, of all things. Honestly, who cared if she danced or not?

She had revealed too much. Blame his handsomeness, the distraction of looks so blond and aristocratic they could be sculpted out of fine Roman marble. His tall frame, elegantly turned out in a dark blue coat and matching breeches, drew every feminine eye in the room. And the way her pulse sped up at the sight irritated Maggie beyond measure, as she should be the one woman to know better.

Why had he mentioned the afternoon of skating? She would rather not remember the Simon of her debut, the charming man who seemingly could accomplish anything. He'd been so gentle that day, so solicitous, and had given her every bit of his attention. They had laughed often, and more than once he'd told her how much he admired her wit.

But too much had changed between them. Too much to ever go back, to be sure.

He opened his mouth—no doubt with some question or insight she had no desire to hear—so she blurted, "You wished to speak with me?"

His jaw snapped shut. After a moment, he said, "Not here, I think. No, I will come to see you tomorrow."

"Will you."

"Yes. The answers I require are best discussed in private."

Oh, indeed? Little doubt what the line of questions would be, then. God knew she'd heard them all hundreds of times over the last ten years.

A small knot of disappointment twisted in her chest. She hadn't expected it, though she should have. Simon was no different from the others. Hadn't she learned that lesson when he'd ignored her after Mr. Davenport—now Viscount Cranford—spread those filthy lies? She'd loved Simon madly once, and he'd proven unworthy of such a powerful and generous emotion.

Yet hearing him say the words would open a wound she'd worked hard to heal. She needed to find a way to dissuade him. Ignoring him hadn't done the trick. Neither had refusing him. There was another path to take.

"You assume I will be home to accept callers. Perhaps I have plans—or perhaps I will be occupied with another guest. The evening is far from over, after all."

The expression on his face changed, hardened, as she'd hoped it would. Satisfaction was short-lived, however, because he returned, "If that is so, perhaps he could see his way to allowing you a few minutes for a friend."

She almost laughed. "*Friend?* Simon, I have nothing to offer or say to you. The idea of a friendship between us is ludicrous for so many reasons, the least of which is your lauded political career. What will people think, the powerful Earl of Winchester with the Half-Irish—"

"Do not say it," he snapped, surprising her.

"Do not say what? *Harlot?*" A dry, brittle laugh escaped. "Come, you know what everyone calls me. There's no getting around it, I'm afraid. And one thing I've learned over the years is that it is better to embrace your destiny rather than try and alter it. Now if you'll excuse me, I must change."

Maggie threw open her chamber door with more force than she intended. Her sister, Rebecca, glanced up from where she sat on Maggie's bed, reading. "My heavens. What is the matter?"

Maggie strode to the bell pull and tugged. She'd need Tilda's help with a new gown. "I stepped in the pool and dampened the hem of my dress."

"Did you? Oh, I wish I could have seen that."

Maggie smiled at her sister. This was an old battle— one Becca would never, ever win. "You know my parties are not for respectable Society ladies. Coming below would ruin your reputation, which I might add already suffers from our being related. It's bad enough you insist on sending your husband."

Becca lifted her chin. "Someone needs to watch out for you. Marcus will never let anything happen."

"What, precisely, worries you? That I'll run low on champagne and fisticuffs will break out?" While Becca's protectiveness was an open source of amusement, it secretly warmed Maggie's jaded heart.

"Jest if you must, but I won't have them hurt you again. Now tell me what actually happened to upset you."

The disappointed set of Simon's full lips when she'd uttered the word *harlot* filled her vision. Better to get it over with, as Becca would hear about it soon enough from her husband. "Winchester is here."

Becca's mouth formed a perfectly round ring of dismay. "Good heavens. Why, after all this time, would he come tonight?"

Maggie lifted her shoulder. "We ran into one another the other day at McGinnis's shop."

"You . . . you did?" Becca gasped. "And you did not tell me?"

A sharp knock sounded before Tilda marched into the room. She tittered when she saw Maggie's dress. "That's what you get from swimming in the pool, my lady. Come with me."

Most ladies would never tolerate rebuke from a servant—but then Maggie was not most ladies. And Tilda definitely was not most servants. Once the wife of a butcher back in Little Walsingham, Tilda had run the shop with iron-fisted efficiency. Her husband had been a spendthrift drunkard, however, and Tilda had ended up with most of the work. The hours long and the job physically demanding, Tilda had been exhausted. So when her husband died, Maggie had asked the childless woman to come and work for her instead.

She hadn't regretted it. Tilda was a gift from heaven. She oversaw everything, leaving Maggie to do what she loved best: her art.

Maggie followed Tilda into the dressing room, leaving the door ajar to continue her conversation with Becca. "It was hardly worth mentioning. We made polite chitchat for a few moments as he purchased some paintings."

"Purchased paintings! Which ones? Not one of—"

"He bought a handful of Lemarc's nature paintings," Maggie cut off her sister. Tilda likely knew of Maggie's sobriquet, but one never knew who else could be listening. While Tilda could be trusted, many other staff members could not.

The gown slid off her shoulders. "Here, step out," Tilda ordered.

The petticoat came next. Then Maggie drew her wet stockings off. "The only reason he attended this evening was because he wishes to speak with me and I refused to answer his notes."

Maggie heard Becca's squeak of outrage from the next room. "And what does he wish to discuss after all this time? The gall of that man. I hope you told him to go to the devil!"

Maggie couldn't help but laugh. "In more polite terms, yes. That is very nearly what I told him."

"You know I do not care for political matters, but Winchester has made quite a name for himself in Parliament. Not that I would ever lower myself to give him any notice—not after what he did to you. And everyone knows he has a mistress over on Curzon Street."

Maggie frowned. Of course he did. She purposely avoided any conversation where Winchester's private life was discussed, but a mistress was de rigueur for male peers and politicos. Of course proper wives and ladies were supposed to sit home and drink tea . . . alone. And how, exactly, was that not a recipe for a woman to go stark-raving mad?

The restrictions placed on women in Society were unfair and infuriating. Thank God for the outlet Lemarc afforded her to point out such injustices. It was the only reason for these fêtes: they were a means of gaining access to the *ton*. Most of her invitations had dried up ages ago. Not even marriage had made her respectable, forgiven for all of her supposed transgressions, so she used lavish events to bring the *ton* to her instead. After all, the two things Society adored were scandals and champagne; Maggie had already given them the first and kept supplying the second. Little wonder her parties had become fashionable with a certain set.

And the evenings had proven quite fruitful, if the popularity of Lemarc's cartoons were anything to go by. Each event produced at least one delicious *on-dit*, sometimes more. In fact, Maggie's fingers itched to get her paper and pencils, the idea for a new cartoon already swirling in her mind.

"Did you hear me, Maggie?"

"Yes, I heard you," she called as Tilda reappeared with stockings and a clean petticoat. Once they were on, Tilda helped Maggie into a fresh gown. This one wasn't quite as lovely as the ruined costume, but the green silk would flatter her eyes.

With arms in the sleeves, Maggie held it as Tilda fastened up the back.

"There. Now, no more swimming, my lady."

"I shall try, Tilda, but I make no promises." Maggie strode back into her bedchamber. "Becca, I must return to the ballroom."

"I do not like it," her sister said, a heavy frown transforming her pretty face.

"What, the dress?"

"You know that is not what I am talking about." Becca crossed her arms. "I do not like that he is here, upsetting you. Will you be able to ignore him?"

Maggie smiled at her overprotective yet sweet younger sister. Becca had always been Maggie's biggest champion, even when the rest of the world had thought the worst. "Of course. After all, I've ignored his existence for ten years. How hard could a few more hours be?"

Chapter Four

"Better not have too many, Winejester!"

Three young men dissolved into laughter, and Simon forced a smile and raised his glass toward them. He recognized each one, the fools. "Appreciate the warning, Pryce."

Colton made a noise. "The reason you should humor those walking cocks is unfathomable to me. It's as if your bollocks have shriveled up and fallen off since you started up in Parliament."

"Pryce's father is the Earl of Stratham, one of my biggest allies. Pulverizing his son for a drunken jest is not how the game is played, Colt."

"Exactly why I never took up my seat in Lords. Too many favors and slaps on the back. No one saying what they truly mean. I don't know how you tolerate it."

Simon sighed. Colton knew him better than anyone, but not even his childhood friend would understand. Colton's father had been a cold-hearted bastard, not particularly well liked in either Parliament or Society. But Simon could perceive his family's legacy everywhere he turned. Some men came from a long line of butchers or blacksmiths; the Barrett men were statesmen, helping to shape the policy and future of the realm since Henry the Sixth. The fifth Earl of Winchester had once served as Lord President of the Council. And Fox himself had taken counsel with Simon's father on occasion.

His father had died at forty-five. Rare heart condition, they'd said. Simon had no idea if his own health would follow a similar path—if he were going to keel over and expire, dear God, let it be a surprise—but he did intend to do something worthwhile in the time he had left.

So six years ago, he had taken up his seat in Lords. Turned out he had the family knack for politics as well, and he'd quickly gained a reputation for backing the winning side. He enjoyed the competitiveness of Parliament. The thrill of success. The challenge of exploiting an opponent's weakness to get what he wanted.

"I rather like the Winejester cartoons," Colton continued. "At least I'll always have those to remember our drunken escapades."

Simon turned sharply. "Have you purchased one?"

Colton's lips twitched. "I've tried. Twice. Curst shopkeeper won't sell it to me."

"Well, I wish they would stop. Certainly there are more interesting subjects to skewer."

"Doubtful." Colton followed Simon's gaze to the circle of men on the other side of the room. They both knew who stood in the center of that pack of jackals. "Do you plan to stare at her all night, my friend? You're glowering like an elderly chaperone, ready to pounce at a moment's notice."

Simon took a healthy swallow of champagne, wished

for something stronger. "I'm trying to reconcile the somewhat shy and sweet girl I knew with this confident and brazen . . ."

"One can change," Colton murmured. "Or perhaps you never really knew her at all—you only assume you did."

Yes, she had certainly duped him. How many men had she taken to her bed before Cranford had revealed her true nature? And to think, he'd even asked his mother for the Winchester rubies as a betrothal gift.

Watching her flirt and entertain her circle of admirers put him in a foul mood. Which must have shown on his face because Colton asked, "Wondering whom she may choose tonight?"

"The fortunate sod," Simon growled.

"Who says she'll take only one? There were plenty of nights where I—"

"God, don't say it. You know how much I loathe it when you attempt to be insightful." Simon threw back the rest of his bubbly. "I'm off. Give Julia my excuses and I'll see you on the morrow, if you're about."

"Allow me to guess," Colton drawled. "Curzon Street."

No need to answer. Colton was right and they both knew it. He shoved his empty glass into his friend's hand and headed for the door.

Outside, Simon set a brisk pace for the small house where his current mistress, Adrianna, resided. Curzon Street was not far, so he told his coachman he'd rather walk. If nothing else, he needed the cold air to clear his head. The sight of Maggie surrounded by her throngs of admirers gave him a pounding ache precisely behind the eyes.

He knew what those men saw because he'd seen it once, too. Maggie could hold the attention of a room merely by lifting a dainty finger. Heart-stoppingly beautiful, her unique looks and confidence could bring a man to his knees. It had taken him years to forget her.

So Adrianna was precisely what he needed at the end of this evening. A soft, warm, and willing body to take his mind off everything else. He'd first met Adrianna at Drury Lane, where she'd upstaged Kean in a production of *Brutus*. It had taken some doing to get her away from her former protector, but Simon had charmed her until she relented—charmed as well as promised better lodgings and more money.

They got on well and she was an enthusiastic and adventurous lover. He hadn't planned to see her this evening so he had no clue whether she was in. Approaching the tiny brick house, he noticed the lamps were on. That boded well. He took the front steps quickly, rapped on the door.

Adrianna's maid, Lucy, answered. She confirmed Adrianna was in, took his things, and asked him to wait in the small sitting room in the front. Odd, since he normally would venture directly to Adrianna's bedchamber. Instead of trying to understand the workings of his mistress's mind, Simon used the opportunity alone to get a strong drink. He splashed a liberal amount of his favorite scotch whisky into a tumbler. Imported from an illegal distillery in one of the Inner Hebrides, the whisky did not come cheap. *But it's worth every shilling,* he thought, taking a swallow as he settled on the small sofa to wait.

Why did Maggie not dance any longer? She had loved to dance all those years ago. He knew because he had partnered with her at least once during every party. And each time he'd arrived to claim their set, her eyes had sparkled, a secret joke between the two of them—

The latch sounded and Adrianna burst through the door. Her long, brown hair swirled down her back, a black silk dressing gown covering her petite, but generously endowed, body. By the way her breasts bounced and swayed, it was clear she was naked under the thin fabric. Excellent. That would certainly expedite matters.

"Darling! I had no idea you planned to come tonight." She crossed to the sofa and sat down, leaning over to kiss him. "Is something amiss? You know how I worry when you stray off your routine."

He frowned. Was he so regimented, then? So predictable and boring? "Everything is fine. I was out nearby and thought I would see if you were home. Were you going out?"

"I have a late supper with friends, but I'm more than happy to cancel my plans."

"No, it's unfair of me to come unexpected. I was just in a mood."

She lifted her brows and gave him a sultry smile. "Is that so? What kind of *mood*? The kind of mood where I get on top and—"

He laughed. "You are incorrigible, you saucy wench. I'm only staying for the drink." He finished the whisky and leaned forward to place the glass on the table. "I'll see you this week. Tuesday, as always."

Adrianna threw a leg over his waist, lifting her dressing gown to sit astride him. "Maybe I better give you a reason to come back, then." She wrapped her arms around his neck and placed her mouth on his, kissing him deep and hard. The soft, enticing weight of her heavy breasts rested on his chest. He felt his body begin to respond, so he gently put some distance between them.

"Tuesday," he told her. "We'll finish this on Tuesday."

"I can hardly wait," she said, grinding down on his growing erection. "Why don't I suck you now? You know how much you love my mouth. I'm certain it won't take long."

He considered it. Adrianna was incredibly skilled. But every time he closed his eyes he saw midnight hair and flashing green eyes. Imagined it was Maggie on her knees, taking his cock between her luscious—

"I see you like that idea," Adrianna purred, her clever fingers working their way to the buttons on his breeches.

He grabbed her hand. "Not tonight. Not if you're on your way out." And definitely not when all he could think about was Maggie.

What in God's name was wrong with him? He'd never been distracted by thoughts of another woman while enjoying Adrianna's charms. Ever. However, Maggie kept invading his brain, even at the most inopportune moments. He did not want Adrianna; he wanted another woman. Craved her with every molecule in his body.

No doubt there were other men in London likely experiencing the very same reaction.

"Fine." Adrianna pouted, regaining his attention. "I'll see you on Tuesday, then." She kissed him once and then stood up. Not that he'd expected her to argue, but her easy acceptance had him frowning. Was she so eager for him to leave? When he'd first set her up in this small house, they had enjoyed many evenings together, but over the last six months he'd settled into a pattern of twice weekly visits. He hadn't given a thought about what she did on those other five nights.

Smoothing down her dressing gown, she added, "I best get to it. It will take some time to finish dressing."

A rap on the front door sounded. Simon heard Lucy, the maid, hurry down the hall. A single male voice drifted through the walls. Adrianna's eyes darted to his face and Simon registered the guilt there.

"You're not going out, are you?"

Her fingers twined in the loops of her dressing gown, and she swallowed. "No," she said, quietly.

He sighed. "Hell."

The sun peered out from behind a large cloud just as Maggie entered the park. She'd offered many times to host these meetings at her own house, but her companion staunchly refused. As if Maggie gave a whit for propriety. Besides, did anyone truly care with whom the Harlot associated with these days?

She had no trouble spotting the carriage. Though plain and without distinguishing marks, it was the only conveyance with the curtains drawn on such a lovely winter day. She slowed her mare, dismounted, and threw the reins to her groom.

The driver jumped to the ground at her approach. "Morning, my lady."

"Good morning, Biggins. How's her mood today?"

"Excitable, my lady," he answered with a smile and opened the door. "But I am used to it."

A volume of purple silk rustled as Maggie climbed inside.

"Quit complaining, you puppy. You have the easiest job in all of London," the woman snapped and then gentled her voice. "Come in, my lady. Please, have a seat."

The lamps in the carriage gave off a warm glow, revealing the delicate face of Pearl Kelly, London's current reigning courtesan. Swathed in a resplendent violet morning dress and expensive jewelry, Pearl could easily have passed for nobility if one didn't know her background. Born in the slums of London, she'd used her unparalleled wit and quick mind to make an illustrious name for herself.

She and Maggie had become friends of a sort. When Hawkins died, Maggie had moved back to London a much different woman. No longer a sheltered innocent, she now understood the difficulties women faced in a man's world—especially those without money or family connections. She'd decided to help other fallen women, even if the label was earned. Women had so few choices in this world, a fact she understood better than most, so should she not try and help those less fortunate?

Through Tilda, Maggie had learned of Pearl's wretched childhood. As a girl, Pearl had suffered abuse and left home at eleven years of age. No one quite knew what had happened to her between quitting home and finding her first protector. Pearl never said, but one could assume they had not been the happiest of times. After learning of Pearl's struggle, Maggie had believed the courtesan to be the perfect choice for her plan. She'd approached Pearl with a proposition: If Maggie provided the money, would

Pearl see it used to help the London girls and women who traded their bodies for coin?

Pearl had jumped at the opportunity. The courtesan provided knowledge of the brothels and how best to help the girls earning a living there. She was acquainted with the owners, aware of who would be receptive to new ideas, and who would use additional funds in the intended manner. And when they were fleeced by an owner, which had only happened once, Pearl employed a few large men to send a message.

Maggie liked to hope the efforts made a difference. While one could never prevent a girl from making a living on her back, Pearl and Maggie did try to keep them healthy and safe.

"Good afternoon, Pearl. You look stunning, as usual."

Pearl waved the compliment away, though Maggie knew it pleased her. "I feel tired, my lady. I am considering a young man and he is much more . . . energetic than I'm used to. Though I must say, one learns to appreciate exuberance at my age. It far outweighs experience."

Maggie chuckled. "Considering Hawkins was nearly thirty years my senior, I understand. In my next life, I hope to be blessed with a young buck."

Pearl made a disbelieving sound. "Next life? If your ladyship will forgive my impertinence, you are young, beautiful, rich . . . what in heaven's name are you waiting for?"

Maggie had no idea, to tell the truth. At twenty-eight, she'd had two lovers: her husband and a Frenchman she'd met while studying in Paris. Both experiences had been disasters.

"I can see I have brought up unhappy memories, so

my apologies," Pearl said. "And I did not arrange this meeting to discuss our current amours—though should your ladyship ever seek advice, you only need ask. What I don't know about men could fit on the head of a pin."

"Thank you. I may take you up on your offer one of these days."

"Indeed, I hope so. Talking about men is my very favorite thing to do." She smirked. "Well, second favorite anyway."

They both laughed, and then Maggie asked, "So if we aren't discussing men, what are we discussing?"

Pearl smoothed down the folds of her skirt. "A few matters. The first, my lady, is I have spoken to the owner of The Goose and Gander. She has accepted our terms in exchange for the money."

"Excellent. I'll send a bank draft later today."

"That is most kind of your ladyship."

"I am happy to do it, as you well know. What else?"

Pearl toyed with her fan. "I have heard rumors that your ladyship is acquainted with the Earl of Winchester. Are they true?"

Maggie blinked. "Yes, I am. That is, our mothers were friends and the two of us were close during my debut. Why?"

"But you've seen him? Recently, I mean."

Yes, unfortunately Maggie had. *The answers I require are best discussed in private.* His words from the previous evening still rankled. Did Simon truly plan to proposition her? She hadn't decided whether to admit him to the house if he presented himself today. He deserved to be left waiting on the stoop.

Pearl was staring so Maggie answered, "Indeed, only last evening. Why?"

"Has your ladyship been informed about the proposal he plans to present?"

Maggie shook her head. She never paid attention to political matters. Pearl, however, was better informed than most when it came to Society gossip and politics. She'd once told Maggie that information proved almost as powerful a currency as money.

"The proposal has to do with rape. Forgive me for speaking plainly about an indelicate matter, but—"

"No, please do so. There's no need to dance around it with me. Pray go on."

"As you know, the facts can be hard to prove to a magistrate. Many times the woman may cry rape, but the man claims the act to be consensual. Lord Winchester's law would, in such cases, force the man to provide compensation to the woman. An annual sum. Into perpetuity."

Maggie's jaw lowered. "A yearly stipend? No woman would want to be tied in such a manner to a man who'd violated her. A yearly reminder of what's been done, and her attacker knowing where she lives . . . it's terrible."

"Precisely, my lady."

"Why on earth would anyone even assume it to be a good idea?"

"I could not say. But perhaps your ladyship can set his lordship straight?"

The last thing she wanted to do was engage Simon in a political discussion. Perhaps there was another way, however. Many members of Parliament attended her parties, providing any number of opportunities to undermine Winchester's efforts. "I'll see what I can do."

"I shall leave it in your ladyship's capable hands, then. I'll certainly use whatever influence I have with my meager connections."

Maggie suspected Pearl's influence remained considerable, though she currently had no protector. "Excellent. I will do the same."

"Now, I have one last request. One of our houses, over in Long Acre, has thrived with the embroidery instruction, so much so that a few girls would care to apprentice with a dressmaker. Perhaps your ladyship knows of a modiste who would appreciate a somewhat sullied pair of helping hands."

"How many girls?"

"Three."

Maggie bit her bottom lip, thinking. Possibly she could browbeat her own modiste into taking one girl, but she did not spend much on clothing or fripperies. And her social rank, while titled, was not as powerful as that of a lady without a scandalous past. That left her with little leverage. "I fear my position is not powerful enough for such a feat. It would take a lady with tremendous cachet to convince a modiste to take on these girls."

"I know a lady who qualifies," Pearl said. "And she happens to be in my debt. I once did her a favor and she was exceedingly grateful."

"Wonderful. Let's ask her."

Pearl shook her head. "I cannot. For many reasons, I must not approach her directly. But your ladyship can. . . ."

* * *

Simon presented his card at the door, unsure of his reception. Would Maggie refuse to see him? She'd been politely cool the previous evening after changing her costume, and there was every possibility she had a guest in the house.

His hand tightened on the crown of his walking stick.

One glance at his card and the servant ushered him inside. He noted she was the same woman who had admitted them the previous evening. Had Maggie no butler, then? He quickly handed over his things and followed to a comfortable sitting room in order to wait.

Aside from her lavish parties, it seemed Lady Hawkins lived responsibly, even frugally. The furnishings exhibited some wear. The rugs were serviceable plain wool rather than fashionable Aubusson carpets. True, an ample amount of coal sat in the grate, giving off a nice amount of heat, but it was a comfortable space without pretension or artifice. It suited her, he thought. Certainly a refreshing change from the extravagance of the other women he'd consorted with over the last few years—though, to be fair, mistresses were not exactly known for pinching a penny.

After a few moments, a small landscape portrait on the far wall caught his eye.

He closed in for a better inspection. A watercolor seaside scene. Quite smartly done, in fact. Waves pounded the beach and a selection of birds littered the sand, perfectly capturing the vibrancy and serenity of the location, as well as the chaos of the ocean. The artist had skill. Odd there was no signature in the corner. It had the look of a Gainsborough or Sandby, to his eye.

Art normally bored him to tears, but this . . . this *calmed* him. He could stare at it and not grow to hate it day after day. There was something about it, though, something familiar about the image. He couldn't put his finger on it. Not the location, exactly—

The door opened, startling him.

"Good afternoon."

And there stood Lady Hawkins, every bit as vibrant and lovely as the painting he'd just been studying. The combination of black hair, luminous green eyes, and porcelain skin made his breath catch—just as it had all those years ago. Only she wasn't a girl any longer, but a woman with fuller curves. He wished he could have witnessed her transition, he realized.

She dropped a quick curtsy. "My apologies for keeping you waiting."

He bowed. "I have not been waiting long. I've been admiring this picture here." He gestured to the watercolor. "I was attempting to discern the artist, but it's unsigned. Do you know who painted it?"

She smoothed the folds of her dark blue gown and drew near, her eyes on the painting. "Do you like it?"

The hesitation and attention to her clothing gave him the impression the question unnerved her. His first thought was that someone close to her had painted it. A lover, perhaps? "I do, very much. I'm not an expert when it comes to art, but this is well done."

Satisfaction curved her generous lips. "Excellent."

Definitely a lover. A dark, irrational jealousy churned in his stomach. Would he forever be reminded at every turn just how many men had graced her bed? "Shall we sit?" he bit out.

"I painted it."

"You?" He couldn't hide his surprise, and a strange look passed over her face before she could hide it.

"Shocking that a woman possesses talent, I know."

"I meant no such ridiculousness. You're quite gifted."

"You are too kind," she murmured, though there was a tone in her voice that sounded . . . offended?

"Would you care to sit?" he heard himself ask again.

She cocked her head, studied him with an enigmatic expression. "I'd rather stand. I suppose it's only polite to offer you refreshment. Shall I ring for tea?"

He refused as Maggie drifted away toward the armchair by the fire. Instead of sitting in it, she ran her fingers over the high back, stroking the fabric and regarding him thoughtfully. "Have you come to see if I live up to my name?"

"What?" he blurted. She couldn't mean—

"We're both aware of what everyone calls me, Simon. I've heard the word nearly every place I have turned for ten years. One would not think the residents of Little Walsingham to be so current on gossip, but"— she shrugged—"there it is. So have you decided to find out if I have earned the title?"

A vivid image flashed through his mind—one of Maggie on her back, skirts hiked up to her waist, legs spread invitingly—and lust swept through his groin. He had to force the arousing picture from his mind. "You believe I've come to try and fuck you." He was deliberately crude.

She didn't flinch. "Yes, I do. Why else would you visit? Or perhaps you wanted to see if I decorated my house with nude frescos. Or if I keep young men tethered in my chambers to have my wicked way with them whenever I want. You would not be the first to ask if the rumors were true."

Astonishment rocked him back on his heels. Hard to say which he found more distasteful: that she'd said it, or that she thought so little of him in the first place. "And yet you seem determined to feed those rumors. With extravagant parties and dancing in pools, is it any wonder they talk about you?"

"If I give them something to talk about, at least they cannot fabricate stories out of sheer boredom. But really, this is all beside the point. Perhaps you should arrive at the purpose for your visit."

Hostility and bitterness did not suit her. If anyone had cause for those emotions, it was Simon. "What has happened to you? What has given you cause for such venom?"

"*Life* happened to me, Simon. Everything you likely hoped for and worse."

"Me? Hoped for?" He blinked. "I never wished you harm."

"Did you not?" she asked, calmly.

"Maggie, you are not making sense. It's as if you are blaming me for the affair with Cranford. And the others."

"*Others?*" She gave a dry chuckle. "Of course. The others. How could I possibly forget them? Men, women, livestock . . . with so many, it has been difficult to keep them all straight."

Simon clenched his jaw. She'd damn near broken his heart and that was cause for jests? "Do you think to make light of it?"

"The truth is rarely as humorous as fiction," she answered, standing taller.

This conversation had gotten away from him. He rubbed at the tension settling at the nape of his neck.

"I think it best if you go." She lifted the hem of her skirt and moved toward the bell pull behind him.

Surprising even himself, Simon's hand darted out to catch her wrist. "Wait." He glanced down at her small, gloved hand. For an insane moment, he wanted to feel the softness of her bare skin, to have her delicate fingers touch and stroke him in return. Once, she'd removed her gloves to trace the edges of a painting at an exhibit all those years ago and it had nearly driven his twenty-three-year-old body mad with desire.

Now why had that insignificant memory resurfaced?

He dropped her arm. "Wait. I need your help."

She took a step back and one black eyebrow shot up. "I am fairly certain you have a mistress for that."

Annoyance rippled through him. Why did she assume everything had to do with fornication? "As it happens," he ground out, "this is an entirely innocent request."

She put more distance between them but did not reach for the bell pull. He folded his arms across his chest to keep from touching her again and got to his purpose. "Do you recall the cartoon in the print shop window, the Winejester fellow?"

"Yes," she said after a beat.

"They were all drawn by the same artist, this Lemarc. I would like you to assist me in finding him."

Chapter Five

A very good thing they were not sharing tea because Maggie surely would have choked. As it was, she could hardly breathe. Did he say . . . find Lemarc?

Good heavens.

He awaited her response, those cerulean eyes trained on her, when all she wanted to do was laugh at the absurdity of it all. *Oh, what a tangled web we weave . . .*

Through sheer perseverance, she hid her shock behind a mask of cool indifference. "You wish to find Lemarc? Whatever for?"

Simon shifted on his feet. "I find these Winejester drawings to be bothersome. For a number of reasons, I should like to see them stop."

"And you believe you can convince Lemarc to stop producing them?"

"Yes."

The arrogance in that one word astounded her. Did Simon think Lemarc would bow to an earl's whims merely because of his station? It was well known that artists were temperamental creatures, herself included.

The idea that he could dictate to Lemarc what she could and could not draw was ludicrous. And irritating.

"Why should he cease to draw such a popular character? Winejester is one of the reasons Lemarc has been discussed so often over the last year."

"I plan to convince him."

She swallowed a snort. God save her from male vanity. "I do not doubt it, but no one knows the identity of Lemarc. It's a well-guarded secret. What makes you believe I would be able to help find him?"

He lifted a broad shoulder. "A suspicion, really. Your knowledge of art and techniques may lead to a discovery. I have a number of Lemarc's paintings at my disposal. Perhaps you could look at them and see if something strikes a chord. A tidbit you've heard at a lecture or seen at an exhibit. It's likely a waste of your time, but I would be grateful for your assistance."

Waste of time, indeed. No one could unearth Lemarc by merely looking at some bird paintings, especially not that particular series. They had been painted four or five years ago near the shore and contained only birds and water—no people or buildings. If there were distinguishing marks in her paintings, she would've been found out long before now.

And truly, helping him was the very last thing she wanted to do. It was bad enough he had attended her party and cornered her there. "I am afraid I cannot."

"May I ask why?"

She hadn't expected him to press. What excuse could she give? Because she knew the effort to be a futile one? Because he deserved whatever inconvenience Lemarc's cartoons produced a thousandfold?

Or because, after all he'd done, he still made her heart race?

Into her silence, he said, "One afternoon, that is all I ask. If you do not see anything relevant, we'll forget it entirely."

"If I cannot discover anything, you shall give up searching for Lemarc?"

Simon shook his head. "Absolutely not. I plan to find him by any means at my disposal."

That set her back. He did seem rather . . . determined. Hmm. Such tenacity did not bode well. Though she believed her secret safe, there was a kernel of panic inside her that he might succeed. Simon had a reputation for doggedly wearing down his opponents until he got his way, of using whatever means necessary to win. The notion of her career as Lemarc being exposed . . . ruined . . .

A sliver of dread slid down her spine.

Of course, staying involved in Simon's quest meant she could throw him off the scent with misleading information. Keep him guessing. The more she thought about it, the more she liked the idea. "Fine," she agreed. "I would be pleased to aid in your search. To be fair, there are many more qualified than I to lend assistance. Perhaps you should think about asking another—"

"That is quite unnecessary," he interrupted smoothly, smiling in triumph. "I think you are more than capable of the task."

In a strange way, his faith in her was flattering. Little did he know she planned to undermine his efforts, ensuring his failure. In finding her. She had to bite her lip to keep a hysterical bubble of laughter from spilling out. "Very kind of you, my lord. When shall we begin our investigation?"

"As soon as possible, I think. I'll send a note, if that is acceptable."

"Yes." Maggie tried not to think about how impossibly handsome he was. Of course, the light blue jacket and breeches did offset his fair coloring, making the blue of his eyes even brighter. His shoulders—

Curse her feminine biology. Being a woman was decidedly unfair.

Instead, she concentrated on the smug, satisfied smile he now wore. Yes, he'd gotten precisely what he wanted today. Oh, how she longed to wipe that expression off his face. "Does anyone ever say no to the Earl of Winchester?"

"Rarely. I can be very persuasive."

"So I have heard. You have a reputation in Lords for getting your way. I suspect you could talk a nun into giving up the cloth and throwing in with a band of gypsies if you wanted."

The edge of his mouth kicked up. "That charming, am I?"

She could've bitten her tongue. "More like full of useless wind."

His head fell back and he let out a deep, rich laugh. She loved his laugh. It was the kind of sound a woman felt deep in her belly, warming her from the inside out. She now knew what those stirrings represented, the kindling of desire. Her husband had never elicited passion from Maggie; their few couplings had been quick and perfunctory. Then Charles had taken ill and any obligations in the marriage bed had been rendered impossible. A relief to both parties concerned, to be sure.

But when Maggie went to study in Paris, there had been another man. She'd been attracted to the handsome and worldly Jean-Louis and, God save her vain soul, the attention had been quite nice. Her friend Lucien had encouraged her to take on a lover, one closer to her own age, and she'd liked Jean-Louis, so where was the harm? It had been an unholy disaster, however. The heavy breathing, the sweating, the embarrassment . . . it had all served to convince her of one terribly ironic thing:

The Half-Irish Harlot was frigid.

She'd come to accept it as fact, especially since every sort of lewd invitation had been issued during her parties and she'd felt absolutely nothing. No twitches or flutters, no racing of her pulse, or anything else the poets waxed on about.

She knew she should feel *something*. In fact, it had been Simon who'd provided a hint of what a woman could feel for a man all those years ago. Through the rose-colored spectacles of youth, she'd noticed things about him: the unique color of his eyes, his quick smile, the fall of hair over his forehead. It had all made her quite breathless.

She was no longer a girl, however, and with a woman's perspective she could well picture what was under his fine clothing. Broad shoulders atop a sculpted chest, slim hips, and long, muscular legs, a shaft jutting out proud and hard—

Heat suffused her entire body, blood thrummed in her veins, and moisture pooled between her thighs. Swallowing, she closed her eyes. Heavens, she wanted him. Lusted after him, even.

Absolutely intolerable. She would not allow it. *Could not* allow it.

The room had grown unnaturally still. She found him studying her, his gaze locked on her hands. Maggie looked down. Her fingers were clutching the top of the wingback chair in a white-knuckled grip. She would not be surprised to find indentations from her nails in the fabric. She forced her hands to relax.

He lifted one supercilious brow, a knowing smirk on his lips, and mortification burned in her chest. He was aware of, or suspected, the direction of her thoughts, the blackguard.

Straightening, she asked, "Is that all?"

"You appear"—he gestured to his face and neck— "flushed. Is it overly warm in here? I should hate to think you're coming down with a fever of some kind."

Unbelievable, his impertinence. "A *gentleman* would not comment on the color of a lady's skin."

"Shall I open a window, Maggie? Fetch a cool cloth? I shouldn't want you to—"

"All I need," she bit out, "is for you to *leave*."

He smiled, bowed. "As you wish, my lady."

So the attraction was reciprocated. Interesting.

Simon knew the signs of a woman's desire—high color, heavy lids, rapid breathing, tight, beaded nipples poking through cloth—and Maggie had exhibited those and more. His own body's reaction to her lust had almost knocked him to his knees. Christ, he'd wanted to take her right then on the small sofa. Rutted like an animal in heat until he lost himself in her.

But he had been duped before. What a clever actress

she'd been ten years ago, with her coy smiles and lingering glances. He hadn't questioned her feelings until he'd seen the irrefutable proof of her perfidy. So he would not allow her to humiliate him once more—or have her questionable standing damage his reputation in Parliament. Hard to argue for preserving morals for future generations when linked to the most scandalous woman in Society. *As an earl,* his father had said, *people will depend on you to do the honorable thing.* Without a doubt, the honorable thing would be to keep his distance from Lady Hawkins.

Therefore, as he returned to his study at Barrett House, he put the idea of tumbling Maggie firmly out of his mind. There were other matters to attend to today.

First there were meetings with members of Liverpool's circle to outline Simon's upcoming proposal, a law that would force men convicted of rape to pay financial restitution to their victims. Then he sat with his secretary to deal with correspondence before his solicitor arrived to review a contract for a parcel of land in Scotland. By the time late afternoon crept over the city, he was starving.

His housekeeper, Mrs. Timmons, arrived with the footman bearing provisions. "My lord," she said, "a Mr. Hollister is here to see you. But before you begin your meeting, may I have a moment of your time?"

"Of course, Mrs. Timmons. Thank you, Michael," he told the footman, dismissing him.

"My lord, a girl presented herself at the back door last night, a cousin to one of our lower housemaids. I've taken her on, which means I must place one of our older girls in another residence. I sent a note to the viscount's housekeeper, but I believe she's new and not yet acquainted with our staffing arrangement."

Simon sighed. "I'll speak to Quint. His housekeepers do not last, as you well know."

"Thank you, my lord. That would be most helpful. The duchess's housekeeper, however, was only too glad to take Annie. I've got the girl packing her things now. Shall I give her the usual reference and severance?"

"Yes, please, Mrs. Timmons. And thank you for your diligence."

"It is my pleasure, my lord. It's a sorry thing, to see a twelve-year-old girl with bruises all over her face and body."

"The girl from last night?" Mrs. Timmons nodded, so Simon said, "Tell the staff to give her some time to heal before putting her to work, then."

"I will, my lord."

"Thank you, Mrs. Timmons. Show Hollister back, if you please."

She returned a few minutes later, a beefy, unremarkable man behind her. The man entered and gave a polite bow. "My lord. It is an honor."

Simon's approach to finding Lemarc had many facets. Quint would study the bird paintings to narrow down a possible location, and Maggie could examine the works for any clues in the artist's technique. But the most likely method to elicit results would come through an investigator.

Hollister came highly recommended. He'd toiled for Bow Street for years, more recently taking on discreet work for members of Society. On looks alone, he seemed well suited for it; one could imagine the man blending in anywhere.

"Thank you for coming, Mr. Hollister. If you'll have a seat." He gestured to one of the chairs opposite the desk.

Hollister, limping ever so slightly, came forward and lowered into a chair.

"I'll get to the point," Simon started. "I need you to find someone. Have you heard of the artist Lemarc?"

Maggie arrived fashionably late.

The stone monstrosity that passed for the Duke of Colton's residence loomed like a setting in a gloomy Gothic novel. The lamps and torches blazed in the darkness to illuminate the pointed arches and flying buttresses. Good heavens, were those gargoyles? She often sketched buildings and churches, and her fingers itched for her charcoals as she waited on the stoop.

Hard to believe she'd been invited tonight. It'd been quite some time since she'd been asked to a dinner party of this caliber. Of course, she had reached out to the Duchess of Colton first, to request an audience, when the duchess replied with a dinner invitation.

One could only hope for an intimate gathering or, at the very least, that the guests had been warned of her attendance. Perhaps then the whispering and snickering would be kept to a minimum.

The door swung open and she was shown in. At first glance, the inside of the structure was nothing like the outside. Warm and comfortable, the home had fresh flowers and plenty of bright candlelight. As Maggie climbed the stairs, she noted a Greuze painting on the wall. Impressive. The duke and his duchess had excellent taste.

When she stepped into the salon, the first person her eyes found was Simon. He stood across the room, tall, lithe, and handsome. The shock of his appearance felt similar to a kick to the stomach, and she appreciated it about as much.

Blast it all. She should have expected him to be in attendance, considering his relationship to the duke. If she'd known, however, she certainly would have refused the invitation. The memory of their last exchange still haunted her. Why did he, of all men, elicit such wanton, lustful feelings from her?

A blond beauty in a pale pink gown rushed forward to clasp her hands, diverting her attention. "Lady Hawkins," the duchess exclaimed. "I am indeed grateful you decided to attend our motley gathering."

"Truly, I am honored," Maggie replied, with a genuine smile and a proper curtsy.

"None of that," the duchess said. "We're amongst friends. Well, mostly friends anyhow."

"Lady Hawkins." The Duke of Colton arrived at his wife's side. A dark and handsome man, one could easily imagine how he'd earned his reputation as the Depraved Duke. "How lovely to see you. My wife has been speaking of you all week."

"Good evening, Your Grace. I am happy to be included." Not to mention baffled.

"Come along," the duchess said, "and I'll introduce you to tonight's group." Slipping her arm through Maggie's, the duchess thankfully steered them in the opposite direction from where Simon stood.

The introductions took several minutes. Most were familiar faces—the men, at least. When the duchess excused herself to check on the other guests, Maggie found herself with Lord Quint. The viscount gave her an elegant bow, stood, and pushed overly long brown hair out of his face. "Lady Hawkins. I look forward to more discussions on painting this evening. Do you plan on attending the Bathmore exhibit in two weeks' time?"

"I do, indeed. I am curious to see if this new batch of paintings solves the perspective issues in his last exhibit."

Quint chuckled. "You are a harsh critic."

"I suppose that is true. I am much more interested in the technique and the choices an artist makes rather than the end result."

"I quite agree. I find myself fascinated by the whys and hows of things."

Quiet and whip-smart, Quint had a subtle handsomeness under that rumpled exterior. Even his appalling fashion sense was endearing. So why did she not get fluttery in his presence instead of Simon's? Quint would be better suited to her, with his keen eye and perceptive nature, and he seemed much too reasonable to mind her blackened reputation.

Not that it mattered, as she intended to avoid the male species.

Another familiar face joined them. A bit older than the others, Lord Markham's presence tonight had been an unwelcome surprise. He'd attended a few of Maggie's recent parties, never failing to issue at least one not-so-veiled invitation to her during the evening. She never encouraged him, but some men were more determined than others.

"Lady Hawkins." Markham bowed, his smile a touch too wide as his eyes traveled up and down her form.

"May I say how happy I am to find you here this evening? I had no idea you were on such intimate terms with Colton."

The gleam in his gaze said exactly what intimate terms he assumed. From everything Maggie knew, the duke and duchess were happily married, and there had been no rumors regarding the duke and another woman since his return from the Continent. But even if Colton did have discreet affairs, did Markham truly think the duchess the sort of woman to tolerate her husband's conquests at her dinner table?

"Her Grace issued the invitation after she attended my party last week," Maggie told him.

"Indeed," Markham said, giving her an audacious wink that caused bile to rise in her throat.

Yes, why else would the Half-Irish Harlot be invited? Markham's assumptions were likely being made by everyone here, save Colton and his duchess. She straightened her spine to stand a bit taller. Let them think what they would; they always did.

"Excuse me," Quint murmured before sliding away. Maggie considered clutching his arm in order to prevent his escape, but Quint proved too quick.

Markham took this as an invitation to move closer. Desperate for help, Maggie glanced wildly around the room. Her gaze swung in Simon's direction, then stopped. Sharp blue eyes were locked on her, the irises bright with cold fury. She'd never seen him so furious. What in heaven's name?

"Lady Hawkins," Markham whispered, boldly reaching out to touch her hand.

Simon didn't miss Markham's audacity either. A muscle in the earl's jaw clenched before he pointedly turned away. An idea occurred. Perhaps if she kept

Markham close this evening, Simon would maintain a distance. The notion was a harsh one and would ensure a tedious evening—but a woman must do what she must, after all.

She gave Markham a blinding smile. "Yes, my lord?"

The viscount blinked. "Oh, yes. Well, I had hoped to escort you to dinner. You never—"

"Yes," she blurted. "I meant to say, I would be honored."

"Excellent." Markham puffed up, his ruddy face turning a bit ruddier. "I quite enjoyed your last party. Interesting how Rowlandson had that cartoon about the mermaids."

"Lemarc," she corrected.

Markham's brows dipped. "I beg your pardon?"

"The cartoon was drawn by Lemarc, not Rowlandson."

"Oh, yes, Lemarc. Clever gents, those cartoonists. I wonder how they're privy to the *on-dits* used in their drawings."

If they're smart, they host parties. "Who knows? Perhaps they are more resourceful than we give them credit for."

He leaned in, as if to share a great secret. "All you need is to press a coin into the right palm, m'dear. Any information can be bought."

That comment gave her pause. Markham was active in Parliament, so was he speaking from experience? More to the point, perhaps she could use this opportunity to undermine Winchester's proposal. Yes, this evening was looking up.

At that moment, the duchess announced dinner. Markham presented his arm. "Shall we?"

Chapter Six

"Simon, really. You must stop glaring at her," Julia said.

Simon and Julia were making their way down to dinner, last in the line of guests. He clenched his jaw and forced his gaze away from Maggie and Markham. Anger still burned in his gut, however. Markham had attached himself to Lady Hawkins like an apothecary's leech from the moment she'd arrived. Did the man have no shame?

"And you are the one who insisted I invite Markham," Julia continued.

"Thank you for the reminder," he muttered.

"I don't believe I've ever seen you jealous. This is quite interesting."

He made a dismissive noise as they reached the stairs. "I'm hardly jealous of Markham. There's a reason his wife stays in Cornwall and no mistress will tolerate him for more than a few weeks. The man wouldn't know what to do with a woman if she dropped, naked, into his lap."

"A good thing we've been friends forever, otherwise

my husband might take offense to the nature of this conversation."

"Colton hardly scares me. After all, I'm the reason you two reconciled. He should thank me every chance he gets."

"Oh, it was your doing, was it?"

He grinned down at her. "You never would have made it to Venice without my assistance."

"True, but I had the hard part."

"Please." He held up his free hand. "Let's not discuss Colton's virility before I've food in my stomach. I'm likely to lose my appetite."

Julia chuckled. "You are incorrigible. It's a wonder anyone takes you seriously in Parliament."

"They don't know me as well as you do, that's how."

"Quite so. Otherwise, they would not be so easily intimidated by the illustrious statesman you've become."

They entered the enormous dining room. Colton had taken his place at the head of the elaborate table, Julia's aunt on his right. Simon noted that Markham had, of course, secured the chair beside Maggie. Bloody fool.

"Ease up, Simon," Julia muttered. "You are crushing my hand."

"My apologies."

"You know, you deserve everything she gives you and more," the duchess said under her breath as they took their seats.

"I shall remember you said as much," he returned, "especially when Colton asks me if you've ever visited a gaming—"

She slapped his arm. "Simon! Do not breathe a word of that to my husband."

"Something amiss, Duchess?" Colton called, glancing between his wife and Simon.

Julia gave him a perfectly innocent look. "No, Colton. Merely starving." She signaled to the footman to begin service.

Simon purposely averted his gaze from Maggie and Markham during dinner. Maggie's encouraging grins at the viscount made Simon contemplate stabbing someone with a dinner fork. So he drank more than he ate. Not until the sixth course did he realize he was fast on his way to becoming soused.

It didn't help that she was bloody beautiful, the witch. He wished he'd stop noticing, but he could picture every detail, every curve—even with his eyes closed. All those years ago, he'd spent hours pondering the delicate bones in her wrist. Or the curve of her ear. Imagining her bare, soft breasts would have turned him hard as stone.

Tonight, the tops of said breasts were pushed absurdly high. He found the lush, creamy swells incredibly distracting, as likely did every other able-bodied male in the room.

And why had she come tonight? He hadn't expected to see her here. At the very least, Julia should've warned him Maggie would be attending. Then he could have sent his regrets.

"Would you care to go and lie down?" Julia asked him quietly. "You are drawing stares."

He straightened and forked up a bite of roasted lamb. "Do not be ridiculous."

"Will you ever tell me what happened?"

Everything you likely hoped for and worse. The comment had pricked at him for days. What had Maggie meant?

He noticed Julia studying him and tried to remember her question. Damned wine. "What?"

"I asked if you would tell me what happened between the two of you."

"No."

Julia contemplated his answer while she chewed. "Perhaps I'll get Lady Hawkins to tell me, then."

"Ask her if you wish, but you know what everyone knows. There's nothing more to the tale." She'd made a fool of him. The end. What more needed to be discussed?

"Oh, there's often more to a story than what gossip carries. Look at Colton, the way the *ton* branded him a rapscallion and a murderer before the truth came out."

"Colton *is* a rapscallion," Simon pointed out.

Julia grinned. "Yes, but he's my rapscallion now. And anyway, I am not so sure Lady Hawkins meant to break your heart."

Simon picked up his wine and threw it back. He signaled to the footman for more. "Men don't get broken hearts, Julia. Those are for young girls and poets with nothing but time on their hands."

Julia drummed her fingers on the table. "Is that so?"

"Quite. I figure she did me a favor."

"By all means, then, have another glass of gratitude before the end of dinner."

There were six women in attendance, so maneuvering a seat next to the duchess proved challenging. Yet Maggie managed it neatly. The ladies had all settled in the drawing room, having left the gentlemen in the dining room, and the duchess now began pouring tea.

Maggie accepted her cup and added two lumps of sugar. She relaxed and took a grateful sip. Dinner had been excruciating. Not only had she juggled Markham's attentions, but Simon spent the evening either scowling at her or pretending she didn't exist. Hard to say which bothered her more.

Truth be told, the ease with which Simon interacted with the duchess made Maggie envious. Clearly the two were close friends. Maggie had once enjoyed that same familiarity with him. They had shared jokes and laughed together, and he'd been the first person she'd sought out upon entering a room. Of course, she'd stupidly assumed his attention meant something, that it showed a depth of feeling on his part. She'd been wrong; he'd snubbed her just as the rest had.

"I see you like your tea sweet," the duchess remarked as she sat back. "I do as well, though I can't resist a bit of cream."

"I have a terrible sweet tooth," Maggie admitted. "I've been known to have a slice of cake for breakfast."

The duchess's brows shot up. "How deliciously decadent. You are a woman after my own heart."

"I hope so." Maggie leaned closer, lowered her voice. "Perhaps you'll be amenable to providing help to a friend of mine."

"Oh?"

"Yes, Pearl Kelly." The duchess's eyes widened, so Maggie continued. "She and I have embarked upon an endeavor, and we've encountered a strange request." Maggie proceeded to fill the duchess in on the three girls who wanted to apprentice with a modiste.

"It is a challenge," the duchess admitted. "But I do love a challenge. And because of the baby, I've ordered three new complete wardrobes in two years. My dressmakers are ready to nominate me for sainthood. Tell me, what do you and Pearl hope to accomplish?"

"For the most part, we offer the owners additional funds for better care. For disease and other delicate . . . problems. We also try to help the girls learn, whether it's reading, writing, sewing, or an instrument."

"A worthwhile cause. Indeed, I am a bit jealous she did not ask me to help."

"It was I who approached her originally. However, if you and I had known one another, I would have asked for your involvement."

"Well, you shall be hard-pressed to keep me out of it now. I'll pay some visits tomorrow and let you know. Have you told Simon of this work?"

Maggie frowned. "No. Why would I?"

Julia's lips twisted as if she stifled a smile. "No reason. Amazing how little we know of one another, is it not?"

Maggie shrugged. "Often what we show the world is not our true selves."

"Indeed." The duchess's gaze was far too calculating for Maggie's comfort. Another guest secured Julia's attention, so Maggie took the opportunity to excuse herself. She needed a moment alone, or perhaps some fresh air.

The long corridor outside the drawing room resembled a maze, with doors every which way. Picking a direction, she searched for a footman. Perhaps he could draw her a detailed map on how to find the terrace.

From the shadow of an alcove, a figure stepped into her path. "Lady Hawkins."

Simon. She started, pressed a hand to her chest.

"You scared the life out of me. What are you doing out here?"

He folded his arms, the fine wool of his coat pulling taut across his broad shoulders. "I could ask you the same question—only I suspect the answer. Where did you have it planned?"

"Simon, I think you had better return to the dining room—"

"The music room? The conservatory?" he continued, steady steps bringing him closer. "I happen to know there are hundreds of little spots all over this house where one—or perhaps two—could hide for an extended period of time."

She tried to make sense of his words over the thundering of her heart. Was he insinuating . . . ? Oh, for heaven's sake. Did he always assume the *worst* of her? Feet planted, she stopped moving and lifted her chin. "Are you under the impression I'm engaging in some sort of a *tryst*? In the middle of a dinner party?" It was so absurd, she could hardly speak it.

His smirk confirmed it. "Convenient you and Markham both excused yourselves within moments of one another, wouldn't you say? Let me give you a piece of advice for next time: It draws less attention if you sneak away once the gentlemen join the—"

She came forward to hiss, "You hypocritical horse's arse. I stepped out for some air. Alone."

He had the gall to snort. "Yes, I'm quite sure Markham would offer up a similar story if we were to ask him."

Anger rushed through her veins, settling in her chest like a heavy mound of potter's clay. Simon loomed over her, snarling down in self-righteous fury, and she discovered he'd backed her up against a wall.

She knew in that moment he would never believe her denials; he'd formed his opinion of her ten years ago and there would be no changing his mind.

Fine, she could play the harlot for him. Maybe then he'd leave her alone—though she truly longed to crack him one across his closely shaven jaw.

She exhaled, forced her limbs to relax, and licked her lips. Predictably, his gaze locked on her mouth, so she rolled her bottom lip between her teeth. His chest continued to rise and fall, the harsh exhales filling the room, and his eyes darkened to sapphires. Oh yes, revenge could be sweet. Ever so slowly, she dragged one finger down the length of her bare collarbone. "Did you corner me in hopes of taking his place?" she asked, her voice low and intimate.

Simon shifted closer, the pure male, spicy scent of him filling her nose. She liked the way he smelled, orange and sandalwood with a hint of tobacco. The proximity of his frame distracted her as well. His evening clothes held no padding, and the well-tailored fit hugged him quite perfectly. She could see the outline—

"If I chose to take Markham's place," he started, placing his hands against the wall, one on either side of her head, to cage her in. He leaned in and for one terrifying, heart-stopping moment she thought he was going to kiss her, but he shifted just before their lips touched. The tip of his nose slid across her cheek, tiny puffs of breath heating her skin as he nuzzled her. Maggie's breasts swelled, and her lids fell with a rush of pleasure that rippled the length of her body. "If I chose to take his place, it wouldn't be here," he whispered near her ear. "I'd take you to my bed at Barrett House and show you wickedness Markham could not even begin to imagine. But that is not why I cornered you."

Close. He was much too close. Despite her desire to remain unaffected, her belly fluttered and warmth tingled between her legs. Why on earth had it only ever been this odious man to elicit such feelings? She swallowed. "Then why?"

He flicked her earbob with his tongue, then nipped the lobe with gentle teeth. She inhaled sharply. "What game are you playing at, Maggie?"

"I—" Her traitorous voice caught, so she cleared her throat. "There is no game, Simon."

Her control began melting away. She longed to do every improper thing in the world to him—and for him to return them in kind. Odd since she hadn't ever enjoyed intimacies with a man. Had hated it, actually. But somehow, this was different.

Why had she started this? Oh yes, she'd thought to teach him a lesson, make a fool of him. Have him panting with lust and then leave him begging—only this was turning into something else entirely.

"I like games," he continued, his lips brushing over her throat in a seductive caress. "But I also like to win. I wonder, are you prepared to pay the price when you lose?"

She shivered. There wasn't enough air in the damn room. "I never lose," she rasped. "And you have more at stake."

"Do I?" His nose slid along the sensitive line of her jaw, the skin prickling in his wake. "I think I could take you against this wall. Right now. Right here." His hips pressed against hers, his erection stiff and un-apologetic, and she sucked in a breath. Before she knew it, her hands clutched at his waist to hold him in place.

"But you should know," he continued, his mouth hovering above her lips, "I only play games when there aren't quite so many players. I do not care to be one of many."

It took a few seconds for that remark to sink in. When it did, hurt and anger resurfaced to eclipse whatever else she might have felt. The unbelievable, thick-skulled *swine*.

All of her muscles clenched and she shoved at his shoulder with all her strength. When he stepped back, she pushed by him and strode for the door. While the idea of running had merit, she couldn't resist a last parting jab over her shoulder. "Fitting, then, that we shall never know how you measure up."

Simon needed several minutes to collect himself. The current state of his shaft, now diamond-hard, prevented an immediate return to the party, so he practiced the speech he'd been crafting for Parliament in order to distract himself from his run-in with Maggie. How she'd felt pressed against the length of him. Her sweet scent. The softness of her skin.

Groaning, he reached to shift himself inside his breeches. Christ, he'd never rejoin the others if he kept this up. And what had he been thinking, baiting her in such a manner? He had no intention of tangling himself with her, no matter how enticing the package. Why had he drunk so much wine at dinner?

At least he'd prevented her tryst with Markham.

That brought a measure of grim satisfaction for many reasons. Markham had been invited merely because Simon needed to gain the viscount's support for the upcoming proposal. Yet the old fool had spent the entire evening salivating over Maggie—not that she'd done anything to dissuade him.

As long as Simon lived, he'd never understand what Maggie saw in those other men. While Simon could live with having been thrown over, she certainly deserved someone better than Cranford—or Markham. Had the woman no standards?

By the time he strode into the main hall, Maggie stood in the entryway, fastening her pelisse while speaking in low tones to Julia. The duchess nodded; then the two women embraced. So Maggie had decided to quit the party. Feeling a bit of a voyeur, he returned to the drawing room and found Markham on the sofa chatting with another guest. Had he given up on Maggie so easily, or did he have plans to follow her home this evening? The idea made Simon positively ill.

Colton and Quint were propped up near the sideboard, so Simon made his way over.

"I would ask where you've been," Colton drawled, "but considering the way Lady Hawkins just blazed in and dragged my wife out of here, I'd venture the question unnecessary."

Simon reached for the decanter. "Leave off, Colt."

"What did you say to her?" Quint asked. "She looked bloody furious."

Simon could not begin to sort through the emotions swirling in his head, let alone talk about it. "Do you two not have anything better to occupy your time than to stand around and gossip? You're worse than ladies loitering around a punchbowl."

The duke's eyebrows lifted. "What has your bollocks up your arse?"

"It's Markham, is it not? You think Lady Hawkins
favors him." Simon watched as Quint lifted his tea,
sipped. The viscount never drank spirits. Ever. Said it
scrambled his brain and he hated the dull, numb
feeling.

Simon, on the other hand, needed a bit of numb-
ness. His glass now full of claret, he took a healthy
mouthful and swallowed.

"Doubt anyone missed that," Colton said. "So she
flirted with Markham and, what, it hurt your tender
feelings?"

Simon sighed. "Remind me why I helped you reconcile with your wife? I liked you far better when I
only saw you once every few years."

"It's because the duchess tricked you," Quint put
in. "Both of you, actually."

"Quint," Colton drawled, "there are times when
you are unbelievably helpful. This is not one of those
times."

Because Simon had a clear shot of the doorway, he
noted the instant Julia reentered the room. Glancing about, her gaze locked with his and, mouth tight,
she started forward.

"I know that face," Colton muttered. "That face
means one should run—not walk—the other way.
Winchester, dear God, man, do yourself a favor—"

"Too late," Quint said as Julia joined them.

"May I speak with you?" Julia snapped at Simon.
Her blue eyes narrowed on him and he knew he'd
best get it over with.

He wouldn't go without fortification, however, and

took a moment to refill his glass. When he finished, he turned. "After you, Duchess."

She stomped to the farthest point in the room, lifting her skirts to keep from tripping in her haste. "What in the name of Hades happened? You and Lady Hawkins disappear together, only to have her return in a tizzy. What. Did. You. Do?"

He took umbrage at that. "Why do you assume it was *me*? What about what she did?"

"What are you, a child tattling on your naughty sibling?" Julia pinched the bridge of her nose. "I vow, I have never seen you like this. You're normally so calm, so predictable. It's as if you've been completely replaced by a stranger with the same outward appearance."

"What did Lady Hawkins tell you?"

"Nothing. Merely that she felt out of sorts and needed to get home to rest. But it was clear it had to do with you, since she came back from your tête-à-tête worked up into a lather. I don't like you upsetting a guest, not to mention a friend."

"A friend?"

"Yes, a friend. I like her. And I'm helping her with a little project."

"What project?" He didn't like the idea of Maggie and Julia becoming close. The two women were far too alike and he already knew what sort of trouble Julia could get in to. Hell, he'd rescued her enough over the years from one scrape or another. Now he needed to worry about Maggie as well?

"None of your concern, is what. Honestly, Simon, I know you're carrying a grudge over what happened all those years—"

"Ridiculous. I am *not* carrying a grudge. But did

you see the way she encouraged Markham, flirting with him all night? Fairly disgusting."

"She's a widow and has already earned a reputation for herself. Since most of polite society will not have her, I say she's entitled to partake in fun wherever she can. And it is unlike you to pass judgment on another's liaisons."

He pressed his lips together, unable and unwilling to comment. How could he explain it to Julia when he barely understood it himself?

"Tonight almost makes me regret the small part I played in that fiasco during her debut. Perhaps you should have challenged Cranford after all."

"No, you were right. It would not have changed the outcome and likely could have made it all worse. Cranford may be many things, but a poor shot has never been one of them."

"I don't know. There is a sense of grand romance. . . ." She trailed off. "Anyway, what's done is done. I just cannot understand why you insist on punishing the woman. Hasn't she suffered enough?"

"Suffered?" he scoffed. "You've been to one of her parties. The woman lives like a French aristocrat before Robespierre started lopping heads off. I'd hardly call that a hardship."

"You are obviously more cynical and dim-witted than I give you credit for." Julia blew out a breath. "Being on the outskirts of our Society is different for a woman than a man. I shouldn't expect you to understand, but I do expect you to leave her be, Simon."

"Fine," he snapped, then gentled his tone. "I'll leave her be." He heard the resolution in his voice but wondered if he truly meant it.

Chapter Seven

Early the following morning, the door of Maggie's studio swung open and Rebecca's voice rang out. "I couldn't wait a second longer. I want to hear all about last evening."

Maggie didn't look up. Sitting at the large wooden table she used for drawing, she continued to sketch, determined to get the image down perfectly. She'd been at it for over an hour. "Tilda, bring tea, if you would."

"Yes, m'lady."

Maggie heard the click of the latch and then felt a presence at her back.

"Are you working on the Scottish and Welsh drawings for Ackermann's travel book?" Rebecca asked, up on her toes to peek over Maggie's shoulder.

Maggie hunched and covered the paper with her hands. "No. It's another cartoon for the shop, and you'll see it when it's done, not before."

"Fine. Lud, you're secretive about your work." Becca crossed to the sofa near the tall row of windows. "It's nothing to do with last night, I trust." Silence stretched until Rebecca gasped. "Maggie! What are you thinking? Everyone will know Lemarc attended the duchess's dinner party."

"No one would believe such a thing. People will merely assume he's well informed."

"Still, it is an unnecessary risk in my opinion, but I know you will not listen to me. So what happened between you and Winchester last evening?"

Maggie's hand slipped. Damn. The lower right section would need to be redone now. "Must we talk about this now?"

"Yes, I rather think we must. He must have been there because Tilda said you came home early, madder than a wet hen."

Curse her loose-lipped servant. Maggie put down her pencil and stood to take the chair nearest her sister. "Yes, he was there. Glaring at me from across the room the entire evening. He is the most infuriating man."

"An infuriating man you were once madly in love with. I worry you will not be able to resist him."

The memory of being pressed up against his body last night rushed back. *I think I could take you against this wall. Right now. Right here.* He may have turned her plan to tempt him around on her, but she would not fall for it a second time.

She waved her hand. "He is the very last man I would choose to involve myself with."

"Especially when you could have your pick of all the men in the *ton*. It's not fair; widows get to have all the fun."

Oh, yes. So much *fun*. The gossip, the snickers behind her back. The innuendo and improper invitations constantly hurled her way. Becca certainly had romantic visions of Maggie's life, and Maggie loved her too dearly to ever crush them with the harsh reality. So she smiled and said, "I think you mean men get to have all the fun."

"Well, no one could argue with that statement. Tell me who else was there."

Tilda returned with tea just as Maggie began a recounting of the evening, starting with a description of the Colton town house. By the time tea had been poured, she'd told almost all of it and ended with her decision to come home early.

"You've left out the most important tidbit," Becca said. "What caused you to leave prematurely? Something—or some*one*—obviously upset you."

Maggie lifted a shoulder and took a sip. "A small disagreement. Nothing worth mentioning."

"Liar. What did he say to you? I swear, if he was cruel—"

"I love that you worry, dear sister, but there's nothing you can do to change the minds of the stubborn."

Her sister tapped her toe, a sure sign Becca was deep in thought. Maggie sipped her tea and kept silent. Finally, Becca's eyes grew wide, then narrowed. "So Winchester believes all those terrible rumors about you? He should be the one man to know better. I swear, I will never forgive him for not standing up for you when—"

"Oh, Becca." Maggie sighed. "What's done is done. Many times we expect more from our friends than they are prepared to give. Or capable of giving, really. I'm grateful I learned where I stood when I did. Otherwise, I could have spent many miserable years with a man who cared so little for me."

"Instead you spent many miserable years with a man old enough to be your father."

"They were not miserable. Lonely, certainly, but not miserable. Hawkins preferred his mistress and I had no arguments to the contrary."

Becca leaned over to grip Maggie's hand. "And you do not see that as miserable?"

Maggie smiled, shook her head. "No, I certainly do not. Not everyone finds love as you and Marcus did. You are one of the rare examples of a happy marriage, Becca. And while I could not be more pleased for you, not everyone is so fortunate."

"And I have you to thank for my marriage to Marcus. Had you not married Hawkins, I never would have found my husband."

Maggie squeezed her sister's fingers affectionately. After the scandal, Maggie had the choice to marry Hawkins or bring shame on her entire family, including her innocent younger sister. Under no certain terms would Maggie have deprived Becca of the ability to debut and find a husband, no matter what it cost her personally. So she'd married Hawkins, endured the painful and embarrassing wedding night, lived in the little town where the whispers and innuendo followed, and buried herself in her art. But Becca's gratitude and happiness made the past ten years worthwhile.

"I only wish Papa had lived long enough to see how successful you've become," Becca continued. "He would be so proud of you."

Tears pricked Maggie's eyes before she could prevent it. She missed her father, whose sensitive artist's soul had been so much like her own. It hurt to think his final memories of her were of shame and disappointment. All she'd ever wanted was to make him proud, and she'd failed miserably while he'd been alive. Perhaps now, from wherever he rested, he would see all she'd accomplished in a short amount of time.

She exhaled, released Becca's hand, and sat back. "At least he saw you happily married. He knew how much you loved Marcus." Watching her father's grin during Becca's wedding ceremony had been bitter-sweet for Maggie; Papa's joy at Becca's match only sharpened the contrast of his unhappiness during Maggie's hasty wedding.

"Yes, but you were always his favorite. And he knew how talented you were, even then." Cup in hand, Becca relaxed on the tiny sofa. "I do so love this space. It's quite relaxing up here."

"I spend most of my time here," Maggie said, "as you know. Just look at the stains on my hands." Maggie had purchased the town house with a portion of her jointure. The best feature of her town house by far was the small glass room on the upper floor.

The previous owner had been a sculptor and he'd joined the top-floor nursery and smaller bedroom into one giant windowed studio. The space was an artist's dream. Two dormer windows had been com-bined to form one long row of windows—each com-prised of small squares separated by thin glazing bars—for maximum light. All of them opened with hinges to allow for fresh air when she painted. There were glass windows in the ceiling as well, and they could be vented and propped open using a long pole. With its high ceilings and privacy, the room was quiet, airy, and bright. Maggie loved it.

All she needed was this space and her paints. A

pencil and some canvas. Simple things that in no way included the Earl of Winchester.

"Maggie," Becca said, regaining her attention. "You know the work I've been doing with the Foundling Hospital in Bloomsbury. The committee has planned an event to raise money and I hoped to use some of your artwork, if you're amenable. They've some other pieces, by Rowlandson, Pugin, and the like, and Lemarc's work would surely generate some interest as well."

"Of course. Whatever you need. I would be honored."

"What do you think about donating some pieces under your own name? You've dreamed of establishing a more respectable career outside of Lemarc. This could be a most advantageous opportunity."

The idea had merit. It would allow her greater freedom to admit her passion to the world. She would no longer need to keep her work a secret. But would Society accept her? Women artists were not as well received as their male peers. Patrons were harder to come by and commissions were scarce enough as it was. It was easier in France, where a few women, such as Vigée-Lebrun and Ducreux, had already succeeded. The English had not been as quick to embrace female artists, however.

Still, if she could do her own pieces and continue on as Lemarc as well . . . But who would purchase art by the Half-Irish Harlot? Hard to guess whether her reputation would make the art more popular or herself more of an outcast.

"I will think on it. When does this event take place?"

"A few months yet."

"If I start working under my name, there is a chance of social recrimination, which could affect you and Marcus."

"I shan't mind a bit. You have a gift, Maggie, and it should be celebrated, not hidden away. Let them gossip all they like. You know the talk only leads to the sale of more pieces."

"Afternoon, Quint. Nice of you to tidy up for me."

Simon stepped over the usual stacks of papers and books along the floor on the way to the viscount's desk, where his friend was studying something. Quint straightened, giving Simon a good look at today's sartorial transgression. A violet coat over a green striped waistcoat, topped with a cravat so loosely tied it more resembled a sash. Simon cringed. He loved Quint, but the way his friend dressed would have Brummell fainting dead away in the street.

Last evening, Quint had revealed he'd made progress with the birds and asked that Simon call today. Even still, it seemed Quint was entirely taken off guard by Simon's arrival.

"Winchester! Glad you're here. I'd offer you a chair, but . . ." Quint gestured to the two across from the desk, which were filled with books. "Hold on and let me just get the—" Quint shuffled about, then carefully laid out seven framed portraits on the desk. When he was done, he waved a hand. "Your bird engravings."

"Weren't there almost twenty of them?"

"Yes, but I've eliminated all of the usual birds. Ones found anywhere in England, such as the partridge, magpie, woodpecker, and the like. What we have here are the only seven that matter in narrowing down where our famed artist might reside."

"Or once visited."

"Perhaps," Quint allowed. "But as you'll see, some of these birds span seasons. So if the artist only took a short vacation, he likely wouldn't have seen summer birds *and* winter birds. In my opinion, the artist spent a considerable amount of time in this area, watching wildlife."

"Yes, that makes sense."

"Now, let's study the remaining lot. The top row"— he pointed—"are the male golden oriole, female dotterel, and nightingale. All summer feathering, mostly located only in eastern England. The second row, the bar-tailed godwit, plover, redwing, and dunlin, are depicted with their winter feathering. All can be seen in eastern England during the winter." Quint slid two of the frames down to separate them. "What's interesting is that both the godwit and the dunlin are coastal birds, specifically living around estuaries all throughout England."

"We're thinking somewhere in eastern England, near the coast or an estuary?"

"Well, that was my conclusion until I landed upon this one." Quint bent, produced another framed painting from his desk drawer. "This appears to be, at first glance, a type of grouse, which you find up north on the moors. But I can't place it."

"So what is it?"

"The devil if I know. It's no bird found in England."

They both stared at the painting for a long moment. "What if Lemarc got it wrong?" Simon suggested.

"You mean he invented a bird?"

"That or perhaps painted it from memory—only he didn't remember it correctly."

"You might be on to something. Grab that book over there, will you? The black one with the yellow lettering."

Simon followed Quint's direction until he found the book entitled *Birds Throughout England*. He handed it over.

Quint flipped through to the section containing grouses. He rustled through the pages quickly. "Aha. Here, a male red grouse." He placed the book down on the desk alongside the framed painting. The men moved their eyes back and forth to study each image.

"Look here, the bill is all wrong." Simon pointed to the painting. "And according to the book, there should be yellow edging on the wing feathers, which is missing in Lemarc's version."

"But it's close enough we can assume this is what Lemarc attempted to paint. He didn't have one in front of him, however, so did it from memory." Quint slapped Simon on the back. "Well done! I knew you were smarter than you appeared—"

"Easy, man. I am still able to pin you to the ground with one hand tied behind my back."

His friend chuckled and picked up the grouse painting. "I believe we can discount this one altogether, then."

"I agree. Lemarc likely had seen one in his lifetime but didn't have a recollection recent enough to work from when completing the painting."

Quint flipped the picture over. "So, without the grouse, your artist is near an estuary in eastern England. My opinion would be Suffolk or Norfolk, near the sea."

"Which doesn't do much good. Those counties are rife with estuaries."

Quint put a hand to his ear, cupping it. "Beg pardon? Was that a 'thank you, Quint' I just heard?"

Simon grinned and clapped his friend on the shoulder. "Thank you, Quint. This is brilliant, though I daresay I'd hoped for a closer range."

"You are aware that birds *fly*, are you not? The best we could hope for was a small region." Quint pushed a stack of books onto the floor and flopped down in the now-empty chair. "We've narrowed it down to two counties. What more do you want?"

"My apologies. I'm being churlish." He sat on the edge of the desk, the only remotely clean surface in the room. "Hopefully the Runner I've hired can narrow it down further. May I take these with me?"

"Of course. Tug the bell pull, will you? I haven't eaten all day and no doubt my housekeeper is on the verge of hysteria."

Simon strode over and did as Quint asked, remarking, "How long have you had this one?"

"Five weeks. I hope she lasts."

Not likely, Simon thought. Though he could afford to pay well, being in Quint's employ had to be more bloody trouble than the job was worth. The viscount buried himself in projects from time to time, with any normal routine abandoned for his whims. Sometimes he didn't remember to eat until well into the night.

Simon collected the eight frames off the desk, then went to the door. "I shall leave you to it, then. I've got an errand to run. Will I see you later at the club?"

"Doubtful. I've a clock that's running a few minutes slow and I want to—"

Simon held up a hand. Quint could talk details until cock's crow, and Simon was pressed for time. "No need to spell it out for me. Thank you for the information on the birds, Quint. As always, you've been brilliant."

"I'll expect you to have that inscribed on my tombstone."

"Again, my thanks. I shall see you tomorrow, then." Simon lifted the handle and escaped into the hall.

Normally Simon would linger. However, his mother had sent a note requesting his presence for tea and, before that, he wished to deliver the bird paintings for Lady Hawkins's inspection.

The ride to Maggie's did not take long. He had no clue whether she was receiving callers or not, so he bounded up the steps, the pictures cradled in his hands. Perhaps he could leave them with a servant.

He doubted she would see him—not after their exchange during the dinner party last evening. Maggie had been furious when she left; everyone had seen and commented on that fact. And honestly, what had prompted him to act the way he had? If she wanted Markham, why in hell should Simon stand between them?

When the door opened, Simon found the same servant he'd encountered on previous visits staring back at him. He presented his card and requested an audience with Lady Hawkins. The woman eyed him critically before allowing him entry. She held out her hands to take his things, so he rested the paintings on a small table and began removing his greatcoat.

A card on the table caught his eye. The name on it,

easily read even from his height, caused him to gnash his teeth. "Has Lord Markham departed?"

"No, my lord. Her ladyship is still engaged. Perhaps your lordship would care to wait in the salon?"

"That won't be necessary." He gave her his coat and snatched up the paintings. "I am acquainted with them both. Lady Hawkins will not mind if I intrude." A bold lie, if he'd ever heard it—not that he cared.

Having been here a few days prior, he knew precisely where to go. The servant followed closely behind. "My lord," she called, but he walked quickly, an uncomfortable tightness in his chest providing him additional speed.

Seconds later, he threw open the drawing room door, stepped in. Maggie's head shot up and she gaped, while Markham rose and saluted Simon with his teacup. "Welcome, Winchester. Care to join us?"

Of all the wretchedly inconvenient timing.

Maggie watched with dismayed interest as Simon strode farther into the room, a stack of small canvases in his hands. She'd barely begun discrediting Simon's upcoming proposal to Lord Markham when the earl himself strolled in. Surely Simon wouldn't stay, would he?

She observed him from under her lashes. Long legs wrapped in tight buckskin breeches, tall, black boots, wide shoulders framed in a sapphire-blue topcoat. He was every bit as breathtaking and imposing as ever. And just as it had done at eighteen, her silly heart stuttered at the sight of him. She forced her eyes elsewhere.

"I wouldn't want to interrupt," he said smoothly.

"Nonsense," Lord Markham returned and lowered into his chair. "You might well be interested in this conversation."

Simon wasted no time in joining, the lout. After placing the canvases on a table, he made himself comfortable. "Is that so?" He lifted an eyebrow and shot Maggie a look dripping in sarcasm. "By all means, continue. I am trembling with anticipation."

Did he think she was wooing Markham—or allowing Markham to woo her? Likely yes, since he believed her bedchamber to be filled by a never-ending stable of able-bodied lovers. She straightened and did not attempt to hide her displeasure. "Would you care for tea, Lord Winchester? Since you intend to stay, that is."

"No, thank you, Lady Hawkins. Though your offer is most generous." His tone implied entirely the opposite, and she longed to pick up a saucer and toss it at his head.

"The lady was just explaining—" Lord Markham started.

"My lord," Maggie interrupted. "I am certain Lord Winchester has more interesting topics of conversation in mind than our boring matter."

"Indeed," Simon drawled, "I am certain I do not. Pray continue, Markham."

Markham's gaze darted between her and Simon, and then he cleared his throat. "Yes, well, the lady was telling me about your—"

"Estate. We've just been discussing your estate," she blurted.

Markham blinked rapidly but did not contradict

her, thankfully. "Why, yes. That's so. Quite." Maggie relaxed, relieved Markham hadn't given her up. Simon would be furious to learn she was actively working to thwart his idiotic proposal.

"My . . . estate." Simon stripped off his gloves and began drumming his fingers on the edge of the chair, his expression cool and disbelieving. "Truthfully, I am impressed. To be clear, which of the four estates in my care were you discussing?"

Four? Her mind scrambled for a name. "Winchester Towers. But let us move on to other matters. I dislike carrying on serious discussions in a crowd."

"Surprising, since you certainly prefer crowds for everything else."

Her breath caught. Then Winchester's comment from last evening—*I only play games when there aren't quite so many players. I don't care to be one of many*—came back, and anger heated her blood, boiled inside her like a rising tide. His insults were unjustified and tiresome. She wanted to lash out, to hurt him as he'd hurt her. A petty and childish wish, to be sure, but it was very, very real. Only sheer force of will—and Markham's stupefied presence—kept her from giving Simon the tongue lashing he so sorely deserved.

His proposal would fail. She would see to it. Tethering a woman to a man who had abused her, even for financial gain, was wrong. She'd seen women who had suffered cruelty at the hands of men, and most of them wanted to forget the entire experience. An annual stipend would only reopen old wounds again and again. Perhaps another Winejester cartoon was in order, one in which the character rose to even greater heights of buffoonery. Yes, he may think he'd bested her . . . but Maggie would not lose in the end.

"I like crowds," Markham put in to fill the silence.

"I do as well," Maggie echoed, grateful for the distraction.

More drumming, busy digits registering annoyance. "I have matters to discuss with the lady, Markham. Perhaps your visit has concluded?"

Markham gaped. Simon outranked him, and arguing would be fruitless. Maggie, on the other hand, did not care for anyone coming into her home and making a guest uncomfortable. "You overstep, sir. Lord Markham is welcome to stay as my guest."

Simon's lips flattened. "Fine. Let us have a long chat together. I so rarely get the chance to pay social calls." He shifted deeper in his chair. "How is your wife, Markham? I assume she'll be coming up for the start of the Season. Perhaps the two of you could join me for dinner at Barrett House. I'm certain she'd love to hear all you've been up to in her absence."

Chapter Eight

Markham fairly scurried out the door, much to Simon's satisfaction.

"I cannot see how that was necessary," Maggie snapped, placing her cup and saucer on the table.

"Did you honestly believe I would sit and watch while the two of you flirted with one another?"

Her jaw dropped. "I was not *flirting* with him. We were discussing other matters."

"He wants to bed you, Maggie. And it's not as if you weren't flirting with him last night."

"Jealousy does not become you."

He gave a dismissive sound. "I am hardly jealous. I don't care if you want to bed Markham—though I would urge you to set your sights higher. He's not exactly known for prowess in the bedroom."

Her creamy skin turned a pretty pink, and he found himself entranced. Sweet Bartholomew's bollocks, she was beautiful. When she blushed, the traces of cynicism and distrust vanished and he saw the girl he remembered: an intoxicating combination of youthful innocence and a fortitude beyond her years.

Strong, stubborn, and unafraid. Everything he'd ever admired in her. Desire slid down his spine, wound its way through his guts. God, he wanted her. Desperately.

"Allow me to guess," she said tartly, smoothing down her skirts and avoiding his eyes. "Someone like yourself, perhaps?"

"If you are so inclined. I would most definitely enjoy your efforts at seduction." He couldn't prevent his voice from dropping to a low, husky pitch. "And I can guarantee you'd enjoy the results."

Her gaze snapped to his and he saw the confusion there, not that he could offer any explanation for his remark. One man just finished flirting with her, and now here Simon did the same. But he liked to think the comparison ended there. Other men might lust after Maggie, thanks to her exotic beauty or legendary reputation, but Simon *knew* her. Knew how she bit her lip when she was confused. The deep, rich sound of her laughter when she found something amusing. The stubborn set to her chin when she argued.

"I think not," she returned, though the hitch in her voice suggested otherwise. "Did you bring those paintings to show me?"

He cleared his throat. "Yes, I did. These are Lemarc's bird paintings I purchased the other day." Standing, he moved the tea tray to another side table. Then he retrieved the paintings and began placing them in front of Maggie.

"Only eight? I thought there were nineteen in the set."

"Excellent memory. There are nineteen and Quint has the rest. I can have them sent over, if you wish. But I thought these might be a good start."

He purposely slid onto the sofa, close to her, the outside of his knee brushing against her skirts. "What do you think?"

"I like them," she replied.

Chuckling, he said, "Not precisely what I meant, but I'm glad you approve. Quint has used these eight to pinpoint a general location for where they were painted."

He felt her stiffen. "That's . . . remarkable," she said, a strange note in her voice.

"It is, indeed. There is one that caused him no small amount of trouble. I wonder if you can spot it."

"Oh." She held up her hands. "I know nothing about birds, I'm afraid. Why do you not tell me instead?"

This close, he could study each of her features. Green irises, clear and sharp, were locked on his face. The pouty, soft lips that beckoned a man's mouth and tongue. A straight, delicate nose and graceful jaw. It was impossible to miss the pulse that fluttered at the base of her throat or the rapid rise and fall of her chest. God, he was mad for her. And the knowledge that he affected her every bit as much had lust tightening in his groin.

Her lips parted, the pink tip of her tongue darting out to moisten the plump flesh, and blood rushed to his cock, filling it in sweet, steady pulses. It took everything he had not to pounce on her.

A silky tendril of black hair curled by her temple. Without thinking, he reached up to drag the ink-colored strands between his thumb and forefinger. Soft, like velvet. What he wouldn't give to have that luxurious curtain of hair surround them while she rode his shaft.

As if she knew the direction of his thoughts, color dusted her pale skin once more, an enticing blush he could not resist. He felt himself leaning toward her. "Maggie," he whispered. "In the name of all that is holy, stop me now."

Instead of blistering him with her razor-sharp tongue, she lifted her face and met him halfway, giving him the approval to kiss the bloody hell out of her.

Approval he promptly took advantage of, capturing her mouth fiercely and with no hesitation. He wanted to be gentle, to build slowly, but he couldn't. He'd waited a lifetime to taste her. And it was even better than he'd imagined. Her lips were soft, her breath sweet and hot, and he found himself deepening the kiss. Hard to believe this was *Maggie*, yielding to him. Kissing him back with unexpected fervor. But now that he had her, the fires of hell couldn't pull him away.

He could feel her trembling and realized his own hands were none too steady as well. And when his tongue touched hers, it sent a jolt of pleasure straight through him. Sweet, she was so sweet. Her mouth warm and lush, her tongue wicked and slick. His erection throbbed, harder than it'd been in ages. Yet he couldn't stop kissing her. He came back again and again, a never-ending thirst that her kisses both eased and worsened at the same time.

Reason and good sense dictated this as a terrible idea. He shouldn't have started this madness. It was the afternoon, for God's sake. They could be caught at any moment—there were servants milling about, possibly listening at doors. Had he lost his everlasting mind?

But heaven help him, it wasn't enough. Lust clawed

at his insides, a swirling, living animal that craved satisfaction. He pressed her into the back of the couch, trying to get closer. Damned clothes. He'd give his considerable fortune to feel her naked skin next to his. To roll her underneath him and slide into the wetness between her thighs.

His palm covered her breast, cupping it, shaping it, stroking the taut nipple through her clothing. Her back arched, lifted to him, as she made a needy sound in her throat. Urgently, he dragged the bodice of her dress down, reached past the layers of cloth until her small breast spilled out. He broke off from her mouth and bent his head to see her. Gorgeous. A hard, pink-tipped nipple surrounded by a dark areola, a lovely contrast to her creamy white skin. Simon wasted no time in running his tongue over the taut bud, laving and licking, before drawing it deep in his mouth. He heard her sharp inhale and felt her fingers thread through his hair to hold him in place.

As if retreat was a possibility.

He knew she'd had many lovers and, right then, he did not care. It made not a whit of difference because none of those men had waited as long for her as Simon had. Dreamt about it as often as he had. Not one of them craved her down to their very souls. In fact, he'd never lusted after a woman with this much delirium. And now that he had her, with her body soft and pliant under his hands, he planned to pleasure her until she shouted his name. Only his.

So he used his teeth, scraping lightly, biting gently, until she whimpered. He loosened what fastenings he could, clawing at the laces of her dress, and then tugged the fabric down farther to give the other breast the same attention. She moaned, and he didn't stop until she began writhing restlessly next to him. Her nipples were taut and eager, straining against his tongue, and unbelievably sweet.

Rising up, he reclaimed her mouth, drinking her in . . . surrounding himself with her. Her small hands slid up under his coat to clutch at his sides as she kissed him back. God, he needed to touch her—and wanted her to touch him in return.

He drew up her skirts, his fingers trailing up her thigh. She shivered—whether from the sensation or the cool air, he couldn't say, but he didn't stop. He would unlock all her secrets, find out what made her shudder and shake if it killed them both.

Liquid heat met his touch at the entrance to her body. *Everlasting hell.* She was wetter than he'd dared hope, and the undeniable proof of her desire made his gut clench. He held off, however strong his need to thrust deep into that slick heaven. No, he didn't want to lose himself just yet.

"Simon," she breathed, breaking off from his mouth as he slowly slipped a finger in her tight channel.

He bent to nibble her throat, kissing down to the hollow between her collarbones. "Yes?"

"Oh," she gasped when he added a second finger. She was snug. A fine sheen of perspiration broke out on his brow imagining that hot silk squeezing his cock. Somehow he forced himself to stay on task.

He happened to notice her hands gripping the cushion, as if she were afraid to let go. That wouldn't do at all. He much preferred active participation from his lovers rather than a woman who'd lie back and take it. Hell, if he wanted passivity in a bed partner, he'd marry.

Maggie had passion inside her. He'd seen countless

examples, in fact, from glimpses during her youth to more recent skirmishes. And he meant to have it. *Now.*

"Lift your breasts for me," he told her, continuing to work her with his hand, gliding in and out. "Hold them up."

She hesitated only a moment, then shifted to cup the undersides of her mounds, plumping them. The sight nearly made him spend in his breeches like a lad. He rewarded her by laving a nipple with the flat of his tongue before drawing it between his lips. He flicked it, stroked it, worshipped the tip of her breast with every bit of his concentration; then he moved to the second and began all over again.

She was panting, head thrown back, eyes closed in pleasure. He'd never seen anything more lovely in his life. When he felt her inner walls tighten, he stilled his hand.

"Oh, God," she groaned, writhing. "Simon, you must . . . oh. Do not stop, please."

He could finish it now, could use his thumb on the bud at the top of her cleft to send her over the edge. But he had to have more. He needed her complete surrender, to own her, body and soul.

"Come here," he said, settling against the back of the sofa. Wrapping his hands around her small waist, he lifted her up and swung her over his lap, her knees astride his hips.

Ebony hair disheveled, emerald eyes gone dark, her lips swollen and rosy from his mouth . . . He'd put that look on her face, he thought smugly. "Touch me, Maggie. Put your hands on me. Any place. Anywhere at all. Just touch me."

* * *

Maggie knew precisely what he meant. She hadn't much experience with men, but there was one place they all wanted to be touched and, by God, she couldn't wait to touch him there, either.

What had happened to her? In the last quarter hour, she'd gone from resenting his presence to falling under his spell like Persephone *après* the pomegranate seeds. Hardly her fault—talents such as Simon's, she supposed, were not to be underestimated. No other man had ever incited a wicked burn in her belly. Or made her skin itch with need. She hadn't expected it, and yet it seemed she'd waited a lifetime for it. She was consumed, overwrought. Indeed, she had every intention of following through on what was likely to happen on this tiny sofa.

She snaked her hand between their bodies, covered the hard shaft evident in the tight buckskin. He sucked in a breath, and she traced the thick, straining length of him with her fingertips.

"Maggie, please," he pleaded through gritted teeth. "I am past the point of teasing."

Hmm. Though her body throbbed, her heart beating so hard that blood roared in her ears, she thought he deserved to be tormented a little. She scooted back to sit on his thighs. Slowly working the buttons on his breeches, she peeled back the fall to reveal his shaft. Long and rigid with springy, dark blond curls at the base, his erection was more impressive than the two she'd seen before. With a fingertip, she traced the smooth, silky head.

If only she could see all of him in the gray afternoon light. She'd seen enough sketches of the bare human form—both male and female—and had even drawn a few unclothed models in Paris. The hard angles on a man were so different from the soft, roundness of a woman. Protruding hip bones, sharp ribs, the ripple of sinewy muscle under skin . . . they combined into something capable of great power and strength. It would be nice to see how Simon compared—from an artist's perspective, of course.

Still, one must make do with what one had. She swiped her thumb over the tip, fascinated, and heard his groan.

"I want to take you to your bed," he growled. "Lay you down and strip you bare. Please, Maggie. Will you let me?"

No, she nearly shouted, the answer swift and absolute. Stolen moments in her drawing room were one matter. Taking him to her chamber, undressing, allowing a man in her bed—at this hour, no less— was entirely something else. And it wasn't the servants she worried about; it was her sanity.

In this small room, she could pretend that passion had overcome her reason. Pretend that Simon hadn't hurt her terribly all those years ago. Pretend that this burning fever for him was nothing other than a temporary biological condition to be dealt with.

Without answering, she bent forward and pressed her mouth to his. He kissed her back, took her mouth as if it were necessary to his very survival. Spread the seam of her lips with his clever, wicked tongue. Demanding. Impatient. And Maggie melted against him, pliant and desperate to get closer. Her fingers threaded the smooth strands of his hair, holding on under the glorious rush of sensation.

His mouth broke off, and he trailed kisses down her neck. "You stubborn, maddening female," he said into her skin. "I want to have you properly, not in here like a footman—"

Maggie rocked her cleft over his shaft with a roll of her hips, forestalling his words. The resulting pleasure pulsed in her core. "Simon, please. Now."

Simon groaned, his eyes searching her face. He gathered her skirts out of the way to expose her. "Take me inside, Maggie. Let me have you."

She hesitated, questions coming unbidden to her mind. Did he want . . . ? The mechanics weren't unknown, of course, but she'd never . . . well, she'd never been the one on top. Should she merely—

Without warning, he snatched her shoulders and twisted their bodies until she was on her back, Simon cradled between her splayed thighs. His eyes glittered, and she felt the blunt tip of him at her entrance as he lined up. In one smooth thrust, he drove deep, filling her completely.

She squeaked and clutched at his shoulders. Though not a maiden, she hadn't done this often. It hadn't hurt, exactly, but the sensation had taken her by surprise.

He dropped his forehead to hers. "I'm a cad. I took you too fast. But I could not . . . I'm sorry, Mags. Let me make it better." Withdrawing slightly, he angled to slide back inside. "The servants . . . ?"

She gasped, the deliciousness of that one small movement too much to take. "No," she breathed, knowing Tilda well enough that her maid would not allow anyone to disturb them for any reason. "Again, Simon."

He complied, then murmured, "The way you feel

around me . . . so tight." Another rock of his hips, deeper this time. "God in heaven."

She couldn't agree more. It felt less of an invasion and more of a *merging*. Like his body was leading hers to a destination they could only arrive at together. She'd never have guessed, would never have imagined, this bliss. How had she gone her whole life without feeling it until now?

The pace increased, their ragged breathing filling the small drawing room as ghostly afternoon light filtered in through the glass. Simon filled her again and again, increasing the ache, until she whimpered and writhed beneath him. He teased her nipples, rolling and pinching them, drawing them deep into the lush heat of his mouth. When she thought she would die from the intensity of it, he reached between her legs and found the hard nubbin of flesh at the apex of her thighs, stroked. Once, twice, again, and she exploded in a burst of color and light, muscles clenching in a spectacular euphoria.

As she floated back down and tried to catch her breath, Simon's movements grew erratic. Then his head snapped back, and he let out a deep, feral growl, his body shuddering. He pulsed inside her and she held on, savoring the intense force of his orgasm.

Relief washed through her. He'd given her pleasure and she'd returned it in kind.

She was not frigid.

Giddy with that knowledge, she wrapped around him. Strange to be fully clothed and feel so close to a man. She pressed a soft kiss to the rough skin of his throat, above his perfectly ruined cravat. Chest still heaving, he thrust one last time, and her channel, slick from his seed, offered no resistance.

His . . . seed.

Oh.

Her husband hadn't tried to prevent conception during their few couplings, but Jean-Louis had. Therefore, she knew what a man must do when a baby was not the intended purpose, and Simon had not done it. A riotous mix of emotions crashed through her. Everything from panic to fear to longing.

Then back to fear.

She did not want a child—not even one with eyes as blue as a Norwegian fjord she'd seen once in a painting. No, she most definitely did not. Having another man's by-blow would truly confirm what the *ton* thought of her. She'd have to move away, give up her livelihood, give up Lemarc.

And the spiteful women, the horrible ones who snickered behind her back, would win.

It begged the question, why had Simon not taken care with her? Surely he remembered those precautions with his mistress. *Because you do not matter to him. He thinks you no better than a trollop, as does everyone else.* Her insides turned cold.

She pushed at his shoulder, dislodging him. "Get up, Simon."

That roused him out of his postcoital befuddlement. "Oh, my apologies. I must be quite heavy." He withdrew and sat back on the sofa. Maggie felt the sticky wetness between her thighs as she untangled herself and stood up. *Damn it.*

She tucked her breasts back into her stays and gown. She couldn't do the fastenings, of course, so she held the garment over her bosom. Out of the corner of her eye she saw Simon working at the buttons of his breeches. Her hair must look a fright but there was no hope for it now. She'd order up a bath the instant he walked out the door—which couldn't come soon enough for her liking.

He rose and adjusted his clothing. Despite the disheveled hair and ruined cravat, he was impossibly handsome.

When she said nothing, he remarked, "Not much for tender words and a cuddle after the fact, then? Cannot say I blame you. This sofa is deuced uncomfortable for this sort of thing."

Though his tone was light, she clamped down on the furious retort burning in her chest. "Why did you not . . . withdraw?" No doubt she blushed, if the heat under her skin was any indication, but the question could not be ignored, no matter how uncomfortable the topic.

He blinked. "To be honest, I forgot. It felt . . . rather, you felt . . . so perfect and I lost my head. But you needn't worry if it comes to that. I'll—"

"Yes, and while I'm sure a bastard here or there is nothing to you, it makes a great deal of difference to me. Why is it men never think before rutting like a . . . like a . . ."

"Careful," he warned, his gaze gone colder than the North Sea in February. "I am feeling particularly indulgent at the moment, but I would not push it, Maggie."

Who did he think he was, giving her orders as if he were her father? Or, even worse, her *husband*. "Or else what, Simon?"

He thrust his hands on his hips. "Really, you're experienced enough to know what was happening here. And you enjoyed it every bit as much as I did. Need I remind how you begged?"

No, he needn't. Likely those memories would haunt her nightmares for some time to come. And the words only proved that he was no different from the others. Even after what had just happened, he still believed what everyone said, the vicious rumors and packs of lies.

And that *hurt*.

She took a ragged breath. "I am not some mistress to whom you may toss a few coins and send on her way. You assume because of my nickname I've legions of lovers, which could not be further from the truth."

He crossed his arms over his chest and frowned. "I apologized for the carelessness on my part. Rest assured I won't make the same mistake again."

"Indeed, you'll not, because what happened today shan't be repeated."

"Why the devil not?"

Because it was too wonderful. Too beautiful. Too much like everything she'd ever hoped for.

It's what you could have had, if he'd offered for you ten years ago.

But he hadn't. Simon had walked away, had turned his back on her when she'd needed him most. He never asked for the truth. Never once had he sought her out to hear what had happened that night in the Lockheed gardens. He'd cast her into the lion's den without a second thought and she'd spent years crying herself to sleep at night, wondering what she'd ever done to deserve a life such as the one forced upon her.

And when Hawkins died, she'd earned the most precious commodity a woman like her could ever have: freedom.

No one would take that away—not even Simon.

"It was a mistake," she told him, lifting her shoulder with a carelessness she did not feel.

His expression shifted, the stark planes of his aristocratic face turning hard. Dangerous. She took an unconscious step back as he stalked forward but then planted her feet. He would not intimidate her, by God.

"A *mistake*?" he whispered darkly, prowling toward her. "The moans? The sighs? The way you wrapped your legs around my hips? Was that all a mistake, Maggie?"

She opened her mouth to confirm it, but he continued, cutting her off.

"The wetness pooling between your thighs said otherwise. The way you begged me to take you said otherwise." He now stood much too close. She had to wrench her neck to look at him as he loomed over her. "You say you're no doxy; well, I am no untried lad you can chew up and spit out. Nor am I an old man rutting with rheumy eyes and a withered prick. Believe what you must to be able to sleep at night, but what happened was no mistake."

Oh, he was intolerable. "It shall not happen again, Simon."

A muscle jumped in his jaw. "Take comfort, then, that I won't force my attentions on you. There are any number of women who won't cringe at the idea of me in their bed."

"Like your mistress," she couldn't help saying.

Something flashed in his eyes, and she feared it might be satisfaction. "Why, you almost sound jealous, Lady Hawkins."

The idea of Simon and another woman doing what had just occurred in Maggie's drawing room sickened and depressed her, but she'd be damned if she ever let him know. "Hardly. All of those women can have you, as far as I'm concerned."

Shoulders stiff, he took a step back and bowed. "I shall remember you said so, madam."

"Good afternoon, Mother. You look lovely, as always." Simon bent to kiss his mother's cheek.

"I'll overlook the fact you're late because of that compliment—which, I'm sure, was your intention." Still a handsome woman, the countess was tall and thin with features similar to his own. She looked much the same as she always did, in a high-neck violet gown. She put down her embroidery, an activity she only undertook when anxious.

He'd gone home after Maggie's in order to change, which had made him late for his afternoon appointment with the countess. He grinned at her. "I never could get anything by you."

"You still cannot," she retorted. "Please, sit. I cannot strain my neck to converse with you." She requested tea as he settled into a chair. When they were alone, she asked, "Have you been to your club today?"

"No. Why?"

"It's that wastrel, Sir James!" his mother blurted, color high on her cheeks. "I heard the news last night. Lady Keller heard from Lady Peterson that Sir James lost all of their money. All of it! Sybil is utterly ruined."

Oh, Christ. "Wait." Simon sat forward. "There is the money I set aside in her trust, is there not?"

"I confess I do not know, but I suspect that shiftless excuse for a man found out about the trust and convinced her to turn it over. Lord Peterson saw

James drunk at the hazard table inside a gaming hell, babbling on about his investments failing. He was playing with every last farthing they had."

"Unbelievable," Simon muttered, slumping in his chair. "How can he be so stupid? But perhaps Sybil did not turn the money over to him. Surely she would not be so brainless."

His mother shook her head. "Women who love the wrong man are blind to sloth, stupidity, or spite. Precisely why those of our class should never be allowed to make their own matches."

"Seemed a good match at the time, though I wish I'd dug a bit deeper on him before we allowed it."

"It would not have mattered. Sybil was determined to have him. She'd have run off to Scotland if we tried to stop them."

That was true. Sybil had been madly in love with Sir James. Only sixteen at the time, Simon hadn't understood the importance of his role as head of the family and had also lacked the experience to know what men of Sir James's ilk were like. He'd had the title for a mere two years but hadn't even finished school. Still, he wished he'd asked for advice or had James investigated because the man was an utter arse, through and through.

And now Simon had to clean up the mess. Again.

"I'll go and see him this afternoon," he told his mother. "No matter what has happened, I'll not let Sybil suffer because of James's stupidity."

The dowager's shoulders slumped with relief. "Thank you, Simon. I knew when he ran through her dowry in less than three years the man would be trouble." The tea tray arrived and she labored over it for a few moments. "Remember that Greek diamond mine he invested in? Failed to produce a single stone and all the workers quit."

He shook his head. "What about the fleet of merchant ships overtaken by pirates? Or the abandoned Russian coal venture?"

"My favorite was the monkey-breeding scheme where all the animals turned out to be male." They both chuckled, and the dowager covered her mouth. "Oh, it's wrong to laugh, Simon. The man has absolutely no sense and he's ruining Sybil's future."

"I shall do what I can, Mother. Sybil will not end up on the streets."

She picked up her cup. "Your father would be so proud of you."

Simon liked to think so. He had worked hard over the last six years to carry on the Barrett family legacy in Parliament. The three estates he owned all prospered and were well-managed. True, he hadn't married and started producing offspring, but he would someday. Just not anytime soon.

Thoughts of offspring reminded him of this afternoon. Yes, he'd acted abominably. Should have withdrawn, spent himself anywhere but inside her. He never forgot with Adrianna or with any of his other lovers. His father's mistress had borne the seventh earl two bastards, and Simon could still remember the day he'd learned of the existence of his half siblings. While it was not uncommon amongst the nobility, the revelation had confused and hurt him at the time, and Simon had vowed at nine he'd not sire any byblows. And so far, to his knowledge, he hadn't.

No question, then, he'd erred this afternoon. But hell . . . pulling out had been the last thing on his mind at that precise moment. The feel of Maggie clenched around him had been heaven. The pleasure had ripped through him, roared up from the depths of his soul to obliterate everything else.

All of those women can have you, as far as I'm concerned.

Obviously Maggie hadn't been similarly affected.

She had every right to be angry, of course. His actions had been thoughtless. No doubt her other lovers were far more considerate.

"You have the oddest expression on your face right now. What are you thinking?"

Simon glanced at his mother and shook his head. "Nothing of importance."

"Some days I fear you've grown far too serious, Simon." She sighed, and he refrained from comment, reaching out to steal another piece of plum cake instead. "Have you by any chance run into Lady Hawkins since she returned from that godforsaken little town Hawkins dragged her to?"

The cake turned to dust in his mouth. No chance his mother asked that particular question on a whim. Obviously word had gotten round about either his attendance at Maggie's extravagant soirée or the dinner party at Colton's.

He swallowed, forcing the lump of dry cake down his throat. "Yes, as a matter of fact, I have."

She sipped her tea, sharp blue eyes identical to his own watching him over the rim of her cup. "And?"

"And she seems well. Hawkins left her fairly well off, it seems, and she certainly loves to stir up attention for herself."

"Hawkins did not leave her well off," his mother said. "A very modest jointure, I heard. The estate got the rest."

Interesting. He hadn't paid attention to the gossip

when Hawkins died, but the woman lived in debauchery and excess to rival a Bourbon king. How could she possibly afford it?

"Were you kind to her?" his mother asked, and Simon nearly laughed. If he'd been any kinder, the two of them would've melted in a puddle of lust. Without doubt, it had been the most satisfying and intense encounter he'd ever had with a woman.

He didn't care for the way his mother was studying him. "Why on earth would I be unkind?"

The countess sighed. "Because people often are, especially in our circles. She did not have an easy time with her debut, and the marriage to Hawkins could not have been much better. And I know you favored her."

Such a commonplace phrase for the profound depth of his former feelings for Maggie. He had followed the girl around like a beggar, desperate for any word or glance she might throw his way. Hell, he'd almost demanded Cranford's seconds, ready to take a bullet to defend her honor.

What a young, foolish idiot he'd been.

Then Cranford had shown him proof, the letters from Maggie suggesting assignations. How much she looked forward to Cranford's attentions. The truth had nearly crushed Simon. And there had been others, Cranford swore, other men to whom she'd given her favors. But Simon had been the fattest prize that Season, a prestigious title and more wealth than any other unattached man that year.

It had all been a game to her. A game to win the husband too besotted to know better.

And so he'd licked his wounds like any respectable twenty-three-year-old would: the day of her hasty wedding, Simon got stinking drunk in one of London's most exclusive brothels. He'd stayed for three days, hiring enough women to keep him entertained round the clock. Madame Hartley, the owner of the establishment, joked as he left that he should have his cock bronzed in commemoration.

"Simon, are you paying attention?"

He glanced up. "Of course. We are speaking of Lady Hawkins. And I did not shun her, if that is what has you concerned."

"Most of the older women have, I'm afraid. She's not welcome everywhere, as I'm sure you well know, and her mother was a dear friend at one time." She paused. "Perhaps I should have spoken up for the gel. Hard to imagine she'd truly taken to Cranford, not when she had *you*. Anyway, I'd like to have her for dinner. Would you come?"

It took him a second, but he managed, "If you wish. But she might not accept the invitation, Mother." Not after today, anyway.

"Nonsense. Why would she refuse?"

Simon shrugged. "You know how temperamental some women can be. Well, I must go deal with Sir James before this gets any worse." He stood and bent to kiss his mother's cheek. "I'll send a note later after I meet with him."

"Excellent. Thank you, Simon. And I shall let you know what Lady Hawkins says about dinner."

Chapter Nine

Maggie hadn't ever been inside a brothel before.

To be precise, she wasn't truly *in* a brothel—or at least not any part where any of the guests could see her. She'd entered through a private door and had promptly been escorted to Madame Hartley's small office, which, it turned out, had a convenient peephole into the main drawing room—a peephole Maggie immediately made use of.

The opulence surprised her. Granted, this brothel was a cut above the rest, catering to the elite and wealthy men of the *ton*, and the services, she guessed, were not cheap. This was no tug 'n' tussle for a quid. No, the gentlemen clearly came and stayed, enjoying the women, gambling, and spirits in equal measure for a prolonged amount of time. That would be the only way Madame Hartley could afford the Hepplewhite chairs, the lush Aubusson rugs, the silk draperies. The portrait above the mantel looked to be an original Joshua Reynolds, for heaven's sake.

There were Lemarcs here, too. A series of her erotic sketches hung in the bedchambers. Upon her return to London, Maggie had asked Mrs. McGinnis to gift the deliciously lascivious works to Madame Hartley in order to gain Lemarc a bit of notoriety. And it had worked; last Maggie inquired, Madame turned down offers to buy them almost monthly.

In the main drawing room, there were four men relaxing and talking, each with a drink in hand. Some had girls in their laps. It was fascinating, this civilized debauchery. Where were the naked dancing girls, like one saw in Paris? Of course, there could be all sorts of raucous behavior occurring on the second floor. Maggie cursed yet again the fact she'd been born a female. If she were a man, she could discover exactly what transpired in the private rooms.

You know what they're doing up there, her mind whispered. *The same thing you were doing yesterday afternoon.*

"Here, let me see," the Duchess of Colton said, pinching Maggie's arm.

"Ow," Maggie said and slid out of the way. Julia wasted no time in lining her eye up with the tiny hole.

"Look, it's Lord Burke. And Sir Henry. And the one with the woman on his lap is Lord Andover. Oh, I can hardly believe it. It's fascinating, isn't it? Goodness, he's reaching into her bodice!"

"Where?" Maggie gasped and elbowed Julia. "Hurry. Let me see."

"Wait," Julia said, laughing, as she relinquished the tiny window. "Oh, this is too much fun. We should come here more often."

Back at the small hole, Maggie confirmed that Andover's hand was indeed inside the girl's bodice. The girl didn't appear to mind; in fact, she slid the dress off her shoulder, allowing him better access. Andover wasted no time, pulling the plump mound out to bare it. He then began to fondle her, rolling and pinching the nipple, while he chatted with the other gents. The girl leaned against him, head thrown back on his shoulder, her lower lip pulled between her teeth like it was all she could do to keep from crying out. Maggie's own nipples puckered inside her chemise and stays, her breasts swelling. Simon had done that very thing only a day before, and she remembered how extraordinary it felt.

The girl squirmed on Andover's lap, grinding her backside into his groin, which got her a pinch hard enough to make her gasp. Her lids fluttered shut, chest rising and falling rapidly, as she clearly enjoyed the torment.

Unable to tear her gaze away, Maggie recalled the feeling of sitting on a man's lap while her breasts were fondled and caressed. In her recollection, however, Lord Andover was not underneath her. No, this man was taller, leaner, with sand-colored hair and piercing blue eyes. An ache began in her core, an emptiness she'd never experienced before. It was as if her body knew what it was missing. Or rather, *whom* it was missing.

God help her.

In the drawing room, Lord Andover put two fingers up to the girl's mouth. She opened greedily, taking the digits inside and sucking on them. Maggie watched, entranced, as the fingers reemerged, slick with saliva, and traveled to the girl's breast once more to glide easily over the puckered, rosy tip. The girl must have moaned, or made some other sound, because Andover laughed and whispered something to her.

Madame Hartley appeared. She bent to say something in Andover's ear. He nodded, assisted the girl off his lap, helped to right her dress, and escorted her toward the front stairs. It all happened very quickly. Maggie suffered a brief pang of disappointment before noticing that Madame was striding toward the office. The peephole cover had barely swung shut before Madame opened the door.

Madame Hartley's eyes went directly to the cover, and her lips twitched as she curtsied. "I see Your Grace and your ladyship have been enjoying the rare performance in my drawing room."

"It was Lady Hawkins's idea," Julia blurted, all wide-eyed innocence that not a soul in her right mind would believe.

Maggie choked out an embarrassed laugh. "I didn't—I mean, we shouldn't have . . ."

The owner waved a hand. "I can hardly blame your ladyship, but his lordship knows better. I do not run that sort of establishment. That sort of business belongs in the upper rooms."

Maggie spent a moment admiring Madame Hartley's expensive costume. Layers of lace adorned her midnight-blue silk dress, and the sapphires around her neck had to be worth a small fortune. Her lustrous hair styled and coiffed, one could almost imagine her on the way to a box at Drury Lane.

Madame glanced around the small room. "Did Pearl come as well?"

"She preferred to wait in the carriage," Julia said. "She said you would understand."

The abbess sighed. "Indeed, I do. While I treat my girls better than their own mothers, places such as these can be a harsh reminder of a life some would rather forget. And Pearl had it rougher than most. Which brings us to why I sent for her and, by extension, your ladyship." She gestured at Maggie. "Pearl has told me of your ladyship's work at some of the other establishments, the funds for physicians and medical procedures. Additional protection for the girls. I've never needed that here, as I've been able to more than adequately provide for and protect my girls. At least, I did before last evening."

Maggie frowned, a terrible sense of foreboding settling in her chest. "Has something happened, then?"

Madame clasped her hands together and took a breath. "One of my girls was hurt quite brutally last evening. I've had the physician round today and not only was she ridden roughly, the bones in her face have been crushed. An arm broken. Bruises everywhere. It's . . ." She swallowed. "It's terrible."

Julia gasped. "Who was it? Who did such a cowardly, terrible thing?"

The owner nodded. "I have a fairly good idea. I was away last evening, as I'd gone to help my sister give birth out in Hampstead. Otherwise, I would have prevented it. But Your Grace needn't be concerned; I have men in my employ who deal with that sort of thing. He will get his due, no matter how long it takes. I am worried about *her*."

"Of course," Maggie said. "The poor dear. She must be in excruciating pain."

"She is, my lady," Madame confirmed. "We had to sedate her in order to treat her. Now that's worn off and I'm afraid she's . . . well, broken in more than just her body. I sent for Pearl in desperation, that she might know of some way to help the girl. Some place to send her in order to recuperate. I cannot see how staying here in the house is helping."

Before Maggie could speak, Julia said, "I know of the perfect place to send her. Bring me some paper so that I may write a quick note. And send word to the mews that Pearl may go, won't you?"

"Who are you writing to?" Maggie asked her.

"You shall see."

After failing to track Sir James down the day before, Simon entered Brooks's and immediately inquired after his sister's husband.

The attendant confirmed that Sir James was enjoying an early dinner. So Simon parted with his things and came inside.

He nodded in greeting to a few acquaintances as he strode through the subscription room. The crowd here tended to run a bit younger and faster than that at White's, since Brooks's hazard table was the stuff of legend, yet Simon did not spend much time here. He preferred the food and political conversation at White's.

Lamps dim in the dining room, it took a moment to find his brother-in-law. Soon, he spotted the round, balding blowhard near the back, surrounded by three young men. James appeared quite animated, gesturing wildly while the others laughed. Was James telling them about his London orange grove, which had been obliterated in its first frost? Or perhaps the bee colony destroyed by mice?

God save Simon from stupidity.

"My lord, would you care for a table?" a servant asked at his side.

Simon shook his head. "No, I shan't be long."

In seconds, he loomed over James's table. James glanced up, his face registering surprise.

"Winchester," he started. "Why don't you—"

Simon shot a look at the three companions. "Leave." The men gaped and so Simon barked, "*Now.*"

Forks clattered and napkins dropped as the young men flew out of their seats and disappeared. Simon sat in the chair closest to James. He leaned back and signaled the nearest servant. The man hurried over and Simon gestured to the table. "Have all this removed," he said. "And bring me a bottle of claret."

"Yes, my lord."

"Now, see here, Winchester. I—"

"Do yourself a favor and cease speaking, James."

When the table had been cleared and wine poured, Simon took a healthy swallow of claret. "I'd rather been hoping you had the sense to jump a merchant ship bound for India, James."

James put up his hands and huffed a small laugh. "Look here, it isn't as bad as all that. A small stretch of rough road. In fact, I have an idea—"

"No," Simon snapped. "It is *precisely* that bad. Have you truly done it? Have you lost everything?"

Beads of sweat broke out on James's prodigious brow as he leaned in. "I had a bit of bad timing on a few investments. It's nothing I can't recover from. I just need a bit of blunt to keep me afloat until I can get back on my feet."

"Absolutely not. No more money, James."

James's face reddened. "And what of Sybil? You would see your sister out on the street?"

"No, my sister will always have a home. With my mother or even me. You, on the other hand, are more

than welcome to sleep in the gutter, for all I care."
Something flashed in James's eyes, but Simon continued. "Did she turn over the trust? Did you lose the
money I set aside for her protection?"

"My wife and I don't keep secrets, Winchester. She
gave me that money without my even asking for it."

Oh, yes, I am quite sure it was all Sybil's idea.

"Any vowels?" Simon brushed a piece of lint off the
white linen tablecloth.

"A few."

Simon nodded. It was what he expected. He pinned
James with a hard stare. "And the house?"

James swallowed, the muscles in his fleshy throat
working. He dipped his chin in acknowledgment.

Bloody Christ. Simon fought to remain seated, to
rein in the outrage rolling through him. How could
James be so damned irresponsible? At his mother's
behest, Simon had purchased the house as a wedding
present for his sister, then foolishly handed over the
deed to James. But how could he have known—how
could any of them have known—the depth of James's
stupidity?

He took a deep breath and finished his wine.
Poured another glass. Resisted the overwhelming
urge to beat James to a sniveling, quivering pulp.

This was the last time. To bail James out, time and
time again, did no good. The man had to learn, and
perhaps having it all stripped away, forcing him to live
on a stipend, would finally do the trick. There was no
other way. Simon refused to give James carte blanche
to the Winchester fortune for every wild, addlepated
scheme in Britain.

"I won't save the house," he said at last. "I'll cover

the notes, but I won't save the house. You'll be given a small allowance to cover basic expenses and that's all."

"Sybil won't stand for it."

"She won't have a choice. It's that or the street."

James smirked at him. "No, I don't think so. You wouldn't want to tarnish your shiny political career with a family scandal, now would you?"

Simon's voice dropped, low and dangerous. "Are you *threatening* me?"

"Such an ugly word. I think it's more about coming to an understanding that benefits us both. In fact, I could be useful. There are already rumors circulating about you and Lady Hawkins. I could be persuaded to deflect those rumors."

The mention of Maggie's name had Simon stiffening. James noticed and smiled. Cold resolve settled in Simon's chest. He'd not risen to where he was without learning how to conceal his emotions, and he refused to let James be the one to crack the ice. He leaned back, bored. "From threats to bribery in one fell swoop. I am in awe, James. No, there will be no additional funds. I'll have my man collect the notes on the morrow. You'd best run along and tell my sister to begin packing." He flicked his hand, dismissing his brother-in-law.

James shot to his feet, threw his napkin on the table, and stomped out. Simon sipped claret and tried to calm himself. That hadn't gone well. James would need to be dealt with. Perhaps once he settled the debts, he could—

"Winchester," said a voice at his side. "Been some time since you've graced Brooks's with your presence. How fortunate we are this evening."

Simon lifted his head and found Lord Cranford sliding into a chair. *Oh, everlasting hell.* "Evening, Cranford."

They'd kept a healthy distance over the last ten years. Simon hadn't cared to dredge up memories of Maggie, and Cranford tended more toward vice than politics. If their paths crossed at an event or ball, a polite nod had sufficed. So why now? Cranford must have a purpose tonight, else he wouldn't have stopped.

Cranford hadn't changed much. Only a year or two older than Simon, the viscount was not a big man but stayed in excellent physical health. Rumor had it he boxed in his spare time. So had Cranford reacquainted himself with Lady Hawkins after her return to London? The viscount hadn't attended the same party at Maggie's town house, but that hardly mattered. The two would need to employ discretion as Cranford was married. Though Simon's jaw clenched, he told himself he didn't care. Maggie had made herself clear so there was certainly no cause for jealousy.

All of those women can have you, as far as I'm concerned.

Still, the idea of Cranford or Markham—or any other man—resting between Maggie's thighs, sliding into her wetness, making her sigh and scream . . . His hand curled into a fist.

He forced the image away. No matter how many other men were in her life, she and Simon were *not* through. Not by a Scots' mile. So she could pretend indifference all she liked, but he'd seen her eagerness yesterday afternoon, felt it throughout every part of his body. She had wanted what had happened every bit as much as he had. And he meant to have her again, no matter the amount of time it took to convince her.

Cranford signaled for another glass, capturing Simon's attention. "You do not mind, do you, Winchester?" he asked, helping himself to the claret on the table.

Simon waited, watched. He'd learned to let the silence stretch during negotiations; opponents were more apt to trip up that way. And while he'd no inkling of Cranford's intentions, they most definitely were opponents.

Cranford relaxed, cradled the glass in his palm. "So is it true?"

"And what would that be?" Simon kept his face emotionless.

"About Sir James. Heard he lost a king's ransom. But I suppose it shouldn't come as any surprise. Fools and their money, as the saying goes."

No chance Cranford had stopped to gossip about Sir James. "I cannot see how it is any of your affair, Cranford."

Cranford gave him a small smile. "Come, Winchester. We've never kept secrets from one another, have we? I've always shared information when pertinent."

Remembering the love letters Cranford had shown him those years ago, Simon's voice dripped with sarcasm. "Have you? How giving you are. And I assume you've more pertinent information for me this evening?"

"I do, as a matter of fact. I heard of your recent association with Lady Hawkins." Cranford studied the claret in his glass. "I wonder how it will affect that proposal you're crafting. Or those votes you're counting on."

Ah, here is the heart of it.

"I shouldn't think it'll affect anything one way or

another. The lady is an acquaintance, of which I have many."

"Indeed, I've no doubt. But perhaps Lady Hawkins is more than an acquaintance—if gossip is to be believed, that is."

"Gossip you are no doubt helping to spread."

Cranford held up his hands, all innocence. "I am only relaying what I've heard. Some members of Lords wonder how it will look, your *acquaintance* with a woman of such outrageous morals. Especially considering the nature of your proposed legislation."

That set Simon's teeth on edge. "My opponents would, of course, be eager to embrace any weakness—real or perceived."

"Oh, these aren't your opponents making their displeasure known. These are your allies."

Cranford watched him carefully for a reaction, which Simon perversely withheld. He lifted a shoulder. "They will believe what they must. We'll see in a few months' time."

"We will, shall we not? I merely thought I should warn you before you made a terrible mistake. As I nearly did years ago."

"Your benevolence never ceases to astound, Cranford." Simon's tone was dry.

He laughed. "Indeed, I try. So will you finally cut Sir James off from the Winchester financial teat?"

"Winchester."

Tearing his gaze away from Cranford, Simon found Quint standing by the table. "Evening, Quint."

Cranford quickly rose. "Here, Quint, have my seat. I believe I'm done. My thanks for the drink, Winchester."

He strolled away as Quint sat. "What was he going on about?" Quint asked. "When I came in, you looked as if you were about to leap over the table and strangle him with your bare hands."

Simon finished his wine, leaned forward to pour another. "Cranford stopped by to warn me that my association with Lady Hawkins might negatively influence my standing in Parliament."

"I've heard those rumbles. Ridiculous, when every single man of the *ton* has a mistress."

"Except you," Simon noted.

"I don't want a mistress. Too much bloody work."

"Yes, but the very best kind of work," Simon retorted. Which reminded him, he'd need to find a new mistress now that he and Adrianna had parted ways. He'd ended their association on the night he'd learned she was entertaining other men without his knowledge. Shame he couldn't have the one woman he truly wanted in his bed. "And Lady Hawkins is not my mistress. Nor my anything, for that matter."

"Not for a lack of effort on your part, I've no doubt."

Simon drummed his fingers on the table. No arguing that point. He'd be between Maggie's thighs nightly, if she allowed it. Perhaps in time . . .

Simon came to his feet. "Play hazard with me," he told Quint.

Quint shook his head. "You never win. You cannot properly calculate the odds."

Simon clapped his friend on the shoulder. "That is what I have you for. Come along, I need the distraction."

"Winchester!"

Glancing up, Simon saw Colton, still in his greatcoat, stalking across the room, his face thunderous. The duke reached their table and said, "Grab your things. We need to get to Covent Garden before all hell breaks loose."

Chapter Ten

After Julia dashed off her mysterious note, Maggie asked, "May I see her?"

"I do not think it wise, my lady. While I can likely get you up there without being seen, I cannot guarantee your ladyship's anonymity on the second floor. The evenings are no time for a lady to be strolling about in a place such as this."

"We have our dominoes," Julia suggested. She pointed to the cloaks and masks she and Maggie had adorned before coming inside.

"A fine suggestion, Your Grace, but the disguise would not be enough to conceal your identity. And I daresay His Grace would have a word or two to say should you be discovered. Likely he'd have me shut down."

"I would never allow that," Julia insisted. "Colton may be hotheaded, but he is quick to see reason once I strap him down and beat him about the head with it."

Maggie wished she shared Julia's confidence. But she knew better. And exchanging a quick, rueful glance with Madame, it seemed the abbess knew it, too. Men could do whatever they wanted in this world, and women were supposed to keep quiet.

"Have you packed her things?" Maggie asked.

"What little I could, yes."

"How long has she worked for you?"

"A little over three years, my lady. Never had a speck of trouble with her. The rules here are quite strict and my girls are treated well. I have a reputation to uphold and I shouldn't like for this to get out. I know that sounds callous—"

"Not at all," Maggie assured Madame. "You have done the right thing, sending for Pearl. Between the three of us, we can squirrel her off somewhere, get her body healed. Perhaps find her a job in a household."

Madame nodded. "I am forever in your ladyship's debt. Your Grace's as well."

A soft knock sounded, interrupting. Madame strode to the door, a whisper of elegant silk. Pulling it open, she listened at the crack, then mumbled a few words.

"Your Grace, my lady, please excuse me a moment. There is a matter I must see to." She curtsied. "Please make yourselves comfortable. There is sherry in the cabinet against the wall."

With the unwelcome image of a girl battered and bruised stuck in her brain, Maggie walked to the cabinet for the promise of a drink. "Would you care for a sherry?" she asked Julia.

"No, thank you."

Maggie heard the slide of metal and turned to see the duchess at the peephole. "Nothing lascivious whatsoever out there. Just a few overstuffed dandies." Julia sighed and stepped away from the wall.

They chatted of unimportant gossip for several

long minutes, waiting for Madame Hartley to return. Then Julia said, "You surprise me, Maggie."

Maggie sipped her sherry. "Me? Whyever would I surprise you?"

"You must admit, what you and Pearl are doing, it is an unusual cause for a lady."

Maggie didn't like the shrewd, knowing gaze the duchess gave her. She tried to make light of it. "Shouldn't we all strive to assist those less fortunate?"

"Yes, but one could do so in much more . . . acceptable ways. Most ladies hold benefits or serve on the board of various charities. Go knocking on doors to solicit funds for their causes. You, on the other hand, are in the thick of it. Rescuing these women, making sure they are not unfairly taken advantage of. It makes me wonder if this cause isn't"—she waved her hand, searching for the right word—"personal to you."

Maggie sipped her sherry. She hadn't many female friends, had purposely not cultivated those relationships. Women were too intuitive. Whereas men saw what they wanted, the raucous parties and free champagne, women noticed more, which led to questions one would rather not answer.

But the duchess had come along tonight. Pearl had suggested it, knowing the resources at Julia's disposal as well as her social standing, and Julia hadn't even blinked before jumping in Maggie's carriage. And while Maggie did not want to bare her soul, she owed her new friend an honest response.

"It's none of my business, of course—"

"It is personal to me," Maggie answered. "I know what it is like to suffer at the hands of cruelty. To reap consequences one never imagined nor deserved.

You weren't there during my debut, but if it weren't for Hawkins, I very well could be earning my living on my back. Perhaps not in a place such as this, but kept all the same. So I feel a great sympathy toward the women with little choice but to sell themselves."

"Oh, Maggie. My sincere apologies for bringing up unpleasant memories." Julia's quiet tone was heartfelt. "I was led to believe that Cranford . . . that you and he . . ."

Maggie's hands curled into fists. "No. Most assuredly not. He was to marry my friend, Amelia. Said he wanted to ask me questions about her. I didn't know any different. Why wouldn't I believe him? He had seemed nice enough, quick with a smile and a joke. We'd even danced a few times. But he didn't wish to ask questions about his betrothed. He presumed—" She took a very unladylike gulp of sherry. "He presumed I would be amenable to his advances."

"But you were not." Julia stated it as fact, not a question.

"Indeed not. Fought him off, in fact. I got away but became disheveled in the process. And when your dress is torn and the gentleman in question is grinning from ear to ear, no one believes you did not ask for it." She lifted a shoulder. "And the damage is done. The Half-Irish Harlot was born."

"Oh, dear," Julia whispered, a deep frown on her face. "Had he never even asked, the nitwit?" she mumbled.

Maggie returned to the cabinet, intent on a second sherry. She didn't normally imbibe heavily, but why not? This was a week for firsts, it turned out. "Who never asked? Cranford?"

When the latch on the door sounded, Maggie spun, expecting to see Madame Hartley.

A furious Duke of Colton appeared instead. Followed by—

Oh, no.

Behind stood an equally furious Earl of Winchester.

Maggie refused to shrink under his frosty blue stare. He was not her husband or her father. She answered to no one, not even the man who'd given her more pleasure in one afternoon than she'd had in a lifetime. She squared her shoulders as the duke stalked directly toward Julia.

"I ought to paddle your backside, madam," Colton snarled at his wife.

Julia snorted. "As if that would be any kind of punishment. And calm yourself, Colton. No one has seen us and we haven't left this tiny room. Do not make me regret sending for you."

Simon came in to lean against the wall, his large frame making the small room even more suffocating. He folded his arms over his chest, crossed his booted feet at the ankles. While he may appear relaxed to someone unacquainted with him, Maggie knew better. The set of his jaw, the brisk, efficient movements, the light jumping in the depths of his gaze . . . He was livid.

Madame Hartley breezed in behind the men, shutting the door. "Your Grace, my lord, may I offer either of you a glass of port or claret?"

"By all means, and why not play a hand of whist or two while we're at it," Colton nearly shouted. "Have you all lost your minds?" He grabbed Julia's wrist. "Come. We are leaving."

"Wait," the duchess cried, neatly breaking free of

her husband's grasp. "You haven't learned why I needed you and Simon to rush here."

Surprised, Maggie's eyes flew to Simon, whose own steely blues were locked on her face. She couldn't look away. Her skin prickled, a warmth slowly spreading out through her veins, as she remembered yesterday afternoon. She forced it back, buried it deep where she kept all the memories better not revisited.

"Indeed," Colton drawled with a sneer. "This I cannot wait to hear."

"Madame, pray tell my husband and Lord Winchester what you told us earlier."

Madame Hartley gave the men the details, keeping to the facts. As the abbess spoke, Maggie watched the play of emotions over Simon's face. From fury to curiosity, to outright horror, then back to fury—thankfully not directed at her this time.

The duke's anger shifted elsewhere as well. He ran a hand through his hair. "Christ. Who did it? Who was the blackguard responsible?"

Madame shook her head. "I would rather not say, Your Grace."

"Yes, I know. But I'd rather you *did* say, and we both know I always get what I want. You will tell me before I leave."

"I should like to see the girl," Simon said quietly, the first words he'd uttered since entering.

Madame's brows lowered. "With all due respect, my lord, I am not so certain that is wise. She is . . . not in her right mind. I am worried the presence of a man, even your lordship, will upset her further."

"Madame, you know me. I daresay this isn't the first case I've seen, nor will it be the last. If she needs help,

I'll gladly give it, but you must allow me the chance to get her out of here. I will be gentle, I swear."

His statement confused Maggie, but she had to stick to the matter at hand before she lost her chance. "I should like to come as well," she put in.

Simon's head swiveled and blue ice pinned her to the spot. "Over my dead body."

Maggie opened her mouth to argue, but Julia cut her off. "It's best he goes alone, Maggie. Simon will take care not to frighten her. Truly, I wouldn't have sent for him if I thought he could not help."

So Simon's presence here had been Julia's true goal. Not the duke's. What didn't Maggie know about Simon? How could he be the best person to deal with a frightened, broken prostitute?

Madame Hartley nodded. "Very well. Even though you know the way, I'll show you up."

Even though you know the way.

There was no good earthly reason why that statement should upset Maggie, but the words were a barb sliding up under her rib cage. Of course he'd spent time here. Any lord with a few quid in his pocket likely would. She thought about the scene she'd witnessed earlier. What type of girl would Simon choose?

Before she could ponder it further, Simon straightened and trailed Madame Hartley to the door. "Stay here," he turned to say, looking directly at Maggie.

Why did he feel the need to order her about? She clenched her jaw, but gave him a brief nod and watched his broad back disappear into the hall.

* * *

Simon forced his anger down as he trailed Madame Hartley up the back stairs to the second floor. He couldn't think on how reckless, idiotic, cork-brained—

Did the woman care absolutely *nothing* whatsoever for her reputation?

A brothel. Her social standing already teetered on the edge of respectability. How could she—?

He stopped those thoughts, took a breath. He needed to remain calm for the task at hand. Maggie had him knotted up. No female had ever been able to accomplish it, not to the degree and with the expediency to which she succeeded.

They went up another set of stairs, to where the girls roomed. This was a part of the house he'd never explored, and he wished he needn't do so now. Colton would find the man responsible, Simon had no doubt. And while the duke carried out the retribution, Simon would see the girl well taken care of. Perhaps not totally healed, but better off, anyway.

At the far end of the corridor, they stopped. "This is Cora's room, my lord. I'll accompany you." Madame Hartley gave a brisk knock. "Cora, it's Madame. I'm coming in." She withdrew a set of keys from a pocket sewn into her skirts and unlocked the door.

The room was pitch dark. Using the light from the hall, Simon could see the outline of a tiny bed and dresser. A small shape darted to the corner. *Good God.* It was the girl.

Madame opened the door wider, allowing more light in. The sight nearly knocked him to his knees. Her face grotesquely swollen, Cora huddled there, pressed tight against the wall with a large knife in her good hand. The broken arm had been wrapped in a strip of linen, close to her chest to hold it still. She had on a shift that barely covered her, and he could see glimpses of cuts and bruises on her pale flesh.

But it was her eyes that worried him most. Glassy and bright, they darted wildly, reminding him of a feral creature that had been unwittingly trapped.

"Stay back," she breathed. "I won't do it no more."

"Cora, we're here to help you," Madame said gently. "This is—" She glanced helplessly at Simon, the question in her gaze clear. How should she introduce him?

To be sure, his speech pattern and manner of dress would proclaim him quality, but better to ease into it gently. No telling who did this to her. It could be any number of titled men. He didn't want the word "earl" to upset her further.

Simon stepped forward, bent on his haunches. "I am a friend. I'm here to help you. But I cannot do so if you're intent on keeping—"

Cora began keening—a low wail that sent shivers down Simon's spine—and for an instant he assumed he'd frightened her. He straightened, stepped back, only to notice that the girl's stare remained focused on Madame. Could it be the abbess frightening her?

"No more," Cora repeated, shaking her head. "You can't force me."

Simon then knew it was the girl's employer causing the hysterics. Whether Madame Hartley meant to keep the girl wasn't the issue; the girl believed she'd be forced to endure another man's advances.

"Madame," he said gently, "allow me a moment alone with her."

Madame departed and the room fell into gloomy silence. Since there was no chair, Simon sat on the edge of the bed. Cora's harsh breathing filled the tiny space, and Simon waited. Cora had to see that he meant no harm.

After a few moments, when she quieted, he said, "I had a nurse. I was six and had a silly infatuation with her. I used to follow her about any chance I could, trailing her like a puppy. Well, one day, I couldn't find her. Went looking all around and finally discovered her in the stables. A groom had her pinned and was using her roughly. I peeked through the stall and saw how she told him no, how he overpowered her. When I ran for help, they told me not to concern myself, that I would understand when I was a man."

He frowned, realizing he'd never actually told this story to anyone before. The memory was sharp, and it disturbed him how many details he could recall, from the grunting, her cries, the color of her petticoats. He exhaled and continued, "They sent her away after that, but I'd always wondered what happened to her. I never found out until years later. When I left university, I hired some men to find her. Long disowned by her family, she'd bounced from place to place until she settled in Southwark. Scars on her face, body riddled with pox, her entire future had changed because of what happened in my family's stables, a future that might very well have been prevented had the right person taken responsibility for his deeds."

Cora was quiet, her eyes serious but no longer wary. Her grip on the knife had loosened, though she hadn't let it go.

Simon added softly, "Let me help you. I can see you trained as a housemaid, or in the kitchens if you'd rather. A job where you needn't worry about your day-to-day safety. And no one will touch you."

"No one?" she asked softly.

"No one," he repeated.

"Why would you want t'help the likes of me?"

"Because I can." He held out his hand. "But before I can help you, I need to get you out of here. May I have the knife, Cora?"

The girl glanced down, surprised, as if she hadn't even realized she still held it. Carefully, she placed it on the wood floor. Simon stood up and moved closer, lifting his hands so he didn't frighten her. "I'm going to pick you up to carry you down the stairs. I'll put you in my carriage and take you to Barrett House. There, my housekeeper will see you're properly taken care of. I'd like my physician to come and see about setting your arm, perhaps give you something for the pain. Does all that seem acceptable?"

Cora's swollen eyes filled as she nodded. "I don't want t'do this no more."

"I know. I promise you won't have to."

When the door closed behind Simon and Madame Hartley, Colton stalked to the sideboard. "I hope she's got something stronger than sherry in here."

"No doubt she still keeps your private reserve on hand somewhere. After all, you were her best customer for years." There was no jealousy in Julia's tone. It was clear she was teasing her husband.

"Indeed." He grinned at her. "I cannot argue, though it has been some time."

"And that does not bother you?" Maggie asked the duchess, curious about her friend's attitude.

"Not a bit," Julia said. "We were not married at the time. This was years ago, before Colton left for the Continent. All young men sow their oats before settling down. It doesn't mean anything."

"We spent many wonderfully debauched evenings here," Colton said wistfully, now holding a glass of what looked like whisky. He laughed. "Of course, Winchester's three-day sojourn here is the stuff of legend, though it happened, let's see, eight or nine years ago. I wish I could've seen it but I'd just left for France. So it must have been . . . May or June, I suppose."

"*Ten* years ago, husband. You left for France ten years ago. But who's counting?" the duchess quipped.

Maggie frowned. Ten years ago. In May or June? That would have been right about the time of her scandal and subsequent marriage to Hawkins. So when Maggie's life was being irrevocably ruined, he'd been . . . celebrating with a bacchanal orgy to make a Roman envious? For *three* days? She closed her eyes, drew in a deep breath.

"Quint wrote me, though. Told me that Winchester—"

"Nick, darling, do shut up," Maggie heard Julia say and lifted her lids to find the duchesses's gaze trained on her face.

Colton gave Maggie a contrite smile. "My apologies, madam. My comments were in poor taste."

"Everything you do is in poor taste, you devil," Julia quipped. "Maggie, forgive him. Some days I believe my husband to have been raised by wolves."

That got Maggie to smile despite the searing pain in her chest. "No apologies necessary. It was a long time ago and, verily, why should I care?" She gestured to Colton's glass. "Is there any more of that?"

The duke raised an eyebrow. "Plenty. Shall I pour you a dram?"

God, yes. "Please." Maybe the whisky would wash the bitterness and anger out of her mouth.

"Me as well," Julia put in. "I'd say we could all use a strong drink about now."

Seconds later, Colton placed a crystal glass in Maggie's hands, then gave one to his wife. Maggie watched him lean in and whisper something to the duchess that made Julia turn a deep scarlet. It was obvious the two were very much in love, and Maggie felt a sharp pang of envy. Her marriage had been devoid of any feeling, a strict business arrangement with nothing but responsibility and duty. *What must it be like to share your life with someone who worships the very ground you walk on?* she wondered, lifting the whisky to her lips.

As expected, the first swallow burned like the fires of hell. Maggie gasped, waited for her lungs to draw air once more. She'd had some experience with strong spirits, though she never could claim much tolerance for this particular one.

Dimly, she heard Julia coughing and the duke laughing, so Maggie assumed her friend's experience hadn't been much different than her own.

"Gad, how can you men drink such vile stuff?" the duchess rasped.

Once Maggie caught her breath, a pleasant warmth spread throughout her belly. Everything inside her relaxed. Loosened. Like a watch spring wound too tightly, her entire body . . . unfurled.

The second taste went down easier.

Colton raised his own glass in appreciation. "You hardly blinked on the first swallow. My admiration, madam."

"Must be my Irish blood," Maggie said with a rueful smile. "At least it's useful for something."

She hadn't finished half her glass when Madame returned. The abbess explained that Simon planned to take the girl to Barrett House and would need transport since he'd traveled there in the duke's carriage. Maggie immediately offered to take them. Not that she particularly cared to spend any amount of time with Simon. She'd much prefer never to see him again, in fact, but overseeing the girl's care took precedence over any hurt feelings.

Besides, it wasn't as if she'd never had hurt feelings before.

In moments, the two women had reaffixed dominoes and pulled cloak hoods over their heads. The back hall stood empty, so the duke led their small party to the mews.

Both carriages stood waiting, the cattle blowing clouds of impatient breath in the frigid air. Colton handed Maggie up first, had a quick word with her coachman, and then both he and Julia disappeared into his carriage. Maggie huddled against the squabs, the warming brick at her feet, as she watched the duke's carriage lumber off.

At last, Simon appeared, hatless, his greatcoat wrapped around a large bundle in his arms. Maggie straightened as her coachman hopped down and pulled open the door. Simon maneuvered the entrance neatly, not even putting the girl down to step up and in. He settled on the seat, the girl resting on his lap protectively, and the door closed. She rapped twice on the roof and the carriage set off.

Maggie couldn't see the girl's face under the heavy wool of his coat. "Is she awake?" she whispered.

"No," he answered. "She's passed out, from the pain of moving her, I assume."

"I want to help."

"No. I will take her to Barrett House and then see you home."

The dim lamplight outlined the hard set of his jaw. He clearly did not want her along, but that was too bad. Nothing would keep Maggie away. She lifted her chin, not avoiding his piercing blue gaze.

At length, he blew out a breath. "I know better than to argue when you've got that particular look on your face. So come to Barrett House, if you wish. You may assist once she's inside and made comfortable. I've already sent for my physician to be roused out of bed."

A hundred questions burned her tongue, but Simon turned to the window, all but ignoring her. She bit the eager words back, forced herself to wait. Before daybreak, she'd have her answers—both about the girl and the reason for his involvement.

He hadn't expected to find her asleep.

Simon had maintained a respectable distance all evening while Maggie, his housekeeper, and his physician all tended to Cora's injuries. When they finished, Simon spoke at length with his physician regarding the girl's care. Thankfully, Madame Hartley's bonesetter had done an excellent job on Cora's arm. Dr. Gilchrist believed the girl would regain full use of it with no ill effects other than a slight stiffness in poor weather. The physician was concerned, however, about internal bleeding. He'd given Maggie and Simon's housekeeper signs to watch for.

After Dr. Gilchrist quit the house, Simon returned to his study for a brandy.

He needed to gather his wits. Maggie was here. In the house. Just the idea of it made his cock half hard. God, he wanted her in his bed. Wanted her ink-colored hair to fan over his pillows, her pale, creamy limbs gracing his sheets. The picture caused his skin to prickle, need making him restless and randy.

Which was hardly appropriate, considering the reason for her presence in his house. He shouldn't be lusting after the woman, shouldn't be thinking of all the ways he wanted to pleasure her despite all that had transpired tonight. She wasn't here for *him*, he reminded himself.

So he'd kept to his study, drinking. Cowardly, but better to avoid her than do something he'd regret.

Like falling at her feet and begging for the opportunity to slide between her thighs once more.

As the hour grew later, he expected Maggie to barge into his study to pepper him with the questions she'd obviously longed to ask during the ride from Madame Hartley's. Curiously, she hadn't. He wondered if maybe she'd left. Snuck out without a word. He wouldn't put it past her. In fact, he'd put very little past her. The woman had a spine of steel.

So he was surprised at half past one to find Maggie in a chair at Cora's bedside, asleep.

Watching her, he hardly breathed for fear of waking her. She was so lovely, unguarded in her slumber. Black lashes a stark contrast to her pale skin. Full, pink lips parted slightly. Tendrils of hair framed her delicate face like streaks of midnight, her breasts rising and falling gently.

He started when a presence came alongside him.

His housekeeper, Mrs. Timmons, whispered, "Pardon the intrusion, my lord. I've had the yellow chamber made up for her ladyship." She tilted her head toward

Maggie. "She didn't want to leave the girl earlier. Fell right asleep not long after the girl did."

He'd figured as much but he nodded anyway. "Thank you, Mrs. Timmons. I'll see that Lady Hawkins finds her chamber."

"Very good, my lord. I've asked one of the maids to sit with the girl. I'll have your lordship notified should her condition change."

"Thank you, I'd appreciate that. Good night."

"Good night, my lord."

Simon glanced at Maggie, his chest filling with a warmth he'd never experienced. She hadn't wanted to leave Cora, a girl who most women of the *ton* would not even dare look at, let alone speak to. Whatever he'd originally believed regarding the reason for her presence at Madame Hartley's tonight, it was now clear she and Julia had been on a rescue mission. So why the devil would the abbess send for two ladies of quality? Julia was an open book; Simon had known her long enough to be privy to all her secrets. And while there were many, none involved a crusade such as this. But Maggie was a mystery. What was her interest in all this?

One thing for certain: she was unlike any other woman of his acquaintance. He liked that about her. Always had. From the instant he'd met her, he'd liked her spirit, her fire. One had to respect how she refused to cower before the *ton*. Even before her scandal, when they snickered about her Irish blood, her poet father, or her looks, which were so unlike all the other English girls, Maggie had faced them down with her head high.

He knew because he'd been watching. Due to his mother's friendship with Maggie's mother, Simon had been directed to dance with Maggie once each night that Season. Initially, he'd chaffed at the order but found the girl so compelling he could not stay away. In addition to her beauty, she had wit. Not a quality many her age possessed, sad to say, but Simon appreciated it. She made him laugh. Better yet, she made him *think*.

The question, though, was what to do about her now.

He bent, slid his hands underneath her, and, as gently as he could manage, lifted her. She barely stirred, merely threw her arms around him and burrowed her face into the side of his throat with a sigh. As if they'd done this a hundred times.

Suddenly, he wished they had.

Those were thoughts he did not care to entertain at the moment, not when her soft, womanly curves were pressed intimately against him. He carefully strode to the stairs, took them slowly. Though he could claim the fear of waking her had him moving leisurely, the true reason was a reluctance to let her go.

Simon stepped into the yellow chamber. This was his mother's old suite. He'd never had a woman stay in this room; guests normally stayed on the other side of Barrett House. Odd that Mrs. Timmons had chosen it, but he didn't mind. He wanted Maggie here. Close to him.

He lowered her to the coverlet. She rolled away, settling into the pillow though her breathing remained steady. He stood there, deciding. He could leave her fully clothed, but women's garments were not particularly comfortable. And she would require help to get out of them.

Help you'd be more than eager to provide.

He could be practical about it. Wasn't as if he

hadn't undressed his fair share of ladies before. *Just get it done and leave, man.*

The idea nearly made him laugh.

He itched to undress her, but his motives were anything but pure. A familiar ache quickened in his groin as he remembered the previous afternoon's encounter in her drawing room. The warm clasp of her body. How she'd clutched at him, clung so hard he'd felt the sting of her fingernails through his clothing. And when she'd reached her pleasure at last . . . Christ on a pony, he would never forget her expression as long as he lived. As if he'd gifted her with something precious and rare.

He shook himself. Hardly gentlemanly to stand over her like a lecher. And to remove her clothing would undoubtedly wake her. Slippers. He could deal with slippers. Efficiently, he bent, slid them off her feet, and placed them on the floor.

Perhaps he should loosen the fastenings of her gown. No way to get the contraption off without her co-operation, of course, but he could make her a bit more comfortable. Without jostling her, his fingers plucked at the laces, and as the fabric parted, he caught enticing flashes of her undergarments. His hands slowed. What if he—

What in *hell* was wrong with him? He was four and thirty, not four and ten. And a gentleman. Had he completely lost his mind? He forced himself to drop the laces and pull the bedclothes over her still-dressed form. Then he strode to the adjoining door, where he resolved not to think on Maggie any longer.

Chapter Eleven

The adjoining door closed softly and Maggie took her first true breath in a quarter hour. Her heart pounded in her chest, beating so hard and loud that she'd been sure he would notice. But self-preservation had urged her to keep silent.

His ministrations had been so tender, almost . . . loving. He'd made a concerted effort not to wake her and she'd played along. Besides, if she did stir, what would she possibly say? *Touch me, Simon. Kiss me. Prove what happened yesterday afternoon had not been chance.*

It had not been easy. His featherlight touch roused her body, each brush of his hand or press of his finger making her ache. She'd practically purred under his care, like a kitten starved for attention. When he'd unfastened her laces, she'd thought she would melt into a pool of lust before his eyes.

Her breasts heavy with wanting and her core wet with desire, she could hardly breathe with the strength of it. The one spot where pleasure concentrated, the nubbin Simon had stroked to bring her to peak only yesterday, throbbed in time with her heart. He had awakened her in every way, and sleep would not come soon.

She rolled to her back in hopes of alleviating the craving, opened her eyes, and tried to focus on her surroundings. The pretty yellow wallpaper. The bouncing firelight in the grate. She recognized the painting over the mantel as Wilkie's *Village Politicians*. Appropriate for Barrett House, she thought, considering the political legacy of the Earls of Winchester.

Even the masterful Dutch-inspired work could not distract her, however. Her body clamored for relief.

The adjoining door, was that his bedchamber? He'd gone through not long before, so she had to assume he was on the other side of that partition. What was he doing? Relaxing? Undressing? Or, God help her, bathing?

Imagining his tall, lean frame wet and bare, water sluicing over his limbs, did little to ease her suffering. She cupped a hand between her legs over her clothing, hoping to extinguish the flames of desire licking there—only to gasp at the contact. *Decidedly worse,* she noted in dismay and snatched her hand away.

Why had she consumed the whisky at Madame Hartley's? If she had not, under no circumstances would she have fallen asleep at Cora's bedside. Late nights were commonplace for her. She often painted until the wee hours of the morning, not to mention that raucous parties thrown by the Half-Irish Harlot usually continued until daybreak. And if she hadn't nodded off she'd be at home at the moment, not writhing under the grip of deliciously wicked temptation.

Before she knew it, her feet found the hard floor. Her gown hung awkwardly, nearly off her shoulders since Simon had loosened it. Perhaps she could ask him to finish unlacing it. No, no—this was madness. Reckless insanity. She couldn't possibly . . . could she? What would she say?

Very little, with any luck.

What she should do, what any sane woman would do, she thought as she moved closer to his door, was demand he redo her laces and then send for her carriage. But as her fingers wrapped around the door handle, she knew full well she wouldn't.

The partition opened soundlessly and she peeked into what turned out to be a bedchamber. The soft glow of flames bounced off the corners of the massive room, revealing large, masculine furnishings. It was precisely the kind of room she expected—

A soft grunt caught her attention, and her eyes swung to the immense four-poster bed.

Her mouth fell open. Simon, bare as the day he was born, had stretched out on top of the coverlet and he was . . . touching himself. His shaft, specifically. He gripped it, stroking up and down, the muscles in his arms shifting as he worked. Eyes closed, face slackened in pleasure, his hand continued a regular rhythm, pumping from root to tip.

Lord above, he was beautiful.

She watched, fascinated, helpless to look away. There was no extra flesh on him. Flat stomach, broad shoulders, heavy, muscled thighs that bunched and twitched under the strain. Light golden hair dusted his upper chest, forearms and legs. He was breathtaking. She longed for her pencils and sketch papers in order to capture the essence of the purely selfish, purely spellbinding action.

The desire she'd felt in the other room paled in

comparison to the inferno now raging inside her.
His chest rose and fell in rapid bursts as he stroked,
the pressure clearly building. Top to bottom, then
back again. Stronger now, moving faster. She bit her
lip to keep from moaning. Dug her toes into the
carpet to keep from rushing forward. She'd never
wanted to touch anyone so badly in all her years. Her
limbs nearly vibrated with the force of remaining still.

His free hand came off the bed to rest on his belly,
then began to slide lower. It didn't stop where she assumed. Instead his long leg shifted, opened, and he
reached down to cup the sac below. A groan rumbled
out of his throat. Maggie's knees turned to jelly, and
she had to clutch the door frame to steady herself.

A small sound must've carried across the room because his lids snapped open, and Simon's blue eyes,
glittering and dark, pinned her to the spot. His hands
stilled. Maggie held on to the wood, unsure of what
she should say. How could she explain her unladylike,
brazen behavior?

The fire crackled and hissed while she tried to
wade through the murkiness of her mind to arrive at
a coherent thought. One haughty blond eyebrow
rose. No anger or shame in his expression, merely
curiosity. His gaze, however, held wicked promise,
almost as if he dared her to come forward.

"Do not stop," she breathed, her voice a strangled
plea. *Oh, God.* Had she truly said that aloud?

The side of his mouth hitched. Releasing the twin
weights below his straining erection, he crooked a
finger at her. She shook her head wildly. If she got
close, there was no telling what she may do.

"Come here, Maggie."

As if he'd pulled a string tethering her to him,

her feet started forward at his husky command. The closer she crept, the more detail she noticed. The ridges, angles, and hollows along his delectable frame. The fine sheen of perspiration coating his skin. A small scar on his muscled abdomen. At the foot of his bed, she grabbed on to the nearest wooden poster, held it.

"I was unaware I had an audience," he said. The hand began moving once more, drawing her eye below his navel. His palm swept over the bulbous head, then he fisted himself and pumped a few times. "You are so beautiful, all flushed in your arousal. Have you ever seen a man frig himself before?"

"No," she whispered.

"It's plain you've enjoyed the performance. Tell me what watching me makes you want to do."

Dishonesty never occurred to her. "I want to lick you."

His hand stilled and he gave a small intake of breath. "Where?" he rasped.

Her eyes met his. "Everywhere."

He released his erection and it fell, stiff and proud, against his belly. Simon slid both arms above his head, his body stretched out in front of her in all its straining, aroused, masculine glory. Her mouth went dry. In no hurry, he waited. Clearly challenging her to see what she might do. *Sweet heaven.*

Could she do it?

Could she *not* do it?

It wasn't as if she was an innocent; her maidenhead had been lost years ago. But pleasure, the kind Simon had shown her yesterday, was a recent discovery. She never would have believed it if she hadn't experienced it for herself, in fact. And, as if it were a bite of Tilda's lemon cake, she craved more.

Pulse racing, she began to climb onto the bed until he said, "Your dress. I want to take it off." Bracing both feet on the floor, she turned to present him with her back. She heard him sit up, could feel the heat coming off his big body behind her, and she held her breath. His fingers flew over the laces. "There."

She pulled her arms through the sleeves and let the gown fall to a puddle of silk on the ground. Before she could step out, he unfastened her petticoat and pushed the straps off her shoulders. Clasping her hips, he spun her around, reached for the ties of her stays. He removed the garment as quickly as the others and then reclined back on his bed, leaving her wearing only her thin shift.

Simon slid his arms back above his head, almost as if he were trying not to touch her. "Will you remove it, so I can watch?"

Maggie bit her lip. She hadn't removed her clothing in front of a man before; her maid always undressed her, even during her marriage. But she wasn't shy with Simon. Perhaps she should be, but he'd already seen most of her and anyway, what was one more pair of breasts? Male artists had been focusing on them since they first used sticks to draw in the dirt. And she'd seen enough art to know there were all different sizes and shapes. Hers were certainly not unique.

Grasping the hem of her shift, she lifted it over her head and tossed it to the floor.

Simon's heavy-lidded gaze raked over her bare form. Everything inside her melted under his hot, appraising stare.

"Jesus, you are even lovelier than I imagined," he breathed.

"I could say the same about you."

"Show me," he said, though it came out more like a plea than an order.

She climbed onto the massive bed and bent to press her mouth to the inside of his knee. The muscles in his leg jumped. Encouraged, she kissed her way up his thigh. The salty heat of his skin, the slight tickle of the wiry hair . . . She felt drugged on the smell and taste of him as she used her teeth and her tongue to mark her path, while Simon's rapid exhalations echoed in the quiet of the bedchamber.

She nipped his hip bone and he sucked in a breath. Whereas her own experience had been rather limited, the bawdy engravings and illustrations that circulated through London had provided their own carnal education of sorts. The Lemarc sketches she'd produced for Madame Hartley showed couples engaged in all sorts of activities and positions of which Maggie had never dreamed. At the time, she'd dismissed them as fanciful imaginings. But now . . . now she yearned to explore. To discover. To please.

She swiped the tip of her tongue over the head of his engorged penis. His hips jerked.

"Oh, Christ," he groaned. "Again, darling."

She complied, this time starting at the root and working up the entire satiny length. When she reached the end, she wrapped her lips around him and sucked deep, drawing his thick erection into her mouth. His head and shoulders levered off the mattress, then dropped back down with a thud. He cursed, long and fluently, muscles tightening.

Remembering the motion of his hand earlier, she

began to repeat the action with her mouth as best she could. If nothing else, surely it would feel pleasant enough—

"My God," he wheezed. "I won't last if you keep that up."

She wanted to smile, but clearly couldn't, so instead she worked harder, the soft, steely velvet sliding between her lips and against her tongue. It gave her a measure of power to be able to pleasure him this way, to be the one in control. She'd never have guessed as much from the erotic drawings. But this was heady, indeed. The ache between her legs increased as she bobbed up and down over his shaft.

Then she recalled something else from earlier. Her hand glided between his legs to the sac below, where she cupped and squeezed him gently.

"Oh, hell. I cannot—" His hips began rocking, quick, shallow thrusts into her mouth as his fists clutched the bedclothes. "I am going to . . . I cannot . . . God, Maggie!" He ended on a shout, and that's when she tasted the first spurt of thick, ropy liquid on her tongue.

His body spasmed as he spent himself in her mouth, and she held on, tightening her grip on him during the release as best she could. He gasped and bucked, his seed emptying deep into her throat. Finally, when he stopped shuddering, she released him and placed a kiss to his belly. She'd satisfied him. Made him lose control, even. She was nearly giddy with the happiness, drunk on the power.

"Come here," he panted. Large hands slipped under her arms and he lifted her up next to him. Their eyes met, and his blue depths were soft and full of a tender emotion she felt down to her toes.

He swept her hair back off her face, gathering the heavy mass to one side. "Do you know," he asked softly, "what I was thinking of while pleasuring myself?"

She shook her head and he continued, "I was imagining you doing precisely as you just did. And the reality, my sweet lady, far exceeded any of my imaginings." Cupping the back of her neck, he drew her down slowly toward his mouth. "Kiss me. Let me taste you."

Her mouth met his, and he immediately parted her lips with his tongue and swept inside. She kissed him eagerly, aggressively, feeding the spark between them.

After a moment, he rolled her to her back. "Now I must return the favor."

Simon settled between Maggie's thighs, certain he'd never needed to please a woman more.

He pressed tiny kisses over the soft creamy skin of her inner thigh. He could smell her arousal, could see the glisten of desire on her outer lips. For him. The sight could bring a man to his knees.

He took a moment to merely look at her. Pale skin, with blue veins traceable under the surface. A thatch of black hair covered her mound. Legs parted invitingly. The vision struck him as unbelievably erotic. "God, you are lovely," he whispered.

With the tip of his tongue, he traced the outer edges of the plump lips that guarded her channel. "Simon!" she gasped and jumped a bit, so he slid his hands beneath her bottom to hold her.

Her reticence surprised him. Surely one of her other lovers had tasted her here. "Relax, Maggie. Let me pleasure you."

Then he licked her from the bottom of her opening

to the tiny bud at the top, barely registering her squeak of shock. How could he pay attention to anything else when she was bared before him, her sex so wet and swollen and undeniably delicious? The sweet tang of her arousal exploded on his tongue and he nearly groaned. He'd never get enough of the taste of her. Indeed, if a man could choose a way to perish, performing this service would be his dying wish.

She gave an inarticulate sound as he began to focus on that one spot, the small bundle of nerves where a woman's pleasure concentrated. He teased and tormented, using his mouth, his tongue, his hands, and even his teeth, to drive her to madness, listening to her moans and cries to determine what she liked best.

Her hands clutched at his head, fingers threading in his hair to hold him as he continued to work at her. Within seconds, her thighs began to quiver and her body grew tight. He shifted to slip a finger inside her channel and achieved the desired result. She gave a hoarse shout, limbs convulsing while her inner walls clamped down. He loved how she held nothing back, her reaction as honest and enthusiastic as he'd ever experienced. Loved it so much, in fact, his erection now strained against the bedclothes, demanding attention.

When her shudders finally ceased, he crawled up and covered her body with his own. With her flushed skin, tousled black hair, and drowsy, satisfied expression, she was exquisite. He brushed her hair out of her face.

"That was quite wicked of you," she panted.

"My dear lady, I haven't even begun to show you wicked." He bent to suck the hollow behind her ear and rolled his hips, dragging his swollen cock, against her sensitive flesh. "Next time I'll lie on my back, bring you on top of me with your feet at my head. That way we can both give pleasure with our mouths simultaneously."

She inhaled and arched up, obviously in accordance with that plan. He grinned and palmed her breast. "Like that, do you? Shall I tell you what else I'd like to do to you?" He rolled her hard, smooth nipple between his fingertips.

"Simon," she sighed, her lids fluttering closed.

"Perhaps I'll show you instead." Crawling down to her breasts, he shaped the luscious mounds with his hands. So lovely and plump. Perfect nipples that tasted like velvet. Lowering his head, he circled the puckered tip with his tongue. Her back bowed, pushing up toward his mouth, so he drew the bead inside and sucked hard.

She clutched him as he continued to lave the taut points of her breasts. When he had her writhing beneath him, soft mewling sounds in her throat, he rose up over her and slid inside. The warm, wet clasp fit him perfectly, and he closed his eyes against the surge of utter bliss. "Oh, Christ," he heard himself rasp while struggling for control. He needed for this to last.

Her legs wrapped around his hips, pressing closer to urge him on, and instinct took over. Lust and need ripped through him, a force he was unable to resist— much like the woman beneath him. He drove deep again and again, his hips working, their bodies slapping together as he kept them joined. Her nails dug painfully into his back, her sweet gasps filled his ear. He couldn't stop, couldn't slow down.

Suddenly she tightened, held her breath. He groaned,

"God, yes. Take your pleasure, Mags." She let out a shout and her silky walls milked his shaft. Pressure built in the base of his spine, spread through his bollocks, and he withdrew in time to spill himself on the sheets. The release went on and on, waves of incredible euphoria that wrung him dry. When it finally finished, he flopped down on the bed, shaken by the intensity and roughness with which he'd taken her.

He closed his eyes, gathered her against his side. He tried to catch his breath along with his sanity. Had it ever been like this with any other woman? If so, Simon couldn't remember it. Feminine fingers dragged over his chest, exploring and soothing, and for once he remained silent. He didn't trust his voice, didn't want her to suspect how raw he felt. The emotions coursing through him had no precedent. She'd reached in and flipped him inside out, and he wasn't at all sure what to do about it.

"I should go back to my room," she said, starting to pull away.

"Do not dare leave this bed." He tightened his arm around her, pressed her close. "I am not finished with you yet."

"Is that so?" She dragged the soft underside of her foot over his shin.

"Yes, that is so. Give me a moment to gather my strength." *And my wits.*

"Hmm. So if I get up and leave, you are too weak to follow me."

He shifted to stare at her. "I will always follow you, Maggie. You'll not get away from me this time." And he realized he meant it. He'd lost her once; he would not let her go. No matter the past, he wanted her, and tonight was proof of how satisfactory it could be between them.

She bit her lip, her cheeks turning a pale rose color. He could not decipher whether he'd embarrassed her or pleased her. Perhaps both.

"What did you say to Cora? How did you gain her cooperation and trust?"

He relaxed at the change in topic. No need baring his soul on their first night together. The first of many, he vowed. "I told her she would be safe here, that no one would force her to do a thing against her will."

"And she believed you?"

His hand caressed her back, slid down to cup one of her buttocks. "I can be very persuasive. Have you not learned that by now?"

She gave him a wry smile, gestured to the bedroom. "Considering where we are and what just transpired, I am well aware of your skills of persuasion."

"As if you did not enter my bedroom first," he teased. "I believe you seduced me, madam."

Deeper color on her cheeks this time. "It's ungentlemanly of you to remind me."

He rolled them until he had her pinned beneath him. "Darling, it is a fact I shall never let you forget." Without giving her a chance to comment, he kissed her, long and sweet. Then he kept on kissing her until she moaned and begged him to take her.

After they'd exhausted themselves, she curled against him, an arm thrown over his chest. Her breath gusted over his skin rhythmically, and Simon had never felt more content. What did the past matter when he had the woman in his bed now? The other men, the scandal, the lies . . . all forgotten. Tonight was what mattered. And tonight, he'd found everything he ever wanted.

"You're mine now," he whispered into her thick mass of hair.

As he drifted to sleep, Maggie resting in his arms, he contemplated all the naughty things he'd like to do to her in the morning.

By the dawn, however, she was gone.

"My lord, a Mr. Hollister to see you."

Simon sighed and carefully placed his knife and fork on the edge of his plate. He'd come down early with the intention of hurriedly breaking his fast so that he might pay a call on Maggie first thing. A number of questions swirled about in his head demanding answers, starting with why had she skulked out of his bed in the wee hours of the night. He'd learned from Stillman she'd called for a maid to help her dress around half past four, then departed in her carriage after checking on Cora once more.

That she hadn't stayed left a sour taste in his mouth, one not washed away by the morning's flavorful coffee.

And now the Runner had arrived. Simon still planned to find Lemarc, of course, but he had other issues on his mind that were more pressing than hearing Hollister's report. "Tell him to come back this afternoon, Stillman."

His butler bowed and left, and Simon snatched his cup for a deep, grateful sip. Newspapers littered the table, unread. He'd stared at the pages, unseeing, while trying to make sense of Maggie. Last night, she had crept into his chamber and left by the same means the instant he'd fallen asleep. Had she regretted it, then?

No, he told himself. Surely not. Perhaps she had, for once in her twenty-some years, shown a care for her reputation. Servants did talk, and likely she hadn't wanted to be discovered in his bed. He rolled his shoulders, attempting to alleviate some of the tension that had taken up residence there in the last few hours. Yes, that had to be it.

What she did not yet understand was that he planned to marry her. The Winchester rubies were even now waiting in his study, the finely crafted set that had been in his family for five generations. Each Countess of Winchester had worn them on her wedding day, and Maggie would be no exception, despite her past.

Stillman returned, an unhappy expression on his face.

"My lord, I apologize but Mr. Hollister is rather insistent on seeing you."

Simon dragged a hand down his freshly shaven jaw. What could be so bloody important? After all, he'd read an update from Hollister only three days ago. Had he discovered Lemarc's identity in the meantime? Seemed unlikely. Nevertheless, if he could finish this quickly he could deal with more pressing issues. He stood. "Fine. Show him to the study."

He entered as Stillman and Hollister came down the corridor. Simon made his way toward the desk and did not bother to hide his impatience as he threw himself in his chair. "Well, Mr. Hollister. You've got me, so let's hear your pressing news." He drummed his fingers on the armrest.

Hollister stepped in and bowed. His reserved,

serious countenance positively glowed with pride. "I've found him, my lord. Or her, as the case may be."

Simon froze. *"Her?"* He motioned for the investigator to sit.

"Yes, my lord," Hollister said, lowering into the chair opposite the desk. "We've been following McGinnis's errand boy. Henrik is his name. Parents moved here three years ago from Prussia, and he began working for McGinnis about a year after she first opened. Mostly he delivers packages, paintings, and the like, around town. Occasionally runs out for supplies. Then we noticed him taking a trip over to an abbey on Knightrider Street. Went in empty-handed but came out with parcels wrapped in brown paper that looked a lot like canvases and engravings.

"So we watched that abbey for a few days as well. Saw a woman going in, carrying some of the same wrapped parcels. Came out, no parcels. My man followed her back to her big house over on Charles Street."

Simon frowned, thoughts beginning to tumble about in his throbbing brain. Charles Street? *No, it couldn't be.* How? Why? Then it all clicked for him, the pieces falling neatly into place, and his breath caught. Good God. The landscape. Why hadn't he seen it himself? He didn't even need Hollister to finish, but shock had robbed him of the ability to interrupt.

"We got a name from there and started doing some digging. Turns out, this particular woman and McGinnis knew each other in a small town in Norfolk called Little Walsingham. She was the wife of some fancy nob who kicked off almost two years ago." Hollister cleared his throat, carried on. "He left her a small amount of money, and we assume the widow gave a portion of this to McGinnis to start the shop. I have a friend at the woman's bank, and he confirmed monies put in that account by McGinnis over the last two years, presumably for art sold as Lemarc. A nice bit of change, if you ask me."

"Let me guess," he bit out, his jaw tight. "Lady Hawkins."

Hollister blinked. "Well, yes, my lord. Excellent guess. Your lordship may even know—"

Simon's hand slapped the desk, rattling the inkwell and pen tray. Hollister paled but said nothing as Simon silently fumed. Oh, he'd been so monumentally stupid. This whole time, she'd been making a fool of him. Hot, roiling rage clogged his throat. Lord Winejester. *Bloody hell.* He wanted to hit something, someone. Anything.

She'd been humiliating him while he'd been mooning over her. Again. Christ, would he never learn?

The velvet box containing the Winchester rubies sat squarely on the corner of his desk, mocking him. No smarter at four and thirty than he had been at three and twenty. His father, a paragon of intelligence and fortitude, would be sorely disappointed in his son. *People will depend on you to do the honorable thing.*

Simon's eyes pinned Hollister to his chair. "How certain are you?"

"No doubt whatsoever, my lord. I've got proof, if your lordship would care to see." Hollister gestured to a brown leather case resting on the floor.

Simon needed no proof. Deep down, he knew Hollister's report to be true. The painting in her drawing room, her knowledge of technique . . . Oh, she must have had quite a laugh over this. It was all he could do to keep his seat, to not go tearing out of the house to demand answers. "No, that will be unnecessary," he forced himself to say. "Nice work, Hollister. Send me a bill and make sure to include one hundred pounds as a bonus."

The Runner beamed. "Thank you, my lord. And if your lordship ever requires anything else, just send for me."

"I will. Thank you, Hollister."

Simon waited until the investigator left before stomping to the front entry. "Stillman," he bellowed.

The butler appeared from wherever butlers lurked throughout the day. "Yes, my lord?"

"Phaeton, Stillman. Now." Spinning on his heel, he marched back to his study. There was one thing he needed to retrieve before he met the famous Lemarc.

Thus far, it had been an extraordinary day.

In her studio, Maggie had set to work on the landscapes for Ackermann, grinning like a simpleton all the while. Hard to recall a time when she'd been this productive. She felt relaxed and well rested, even though she'd had very little sleep. Her cheeks grew hot, the reason obvious. Last evening, well, she'd been in bed but most definitely not resting.

Simon had fallen asleep first, his patrician face boyishly handsome in slumber. She had watched him for a long time, content to merely drink him in. Full lips parted softly, his chest rising and falling. Blond lashes brushing the tops of his angled cheekbones. A thin layer of whiskers spreading over his jaw. How intimate, to see and feel those sharp hairs sprout on a man's face. How *wifely*.

With her entire being, she had longed to stay in the warm cocoon of his bed, their bare legs brushing one another in relaxed, postcoital doze. But it wasn't real. The contentment was an illusion. He knew nothing about her, not really. In fact, he continued to believe all the untrue, hurtful things said about her. And no matter how tender, how loving he'd been last night, the pain of what had happened during her debut could not be undone.

So she forced herself out of his embrace, to rise and return home. Better that way. Safer. She could not allow herself to feel tenderness or affection for him, not now. Not ever.

Too late, a voice inside her whispered. With her heart a shade too full of feelings this morning, she feared it was true.

Determined to forget, she turned back to her work, the one true solace from the melee of her life. No matter what chaotic mess tumbled down around her, there would always be the art. Her way of bringing joy and beauty into such a harsh, violent, and oftentimes cruel world.

The morning light had just begun to shift overhead when a knock interrupted.

"Yes?" She stretched her fingers to relieve the stiffness.

Tilda appeared. "Milady, that earl is back again, asking to see you."

"Now?" Oh, dear. She had not expected him so soon. Had he come to update her on Cora? Or did he want to discuss last night? A strong sense of foreboding settled at the top of her spine. "Please show him in, Tilda. I'll be down directly."

The maid nodded and withdrew. Maggie spent a few minutes making herself presentable. Washed her hands. Removed her apron and hung it up. Smoothed her hair and pinched her cheeks. Then she found a pair of pristine white gloves from a table drawer and slid them on to hide the stains on her fingers. This routine calmed her, as it was something to focus on rather than the nervousness churning in her belly. She had no regrets about last night, far from it, but she did not wish to see him so soon.

In the sitting room, she found him at the window, his arms clasped behind his back. The very sight of sandy hair and those broad shoulders caused her heart to stutter. "Good morning."

He spun and it immediately became apparent that something was terribly wrong. His bright, crystal blue gaze normally danced, either with mischief or intelligence. Today it was dull. He looked . . . lost. Angry.

She frowned and came forward. "Are you ill? You—"

"I should have known." He stomped over to the wall and pointed at a frame. "This painting here, the landscape. I should have seen it then. I should have recognized your handiwork."

She blinked. "I don't understand. What do you mean, the painting?" She thought he'd come to talk about last night. Instead he wanted to discuss . . . her artwork?

He crooked a finger at her, beckoning. Dread settled in her chest, but she forced her feet to move to the wall. Her heartbeat seemed loud in her ears as she stepped closer.

"Here." A long, elegant finger jabbed at a tiny bird

wading in a tiny pool by the sea. "A plover with winter feathering."

"Yes. That's correct. I saw them quite often in Little Walsingham."

"Obviously." Simon stalked to a side table. He snatched a small painting and held it up for her. An exact match of that tiny plover. *Oh, no.* The bird paintings . . . she'd used the same pencil sketch for both . . .

The pieces fell into place. The air left her lungs in a rush while darkness filled the edges of her vision. She put a hand up to the wall, steadying herself. Heavens, was she going to faint?

"What an honor to finally meet you, Lemarc."

Chapter Twelve

The derision in his voice was not lost on her. "How . . ." she asked, the sound surprisingly strong considering how weak she now felt. "How did you find out?"

"I hired a Runner. He followed McGinnis's errand boy."

"The abbey." She closed her eyes. *Damn.* And here she thought she'd been so clever.

"Yes, the abbey. Really, Maggie, one would think you'd take more care. But then, you've never really tried to hide behind respectability, have you?" His jaw taut and shoulders rigid, he seemed to vibrate with raw fury. "I cannot believe you fooled me again. How you must have laughed at me all these weeks. *Winejester.* Christ!" He tossed the painting down on the table, where it landed with a smack. "I asked for your help in finding *yourself!*"

She flinched but did not shrink under the force of his anger. There was no time for hurt feelings or to acknowledge the fist-sized ball of regret lodged in her chest. No, this had to be managed. Simon was in a position, both politically and socially, to inflict damage on her—either as Lady Hawkins or Lemarc. Not that she cared about the personal side of things—she'd given up hope on that front many years ago. But she refused to see her livelihood threatened or, God forbid, eliminated.

"What will you do?" she asked him calmly.

His brow furrowed as he rocked back on his heels. *"What will I do?* Is that all you can think to say? You offer no apologies, nor even any explanations." He made a dry, brittle sound, a bit like a hollow chuckle. "Of course. Why would you explain yourself? You never do."

"Believe what you will. Everyone always does. No one is ever interested in the facts. But I must know what you plan—"

"I am, Maggie. I am quite interested in the facts. I should very much like to learn why you have proceeded to turn me into the village nincompoop. Was it not enough to make a fool of me ten years ago? You had to come back and do it once more for equal measure?"

A fool . . . ten years ago? Her jaw fell open. "Whatever are you talking about? Ten years ago you turned your back on me when the scandal broke. How, precisely, is that making a fool of *you?"*

"Oh, please. Cranford told me, Maggie. About him and the others."

The words were a punch to the gut. Not a surprise, really, but hearing them said aloud hurt more than she'd ever imagined. Mostly because it was Simon, the one person who really should have known better. Not merely because of their friendship during her debut, but last night she'd given him a piece of herself, opened up to him in ways she hadn't with another living person. And here, mere hours later, he still thought the worst of her. What would it take to win him over? How in Hades would she ever make him believe her?

The answer was evident: He would never believe her. He was like the rest of them, the grasping, malicious so-called gentlemen and ladies who liked nothing more than a good, salacious story at someone else's expense.

A prickling started behind her eyes and Maggie clenched her fists. No tears. Not for him. Not for any of them.

She hardened her heart, putting up a wall of icy resolve while straightening her shoulders. The same protection she adopted every time a lady gave her the cut direct on the street. Each time a rogue propositioned her at one of her parties. When the invitations to the biggest Society events never arrived at her address. Her Irish stubbornness, her father would have said. And for once, she was glad of it. They would *not* win. She would have the last laugh, pointing out their ridiculousness while pocketing their coin. Her success and independence had been hard fought, and she would not give it up.

Simon continued to glare at her, his body poised for a fight with his rigid jaw and aggressive posture. He plainly wanted her angry. Not surprising, since it was what they all longed to do: insult the Half-Irish Harlot enough that she buckled under the strain and carried on like a common doxy shouting down a customer on the streets of Covent Garden. Not damned likely.

So she withheld her anger, buried it deep inside,

and regarded him evenly. Part of her considered maintaining her silence. After all, she'd learned years ago of the futility of trying to change a person's mind once set. And it wasn't as if the facts would change anything. Only Becca knew the truth, her sister being the one person Maggie had confided in.

But she wanted to say it, needed to say the truth, if only to watch Simon's face when it sunk in.

She lifted an eyebrow, doing her best impersonation of a haughty dowager duchess. "I do not know what you were told or what letters you speak of. Ten years ago, I never involved myself with another man."

"I have seen your letters to Cranford with my own eyes. I've seen the proof."

Lord Cranford had letters . . . from her? The idea was preposterous. She'd never written the man a word, let alone an entire letter. "I never wrote letters to a man, most certainly not Lord Cranford. I do not know what you were shown, but they were not from me. I was a virgin when I married Hawkins."

Simon blinked, and she could see the doubt creeping into his piercing blue gaze. "I don't understand. You were caught with Cranford, alone. Disheveled. He told everyone . . ."

"That, thanks to my half-Irish blood, I would lift my skirts for anything in breeches?" she finished.

A muscle twitched in Simon's jaw, but he nodded.

"And everyone in London believed him, including you." She strode to the window. Down on the street, two young girls walked arm in arm toward the park, their maids trailing a respectable distance behind. The two girls laughed, enjoying a carefree day in their sheltered existence, and Maggie felt a stab of envy. What must it feel like, to have your whole life ahead of you, untarnished by hate and judgment?

"Are you saying Cranford lied? Why the devil would he do that?"

Maggie kept her gaze on the cold, gray London morning. "I could not say. I rebuffed his advances, quite vigorously I might add, and I can only assume I injured his male pride."

"Wait, Cranford . . . made this all up? To gain what, your ruination? It makes no sense. And what sort of advances of Cranford's caused you to be found in the state you were?"

She turned away from the street and regarded him. He watched her intently, a frown pulling at his handsome face. "Really, Simon, I'm quite certain you can imagine."

He stiffened, his nostrils flaring. "Goddamn it. Why, Maggie? Why did you not tell anyone?"

"No one would have believed me. Even my own mother did not. You know how it looks when that sort of situation arises. Everyone accepts the word of a gentleman."

"I would have believed you, Maggie. *Me.* I would have listened and tried to help you. You should have come to me with the truth."

Didn't he see? It should have been unnecessary. That was the point. He should have believed her incapable of such terrible duplicity. Simon had been the one bright spot in her Season, when she'd been surrounded by whispers and mocking smiles. She hadn't fit in, her dark, Irish looks far from the superior pale English girls; but next to Simon, her less-than-impeccable pedigree hadn't mattered. One grin from him had made the rest of it endurable. She'd been a silly young thing with a crush on the most handsome man in the *ton,* and the feeling had appeared mutual. Yes, Cranford had lied; however, Simon had never even given her a chance to explain.

"I see," he said, his voice flat. He almost sounded *hurt.* "So Cranford ruins you, you do not trust me enough to confess the truth, and prefer to marry Hawkins instead. So tell me how I am the one turned into a drunken wastrel in your cartoons? What in God's name did I do to deserve it?"

She could not—*would* not—explain the true reasons for that. Would not tell him of her broken heart and foolish hopes for their future together, hopes so wrongfully shattered. It sounded terribly . . . dramatic. *Hell hath no fury* and all that nonsense. She preferred to store up her drama for when it could do the most good.

"Was it because of my upcoming proposal? Was this some sort of effort to discredit me publicly?"

Surprise, followed by relief, swept through her. Heavens, why hadn't she thought of it? Yes, let him think her cartoons were political rather than personal. She latched on to the explanation. "I do not care for your proposal. It will hurt the very women you are trying to protect."

"That is no reason to turn me into London's biggest folly, Maggie."

"Perhaps, but you should thank me. The popularity of the cartoons ensures everyone will remember the name Winchester for years to come."

His eyes rounded. "Yes, but for all the wrong reasons. You've taken a venerable family name and turned it into a something synonymous with drunken irresponsibility. How, precisely, is that a situation that elicits my gratitude?"

She lifted a shoulder. "Perhaps in time you shall feel differently."

"Doubtful. And I cannot help but notice you are surprisingly calm in all this. I should think you would be more concerned, considering I now know your secret. What will the world say, I wonder, when they learn the identity of Lemarc?"

When, he said, not *if*. Her stomach knotted painfully, but she refused to show it. "Is that what you plan to do? Unmask Lemarc? I doubt anyone would care, and it won't exactly help your standing in Parliament to be linked with such a scandalous artist."

He crossed his arms over his chest, the fine wool of his frock coat pulling over wide shoulders and finely honed biceps. She could remember tracing the muscles last evening, committing his well-proportioned torso to memory so that she might sketch it later. The now-bittersweet memory made her chest ache.

He said, "I believe they'll be too occupied discussing how Lemarc is truly a woman—and a lady at that! Are you prepared for what that will do to your reputation? Your future?"

"Do not tell me you are concerned with my reputation," she scoffed.

His lips compressed into a thin line, and he shifted toward the wall, giving her his profile. He did not speak for a long moment. Finally, he said quietly, "I have always been concerned with your reputation. And if I had known—or even suspected—what Cranford had done, I would have stepped in. Prevented you from marrying Hawkins. Challenged Cranford. I would have—"

He broke off, so she finished, "Rescued me?" When he didn't respond, she said, "It's too late, Simon. We cannot change what happened. It's done. And I gained something quite powerful at the end. It took years, but I've achieved my freedom. I won't give it up. Not for you, not for anyone."

"Yes, you've made it clear how you feel about my involvement, both then and now."

The steady tick of the mantel clock echoed in the ensuing silence. Simon's gaze remained fixed on the wall, away from her. Maggie had no idea what to say. Part of her wanted to confess how much she'd needed him all those years ago, but what good would that do either of them now? He was angry with her for a number of reasons, and perhaps that was for the best.

"What will you do, now that you know about Lemarc?" she asked him.

"Is that your only concern, that I will reveal your secret?"

"At the moment, yes."

"Once I decide, I'll be certain to let you know." With his jaw clenched so tight she thought it might crack, he quit the room.

The Black Queen was shabby, much shabbier than the last three locations they'd visited tonight. Simon stopped inside the main room of the gaming hell and let his eyes adjust to the gloom. Smoke hung heavily in the air, making it both difficult to breathe and harder to see. But perhaps that was a blessing, considering the type of patrons who frequented these places.

Men were scattered at the tables, desperation clinging

to them like cloying perfume, while the working girls strolled about waiting for a fare. This was not the sort of semi-respectable establishment that catered to wealthy aristocrats; no, in this place, one risked getting a knife under the ribs over the wrong turn of the dice. And it was precisely the sort of hovel in which Simon expected to find Cranford. Of course, he'd said that about each of the dozen places they had searched over the last two nights.

Colton had been on Cranford's trail since the night they'd rescued Cora from Madame Hartley's, as the abbess strongly suspected Cranford of the violence. The Duke of Colton was not known for his subtlety, however, and Cranford had likely learned of the search before it had even begun. The viscount had all but disappeared. Knowing Cranford's penchant for gambling, however, Simon believed the seedier hells were a good place to start looking.

"Well, where should we begin?" Colton asked, coming up alongside.

"Why don't I find the owner this time? You can search the crowd."

"You certain? Fitz says this one's run by O'Shea and it's his favorite haunt."

"Yes. I'll return in a few moments."

Before he could walk away, a hand caught his shoulder. "Winchester," Colton said. "You've been at it for, what, nearly thirty hours without sleep? I know you want to find him but—"

Simon stiffened. He did not merely *want* to find Cranford; he *needed* to find Cranford. Needed to find him in order to break his jaw. Or his nose. Possibly both. No measure of retribution was too harsh. Cranford had ruined Maggie's life. Hell, he'd ruined

Simon's as well. Without those letters, Simon would have offered for Maggie. He would have—

"Very well." Colton raised his hands up in surrender. "I can tell you won't be talked out of it. I was merely going to suggest getting some rest in the very near future. You're starting to scare even me."

Simon didn't want to sleep. Every time he closed his eyes he could see the hurt on Maggie's face, a sorrow no one could possibly fake. *No one would have believed me. Everyone always accepts the word of a gentleman.* And after Cranford attacked her, the bastard. How frightened she must have been, how heartsick to know she'd done nothing to deserve her downfall. Fury flared in Simon's belly once more, the anger that had kept him going since walking out of Maggie's house two days ago. "I can sleep after I put a bullet through Cranford's heart."

Simon stalked to the man watching over the floor. Nearly every hell was organized the same: the owners remained in the back, away from the action, while men they trusted stayed on the floor to keep an eye out for cheating. So Simon knew this man wasn't the one in charge, but he could help Simon find him. "I need to see your employer."

The keen, dark eyes continued to sweep the floor. "'E's busy."

"Counting money, I've no doubt." Simon stepped closer, his posture threatening. "I need information, and if I do not get what I need, I'll be back each night with authorities from the Crown to shut you down until I do."

The man sighed and glanced up toward a walkway on the second floor. His hands gave a few rapid signals then he waited. Finally, he nodded and told Simon,

"Through the door in the back. Tell 'em Piper said to go up."

Briskly, Simon followed the directions and soon found himself climbing a narrow staircase to the second floor. A large man waited at the top. "Follow me," he said before leading Simon through a series of corridors. He stopped and unlatched a scarred wooden door. "Through here."

Simon crossed the threshold, then stopped. A group of rough-looking men were playing cards around a small, round green baize table. They all raised their heads to stare at Simon.

"Well, well, well." The largest of the men put down his cards and picked up his cigar. "An earl and a duke in my place tonight." He slapped the shoulder of his neighbor. "I must be comin' up in the world, boys." The men all sniggered but watched Simon cautiously.

"Mr. O'Shea, I assume?"

The man's mouth hitched and he sprawled back in his chair. "Just O'Shea. We prefer not to use titles on this side of London. I hear you're interested in a spot of information. Hard to imagine what an earl needs to find in The Black Queen. Unless you're lookin' for a bit of rough trade, that is."

Simon shook his head. "I am looking for someone. Wondered if you might know where I can find him."

O'Shea smirked. "And why do you think I can help find one of your fancy friends?"

"This man is no friend. He's titled, but his tastes run a bit . . . darker. Word has gotten round that my friends and I are anxious to find him, and I think he's hiding out somewhere in London. Perhaps in your part of town."

"Who?" O'Shea asked and blew a smoke ring.

"Viscount Cranford."

Simon saw the flash of recognition before O'Shea quickly masked it. "Not sure. Might be familiar." He idly scratched his neck. "What's it worth to you?"

Land, money, power. He'd give anything on earth, anything within his control to learn the answer—not that he'd tell that to O'Shea. "What do you want?"

O'Shea grinned. "Let's have a drink first." He pointed to one of the men at the table. "Get the bottle from the bottom drawer of the desk, will you? And a clean glass for his lordship."

The man stood and O'Shea gestured to the empty chair. "Have a seat, Lord Winchester."

Simon came over and lowered himself into the chair. As he did, the other men at the table all stood, dispersed, leaving just him and O'Shea.

James O'Shea was a thug but also a crafty businessman. He owned most of the hells, brothels, and gin shops in East London. Rumor had him beating a man to death because the man forgot to pay for a drink. Simon wasn't worried, however. He'd negotiated bills, peace treaties, contracts with mistresses. . . . He could handle O'Shea. The key was to remain calm and let the other side reveal a weakness first.

A glass was placed in front of both of them and the bottle set by O'Shea's elbow. "Now," O'Shea said, uncorking the unmarked bottle and pouring a small amount of light brown liquid in each glass. Simon assumed it to be whiskey, though a strange, sharp odor emerged to make his nostrils twitch. "I'll tell you what I know. After you have a drink with me."

Simon snatched up the glass. Without pausing, he brought it to his mouth and tossed the entire thing back. As soon as the spirits hit the back of his throat, he realized his mistake. *Bloody everlasting hell* . . . It was like nothing he'd ever tasted before, like swallowing a burning ember. All the air left his body as fire scorched his insides. He could feel his eyes water as he struggled for breath. Dimly, he heard O'Shea chuckle as the man drained his own glass.

After what felt like several minutes, but was likely seconds, Simon dragged air into his lungs. He did his best to appear unaffected though flames were roasting him from the inside out.

O'Shea grinned, showing of a mouth full of crooked, yellowed teeth. "My own personal stock. Cooked up by my brother in Dublin."

"To try and kill you, one may only assume."

O'Shea laughed, a deep and booming sound. "I'll be sure and tell 'im you said so. Now, your Lord Cranford. I also have an interest in findin' him." He reached forward and refilled both glasses, which caused Simon's stomach to roil in protest. "He owes me a good deal of money, and I keep an eye on men who owe me that deep."

"And?" Simon prompted when O'Shea fell silent.

"Finish your drink and I'll tell you a bit more."

A game. O'Shea was turning this into a game to see how badly Simon wanted the information. Annoyed, Simon picked up the glass, determined to get answers no matter the cost. O'Shea lifted his own drink and toasted, "*Sláinte.*"

The next morning, Simon stepped down the corridor toward Colton's breakfast room, his movements careful and deliberate. Anything not to jostle his head more than necessary. A blunt hammer would be doing less damage than the current pounding inside his skull. At the very least, he prayed he did not cast up his accounts on the marble floor.

A footman, blessedly averting his eyes from the undignified sight of an earl suffering a hangover, opened the door. Simon found Julia alone, behind a small table, china cup in her hand. "Good morning, Simon. Pray sit down. Would you care for food?"

Simon's stomach flipped. "No, thank you," he managed, then crossed the room and lowered into a chair. "I appreciate the bed last evening. Though I'm not sure why Colton did not drop me at home."

"He was worried about you, you dolt. You couldn't even stand. Now I'm worried about you, as well. We're all *worried* about you. And I mean to find out what is going on."

Simon dragged a hand down his face. "I do not have time for a chat, Jules. I must get home and change. I slept in these clothes. I haven't done that since university."

"Rumpled appearance aside, I think you can spare me a few minutes. And I don't believe this has anything to do with your appearance. No, I believe this has more to do with your search for Cranford. I can see your surprise. Did you think me unaware of what you and Colton have been up to?"

"Yes," he admitted, too ill to lie. "What did he tell you?"

"He told me all of it, including the information you nearly drowned yourself in rotgut to learn last night."

Simon stiffened, searched his muddled brain. What had O'Shea said? That Cranford owed him a large amount of money. And Cranford kept a house his wife did not know about. The house was in . . . Holborn?

Bloomsbury? Dammit, he couldn't remember. "How did Colton find it out?"

"O'Shea told him. And Colton and Fitzpatrick have already checked the location of Cranford's apartments. Cranford is no longer there. Cleared out weeks ago. But you needn't worry; they will continue to turn the city up and over until they find him. There's nothing more to be done. I wish to discuss what you plan to do about Maggie."

He tensed. "About Maggie?"

"Do not play dense. Were you aware she's run off to Paris?"

No, he hadn't known. He rubbed the back of his neck, thinking. Why would she go to Paris? He recalled their last conversation and winced. In his hurt and anger, he'd allowed her to believe, erroneously of course, that he might reveal her as Lemarc. Had she believed him? The idea made him feel worse. "When Cranford has been dealt with, I will find Maggie." *And apologize.*

"Simon, you and I have never kept secrets from one another."

He lifted an eyebrow, causing her to chuckle. "Fine. We *usually* do not keep secrets from one another. Happy?"

"Mildly. And your point?"

"I want to know what's happened with Maggie. What caused her to run off for Paris and for you to kill yourself in a search for Cranford?"

He knew that particular determined glint in her eye. Julia would not relent, and perhaps it might do Simon some good to tell someone. "I'm assuming Colton told you of Maggie's scandal, that Cranford lied, showing me false letters to make me believe the *affaire* consensual."

"Yes. Maggie told me some of that tale as well. At least her side of it."

Simon's jaw dropped. "Maggie told you? When? Why did you not tell me?"

Julia looked down her nose at him—impressive since he towered over her, even sitting. "At Madame Hartley's. And I would not betray her confidence in such a manner. If she wanted you to know, she would have told you."

"Did she also tell you that she is Lemarc? That she is responsible for the Winejester cartoons?"

Julia blinked. She opened her mouth, closed it. "No. She did not. I . . . I never would have guessed. Not in a hundred years."

Simon snorted. "Nor would have I. But there you have it."

"When did she tell you?"

He shook his head. "She didn't. I hired a Runner. He discovered it."

"Heavens. She is . . . well, the work is impressive. The chalk drawings must have been hers. She's a genius."

Yes, a clever, beautiful, infuriating genius.

"And allow me to guess," Julia continued. "You were furious and she was unapologetic."

"At the start. But there's more." Simon recounted the entire tale for Julia, starting with how Maggie hadn't trusted him enough to tell him the truth during the scandal, the creation of Lemarc to discredit him politically, and finishing with his threat of revealing her identity.

"Oh, Simon." Her blue eyes filled with pity. "Do

you not see it? Are you so blind that it has not even occurred to you?"

"See what?"

"Do you not remember doing anything as a small boy to gain a girl's attention? Tugging on her hair or putting a worm in her half-boot?" He must have stared at her blankly, because Julia said, "Well, very likely you never needed to. The point is she wanted you to notice her."

"By making me out to be a ninny? Come on, Jules."

"Clearly you broke her heart. All the more reason to choose you as her target. You should be flattered."

It was close to what Maggie had admitted the day he had confronted her. She hadn't said anything about a broken heart, of course, but implied he should be grateful for his immortalization in cartoon form. He rubbed his jaw, let the idea sink in.

"And let's not forget those cartoons have increased your popularity tenfold. Winejester has not hurt your reputation—quite the opposite. The character has solidified you as one of the premier political men of the age. She's done you a great service."

"Hardly feels as such."

"Because of your pride. And your feelings for her."

"She should have trusted me," he admitted. "During the scandal. If she'd come to me then, I—" He couldn't finish it. But he did not need to; if one person knew what he was feeling, it was Julia.

"I know," Julia said, kindly. "And it's clear I should not have prevented you from issuing a challenge to Cranford. I will need to beg her forgiveness for my role in all this. . . ." She paused to heave a sigh. "What happened during her debut, it gives me shivers. She was so young. I understand you believed Cranford and his false letters, but you ought to have sought her out, Simon. You should have at least given her a chance to be heard."

"Are you saying I deserved Winejester?"

"No. Yes." She threw up her hands. "I don't know. But I'm saying she obviously cares about you. And it's clear you love her. So whatever are you going to *do* about it?"

Love. Did he *love* Maggie? How could one love a woman he neither understood nor even knew? "I need coffee." He got up, went to the sideboard, and helped himself to a cup. After a healthy swallow, he decided not to quibble over the word. What he felt for Maggie was a tangle of emotions too strong to name. And he had no idea how she felt about him. He resumed his seat. "I cannot face her until I've dealt with Cranford."

Julia's brows drew together. "Are you prepared to walk away from her a second time?"

"No," he answered sharply, surprising them both. "I just need . . ."

"Time? I'm afraid you don't have it. She's on her way to Paris right now with no plans to return to London. I'm told she gave orders to close up the town house. Who knows how long she'll stay in France or where else she'll go. Can you afford to let her slip away? Because the longer she thinks you've let her go, the more hurt she'll be when you finally find her."

He had to explain it plainly, so she would understand. "I need to make Cranford suffer, Jules."

She huffed, a sign he recognized as extreme annoyance. "You're making this about *you* and your need for revenge, Simon. This isn't about you. It's about Maggie, and, from what little I can tell, it seems she has made peace with her past. It's remarkable what she's accomplished. You were singled out in those cartoons because you hurt her. Terribly. And now you've hurt her all over again."

He finally saw it. As if a ray of sunlight had burst through the dark sky, he knew Julia was right. Maggie should be his focus. What mattered was finding her and putting the past to rest. Because the thought of losing her forever had a fist-sized ball of panic welling up in his chest.

"Go to her, Simon. She's hurting and you are the only one who can make it stop."

Chapter Thirteen

Not long after, in Paris

"*Ma chère,* relax. You are making me nervous."

Maggie glanced across the small table at her mentor and good friend Lucien Barreau. With his artfully tousled brown hair and delicate features, she often teased him that he appeared more poet than painter. They were close in age, Lucien a year older, but he'd been painting his entire life. Without doubt, he was the most talented, generous, and knowledgeable artist Maggie had ever met.

And right now he was staring at her, his handsome face pulled into a frown.

"Forgive me," she offered, weakly. She lifted a delicate cup to her lips and sipped the warm, fragrant Parisian coffee.

"Maggie," Lucien said gently. His brown eyes were compassionate but resolute. "No more, *s'il vous plâit.* You have been here almost three weeks, and the moping . . . I cannot take it anymore. It is unlike you."

She gave him her haughtiest glare, the one reserved for her critics. "I do not *mope*."

He produced a heavy, put-upon sigh and resumed reading his paper. She settled back in the surprisingly comfortable iron chair and watched the sparse activity on the street through the window.

Lucien had recently moved outside the city walls to the hillside village of Montmartre. Maggie suspected this was for privacy reasons, as well as to distance himself from the growing conservatism and civil unrest sweeping Paris in the last few years. She was glad to see Lucien place more importance on happier pursuits as he aged, rather than the political causes he'd once undertaken. With its windmills and vineyards, Montmartre was a quiescent alternative to his former chaotic life.

The café, situated inside a rooming house a few blocks from Lucien's apartments, was typical of those everywhere in France, with rows of tables, a few comfortable couches, and gilded mirrors gracing the walls. As Lucien often said, the French were like spoiled young girls—they preferred to be surrounded by pretty things at all times.

Most of the morning crowd had already dispersed, leaving only a few customers remaining, and Maggie continued to gaze out the window pensively. She leaned forward and exhaled, a tiny cloud of warm fog forming a perfect little *O* on the cold glass. Reaching up, she traced an intricate pattern in the mist with the tip of her forefinger.

"I noticed you received a letter from Madame McGinnis yesterday. How are things in London?" Lucien asked casually over his copy of *Le Constitutionnel*.

The shopkeeper had written to inform Maggie of

sales, offers, and the gossip of the London art world. At this moment, however, she didn't want to think of Lemarc—or London. "Ever the same. She is anxious about the delivery of my next pieces."

"You have not worked much since you arrived. Perhaps it is time?"

She stuck her tongue out at him, which made him chuckle. But he was right, of course. Life did not stop for a broken heart—a lesson she had learned many years ago. So she did what came as natural as breathing: she removed a sketch-book and pencil from her satchel and got to work. Mrs. McGinnis's concern was not unwarranted; the drawings were almost due to Ackermann. No longer could Maggie allow troubles to keep her from her routine.

Soon, Maggie lost herself in the movement of her hand, the results emerging on the paper. The morning wore on, the bell above the door tinkling here and there, low voices chattering, but Maggie paid no mind. Lucien knew better than to talk to her, and she continued to put idea after idea to paper.

After she'd gotten the sketch the way she wanted, she put down her materials. "What shall we do today?" she asked Lucien, stretching away the soreness in her fingers. "Another museum?"

He folded his paper. "I must go into the city. Henri is rehearsing this afternoon and would like me to give my opinion on his performance. Would you care to join me?"

"That might be fun. You did say I should see Gericault's new piece."

"Oh, *oui. Raft of the Medusa.* It will cause an uproar at Salon this year." Lucien's gaze fairly glowed as it often did when they discussed great art. "You should not leave Paris without seeing it."

"Who said I am leaving Paris?"

Lucien rolled his eyes. "You English, you are so impetuous. One fight with your lover and you run away. I am not complaining, because it has brought you here to me. But at some point, you will miss him enough to go home, or he will come to Paris and fetch you."

"You are wrong," she argued. "Neither of those things will happen. I had perfectly good reasons for leaving London—and not all of them had to do with a *man.*"

"I do not doubt it, *ma chère.*" With a snap, he lifted the paper back up in front of his face. The newsprint rustled ever so slightly, and she suspected he was laughing at her.

Maggie huffed and crossed her arms. "And he's not my lover."

A bark of amusement erupted behind the paper. She glared daggers at Lucien but held her tongue. Yes, there had been the encounter in her sitting room—she would never look at that sofa in quite the same light—and then the one night at Barrett House. That one *magical,* soul-altering night at Barrett House. The heat in his eyes as he'd studied her nakedness for the first time. Moist, rapid breath in her ear, the delicious weight of his body as he slid inside her. The low groan when he found his pleasure. No, she would never, ever forget that evening.

But she and Simon would not be sharing any more magical nights. Regret fluttered in her chest, and she beat it back by sheer force of will.

Leaving London had been the right decision. Paris

served as salve for a wounded artist's soul. She could separate herself from the trappings of English Society here, hide at Lucien's, and focus on her art. In France, she felt more Lemarc than Lady Hawkins. A welcome respite if there ever was one.

But it was time to stop feeling sorry for herself, both for Lucien's sake and her own.

Even so, she had no intention of returning to England. Paris would suit for however long she fancied. Simon could continue his lauded political career, without the hindrance of his association to the Half-Irish Harlot and/or Lemarc. Marcus and Rebecca would settle in the country, and their mother would continue to be well provided for. Lemarc's works would continue to sell at McGinnis's Print Shop. In fact, she could not think of one good reason to hie herself back to London. Perhaps she'd travel the Continent for a few years, as she'd once dreamed.

Her glance swung back to Lucien, who remained suspiciously silent behind his paper. Her friend's earlier words pricked at her pride. *Simon is not my lover*, she repeated to herself. Perhaps he could have been, if circumstances had been different. She would have enjoyed learning more wickedness at his hand. Or hands, more like it.

That made her smile, but her amusement quickly faded when she remembered their last conversation. It hadn't been an argument—well, not an argument of the type Lucien assumed. Simon had been . . . disappointed in her. Not to mention hurt by her duplicity. He'd refused to listen to reason, to accept her explanations, which could hardly be Maggie's fault. Stubborn man.

Granted, she hadn't exactly fought to make him

understand. Maggie plucked the pencil off the table and twirled it in her fingers. Why would she? No one ever listened, in her experience. Simon would certainly be no different. After all, he'd accepted Cranford's lies. Not once had he sought an explanation of the scandal. Yes, Cranford had produced proof, but it had been lies, all lies. Shouldn't Simon have possessed at least a glimmer of doubt?

Devil take them all. Simon, Cranford, all the *ton*. She was tired of trying to fit into a world that neither believed in her nor had any interest in the truth. For God's sake, she was not some hysterical female given to fits of the vapors. She'd endured a scandal, heartbreak, a forced marriage, her father's death, her mother's rapid decline, the entire *ton* whispering and gossiping about her. . . .

She would not hide, licking her wounds and feeling melancholy about all that had transpired. Lucien was right. To do such a thing was *not* like her at all. Which meant one thing.

"I will accompany you into the city today," she told Lucien. "I plan to see if my old house on *l'avenue* Gabriel is available."

"You mean the lodgings you declared entirely too large for one simple English widow?" he drawled.

"The very one. And while the house may be too large for one simple English widow, it is perfect for the outrageous Half-Irish Harlot. It is time to host another party."

Lucien slowly lowered the paper to smile at her. "Ah, at last. Welcome back, *ma chère*."

* * *

Not even residing in a different country prevented gossip. Quite the contrary, in fact. Living amongst foreigners transformed the English into a tight-knit little group, and any news of those from home spread quickly. Therefore, Simon got word of Maggie's appearance the instant she moved into the rambling house on Avenue Gabriel.

He felt overwhelming relief at the news. He'd been in France for over two weeks, unable to locate her despite his best efforts, and the worst possible outcomes started to occur to him: that she'd fallen overboard during the crossing. That she had been kidnapped by a band of thieves. That his information had been incorrect, and she hadn't gone to Paris at all.

He worried Julia's warning had materialized, that he'd lost Maggie for good.

Therefore, upon learning her location, his first instinct had been to rush to her house, apologize, and then kiss her senseless. It had taken Quint a quarter of an hour to convince him otherwise.

"The lady's not receiving, Winchester. I was turned away at the door, and she certainly isn't going to feel any friendlier toward you," Quint had told him, after returning. "Not after the way you acted. Your best plan of attack would be to show up when she cannot escape you, then force her to hear you out. Word is she's throwing a masquerade in ten days' time. We'll go along and you can plead your case then."

So for over a week, Simon paced his top-floor rooms at Hôtel Meurice like a caged lion, doing little but thinking on Maggie. Julia had planted the seed, but now Simon knew it as fact. Maggie was the reason he'd never married. He'd told himself all these years that he preferred being alone, but in truth he'd never found anyone quite like her. No one who made him feel alive the instant she stepped into a room. Who kept him guessing and wasn't afraid to stand up to him. A woman who had caught him pleasuring himself and had not run screaming from the room.

He would not give her up. No more lies, no more mistrust. He would make Maggie believe it, use every bit of charm and persuasion in his possession until she accepted the inevitable.

Now he, along with half of Paris it seemed, had crammed into Maggie's ballroom. Throngs of guests mingled about, all dressed in various revealing costumes. There were satyrs and goddesses, pirates and courtiers. A host of Madame de Pompadours as well as King Henry the Eighths. Quint had chosen to dress as one of his heroes, Francis Bacon, though not a soul would likely recognize the costume. Impractical choice, considering the high heels, wig, and ruff, but it was hard to talk Quint out of something once he'd set his mind.

Though he hadn't seen the hostess yet, he knew her costume. He'd paid handsomely for the information so that his own ensemble would complement hers. He hoped she appreciated his effort, considering his bollocks had nearly frozen off on the way over.

The surroundings were spectacular. Maggie had truly outdone herself. The interior of the ballroom had been transformed into a lush Egyptian oasis, with potted palms and other smaller green plants dotting the space, accompanied by gold columns draped in red fabric. A wall hanging of a desert landscape—mounds of sand under a burning-hot orange sun—covered one side of the room, and he wondered if she had painted it. Tiny sitting areas with divans, pillows, and carpets were set up around the room so guests could relax and watch the revelry on the dance floor.

The footmen were in costume as well, each bare-chested and wearing a black half-mask resembling a jackal. The top portion of each mask covered the men's eyes, with tall, dark ears pointing to the ceiling, leaving their mouths and noses free. Gold bands en-circled their upper arms and thick neck plates of gold and onyx rested against the naked skin of their collars. Black and gold skirts fell to their mid-thighs. Where on earth had she hired these fellows?

Despite the sea of costumes and dominoes, he spotted her with little effort. She stood at the far end of the ballroom, surrounded by guests. Mostly men, from what he could see. Little wonder considering the flimsy, nearly transparent white gown she wore. The cloth pulled tight across her bosom, thrusting her breasts up and out, while ropes of gold beading hung in her black hair, attached to a gilded band encircling her head. Gold shoes adorned her feet, the straps crossing over her ankles. She held a glass of champagne in one hand and a curved scepter in the other.

Cleopatra, exotic temptress of the ancient world. His belly warmed, relief and desire building upon one another until all he could think of was getting to her.

He took a step in her direction, but Quint's hand landed on his arm, stopping him. "Patience, Winches-ter. Let her greet the guests. No sense getting us thrown out before supper."

"She won't throw us out, but you're right. I'll wait until she's had a glass or two of champagne first."

Quint chuckled. "Never thought I'd see the day where your skills with a woman were dependent upon her being soused."

Simon shot Quint a look. "I do not want her soused. I want her amenable."

"Oh, is that all?"

"Winchester!"

Simon turned at the sound of his name. A man in a black domino stood in front of him. With the smug set of the man's mouth, Simon had no trouble recognizing him.

"Markham. Didn't expect to find you here." He turned to include Quint and noticed his friend had disappeared into the crowd.

"London gets frightfully dull this time of year," Markham said. "Thought I'd pop over to see what our French brethren had in store. Imagine my surprise in finding such lively entertainment."

No doubt Markham had followed Maggie to Paris. At one time, Simon might've been jealous, but he no longer cared how many men were in her past. Or in her present, for that matter. Simon meant to have her again. Meant to have her smiles and laughter. Meant to have her quick wit and sharp tongue. And most definitely meant to have her luscious body writhing under his.

A loud clapping cut through the chatter as Maggie stepped into the center of the room. She called for attention and the crowd quieted.

"*Mesdames et messieurs*," she said loudly. "My lords and ladies, welcome. In keeping with our theme this evening, I give you the wonders of Ancient Egypt."

A slow, steady drumbeat started. At the opposite end of the room, two jackal footmen appeared, each holding the poles of a litter. Relaxing on the portable bed was a woman dressed very much like Maggie's Cleopatra. Dark hair swinging to her shoulders, a gold band encircling her head. When they reached the middle of the dance floor, the men lowered the litter and she stepped out, a gauzy white dress falling in pleats to her ankles. The neckline was absurdly low and Simon would almost swear her nipples had been rouged. Lifting her bare arms and hands like an Egyptian statue, she froze. Another litter followed, the same slow procession, and its occupant joined the first woman on the floor, adopting a slightly different position of her hands.

Three more joined for a total of five women, all in identical costumes and wearing serious expressions. Once the jackal footmen retreated, the drum tempo sped up, joined by the tinkling of bells. The dancers' torsos began undulating as their hands moved in quick, efficient bursts. Simon stole a glance at Markham, who stood enraptured by the performance. In fact, Simon wouldn't have been surprised to see a spot of drool on the side of the man's mouth.

Not that he hated the display. Indeed, he'd never seen a dance so uninhibited. So . . . carnal. The women were all rolling hips and bouncing breasts in a blatant depiction of the sexual act. It reminded Simon of Barrett House when Maggie had sat astride him, naked and glistening with sweat, as she worked his shaft in and out of her body. Now, there had been a performance worth savoring.

The dancers began a flurry of coordinated hand motions, then added their feet as well. None wore shoes, so delicate toes whispered over the worn wood of the dance floor as they stepped forward and back.

After a few more minutes, the music swelled to a crescendo, the women spinning in circles to lift their dresses above the knee. Bare legs peeped out, to the delight of the crowd. They each struck a final pose as the notes held, and everyone broke out into riotous applause. Simon grinned and clapped as loudly as the rest. Only Maggie could pull off something this brazen.

The slow drumbeat began once more and the women slowly traveled the length of the room, stepping at the same time. They disappeared and the guests began tittering and talking—marveling at the performance, no doubt.

"I've never seen anything like it," Markham said to Simon. "Well, I feel invigorated. I'm off to find a spot of fluff. Always easier at a masquerade, I find. What will you do?"

"Think I'll wait here." He planned to keep an eye on Maggie.

"Ah, got your sights set on someone already, do you? I'd best hurry, then. Excuse me." Markham hurried away, black cape swirling behind him, and Simon breathed a sigh of relief.

Yes, he had his sights set on someone—a very perplexing, maddening, beautiful *someone*.

"Cleopatra," Lucien murmured in Maggie's ear, "Mark Antony has not taken his eyes off you all evening. Do you, perhaps, know the gentleman, *ma chère?*"

This was the first moment they'd had to themselves since the doors opened over two hours ago. The masquerade was a smashing success, judging by the enthusiastic crowd. Maggie sipped her champagne and looked at Lucien. "Mark Antony? Where?"

"There. On the far side, between the palm tree and Joan of Arc."

She turned in the location he indicated, whereupon her gaze locked with piercing blue eyes the color of the Mediterranean. She sucked in a breath. *Simon.* He wore a gold mask, but she would recognize him anywhere, his intense stare causing prickles all down her limbs. Dear God, what was he doing here?

Pointedly turning away, she told Lucien, "He is no one important. Just a man I once knew." *And loved. And worshipped with my mouth.* The unwelcome thought caused a fluttering deep in her belly.

"I do not know why you bother lying to me."

"Maggie is lying about something?" asked Henri, Lucien's longtime lover, as he joined them. "Is it to do with your lack of costume, Luc? I told you she would be disappointed."

Henri, one of the most popular stage actors in Paris, was fashioned as Hamlet, his favorite dramatic character, while Lucien had refused to dress as anyone other than himself. He claimed to hate masquerades, seeing them as nothing but an aristocratic nuisance. Truly, her mentor could be such a stiff neck at times.

"No. It has to do with the way Mark Antony watches over our fair Cleopatra."

Henri followed Lucien's nod and proceeded to give Simon a once-over. After Henri took a long look, he pursed his lips and leaned in to whisper a rapid stream of French to Lucien. Maggie couldn't catch all of it, but Lucien chuckled and told Henri to stop.

"What did he say?" Maggie asked Lucien.

Lucien's lips twitched. "That Mark Antony has

beautiful legs." He waved a hand absently. "And some other nonsense. So is it he? Is this your English lover, finally come to his senses so that he may sweep you off into the night?"

"Nothing of the kind," she lied. "My English lover is taller. And more handsome."

"*C'est impossible,*" Henri said in a stage whisper to Lucien.

But Lucien ignored the comment to keep his perceptive gaze on Maggie. "*Non,* I am certain it is he. The question is, what will you do about him?"

"We are about to find out," Henri announced. "The Roman invasion is upon us."

Out of the corner of her eye, she watched as Simon wove his way through the guests toward her. A white short-sleeved tunic fell above his knees, a loose belt hanging at his waist, with a purple toga draped over his shoulders, the edges held together with a silver clasp. He wore the ensemble well; he appeared tall and lean, as appealing as any Roman statue she'd sketched, with the precise amount of power and arrogance. Her heart beat hard and fast beneath her ribs.

To her dismay, Lucien and Henri disappeared, leaving her quite alone in the crowded ballroom. She considered fleeing, but Simon would likely catch her. Better to face him down now, when they were surrounded by hundreds of people.

"Cleopatra," he greeted her, bowing and holding a fist over his heart as a Roman might.

So they were to play roles. "Antony," Maggie returned. "And here, me without my asp."

He straightened and regarded her thoughtfully. "You are much too stubborn to choose death at your own hand, I believe."

"But Antony killed himself first. Shall we try it and find out?" she said sweetly.

His mouth hitched. "How I have missed you, my dear Cleopatra."

"Really? I must say, I am surprised. I would have thought you relieved to see the last of me."

"You would be wrong. Will you walk with me?"

Something squeezed in her chest at the idea of being alone with him. Panic, she reasoned. "Why? I think whatever needs to be said is best conveyed here."

A blond eyebrow lifted in challenge. "Afraid?"

"Of strangling you with your tunic? Quite. And taunts are beneath you."

They were beginning to draw an audience, with several of the guests nearby now listening to the conversation with unconcealed interest. Simon noticed and reached out to grab her hand, pulling her along beside him. "Come along, my warrior queen. Let us explore the gardens."

Where they would both freeze. She dug in her heels. "No, follow me."

Plucking a fresh glass of champagne off a tray, she sipped the crisp, sweet liquid while leading him toward the back hall. She had no clue what Simon wanted, but hadn't they said enough during their last conversation? He'd said he missed her. She nearly snorted. Even if it were true, that was hardly a reason to follow her to France.

If he'd come expecting her to apologize for Lemarc, he would be sorely disappointed. She'd no sooner apologize for her art than she would present herself at Almack's on a Wednesday evening.

Lucien appeared in her path, his boyishly handsome

face etched with concern. "Is everything well? Do you need me?" he asked her quietly in French.

"I am fine. I'll only be a moment," she returned in English and continued on.

Behind her, Simon and Lucien had a quick exchange she was too far away to overhear. No doubt Lucien was warning Simon not to upset her, which was so like the Frenchman. Lucien had few friends but fiercely protected each one. Of course, he would have no recourse against the powerful Earl of Winchester, who could get away with what he pleased short of murder. Nevertheless, it touched her Lucien cared enough to try.

Simon caught up as she reached the threshold to the music room. "Have you seen the display?" she asked him.

"No. I've been occupied."

"Then, come along. You must see the artifacts from ancient Egypt I have on loan just for the occasion."

They entered the room, which had been transformed into a miniature collection of Egyptian art. Tables formed a semicircle with screens set up behind them. The screens had all been painted with various Egyptian themes and landscapes. The tables displayed the sculptures Lucien had procured through his web of collectors expressly for the masquerade. Maggie had laughed until her sides ached when the objects were unpacked; no display could have been more perfect for a woman with her reputation.

A small number of guests, mostly men, mingled throughout the room. A few women tittered and pointed, clearly embarrassed by the subject matter. She felt Simon's subtle recognition as they drew closer to the first table.

"Are those . . ." he started. "Ah, fertility statues. I should have guessed."

"Very good. Most of these are variations on Min," she said, pointing to the stone carving of a dark man with a fully erect penis in one hand and a flail in the other. "The Egyptian god of fertility."

There were close to thirty wood and stone carvings, each with large, proud phalluses the Egyptians believed carried virility. Simon said nothing, merely continued around the tables slowly while examining each piece. He would be disappointed, of course. No doubt he'd use the opportunity to chastise her for disregarding propriety and decency. What he didn't understand was that she had no plans to be like the rest of Society. She couldn't do it. Give up Lemarc and take up stitching by the fire, awaiting her husband's return from a night of drunken carousing? Unthinkable.

There had been a time when she'd dreamed of being a proper wife to a man with good connections and an even better fortune; but now she knew the world contained so much *more*. She would not give up the freedom to do as she pleased.

"And this one?" Simon pointed to a wooden statue of a half crocodile, half hippopotamus, her large, swollen belly protruding below bare breasts.

"Taweret. Goddess of childbirth and fertility." She studied him for a hint of reaction but couldn't tell what he was thinking. "The carving is quite well preserved. You can still see the pattern of the scales on the tail."

"Why did you bring me in here?" he asked, never taking his eyes off the tables. "Did you hope to shock me, Lady Hawkins, or perhaps arouse my baser instincts?"

Chapter Fourteen

Her jaw fell before she could stop it. "A-Arouse you?" she sputtered. "Do not be ridiculous. I merely thought you should see them."

"Pity."

He did not sound appalled. Or bothered. Which irked her beyond measure. He seemed . . . amused.

While she mused over his lack of reaction, he picked up her hand and drew her behind the screens, toward the dark recesses of the room. "Simon, where are we going?"

"Now it is your turn to follow," he said, tugging her to a far corner where the pianoforte rested, gathering dust. In the semidarkness, she could not see his features clearly so her other senses heightened in compensation. The brush of her skirts against his legs. The familiar smell of him, citrus and a hint of tobacco. He stood so close they were nearly touching, his large presence enveloping her. Her mouth went dry.

She had replayed their evening at Barrett House in her mind so often that she could recall almost every detail. Every glide of his hand. Every nibble of his lips.

Her body had been his canvas, and with expert strokes and bold sweeps he'd created something that hadn't existed before. Something only his masterful eye had seen the potential for. She had been transformed.

But it would be a mistake to allow lust to cloud her thinking, no matter how extraordinary it had been between them. There was too much at risk.

Did he plan seduction in this corner? If so, she needed to quickly dissuade him of the idea. Withdrawing her hand from his grasp, she asked, "Why have you come to Paris? To inform me in great detail on how you plan to ruin Lemarc?"

His fingers tucked an errant strand of hair behind her ear, the small touch making her shiver. "No more lies between us," he said. "You deserve honesty from me, and I should like you to do the same. I was unbelievably angry with you, but I never had any intention of revealing Lemarc."

She knew the feeling well. Fury still simmered in her blood when she recalled their final exchange.

"But I now understand why you created Winejester and made a fool of me," he continued. "I am willing to put it behind us in order to move forward. I have forgiven you."

Had he really . . . ? A thrum of disbelief pounded in her ears. "*You* have forgiven *me*? You . . . you insufferable man." Gad, he should be on his knees, begging her pardon and renouncing all his cruel words and deeds. Granted, as an earl, he'd probably never apologized to anyone in his life—but that didn't mean she didn't deserve it. Disappointment burned in her chest, sharpening her tone as she stabbed a finger at his chest. "It hardly matters that you have forgiven me, Simon, because I haven't forgiven *you*.

And it's unlikely I ever shall. Return to England. You are wasting your time here."

He caught her hand against the hard plane of his breastbone, his brows lowered in confusion. "I've already explained Cranford duped me with the letters. And believe me, I mean to get an explanation as soon as I can locate the man. But you've made me pay time and time again for my sins with those cartoons. Can we not get past it and move forward?"

How could she begin to explain all the ways he'd hurt her over the years? At the very least, he continually assumed the worst of her. Cranford was merely a small drop in the vast well of all that stood between her and Simon. "I would not even know where to begin. I cannot forget what's happened and it's doubtful I'll ever forgive you."

He shook his head. "I do not believe that. The woman in my bed at Barrett House was anything but bitter and resentful. I want honesty from you, Maggie," he said, his tone entirely too reasonable. "I've had precious little in all the time we've known one another. Do you not think I deserve the truth?"

"Honesty?" she hissed and snatched her hand out of his grasp. "You do not want honesty. If you had, you'd've found me after the scandal broke in order to find out what happened. Instead, you closeted yourself off at Madame Hartley's for the better part of a week in a drunken orgy."

His face slackened in surprise. "How the devil did you—?"

"Maggie," a gentle voice interrupted as a hand touched her shoulder. She turned to find Lucien at her side. "The two of you," her friend said, looking between her and Simon, "you are attracting an audience. Perhaps you should retire to somewhere else in the house, *non?*"

Near the screens, a number of faces were not-so-discreetly turned toward the back of the room. *Blast.* Well, the guests certainly could not complain about a lack of entertainment this evening.

"No need," she told Lucien. "We're quite done here. Lord Winchester was just leaving."

That had not gone well.

Simon scrubbed a hand over his jaw and watched Lucien escort Maggie toward the lights and revelry of the masquerade. He forced down his frustration, heaved a sigh. He'd erred tonight, no question. Perhaps he should have discussed his approach with Quint before their arrival. Well, too late now. He'd have to repair the damage—after he figured out what had made her so angry in the first place.

And how had she learned of his infamous sojourn at Madame Hartley's all those years ago? Colton? Julia?

He rejoined the party. There would be enough time to think while standing watch over her. He wasn't comfortable with her out there, unprotected. Some of the male guests had been overly attentive, hovering near her. Simon didn't like it.

He found Quint as soon as he stepped into the ballroom. A waltz played and dancers crowded the floor, some using the proximity for more than dancing. An overweight Nero leered down at Boudica, his palm firmly on her buttocks.

"Back from your defeat at Actium, Mark Antony?" Quint drawled before lifting a teacup to his mouth.

"Hardly. Merely a minor setback."

"Not from what I heard. Half the damn place is tittering about it." Quint replaced the empty cup in the saucer and handed it off to a passing jackal footman. "So, what is your next plan of attack?"

"I am not sure. I hadn't expected her to be so . . ." He couldn't quite put it into words, all that anger, bitterness, and hatred. How to chip away at such a mountain of female pique?

"I suspected. God knows I cannot offer insight into the female brain. They all want to be wooed. And talked to. It's . . . boggling."

Wooed. Hmm.

"Do you plan to stay?" Quint asked.

"Yes."

"You're worried with all this debauchery around her," Quint deduced. "Can't say I blame you. Well, I'm off to find the very pretty Margaret Cavendish I saw earlier. I'll see you in the morn."

"Wait, who?"

Quint sighed, no doubt appalled. While Simon wasn't stupid by any means, not many could rival Quint's rapid intellect. "Duchess of Newcastle under Charles the Second. Poet, playwright, *et cetera*. Read a book once in a while, will you?" The viscount strode away, melting into the sea of ostrich feathers and tricorns.

Simon turned his attention back to Maggie. She stood on the far side of the room, near the open terrace doors, surrounded by a small circle of guests. Smiling and laughing, she had entranced those around her, if their rapt expressions were any indication. Simon could hardly blame them; her vibrancy had been one of the traits that had initially drawn him to her.

He sipped champagne and watched the men fawn over her. She didn't encourage them, exactly, but participated enough to give a man a glimmer of hope. Long looks, meaningful smiles, small touches . . . she made sure to give attention to each man in the group. Simon's chest tightened, but it wasn't exactly jealousy. No, it was much more complex than that. He felt proprietary toward her, like he wanted to stand on a chair and announce to the room that she was *his*.

One man, dressed as Don Quixote, reached to open the terrace door. Maggie started for it, and Simon's back stiffened. Was she truly so reckless as to allow a man to escort her outside, alone, where any number of things—

"Enjoying your evening, Winchester?"

His attention was briefly pulled away from the terrace to the man hovering an arm's length away. "Indeed. And you, Markham?"

"Oh, yes. I daresay this exceeds any of her parties in London. Though you wouldn't know, seeing as how you never attend the Harlot's parties."

"Do not call her that," Simon said sharply.

Markham's eyes rounded. "What? Why the devil not? She's referred to herself as such many times in my presence. I cannot see that it's offensive if she's adopted the name as well."

Simon clenched his jaw. How could he explain it without appearing a lovesick fool? He regarded the closed terrace doors. Had she gone outside? If so, to what end?

"And we are on rather intimate terms," Markham boasted in a conspiratorial tone.

"What?" Every muscle in his body drew tight. Had she and Markham. . . .

"Well, not yet. But I do have high hopes, especially since she's decided to woo me into joining your opposition."

Simon's jaw nearly fell open. Maggie, woo Markham? To the opposition? As far as Simon knew, she used Lemarc to undermine politicians and their causes—namely his. He'd never realized she would go to these lengths, of actually campaigning to thwart this upcoming legislation.

"Anyway," Markham continued, "perhaps we should meet here in Paris, discuss your proposal in more detail."

A few weeks ago, Simon would have leaped at the chance to bend Markham's ear. The proposal needed all the support it could garner, and Markham was renowned for allowing his vote to be swayed by an evening of cards and spirits. But there were more important matters on Simon's mind than politics at the moment. Like an answer as to what Maggie was doing on the terrace.

Still, an outright refusal wasn't how the game was played. And few played it better than Simon. "Indeed, we should, Markham. I'm at the Hôtel Meurice. Why don't you join me one evening for dinner?"

Markham's chest expanded, pleased with the invitation. "Very good. Next week, perhaps. Did you see the collection?" He chuckled, then stopped short. "Oh, my apologies."

Simon stifled a sigh. Seemed Quint hadn't lied when he said half the party had heard of his and Maggie's conversation in the music room. His eyes found the terrace doors once more. What was she about? Neither she nor Don Quixote had returned. The skin on the back of his neck prickled. Surely he was overreacting. Likely she'd taken air, become engrossed in conversation. Nevertheless, he would rest easier if he could at least see her.

"Excuse me, Markham. There's a matter I must attend to outside."

"*Mon chaton*, you are even lovelier than you were three years ago."

Maggie smiled at Jean-Louis, a man every bit as charming and handsome as she recalled. A friend of Lucien's, Jean-Louis had been her one lover during her marriage. While she wasn't proud of dishonoring her marriage vows, she'd been starved for any kind of affection during those lonely years. Charles had long since stopped any sort of contact between the two of them, awkward as those encounters had been. As her husband's health deteriorated, he'd preferred the company of his longtime mistress and Maggie had been glad of it.

Her ineptitude and guilt, however, had proved a recipe for disaster in the brief affair with Jean-Louis. At least they had remained friends. "Your skill with pretty words rivals your abilities with a brush, *mon ami*. How have you been since I last saw you? Lucien tells me you've taken to portraits."

"I have," he said. "I find it's more lucrative and reliable than anything else. I've just returned from Spain, where I spent months painting the new queen."

"And entertaining the pretty Spanish ladies at court, no doubt."

He smiled, his teeth even and white. "But of course.

What sort of Frenchman would I be if I did not demonstrate all my skills in their backward little country?"

She laughed. "How generous you are."

"Indeed, I try." His expression sobered as he reached out to grasp her hand. "I regret that our . . ." He paused to search for the right word. "That our acquaintance did not continue. I find you very beautiful, Lady Hawkins. Should you ever need me, all you must do is ask."

How she wished she felt something more for this sweet and charming man. When they had met, she'd had visions of setting up a studio overlooking the Île de la Cité, where they would paint each day and make love all night. Those hopes had been dashed, however, when it had become clear that something inside her was missing—something only one man had ever coaxed from her, damn him.

Stepping forward, she kissed his cheek. "Of course. And thank you, Jean-Louis. You were a wonderful friend when I desperately needed one."

"I can be one again. Do not forget it."

"I shan't. Now run along or your lovely companion might wonder where you've wandered off to. I plan to take a few more minutes of air out here."

"Alone? *Non*, I cannot allow it. A pretty woman should not remain out here by herself."

She waved her hand. "Touching but unnecessary. I'm quite safe here, I assure you. Not to mention, I have no reputation to worry over. Go." She tilted her chin toward the house. "I'll follow in a moment."

Still looking unsure, Jean-Louis returned to the party, and Maggie took a deep, cleansing breath. Entertaining guests while trying to ignore Simon's penetrating stare had resulted in a persistent throbbing in her temples. Did the man not have a thing to do but watch her all evening? She wished he would return to his hotel, pack, and depart on the first steamer to London.

Didn't she?

She rubbed her bare arms for warmth. The torches lining the edge of the terrace were more for decoration than heat; still, she found herself drifting toward them. How long did Simon plan to stay in Paris? *I want honesty from you, Maggie.* The idea made her both want to laugh and cry. No one in their world wanted honesty—the *ton* was built upon appearances and deceit, for heaven's sake.

Even if he did want the truth, she'd been playing as someone else for so long she couldn't begin to remember her former self, the Maggie he'd charmed during her debut. That girl no longer existed. In order to survive, she'd become another person, one who was stronger and more confident. One who kept her own counsel. Simon knew of Lemarc and she'd denied Cranford's accusations. What more did he want from her?

A boot scraped over stone and she froze. Was someone else here? Another sound grated, this time near the stairs to the gardens. She forced herself to relax. Most likely it was a pair of lovers now returning to the party. She turned her back to give them privacy.

"Lady Hawkins," a strange, deep voice said seconds later. "How utterly delectable you look this evening."

Her breath caught. That voice. It was distorted slightly, but a memory nagged at the back of her mind. Maggie spun to find a man in a heavy greatcoat wearing a Black Plague mask. The elongated beak protruded from the face, the dark, soulless eyes staring at her from across the short distance.

"Who are you?" she asked, ignoring the talons of discomfort sliding down her spine.

"You do not recognize me? I am crushed."

Heart hammering, she focused her artist's eye on the details. He was English, she could tell both from the accent and his clothing. Slightly shorter than Simon and in good physical condition. Well dressed. She hadn't noticed this particular costume earlier, and she was fairly certain she would have remembered it. "I am afraid I do not. Will you reveal yourself?"

"In good time, my dear, all in good time. You are a hard lady to find alone."

The idea that he'd been waiting to catch her alone did not bode well. Her location, so removed from the house and the protection of the crowd, now slapped of overconfidence and hubris on her part. Still, she would not cower. "If you mean to do me harm, sir, you shall have the devil of a fight on your hands."

"Oh, I like a good fight, Lady Hawkins. Nothing gets a man's blood pumping faster, believe me."

She swallowed the bile rising in her throat. "What is your purpose here? To frighten me?"

"Are you frightened? And here I had thought nothing would scare the great Lemarc."

All the air whooshed out of her lungs. How . . . ? Had Simon told someone? No, she knew he hadn't; he wouldn't want it known he'd been mocked so publicly by a woman. A man's pride could only take so much. She forced down the panic and straightened. "You are wasting my time with your nonsense. Either reveal yourself and your purpose, or be gone."

"And if your hands were not shaking, I might believe you."

She wrapped her arms around herself. "That is from cold. I do not fear cowards who hide behind masks and lurk about in the shadows."

"Yes, you prefer men such as Winchester. The next great politician, they say. Could even rival Fox, perhaps." The sneer in his voice was evident despite the grotesque mask.

"I've grown weary of this conversation. Excuse me." She started for the door, more than eager to put an end to this bizarre exchange.

"I suppose with your reputation, you've likely heard it all by now. He will use you, you know."

Maggie stopped, spun around. "What?" she asked before she thought better of it.

"Winchester. He won't live up to his promises, whatever they are. The consummate liar, he'll take what he wants and move on."

"How do you—"

The terrace door opened and Simon appeared. His glance volleyed between Maggie and the man in the death mask, and then he strode forward. "Lady Hawkins, may I be of assistance?"

Before the sentence had finished, her mystery companion bowed with a flourish and hastened toward the house. Simon stepped aside to allow access to the terrace door and approached her. "Maggie," he said, a deep crease between his brows. "Your lips are blue. Why are you out here? Who was that man?" He slid his hands up and down her arms, the motion nearly painful on her frozen skin.

She shook her head. "I do not know. He wouldn't tell me."

"Wouldn't tell you? That's utter nonsense. Did you recognize him as one of your guests?"

"No."

Simon stared at the door through which the man had disappeared, a muscle jumping in his jaw. "Come inside and get warmed up. Then you must tell me what he said to put such an unhappy look on your face."

Chapter Fifteen

Maggie accepted a healthy glass of brandy from Lucien. They had the library to themselves—after she encouraged an enthusiastic Hera and Dionysus to scale Mount Olympus elsewhere. "Thank you." She lifted the brandy to her lips and took an unladylike swallow.

"What was Jean-Louis thinking, to keep you outside so long? *Mon Dieu,* but you are frozen."

"Jean-Louis did not keep me outside. Truthfully, he insisted I come inside, but I wanted a moment to myself. There was another man. He came up from the gardens."

Lucien pushed his unruly mass of hair back from his face and dropped into a chair. "From the gardens? Who was it?"

Maggie shrugged. "I do not know. He wore a mask and would not give me his name. He'd been waiting to find me alone, he said."

"I begin to see why your earl left you with me and dashed off into the crowd. This man, did he hurt you?"

"No. He merely wanted to frighten me, I think."

She took another swallow of brandy. "He knew of Lemarc, Lucien."

Her friend's eyes rounded. "Knew that you and Lemarc are one and the same?" When she nodded, he asked, "*Comment?*"

"I do not know how. Only a small number of people are aware of Lemarc's real identity and they are all trustworthy. I would never suspect you or Rebecca. Or Mrs. McGinnis."

"What about your earl? You said he knew. What would he do with such information?"

"Stop calling him 'my' earl," she snapped, then softened her tone. "And it's not Winchester. Lemarc as a woman makes him appear an even bigger fool, which he would want to avoid with his proposal going to vote this spring."

"You cannot be sure, *ma chère*. Perhaps he—"

"No, he would not."

Lucien's face gentled while his eyes remained sharp. She remembered the look well, the master softening a blow for the pupil. He never liked to hurt her feelings. "Maggie, do not let your *tendre* for him blind you to the most obvious of things. For two years, you have maintained the secret. But in a few short months your earl reappears and learns you are Lemarc, and now someone else knows as well. This appears more than coincidence, *non?*"

The door swung open, sounds from the party spilling inside. Simon strode into the room, his handsome face pulled into a deep frown as he stalked to the sideboard. Maggie allowed herself a moment to appreciate the sight of his lithe body in the Roman costume. Henri was right; Simon did have very fine legs.

Were her feelings for Simon preventing her from seeing the truth, that he'd spilled her secret to another? Perhaps he had confided in Quint, who had in turn told someone else. If that were the case, half of London could know her identity by now. The pain behind her temples increased twofold, and she began to massage the area with her fingers.

He'll take what he wants and then move on.

What had the stranger meant by such a statement?

"He's gone," Simon announced. "Jumped into a waiting cabriolet and disappeared. The staff only took note of his exit, not his entrance." He turned, a glass of claret in his hand. "Will you tell me what he said to upset you?"

Maggie had no intention of telling him the truth. The only person she fully trusted was Lucien, and even he had not learned all of it. Some details were best not shared. She lifted a shoulder. "Nothing of consequence. I suspect he was returning from a tryst in the gardens and stopped merely to be polite."

Simon swallowed the rich, dark wine, all the while leaning against the sideboard and watching her over the rim of his glass. "You are lying," he finally said. "Did he proposition you? Is that what you are hiding?"

A choking noise of disbelief came from Lucien's direction, but Maggie kept focused on Simon. "Why must you continue to believe the worst of me?"

His brows drew together. "It has nothing to do with you, and everything to do with the situation. If a man finds a beautiful woman alone on a terrace, it's hardly unheard of to deliver a proposition."

"The voice of experience, no doubt," she snapped.

Lucien came to his feet. "I believe it is time for me to excuse myself and return to the party."

"Lucien, wait," she told her friend. "My head is pounding. If I decide to retire, will you see to the guests?"

"Of course, *ma chère.*" He sketched a bow and whirled toward the door.

When they were alone, Maggie sighed. Too many emotions warred inside her, and she was exhausted. Her head throbbed, as if a carver were chiseling away at the hard planes of her skull, a sure indication she needed rest. She rose. "You have wasted your time in coming to Paris, Simon. I am weary of our battle and it's plain it cannot be resolved."

He straightened and set down his wine. "That is nonsense. The only battle is your refusal to be honest with me or to trust me. Like not telling me you were undermining my proposal behind my back."

The surprise must have shown on her face because he said, "Yes, madam. I have learned of your efforts to woo Markham."

"I did not *woo* him, Simon. I merely expressed my concerns about your proposal and pointed out its flaws."

"And why would you not discuss these concerns with me?"

"I told you I did not care for it."

Frowning, he placed his hands on his hips. The motion showed off the ripple of muscle along his bare forearms and biceps. Oh, God. Even with a headache she still noticed things she should not. Annoying how very *aware* of him she was at that moment.

"This is a perfect example, Maggie," he continued.

"You are determined to thwart me and hold me at arm's length. If you would only trust me—"

"Trust you?" she scoffed, her voice sharp. "Why the devil would I ever do something so foolish? No, you broke my heart once. I shall not give you the chance to do it again."

The aristocratic planes of his face slackened, and Maggie could have bitten her tongue. Curse her Irish temper. She'd never meant for him to be privy to that information. Damn it all.

He appeared speechless—a blessing since the condition would give her time to retreat before he could gather his thoughts. "I am unwell. Forgive me, but I must retire. Please go back to London, Simon. There's nothing more to be said here."

Ablaze with lamplight, the Salle Feydeau towered over the street. The imposing brick and stone theater had large figures carved into the façade reminiscent of an Egyptian temple. Patrons dodged the assemblage of carriages, horses, and servants as they hurried to the entrance, indicated by the words *Opéra-Comique* stretched over a series of open doors.

Lucien hadn't wanted to risk a late arrival. When traffic had slowed, he'd insisted they leave the carriage a few blocks away and walk instead. Maggie held the hem of her opera cloak out of the Parisian dirt, though there was no hope for her ruined slippers.

She could not blame Lucien for his anxiousness, not tonight. Henri had the lead role in this production, and Lucien did not want to miss the opening performance.

Once inside, the two of them were shown to an

upper box with an excellent view of the stage. As Lucien chatted with the usher, Maggie stepped down to the front and gazed over the rail. With gilded surfaces, red velvet curtains, and marble accents, the theater was the most beautiful building she'd ever seen. Wooden puppets on strings danced on the stage, but the crowd largely ignored this small performance. Instead, a sea of black topcoats and tall ostrich feathers rippled throughout the boxes as the crowd talked amongst themselves.

"Shall we sit?" Lucien asked behind her.

Maggie nodded. "Does Henri always procure you a box?"

"He insists for opening night, though I'd much rather be down there." He gestured to the floor. "He says it relaxes him to find me whenever he becomes nervous." Because the true nature of their relationship must be kept secret, Lucien posed as Henri's theatrical instructor in public. Maggie suspected the tedium of maintaining the ruse had been one of the reasons the two had moved to Montmartre.

"How lovely you two are to one another."

"Not always," he admitted, the side of his mouth lifting slightly. "We are both artists, so we tend to be stubborn." He knocked his head with his fist. "As you know only too well, since you are of the same temperament."

She chuckled. "True. But if we were not stubborn, we might listen to our critics and never paint again."

"Or perhaps we would acknowledge our mistakes in hopes of never repeating them, *n'est-ce pas?*" He gave her a pointed stare that left little doubt to his meaning.

"You are wasting your breath. Save it for Henri's

ovation." She lifted her opera glasses and began searching the crowd.

"You must admit, it is *très intéressant*. I would never have expected your earl to try and court you. First with flowers, then the paint. What did he send today?"

Maggie shifted in her seat. While she hadn't seen Simon since the masquerade three nights ago, gifts had been delivered in his name every morning. First, an enormous bouquet of white roses arrived. The fragrance, Simon wrote, smelled like her skin. Next came green pigment, a shade she happened to know not many colormen carried. He claimed the color was the same as her eyes in the throes of passion and asked that she think of him between her thighs whenever she used it.

Today's offering had been bawdier. A bronze statue of Priapus, the Greek god of male genitalia, with his huge erect phallus, had both shocked and amused her. Heat suffused her face when she recalled the note.

> *My lady,*
>
> *Your hands have precisely the same effect on my person. Should you want to watch once more, I am most happy to oblige.*
>
> > *Yours faithfully,*
> > *Simon*

She'd memorized every word before tossing the paper into the fire.

"Well?" Lucien prompted.

"Merely a statue." Maggie pretended to peer through her opera glasses, if only so Lucien wouldn't notice her discomfort.

"If merely a statue, then why have you turned red?"

She lowered the glasses. "I do not know what I am supposed to do," she admitted. "Does he plan on sending me something each day until I . . . what? I have no idea what the rules are."

"Ah." Lucien sat back and crossed his legs. "I see. You have never been pursued and the idea makes you uncomfortable. Can you not just enjoy it, *ma chère?* In a dress as beautiful as that, you deserve to have the men of Paris slavering at your feet."

Maggie smoothed her low-cut silver and white opera dress while she considered Lucien's words. No man had ever tried to win her. During her debut she'd received a few bouquets, but no suitor had ever seriously courted her—not even Simon. Her husband had given her a perfunctory gift on each birthday, no doubt picked out by his secretary. She could not even recall them.

This kindness from Simon unnerved her. When the two of them were at odds, she could easily find her footing. Gifts and adoring words, however, were harder to navigate. Discounting them made her a shrew, but did he honestly believe a few tokens would heal wounds long scarred over? And what did he hope to accomplish?

She fervently wished their conversation the other night had not taken place. Without that infernal headache, she never would have revealed the fact he'd broken her heart. Silly female notion anyway, a broken heart. No doubt he thought the revelation ridiculous.

"I could enjoy the attention if I knew what he hoped to gain," she told Lucien.

"It is obvious, *non?* Your earl intends to lure you back to his bed."

The performance began, leaving Maggie to contemplate Lucien's statement. Could it be as simple as that? If he merely wanted to bed her again, would he go to so much trouble? It wasn't as if she were a maiden, for heaven's sake. Not that it mattered. She could not allow her resolve to weaken. Any association between the two of them must be avoided. His political career would certainly suffer from her reputation, and she had no plans to curtail either her behavior or her career as Lemarc. No one would take away the freedom she'd worked so hard to achieve.

The first act had been bloody torturous. Maggie's box was not far and Simon had hardly taken his eyes off her, drinking her in like a man dying of thirst. She looked devastatingly beautiful. The silver and white opera dress showed off the creamy, rounded tops of her breasts. Her long, black hair was fashioned into rings of curls held away from her face with a silver band, exposing the long column of her throat. He wanted to nibble on that soft pale skin.

When they reached the first break, Simon turned to his companions. "Lady Sophia, Lady Ardington, if you'll excuse me, I see someone I must speak with."

Lady Sophia stood, her brown eyes shrewd and knowing. "I shall come with you."

Simon blinked. Sophia was the Duchess of Colton's closest friend, which meant she enjoyed trouble every bit as much as Julia—only Sophia had no husband to keep her in line. Under normal circumstances, Simon avoided her, but she'd requested his escort to the

Opéra-Comique this evening. Since he'd already planned to attend, there had been no reason to turn Sophia and her stepmother down.

Of course, he hadn't counted on Sophia dogging his every step tonight. He needed to have a private conversation with Maggie, one no unmarried lady should overhear. Impatient to leave, he frowned at Sophia. "No."

Sophia waved her hand dismissively, then said, "Stepmama, Lord Winchester and I will return shortly." She grabbed Simon's arm and began tugging him out of the box. "Come on. I am dying to meet her."

Once in the corridor, he placed her hand on his sleeve. They started in the direction of Maggie's box. "How do you know where I'm going?"

"Please. You have been staring at her all night and I read the broadsheets. Everyone talks about her. I was desperate to go to her masquerade, but my stepmother wouldn't dare let me. Were you there?"

"Yes." He recalled Nero fondling Boudica's buttocks. "And the marchioness was right not to let you attend."

"Et tu, Brute?"

He laughed. "I pity your future husband."

"Me as well. Papa is growing more irritated every Season. I fear he may put his foot down this year."

"So just pick one and be done with it. Marriage might not be as bad as you think."

"Or it may be much, much worse—and I'd hardly take your word for it. You've certainly been in no rush to take a countess."

"Julia and Colton are very happy," he pointed out.

"Disgustingly so," she agreed. "But she's stuck with him so why not make the best of it? No, I think I'll wait a little longer. What is going on between you and Lady Hawkins?"

"As if I'd tell you. The marquess would have my head on a stick."

"You're wrong. Papa likes you. Says there's talk you may replace Liverpool one day."

Simon drew back the curtain on Maggie's box, held it open for Sophia. "I think that talk is vastly premature." Especially if anyone ever discovered Lemarc's true identity.

They stepped inside and found Maggie conversing with a man, their bodies in close proximity, her hand placed familiarly on his arm. Simon recognized him as Don Quixote from her masquerade, the one who had led her out to the terrace. His gut clenched, the jealousy swift and fierce. He'd expected to find her with Barreau, not one of her admirers. Forcing a smile, he continued on. "Lady Hawkins."

Her head shot up, emerald-green gaze locking on him. Surprise flickered across her features before she schooled them, and she gave him a polite nod. "Lord Winchester."

Introductions were made all around, during which it became clear that this artist, Jean-Louis, and Maggie were lovers. She was uncharacteristically skittish and talkative, and color stained her cheeks. The Frenchman kept his hand atop hers, where it lay firmly on his arm. Simon barely restrained himself from hauling Maggie over against his side.

Lady Sophia held up the conversation. "Lady Hawkins, the Duchess of Colton is one of my dearest friends and she insisted we meet. How fortunate you attended the premiere tonight."

This resulted in a long exchange about Paris and

shopping, the sort of discussion a man could safely tune out. It was then Simon noticed that Maggie made several subtle attempts to pull her hand off Jean-Louis's arm but the Frenchman held fast. Had Simon misread the situation, or was she merely trying to employ discretion? The idea nearly made him laugh. Maggie, discreet?

Nevertheless, who was this man? How had she come to know him? Even after all that had happened between them, he still didn't know much about her. Well, he was of a mind to change that, starting tonight.

He waited for a break in the conversation. "Lady Hawkins," he interjected, "might I have a word in private?"

Awkwardness descended until Sophia said, "Indeed, I must be getting back to my box. My stepmother will be looking for me. Jean-Louis, would you mind escorting me back? I would love to hear more about the type of paintings you create."

They said their good-byes and Sophia fairly dragged the Frenchman away, much to Simon's relief. Now alone in the box with Maggie, he clasped his hands behind his back. "Are you enjoying the performance?"

"Very much. Henri is marvelous. And you?"

"Yes, though truthfully I haven't seen much of it."

"Did you arrive late?"

"Seconds after the curtain rose. The mob outside was like nothing I've ever seen. I was referring to something else entirely, however."

"Oh, the lovely Lady Sophia. I suppose she could be quite dis—"

He couldn't help but laugh. "You know very well she is not the reason I am here tonight. I came for you."

She bit her lip, the soft, plump flesh disappearing between her front teeth. Simon remembered her mouth and the extraordinary sensation when she'd used it on him. Heat flared in his groin.

"Simon, these arguments are exhausting, and I cannot see why we should continue. You have my gratitude for the presents, but you needn't send any others."

The words she'd flung at him the other night flickered in his mind. *You broke my heart once. I shall not give you the chance to do it again.* Julia had alluded to it in London, but hearing Maggie admit it changed everything. No longer would he wait. He meant to break down the walls she kept up between them. If she'd cared for him once, she could do so again. He merely needed to wage a clever, careful campaign.

So for the moment, he chose to avoid disagreeing with her. Instead he would employ strategy, much as he did when trying to win votes. "Have you seen Notre Dame?"

She blinked. "Of course. Many times. Why?"

"Will you accompany me there? Tomorrow?" Confusion wrinkled her brow and he fought the urge to grin.

"Tomorrow?" She frowned. "Positively not. I cannot go traipsing about Paris with you tomorrow. I am too far behind in my work."

He reached for a silken black curl gracing her cheek, gently tucked it behind her ear. "Bring your work along. I promise to find you a quiet spot and leave you alone."

"But why would you—?"

Before she could finish, the performers returned to the stage. Without waiting for permission, Simon took her hand and led her to her seat. Once she sat, he brushed his lips over her gloved fingertips. He noticed the color that stole over her cheeks. "Until tomorrow," he murmured and then strode out of the box, enjoying his small victory.

Chapter Sixteen

Maggie winced as the carriage bounced into another rut in the road. Simon rested across from her, his long legs stretched out as far as space would allow. As promised, he'd arrived early this morning to collect her for this mysterious journey. She had tried to refuse and send him away, but even Tilda seemed to be on his side, marching Maggie out the door like a side of beef off to auction.

They'd been traveling for nearly an hour, having left the city proper some time ago. Obviously Simon had fabricated the story of visiting Notre Dame. She should have known he would pull a trick on her. At the very least, she wished she'd packed more of her painting and drawing supplies before agreeing to this kidnapping. The devil only knew where he planned to take her and how long they would be gone. She supposed she should be worried, demanding to know what he was about. But it was too late to turn back, so what was the point? At least the warming bricks kept the temperature cozy despite the cold outside.

She gazed out the small window, admiring the

French countryside with its quiet wheat fields awaiting spring. The sky held no color, a blanket of mottled shades of gray, and she enjoyed the bracing fresh air outside the city walls. Wide open spaces with their dormant trees and shrubs always relaxed her, and it had been much too long since she'd allowed herself this small indulgence.

Even so, why in God's name had she agreed to accompany him today?

"How did you meet Barreau?"

Simon's question startled her, both the interruption of the silence and the topic. She shifted to face him. "I came to Paris with my sister and her husband. Every morning, I used to walk down a certain section of the Rue de Rivoli and I noticed an artist there each day. He painted the crowd, lost in his work, but now and then I'd see him sketching a portrait for a customer. I began watching him and noticed he never took money for the sketches. And his work . . . oh, it was extraordinary. Truly extraordinary. So vivid and realistic. So one day, I approached and asked him why he never accepted payment for his sketches." Her mouth turned up in amusement. "That sparked a long and passionate diatribe about how art belongs to the people and it is an artist's duty to share that gift with everyone *gratis.*"

"Ah, a Jacobin."

"No doubt, had he been born earlier. So I complimented him on his work and we discussed art. He handed me his charcoal and some paper and instructed me to sketch him. Testing me, of course. When I produced the sketch, he nearly fell out of his chair." She chuckled. "He asked what artist I had apprenticed under. For weeks, I could not convince him

I was self-taught. He suspected me of lying until my ineptitude about business matters became apparent. Lucien may be jaded to the ways of the world, but he is not ignorant. He's taught me a great deal over the years."

"What did he do with your sketch of him?"

Heat suffused her face. "He framed it. It hangs in his apartments in Montmartre."

"And that embarrasses you? I should think you would be filled with pride over impressing him."

She waved her hand. "I've offered many times to redo it. Lucien won't hear of it."

"I cannot say I blame him. Sometimes the memory means more. Will you sketch me one day?"

She bit her lip, trying not to giggle. He sighed, reading her perfectly. "I meant a *true* sketch. Not Winejester. I've had the obligatory portrait done when I took over the title. Hangs at Winchester Towers and I can hardly stand to look at the thing. I should like to see what you see."

Her first instinct was to refuse. Drawing could be quite personal, an intimate connection between artist and subject. She made a study of her model, noticed every hair, every shadow, to create the most true representation possible. With Simon, however, there would be no need to study; she had every inch of him committed to memory. "Perhaps," she finally answered.

"How did you first start drawing, or notice you had a passion for it?"

She grinned at the memories. "Rebecca. She noticed my propensity for sketching during the lessons with our governess. Instead of learning my figures or practicing my penmanship, I was nearly always drawing. She encouraged me, along with my father."

"The poet, correct?"

"Yes. He pushed me to express myself through paints and sketches. Even tried to convince my mother to let me travel abroad instead of coming out. But she wouldn't hear of it. She was determined to see me molded into a proper English lady." *And look at how well that turned out.*

"You never mentioned your hobby all those years ago."

She shrugged. "Mother warned me not to reveal my unusual interests. She wanted me to appear just as demure and dim-witted as the rest of the girls debuting that year."

He chuckled and silence descended for a long moment. Since they were asking questions, she had a few of her own. "Why politics?" she asked. "You never gave a fig about Parliament all those years ago."

"It's what is expected of me. The role of the Earl of Winchester." He lifted a broad shoulder. "And I am adept at it."

"So I have heard many times over. But do you love it? Feel any passion for it?"

His brows drew together. "One does not need to romanticize a task in order to do it well."

"But if it does not make you happy, why do it?"

"Because I like to win." His mouth kicked up. "Have you not learned that yet?"

The carriage began to slow. Simon leaned to see out the tiny window. "Ah, we must be arriving at our first stop. We can stretch our legs while they deal with the cattle."

Minutes later, Simon helped her out of the carriage. The hanging sign read L'ANNEAU D'OR, or The Golden Ring. It was a modest, provincial structure, constructed of white stone and faded wood. The courtyard stood empty, save their carriage, and the two of them hurried inside.

Simon procured a table while Maggie took care of personal needs. When she found him in the common dining area, he had settled at a table near a small window, his gaze trained on the yard. The soft, gray light cast shadows on the familiar planes of his face, a play of chiaroscuro that fascinated her. He was annoyingly beautiful for a man.

Soon they were fortified with tea and ale, which they drank in companionable silence. A thought struck her and she had to stifle a giggle.

A tawny eyebrow quirked. "You find something amusing?"

"It just occurred to me, this is the longest amount of time we have spent in each other's presence without arguing."

"Not quite," he murmured, leaning forward. His eyes grew sleepy and dark. "There was another time as well. When you spent the ni—"

"Simon!"

He grinned. "Do not tell me I've embarrassed you. Not the woman who flaunts convention with every breath she takes."

It had nothing to do with propriety. She did not need another reminder of that night; the frequent dreams were enough.

"How is Cora?" she asked instead.

"Much improved when I left. My housekeeper will keep a sharp eye on her. The girl expressed some interest in the kitchens, so she'll be trained below

stairs when she's ready. If we cannot use her, she'll be
sent to any number of households nearby."

"You sound as if you've done this before."

"Many times," he answered after a swig of ale.
"Barrett House is generally full to overflowing with
housemaids and kitchen maids. If we cannot house
any more, Mrs. Timmons sends them to Colton or
Quint."

"Ah."

"What do you mean, ah?"

"That is why Julia sent for you, is it not? And why
Madame Hartley turned the girl over to you."

"Yes."

She sipped her tea and tried to fit this newfound
knowledge into the image she'd established of him in
her mind. Any way she turned it over, she could not
understand a reason for his generosity. She had a
hundred questions—did he truly hire any girl who
presented herself? How did his staff manage it all?—
but the one that emerged was, "Why do you do it?"

He twisted the tankard in his hand, making small
circles on the scarred tabletop. "Because I can."

"So could any number of wealthy households, mine
included. Yet it never occurred to me. Why did you
begin?"

"Several years ago, a girl presented herself at the
back door, bruises covering her face and desperate to
escape an unpleasant home. My housekeeper came to
me with the situation and we decided to hire her.
Word traveled amongst our staff, and friends and
relatives began appearing regularly to request em-
ployment." He shrugged. "My housekeeper has a soft
heart."

Not merely his housekeeper, apparently.

"Come, the carriage is ready." He stood and held out his hand. "Let us return to our journey."

"Do we have a destination in mind?" she asked three-quarters of an hour later. "Or are we to stop when the mood strikes us?" They had made polite conversation since the inn, but he'd still said nothing of where they were going.

He folded his arms and smiled. "There is a destination, but wouldn't you rather be surprised?"

"I cannot say that I care for surprises."

"That is merely proof you need more of them. Life is terribly tedious if you know what is coming."

"Who would have guessed the Earl of Winchester to be a philosopher?" she teased.

"I am a man of many talents, Lady Hawkins. As you might recall," he returned, his blue eyes sparking with mischief.

She could not help it; she laughed. The rogue was impossibly charming, a fact he knew full well.

"I adore your laugh, Mags. I always have. You light up a room with it."

Her chest tightened. The mirth stuck in her throat as emotion welled. Was it the use of his old nickname for her or the compliment that turned her inside out? She had no idea. Unsure how to respond, she returned her gaze to the window.

"Do my revelations unnerve you?"

"Yes," she blurted. "I cannot think clearly when you say such things."

He shook his head. "Exactly the point, my dear lady. I do not want you to think. I want you to *feel*."

Leaning forward, he plucked her hand out of her lap and tugged.

Before she could muster resistance, she ended up on his side, directly next to him. Her heart began slamming against her ribs. Heat surrounded her, his nearness sucking all the air from the carriage, and he slid a bare hand up to cup her jaw gently. Everything inside her tingled, a rush of awareness in each nerve ending to serve as a reminder of the delights at Barrett House—heady, wicked delights she craved late at night.

"Simon, stop." The plea sounded half-earnest, even to her own ears.

"I cannot help myself. I've been attempting to resist you all morning. It is too much to ask." He pulled at the ribbons of her bonnet, undid the bow, and lifted it off her head. She heard it hit the empty seat. "You are so very beautiful," he murmured, twirling a loose strand of her hair around his fingers. He let it go, watched the curl fall to her cheek. Then he bent closer and she held her breath. "I ache for you, Maggie."

His mouth covered hers, warm and firm, while his hands clutched her closer. She considered shoving him away, but the kiss was slow and coaxing, a sweet mixture of breath as their lips melded and shaped together. She closed her eyes and let sensation wash over her, clearing her mind of anything but the feel of his mouth dragging over her own. God, she'd missed this. She had not even realized how much until this very moment.

He nipped and teased, keeping the kiss nearly chaste, until she squirmed, ready to crawl into his lap to get closer. Each time she tried to deepen the kiss, he pulled back slightly. Determined, she reached up, slid her arms around his neck, and slipped her tongue into his mouth. The result was an instantaneous spark, as if she'd dropped an ember onto a pile of kindling. Simon took over, opening her mouth wider to thrust his tongue inside, invading, tasting her with relentless intensity. Maggie's head swam as her fingers threaded the silken strands of his hair.

He broke off to rain kisses along her jawline, then traveled down the sensitive column of her throat to nibble and suck the skin under the high collar of her cold-weather pelisse. Nimble fingers worked the fastenings and the heavy fabric fell apart. Simon's lips slid along her collarbone, and anticipation caused her breasts to swell inside her chemise and stays. His breath gusted over the fichu of her lilac traveling dress as he strayed lower.

"All this curst clothing," he muttered, his hand gliding up over her corseted rib cage. "I want to see every inch of you."

"That would prove challenging, considering our surroundings," she breathed.

"But not impossible. And I do love a challenge." He plucked the fichu from her décolletage. "Perhaps I shall work my way down."

She thought of any number of reasons that she should push him away, including all the ways he'd hurt her, could hurt her still. But as his mouth traced the tops of her breasts exposed above her neckline, rational thought escaped her. Besides, when had she ever done as she *should*?

With efficient presence of mind, he flicked the curtains on the carriage windows, plunging them into semidarkness. Her eyes were still adjusting to the dim light when he yanked on the edge of her dress enough to free one breast from her clothing. Her arms twined around his neck while they shared another blistering kiss. His thumb and forefinger found her nipple, squeezed. She gasped into his mouth, the sensation sending white-hot sparks down her spine. *Sweet heaven.* He rolled and tweaked her nipple until she writhed against the seat, the hunger nearly unbearable. Did he want her to beg?

Slow sweeps of his tongue. Maddening pressure at her breast. Her entire focus became nothing except Simon. Highwaymen could stop them and Maggie would not care as long as Simon kept kissing her. She sucked in breath when his lips trailed to her jawline.

"Do you know," he whispered before sucking the lobe of her ear into the slippery, lush heat of his mouth, "how long I have wanted you? How many nights I dreamt of your mouth or your breasts? I want to make this last. I want to—"

She turned her head and found his lips with her own, effectively cutting him off. His revelations brought memories, and this was no time to relive the past. Instead, she pressed up, attempting to get closer. He groaned and deepened the kiss.

Clever fingers disappeared from her breast, and cool air hit her legs as her skirts began to lift. Her body felt feverish, impatient with need. He stroked the skin of her inner thigh while his tongue continued to tangle with her own, and her knees fell open to afford him better access. *Please,* she wanted to scream, then let out a long moan as he finally—God, finally!—probed the entrance to her body.

"Christ, Maggie." He broke off to pant against her

throat. "You are so wet, so ready to take me. Do you want me inside you, darling?"

His finger worked inside her, a delicious fullness that made her shiver. She threw her head back, closed her eyes, and gulped air.

"Ah," he breathed. "You like that. Perhaps one more, I think."

He pulled back, then returned to stretch her further, and her back arched against the sweet invasion. A firm pull of his lips drew her nipple into the hot recesses of his mouth. He sucked hard and used his tongue to soothe before gently scraping the bud with his teeth. Each tug and lick stoked the flames burning her insides. Her muscles tensed as he continued with his hands and mouth, the pleasure nearly unbearable. She could do naught but react; he was a master applying his art, her body the canvas.

"Simon, now." Her nails dug into his shoulders.

"Shhh." He lifted his head. "We're likely to overturn the carriage if we try anything adventurous. This is enough. Let me give you pleasure, Mags."

"No, we will not. We'll be gentle. Please," she begged. Desire had made her desperate, but Maggie was too far gone to care. She snaked her hand down the front of his clothing until she found him, hard and hot, under her palm.

He hissed through his teeth and caught her wrist. "Stop. There's no telling what may happen if you keep that up."

She wiggled her fingers to lightly stroke his erection as best she could. "Did you not say I needed more surprises in my life?"

With his jaw tightly clenched, Simon clearly fought for control. "The stiffness of my cock should come as no surprise to you. I swear, you walk into a room and I grow hard."

His grip on her wrist weakened and she took advantage. Traced the outline of him through his trousers. Dragged the heel of her palm down the thick length. He visibly shuddered. "Maggie, I—"

"Stop talking, Simon," she whispered. "Just *feel*."

Arms braced against the seat to prop himself up, he loomed over her. His chest heaved as she skimmed over him, and she carefully watched his face, gauging his reaction. While she had drawn him many times, the fierce expression he now wore, half-pleasure and half-pain, was one she had never seen. She loved that her touch affected him so deeply.

His harsh breathing echoed in the enclosed space as her touch grew bolder. When her fingers brushed his bollocks, he inhaled sharply. Leaning up, he reached for her waist and lifted her over him. Her knees slid to the outside of his hips, skirts pooling around them. With frantic hands, he worked the buttons on his trousers while she leaned forward to press her lips to his brow, his temple, his cheek, the tip of his nose. He gathered her skirts up with one hand, exposing her, and used his free hand to position himself at her entrance. Maggie wasted no time, bearing down, eager to take the full, heavy length inside.

"Wait." Hands on her waist, he stopped her. "I want to watch. Lean back. Place your hands on my knees."

Tentatively, she reached back with one hand to support herself but still held on to his shoulder.

Eyes dark and serious, he told her, "Go ahead. I've got you, darling. I'll not let you go, I swear."

The weight of that promise settled around her heart. Had she imagined it, or had there been another meaning behind those words? She released her grip on his arm and angled away from him. Thank goodness she'd worn her short stays for the long carriage ride; as it was, she could barely breathe.

He began a maddeningly thorough invasion of her body. Her lids fluttered closed. *Oh, yes.* God, yes. The impossible stretch, the slight sting of his length filling her . . . it was even better than she remembered. The carriage bounced and rocked beneath them, but Simon would not be hurried. He lowered her carefully, deliberately, until he'd fully sheathed himself inside her.

"Damn, but you are lovely. The way you feel around me . . ."

He trailed off and rolled his hips for a gentle thrust. They both groaned. Another slide, deeper this time. She gasped, sparks racing up her spine. He pulled her forward for a long, desperate kiss. The natural motion of the wheels knocked their bodies together, but it wasn't enough. Seemingly of their own accord, her hips worked to create the delicious friction she craved. Simon broke off from her mouth, his head falling back against the squabs. "Christ, yes. Ride me, Mags."

Encouraged, she braced her arms on the back of the carriage and undulated atop him. The swollen bud at the apex of her thighs dragged against him with each roll. When his mouth sucked on her exposed nipple, she moved faster, racing toward the bliss she'd only ever encountered with Simon. She no longer questioned what he was able to do to her. Something about the two of them blended together to create an incendiary reaction, like mixing two completely opposed colors and achieving the perfect hue.

An orgasm, both fierce and sweet at the same time, ripped through her. She gasped and shook, the walls of her channel clamping down on his erection as he continued to thrust up from underneath her. When she stopped convulsing, Simon's grip tightened and he jerked away from her. Muscles taut, he fisted his shaft and pumped once before spilling his seed onto his belly. He groaned, eyes closed in bliss, as he spent himself.

At that precise moment the rear axle snapped in half.

Simon folded his arms and regarded the damage. He and Maggie were unharmed, a little shaken but otherwise unscathed, but the carriage was in a sorry state. Turned on its side, with a broken axle, and missing one wheel, there would be no more riding inside the vehicle today.

It had been a near miss. He'd barely regained his bearings after a spectacular orgasm when a loud *pop* rang out. Thinking quickly, he'd clutched Maggie and braced the two of them as best he could. No telling how adept the French drivers would be at remaining calm during an accident, and if they lost control of the horses then someone could be killed.

The drivers had been impressive, however. By the time the vehicle had lost the back wheel and flipped to the side, they'd considerably slowed the team of four. Everything had ground to a stop. Simon had righted his clothing, helped Maggie with hers, and then assisted her out the top of the vehicle.

Maggie, now in her bonnet, pelisse, and winter cloak,

stood by his side on the road. He leaned over. "I told you we would overturn the thing, you insatiable minx."

She let out a bark of laughter, her green eyes sparkling, and his chest expanded with emotion. He loved to see her happy.

No, he *needed* to see her happy. For years, he'd thought her devious and cunning, entertaining Cranford and the others while he pined for her. But Cranford had lied. Maggie claimed there had been no trysts during her debut, that she'd been a maid when married off to Hawkins. Which meant Simon should have believed her ten years ago, should have defended her. He hadn't, and most of Society turned its back on her, himself included. Could he ever make amends for such unforgivable stupidity?

Possibly not, but he would die trying.

"Well," she said, "what are we to do now?"

"We walk."

Her head swiveled, taking in the barren fields and hills surrounding them. Thankfully no snow covered the ground, he thought.

"To where?"

He lifted a shoulder. "To the nearest town. I'll find out from our driver."

In French, Simon spoke to one of the drivers and learned their original destination, the town of Auvers, was not far. He and Maggie could reach it in less than an hour. The driver wanted to show him the source of the trouble, so Simon went to the rear of the carriage where the man pointed out the twisted, severed axle. The break was even. It could only mean one thing.

"*C'était délibéré*," Simon said.

"*Oui*," the driver concurred.

A long string of curses went through Simon's mind.

Someone had planned this carriage accident, most likely tampering with the vehicle at their last stop. But whom? A bitter wind kicked up, flapping the edges of his greatcoat, and he decided to worry on this later. Maggie would catch her death if he did not get her to shelter.

He found Maggie's supplies and gave the drivers more than enough money to cover their troubles. With a promise to send assistance as soon as he and Maggie reached town, Simon led her along the road.

They walked quickly and said little. The two of them had reached a peaceful accord today, and he was loath to break it. They needed to spend time together, come to know one another, and an argument could destroy this fragile bond. So he traveled in silence, happily focusing his mind on what had occurred in the carriage moments before the accident. The decadent picture of her on top, arching back to rest against his knees, his cock sliding into her delicious wetness . . . now there was a portrait he wouldn't mind owning. Perhaps he could commission Lemarc to paint it, he thought with a smile.

"What are you thinking about?" she asked, her sharp gaze trained on his profile.

He looked down at her. "You."

"Me? What about me?"

"You, on top. Riding me with your hands behind you. Breasts high and tight—"

"Simon!" She shoved at his shoulder. "Have you gone completely mad?"

He grinned. "There's no one about to hear us. And did I not tell you I want complete honesty between us? I will not ever lie to you, Mags."

"No lies? Ever?"

"Not a one."

"Hmmm." That noise should have warned him for what she asked next. "Why haven't you married? I would have expected you to have secured the family legacy by now, with three or four children tucked out in the country somewhere."

A strangled sound of surprise emerged from his throat. Of course she would ask the one question he would resist answering truthfully, the clever chit. But omitting details was not exactly lying, was it? "I almost did once. Even asked the countess for the Winchester rubies. In the end, it didn't work out."

"What happened? Did she turn you down?"

"Never got around to asking. She ended up with someone else."

She nibbled her lip, something he found adorable. "Will you tell me who?"

"No." She frowned and he chuckled. "Come now, what does it matter who?"

She straightened a shade too quickly. "Oh, it doesn't. Matter. To me, that is."

Interesting. Since she'd started down this conversational path, he forced himself to ask the one question he dreaded the answer to. "Did Hawkins . . . treat you honorably, as a proper husband should?"

She remained silent a long moment, kicking at a pebble with her boot. "He was not cruel, if that is what you mean," she finally said.

Now she was being evasive. "Was he kind? Did he . . . care for you?" His chest constricted, but he needed to know the truth. He'd wondered over the years how she'd got on with a husband old enough to have been her father.

"He avoided me, mostly. I do not think he knew

what to make of a young girl, ruined by scandal and yet not ashamed. He never understood my love of drawing and painting but never disallowed it. To be truthful, he spent most nights with his mistress and that suited both of us perfectly."

"Were you happy?"

"Not particularly, but I also was not unhappy."

"And you say I am gifted with words."

The corner of her mouth lifted. "But it's true. For the most part, I could do as I pleased. A few of the women in the village became my friends. Artists like to spend time alone, and I had plenty of time to myself during my marriage. I used it to study and read and practice. I do not regret it."

A small knot he'd been carrying in his belly since learning of Cranford's deception eased. However, Simon hated that Hawkins had not cherished Maggie. Any man in his right mind would thank the saints she graced his bed and spend a lifetime devoted to her pleasure.

Not to mention Hawkins had been her first instead of Simon. Cranford would suffer, if only for that fact alone.

"And what of your mistress?"

Simon nearly stumbled at Maggie's question. He could comment on the inappropriateness of the question, but such observations were pointless with Maggie. Boldness was never in short supply around her. "Adrianna, you mean. She's an actress I met at Drury Lane. What else should you care to know?"

"Is it true you visit her every Tuesday and Friday evening?"

He did stumble then. He caught himself from falling and stopped to glower at her. "How in God's name do you know that?"

"Then it's true."

He offered his arm once more. "It was true but no longer. Adrianna and I have parted ways."

"Hmmm."

"I am coming to fear that sound out of your mouth. May we cease speaking of my former mistress?"

"Who would have guessed you would turn out to be such a prude?" she teased.

"Oh, you think so?" He leaned closer. "I'll show you prudish in the carriage on the way home, madam. We'll see who is laughing then."

She pursed her lips, her lids falling seductively. His cock leaped when she murmured, "I can hardly wait."

Chapter Seventeen

"See?" Simon pointed up at a small stone cathedral on the hill. "Église Notre-Dame d'Auvers."

They finished climbing the narrow steps and stood in front of an elegant church that did, in fact, resemble the great gothic masterpiece in Paris. She'd spent many hours sketching the original Notre Dame, so the comparisons in this smaller stone version were instantly obvious. The buttresses, the strange animals, the human figures, not to mention the apse and bell tower . . . absolutely remarkable, the similarities.

Maggie had to laugh. "And here I thought you had lied."

He shook his head, saying, "I told you, no more lies."

"Yes, but you purposely misled me into thinking we were staying in Paris."

"No, that is what you assumed."

She rolled her eyes. "I should know better than to quibble with a man who can bend Parliament to his whims."

He put his lips near her ear. "Which is not nearly as much fun as bending you, I'm learning."

From the heat under her skin, she knew she'd turned scarlet. The rogue. She wandered closer to the building, grateful they'd enjoyed luncheon at a small café first. Her toes were nearly frozen by the time they arrived in Auvers-sur-Oise. Now that she'd properly recovered from their walk, this majestic structure demanded a sketch.

"Here." Simon thrust the case containing her supplies into her hand. "I can tell by the look on your face that you want to study it." He dropped a kiss on her nose, then turned to leave. "Enjoy yourself."

"Wait," she called after him. "Where are you going?"

He waved his hand. "Around. Never fear, I shall collect you before it grows dark."

She watched his broad shoulders disappear down the stone steps. Was he truly giving her the afternoon to herself?

Excited, she carried her supplies to a small bench. The sun had peeked through the overcast sky, giving her a bit of warmth in the winter air. Remaining outside would not be possible due to the weather, but at least she could get a rough sketch done and then finish it inside.

She removed her gloves and selected a piece of charcoal. The sketch-book came next. It was time to work.

As promised, Simon found her in the late afternoon as dusk began to settle. She had moved inside the church hours before to stay warm. While there, she finished sketches of her surroundings and then resumed work on the landscape pieces.

"And how was your afternoon, darling?" He slid into the row in front of her, skin pink from the cold, his piercing blue eyes searching her face.

She stretched and rolled her shoulders. Lud, these wooden pews were not built for comfort. "Lovely. And productive. But I am ready to return to Paris."

His gaze slid away. "May I see what you are working on?"

She clutched the papers to her chest. "Absolutely not."

A shadow passed over his face, and he went to stand. "Shall we?"

"Simon." She rose to touch his sleeve. "I never show my work to anyone until it is done—or at least I am reasonably satisfied with it. It is not personal."

"It isn't another Winejester cartoon, is it? Causing a carriage accident on a rural road in France?"

"Absolutely not. I am sketching Welsh landmarks."

He nodded and gestured to the door. "I shall wait for you just outside, then."

Something about his demeanor bothered her. He'd been so flirtatious and agreeable earlier. Now he seemed out of sorts. Was he truly worried she would draw Winejester again? She hadn't put up a Winejester cartoon since the day she'd run into him at Mrs. McGinnis's shop. In fact, the one she'd drawn after the Colton dinner party had found its way into the fire. With all that had happened between them, she did not feel comfortable with the characterization any longer. It smacked of disrespect and Simon—

She dropped back on the pew, then winced at the pain shooting through her bottom. Goodness. She had sworn never to allow anything or anyone to interfere with her art. When had he become so important to her that she'd adjusted her plans? Granted, she no longer had just cause for revenge against Simon; he'd been duped by Cranford as well. But the bitterness, the anger, the hurt over all the unfairness thrust on her . . . it did not pain her quite as much.

Strange. Perhaps it was Simon's recent attentions. Or their fragile rapprochement. Art would always be the most important part of her life, but perhaps room could be made for other . . . pursuits. She bit her lip to keep from giggling. *Giggling.* She—the fearsome Lemarc, who had politicians and the *ton* quaking in their fashionable boots—nearly giggled. It was unheard of.

Of course she wasn't merely Lemarc; she was a woman, too. And this particular woman had learned that one particular man liked her laugh. He seemed to like quite a bit about her, the poor misguided fool. Unbelievably, she'd shown him the worst and he hadn't run screaming.

She quickly packed up her things and strode to the entrance. Pushing open the heavy wooden doors, she saw him relaxing against the facade, booted heel propped up on the stone. Tall, athletic, well-proportioned, with a face so beautiful it made her heart hurt. She found herself smiling as she strolled over to him.

He dragged his eyes down the length of her. "You are exceedingly happy for a woman who just spent three hours inside a church."

"It was quiet and I had enough space and light. How can I possibly complain?" He reached and took the case out of her hands, and she asked, "And how did you spend your afternoon?"

"This and that. Nothing worth retelling. Watch your

step," he said as they began down the narrow stone set of stairs. The sun, now a burnished orange, had just begun to set, and there were lights glowing in the windows of the town below. The streets appeared deserted, with everyone likely off to enjoy *pot-au-feu* or a *cassoulet* with their families. Suddenly, she was starving.

They reached the bottom of the stairs and he remained quiet. When she took his arm, she said, "You should know there will not ever be another Winejester cartoon."

His brows rose. "Is that so?"

She nodded. "I have decided to give him up."

"I wish I could say I will miss him. But whatever your reasons, I am grateful."

Since she did not care to tell him those reasons, she asked, "Are we to eat before we leave?"

"About that," he started. "We are not leaving. At least, not tonight."

Feet planted, she faced him. "What do you mean, 'not leaving'?"

"It is too late to travel back. So we shall spend the night here in Auvers. I've procured us a room."

"But it is barely dusk. We could make it back in a few hours. Why not leave now?"

He shook his head. "No. I do not want to travel in the dark. Not with you. It is not safe. We shall go back in the morning."

Maggie crossed her arms over her chest. This was a sudden development . . . or had he planned this all along? First he'd practically kidnapped her and now stranded her in rural France. "Was this your goal all along?"

"Don't be ridiculous—and keep moving before we

both freeze." He took her arm and led her toward town. "I did not plan the carriage accident, Maggie."

"When you say you have procured a room, do you mean one room? Or two rooms?"

He sighed, the burst a white plume in the cold air. "If you would prefer separate rooms, I can easily get another one."

She thought about it. "I have no ladies' maid."

His mouth twitched. "This is true."

"I suppose you'll have to do, then."

His teeth shone in the near darkness, a predatory smile that made her heart skip. "Yes, I suppose I will."

The following morning, Simon woke to a soft, feminine body pressed against his side. *Maggie.* He had to stifle a grin. Roses and a hint of vanilla. He would never tire of that smell. Twice he'd had her last night, and apparently his cock was putting in a bid for another round this morning. Of course, it might have a bit to do with her luscious bottom resting against his hip. How could she be so tempting, even while asleep?

An overwhelming urge to wrap her in his arms, to protect her from the slightest bit of pain, stole through him. Ridiculous considering Maggie was the strongest woman he'd ever met; she needed no champion. But Simon found himself longing for the role nonetheless.

Perhaps it was the disturbing news he'd learned yesterday that brought about these curious and bothersome emotions. The carriage accident had been deliberate. Once the vehicle had been brought to Auvers for repair, Simon had spent the better part of the day going over it with the two drivers, attempting to discern clues as to the culprit. Someone had damaged the axle and Simon would learn who was responsible.

But for now, there were other matters that deserved his careful attention.

Not all women were amenable to amorous encounters in the morning . . . but one never knew unless one tried. He aligned them carefully, Maggie's back to his chest, his erection nestled between her full, plump buttocks. Then his fingers moved to her breast and set about rousing a nipple. It puckered quickly, almost begging for his touch as he teased it. Soon he ministered to the other, giving it the same treatment. Maggie's breathing changed, no longer slow and deep but turning shallow. *She's awake.*

He bent to kiss and nip the sensitive skin behind her earlobe, something he happened to know she particularly liked. In no hurry, he played with her breasts, molding and caressing them, filling his hands with the soft, womanly shape of her. Creamy skin. Heavenly curves. A mouth to tempt a saint. He could not get enough of her, his erection now so hard it hurt.

Unable to wait, his fingers found the slickness pooling between her legs. She gasped, her hand clutching at his hip to pull him closer. *She's ready.* Lust swept through his belly and the need for her became essential, like breathing. He lifted her leg slightly, lined up, and entered her in one smooth thrust. She fit him perfectly. Hot. Tight. He gritted his teeth, stopped to take a moment. No sense in rushing it. He wanted to enjoy this. Then Maggie squirmed and pushed back, bringing him in deeper, and Simon was lost.

It quickly turned into something less playful and more serious. His hips slapped against her delectable backside with each powerful thrust. When he felt his own climax threaten, he worked her tiny bud of pleasure in small circles, rhythmic and fast, until she dug her nails into his arm, moaning. Bloody hell, he loved the way she reacted to him.

Her inner walls clamped down on him, and she gave a cry, her body shuddering. He tried desperately to hold out until she stopped shaking, to let her ride out her orgasm, but it proved impossible. Beginning at the base of his spine, the pressure built and he barely pulled out in time to spill on the sheets.

Fighting for air, he dragged her close. The fire had died down overnight, so he gathered the coverlet and covered them both.

"What a lovely way to say good morning," she said, raising her arms and stretching back against him.

"Mmm, I thought so. My favorite way, anyhow."

After a pause, she said, "Wake up with a woman often, do you?"

He heard the edge to her voice. Pushing on her shoulder, he brought her around to face him. "No, Maggie, I do not. There haven't been that many women in recent years and none who meant anything substantial." That must have satisfied her because she closed her eyes and snuggled against him. "What about you? Have you never had a man in your bed come morning?"

"Never."

"Ah." So she did not care to keep her paramours overnight. Oddly enough, that tidbit pleased him. He liked knowing he was the first to hold her while she slept. His palm stroked the velvety softness of her hip. "They did not realize what they were missing, then."

She was so still, so quiet, he worried he'd offended

her. Then her lids lifted. "There have only ever been three men. One was my husband and you are another."

A weight settled on Simon's chest, pressing down on his lungs and making it hard to breathe. Thoughts swirled in his mind, things he'd said, assumptions he'd made. But the truth was right there in her clear, serious green gaze. No, this couldn't be right. "Three?" he rasped.

She lifted a dainty shoulder. "One would presume more with my nickname, but there have only been three."

"Myself and Hawkins. So who was the third?"

Her lips compressed and he guessed the question made her uncomfortable. But he needed the answer. "Tell me, Maggie," he urged gently.

"An artist. You met him at the opera."

"Ah." So he'd been correct. The proprietary way the man had touched Maggie hadn't been Simon's imagination. He hardly found this reassuring, however. Moving to his back, he folded his hands behind his head and fixed his stare on the ceiling. "No wonder you reacted so strongly when I told you I forgave you. You must have been ready to throttle me. I made terribly unfair assumptions about you."

"Yes, you did. And I did consider throttling you. Many times." The silky glide of her hand swept up his belly and along his rib cage. "But I am glad I did not." Her fingernail flicked at his nipple, and he drew in a sharp breath.

"Stop," he told her. "We need to discuss this."

"No," she returned. "We most definitely do not need to talk." She lifted up to place her mouth, lush and warm, over one of his nipples, laving it with her tongue and gently scraping it with her teeth. Pleasure streaked down his spine.

"Maggie," he groaned. She was attempting to distract him from the conversation. He started to unfold his arms, to reach for her, but her hands stopped him.

"Stay there. Let me have my wicked way with you."

His pulse picked up. "As I just had my wicked way with you mere moments ago, I doubt I can be roused so soon after."

Her mouth began to travel over his ribs and down to his stomach, pressing deliciously soft kisses that had him shivering in anticipation. "Is that so?" she murmured before shifting to settle between his legs.

His cock twitched as her warm breath gusted over the sensitive flesh. Memories of the way her mouth had taken him deep last night resurfaced. The slick, moist suction, her determination in keeping the perfect rhythm . . . That she, a proper lady, deigned to pleasure him with her mouth, seemed to like it even, had him nearly weeping in gratitude. He felt himself begin to swell.

"Hmmm," she said and licked her lips, her eyes flicking from his burgeoning erection up to meet his gaze. "And you doubted yourself."

His lids fluttered shut as she suckled on him, drawing his semi-erect shaft over her tongue. Heaven. Absolute heaven. "A man does require some recovery time," he mumbled. Then her nails gently raked the thin skin covering his bollocks and he bucked. Blood rushed to his cock at the exquisite torture. "But I never should have doubted you, apparently."

* * *

Several days later, Simon strode into the crowded dining room of his hotel, unsurprised to find most of the tables were occupied. Hôtel Meurice served both English and French fare, which made it a favorite with British travelers eager for a taste of home. His guests, he noticed, had already arrived. Excellent. The sooner this meal concluded, the sooner he could hie himself to Maggie's house.

Heat spread through his loins. The past sennight had been one of the best of his life. Each evening since returning from Auvers, he and Maggie had enjoyed dinner together and then retired to her chambers. He departed in the mornings before the household awoke, though she swore it unnecessary. However, he wanted to spare her any further gossip, at least until they could be married. Not that he'd asked her yet, but that was a mere formality. She cared for him, and under no circumstances would he let her go—not after he'd found her after all these years.

Markham brightened when he saw Simon approach. "Winchester! Excellent timing. We've just ordered a bottle of claret."

"Markham has ordered claret," Quint corrected. "I have ordered tea."

"Of course. And thank you for the clarification." Simon lowered into the empty chair. "Glad you joined us, Quint."

"I suspect this may be my only opportunity to see you."

"Why's that?" Markham asked. "I thought you both were staying in this hotel."

"One of us is," Quint said under his breath.

"Oh, ho. Did Winchester find a bit of sport here in

Paris? Tell me"—Markham leaned closer—"are the Frenchwomen as forward as I've heard?"

Simon thought of Maggie, who'd practically coined the word *forward*, and could barely prevent a grin. Though it was not lost on him how Markham had hoped to tumble Maggie himself, and the notion erased any mirth from the conversation. "I'd hardly be a gentleman if I talked after the fact," he said as a member of the staff poured glasses of claret.

They ordered and discussed nothing of import until the food arrived. Based on experience, Simon knew serious discussions were best carried out with full bellies and quenched thirst. So they listened to Markham rattle off a litany of detail regarding how he'd spent his time in Paris. Quint asked polite questions while Simon tried to keep his mind from wandering. Not so easy considering he'd introduced Maggie to a new position for lovemaking, one she'd now declared a favorite. The memory was so vivid, so enticing, he was grateful to be covered by the table.

"Do rejoin us, Winchester," Quint said as their meals were delivered.

"My apologies," Simon told both men. He really must stop recalling the picture of Maggie's delectable backside as he pushed—

"Must be that bit 'o French fluff you're thinking on," Markham said. "Though I am surprised. Half of Paris speculated you were tumbling the Harlot."

Simon carefully placed his knife and fork on the edges of his plate and leaned forward. "Markham, if you speak of the lady in such a disrespectful manner again, you and I shall be meeting on a French field at dawn." He ignored Quint's heavy sigh from the opposite side of the table, continuing to focus his attention on Markham.

Markham blinked, his fleshy jowls quivering. "Damn me. It is Lady Hawkins, ain't it? The rumors are true."

Simon resumed eating. "My romantic endeavors are hardly anyone's concern."

In the ensuing silence, the other man's disposition changed, Markham's jocularity vanishing as quickly as the roasted pigeon on his plate. Lips compressed into a tight, thin line, it was clear he was unhappy. No secret why. Markham had made his intentions toward Maggie clear—he'd hoped to bed her. But Maggie had not returned his interest. That could hardly be Simon's fault, could it?

Quint cleared his throat. "I wonder if we'll see more rain."

Markham, still devoting his attention to his meal, grunted in response. Simon and Quint exchanged a look. Damnation, this was going badly. He needed Markham's support; the man had a small contingent of followers in Parliament and could wield considerable influence over them.

By the time their plates were cleared, Markham had turned downright surly. Still, Simon knew he had to try to win him over.

"Shall we discuss my proposal, Markham?" Simon suggested. "You may tell me your reservations and we'll try and work through them."

Markham finished off his claret, set the glass on the table. "Quite unnecessary. All my questions have been addressed." He pushed back from the table and straightened his frock coat. "And I shan't be supporting you, Winchester."

Simon clenched his jaw. "And may I ask why not?"

"The reasons hardly matter. But I will do everything in my limited power to ensure you fail." He turned and toddled off without a backward glance. Stupefied, Simon watched him go. Could petty jealousy have caused Markham's shift in attitude?

"Well, it seems the Harlot just cost you your first vote."

Simon pierced Quint with a hard stare. Quint held up his hands. "I meant no disrespect. I hold the lady in the highest esteem. But it's clear Markham hoped to win her affections and cared little for the fact you'd beaten him to it."

"It's absurd, especially when the lady has never shown him the least bit of favor."

"Not precisely true, if you will recall Colton's dinner party."

Simon drummed his fingers on the table, unhappily recalling how she had encouraged Markham that evening. That she'd done it as merely a way to irritate Simon did not lessen his annoyance.

Quint said, "I know you do not want to hear it, but are you prepared for what your association with her may cost you? You've worked years to get where you are. Think of all you might accomplish, if you are careful."

"No one other than Markham will give it a moment's thought."

Quint's brows lifted. "Are you so certain of that? It is one thing to have the usual mistress quietly tucked away over on Curzon Street. It's altogether different to be linked to the most scandalous woman in Society, widow or no."

"I plan to marry her," Simon snapped.

Quint appeared even more surprised. "And you think such an alliance won't reflect on you either socially or politically? You are fooling yourself. Are you prepared to let her throw those types of parties at Barrett House?"

Simon had to admit, Quint had a point. He hadn't given much thought to Maggie's lifestyle and if she planned to change it once they married. But if she would have him, sleep next to him every night, bear his children . . . he'd let her do whatever she damn well wanted. He'd be proud to stand at her side. "Yes," he told Quint honestly.

Quint toasted Simon with his teacup. "Then I wish you luck."

Chapter Eighteen

Maggie rolled over when something dragged slowly over her bare skin. A deep inhale filled her head with the scent of orange and sandalwood and just a hint of tobacco. *Simon.* She fought the cobwebs to come awake, aware that a very good reason awaited her. Then the mattress dipped and his warmth wrapped around her, strong arms pulling her near.

"Are you awake?" he asked into her ear. Rough end-of-day whiskers teased her skin.

"Hmmm," she answered, wriggling into the delicious male heat and strength behind her. "Almost."

He chuckled. "Very well. Let us see if I can hasten your progress."

Maggie smiled, even though he could not see it. His presence in a room turned her positively giddy. Good thing she'd given him a key to the house. His lips found the top of her shoulder, gentle kisses whispering over her flesh like the silky bristles of a paintbrush. "How was your dinner?"

"Disappointing."

There was an edge in his voice that caught her

attention. Turning, she searched out his eyes. "You were to dine with Lord Markham, no?"

"Yes. Quint came as well."

"And that made it disappointing?"

"No. My evening is unimportant. I'd rather we spent our time together on more worthwhile pursuits." His hand swept over her bare hip and up her rib cage to settle on her breast. He squeezed gently, plumping her. "I am so very glad you didn't bother with nightclothes."

Momentarily distracted, she enjoyed the sensation. Then she asked, "Were you able to sway Markham, as you'd hoped?"

He bent his head to swirl the tip of his tongue over her nipple. She moaned and arched up. Though tingles shot all over her body, she forced herself to stay on task. "Are you attempting to evade my questions?"

His lips closed over the taut tip and he drew it inside the lush heat of his mouth. *Sweet heaven.* Her lids drifted shut and she threaded her fingers through his silky hair. Everything inside her began buzzing, a heady thrum of desire only Simon could produce. But he had not fooled her.

After enjoying his attentions for a few more minutes, Maggie sucked in a deep breath and pulled away. Simon's bright blue eyes had gone sleepy and dark, her very favorite. She bit her lip and tried to ignore how much she wanted him to ravish her. *Soon,* she promised herself. There was one issue to address first. "Simon, tell me. I know you are distracting me in order to avoid answering."

"Markham will not be voting for my proposal. I was unable to convince him." He angled his head to resume his ministrations to her breasts, but she tightened her grip to stop him.

"Why do I sense there is more?"

"May we discuss this later?" He rolled his hips, the hard length of his shaft urgently pressing into her thigh. "I want you, Mags."

"Simon," she admonished.

"Fine." He flopped back and folded his arms behind his head, displaying the lines of his upper arms nicely. "Markham carried a *tendre* for you, madam, and seemed to resent that your affections were engaged elsewhere."

"Meaning with you."

A brief nod. "With me."

She thought about that. Markham, a *tendre*? They had not spent much time together, but she had encouraged him at Julia's dinner party to irritate Simon. And then there was the meeting to discuss Simon's proposal. A pang of guilt slid through her belly. Many women flirted and pretended interest to get what they wanted; she'd seen it time and time again over the years. But she hadn't ever done it, not before Markham, and the results did not sit well with her.

More to the point, how had Markham learned of her and Simon? This . . . connection between them began only recently. Who else knew?

"What are you thinking?" he asked.

"How did Markham know about us?"

"Apparently half of Paris wagered on it."

Maggie gaped. "You jest."

"Hardly surprising. You are one of Society's favorite topics to speculate on, after all. Even still, half of Paris might be an exaggeration. I'd say more like a third."

She pushed his chest. "Be serious."

"Darling." He reached out to cup her jaw, and the strength and comfort in that simple gesture warmed her down to her toes. "Who cares what anyone thinks? You've certainly not worried before, so do not let us start now. Everyone was bound to find out eventually, and I, for one, do not give a damn about the gossip."

His sincerity calmed her somewhat, but did he not see? Markham refused to support Simon because of her. How many others would there be? How many of Simon's causes would be thwarted because of their association? His political influence would wither as long as the two of them were linked. A mistress would be acceptable, but a lady tainted by scandal and impropriety was another. Quite irresponsible on both their parts to think this liaison would not cost him.

At some point, if they continued, he would come to resent her. She was certain of it. He'd look back at all he might have accomplished if not for her—and that would kill her. For him to regret the time they spent together, to wish she were someone other than herself, would crush the part of her soul that had yearned for him all these years.

He wrapped her hair around his hand and gently tugged her down, drawing her away from those morose thoughts. His other hand steadied her above him. "Do not fret over Markham, Maggie. There are plenty of other ways to get what I want." He shifted her on top of him, the hard planes of his body melding against her softness in all the best places. "And right now, what I want is you."

She studied his face, saw the raw honesty and desire there, and her heart turned over. Emotion swelled inside her, an emotion she'd never expected to feel, and she quickly kissed him so he would not see it. He growled and settled her legs astride his hips, and she rocked over the heavy, hard length of his erection. They both shuddered.

"Besides," he said against her mouth, "you hated my proposal. I should think you'd be glad to see it fail."

No denying she did not agree with his idea. But she did not want to see him fail, not because of *her*. "I know you think your proposal shall protect ruined women who might otherwise be cast aside, forced to earn their livings by less than desirable means. But think about what you are telling her to endure: a tie to the very man who abused her. For the rest of her life, a reminder every year of what she suffered. Think of me. If Cranford had followed through on what he intended—" She paused as Simon's face darkened. "Wait, let me finish. If Cranford had taken me against my will, I might be forced to accept his money. Even such an insubstantial thread would be untenable. No woman would want any tie to the man who'd hurt her in that manner, not even for money."

His mouth settled in an unhappy line. He stared at her, and she could see his brain arguing the emotion against the logic. He'd been so sure of his position, but hopefully she could make him understand the other side.

"I could kill Cranford for hurting you."

She traced the slight dent at the end of his chin with her fingertip. "As could I. And I'd rather starve than accept one farthing from him."

He stroked the small of her back and ran his hand down over her buttock. "Starve?"

"That is how strongly I feel, Simon. Do not pursue

this piece of legislation. There are other ways, better ways, to offer assistance to women in need."

His face softened. He rose up to kiss her quickly, one hand sliding up into her hair. "Whatever you want, darling. You may help me redraft another proposal. A different one this time."

"You would allow me to help you?"

"Of course." He slid a hand between her legs and began to tease and torment. She gasped at the rush of sensation, and he said, "I will always listen to you. Like right now, I want to listen to you say my name in that particular way where . . ." He twisted his fingers to hit the precise spot he wanted.

"Simon," she sighed.

"Yes, just like that."

A few afternoons later, Maggie and Lucien stood in her studio. Lucien had brought along some paintings to show her. A long, involved conversation regarding technique ensued.

"Lucien, these are stunning. Truly." Maggie bent to inspect the detail a bit further. "The unusual angles and the movement you've captured here are breathtaking. The thin brushstrokes . . . it must have taken forever. I love it."

"I doubt they will sell."

"When have you ever cared about whether your work will sell or not?"

He shrugged, his overly long, brown hair brushing his shoulders. "I do not care for notoriety, as you do, but even I must admit money is helpful."

"How positively enterprising of you," she teased. "I must be rubbing off on you."

"You have done very well, *ma chère*. I cannot be prouder of you."

She threw her arms around him for a hug, something she happened to know he hated but tolerated from her. "That is the sweetest thing you have ever said to me," she whispered into his cravat. "And I could never have done it without your help and guidance."

He patted her back awkwardly and made a dismissive sound. "I did very little. The talent is all your own."

Pulling back, she wiped at the moisture forming in her eyes. "Are you attempting to make me cry?"

A knock at the door interrupted them. Tilda appeared, a square, brown parcel in her hands. "My lady, a delivery boy just dropped this off for you."

"Thank you, Tilda." She accepted the parcel, felt the ridges with her fingers. A canvas. She carried it to a table and began unwrapping the paper.

"*Qu'est-ce que c'est?*"

"A painting."

The heavy paper opened and Maggie withheld a seaside scene. One of hers, actually—but not *quite* hers. Yes, the scene was hers, but the shading was not the same. Also the strokes were from a fatter brush, and the hues were a bit darker. Close, but not an exact match of the landscape she'd once painted—though likely no one would know it but her. The work was *that* good. And there was her—Lemarc's—signature at the bottom, which appeared almost correct even to her. Was this an attempt at duplicating a Lemarc? Who in the name of Hades had done this?

"It's a copy of one of my paintings," she told Lucien.

He peered down, studied it. "It is good. I think if I did not know you so well, I might believe it."

"Why would someone bother copying *me?*" Turning her attention to the letter included within, she skimmed Mrs. McGinnis's clear handwriting. The more she read, however, the more her discomfort grew. By the time she finished, her hands were shaking.

"Maggie, you are as white as flour. What did she say?"

Staring down at the painting, she willed air into her lungs. "I am being blackmailed."

"*Mon dieu!*" Lucien ripped the paper from her hand and began reading for himself. No doubt he would be equally horrified by the contents of the letter.

Someone had uncovered her identity as Lemarc, hired a forger—a damn good one by the looks of it—and was now circulating drawings throughout London. But not ordinary drawings—no, these pieces were aimed directly at the Prince Regent and his father, King George III, who was rumored to be on his deathbed. Hateful drawings meant to incite controversy, such as the inference that Prinny would bankrupt England when his father died, or that he suffered from the same mental deficiencies as the king. The most damaging one, according to Mrs. McGinnis, showed the carnage of Peterloo from the year before—where soldiers had ruthlessly squashed a rebellion in Manchester, killing many protesters—and urged the middle class to take up the cause of political reform once more, to not let their countrymen die in vain.

Someone was attempting to get Lemarc arrested for sedition.

Agents from the Crown had already paid a visit to Mrs. McGinnis, asking for personal information about

Lemarc. The shopkeeper hedged and told them she didn't know Lemarc's true identity, but a meeting might be arranged when the artist returned from the Continent. Even though that appeared to pacify the agents for the moment, Mrs. McGinnis was frightened—with good reason. If they discovered she had lied to protect Maggie, the shopkeeper could be implicated as well. The only way to stop it, according to the forger, was for Maggie to hand over two thousand pounds annually—an absolutely outrageous amount of money.

"Did you see the other letter? The one Madame McGinnis said is on the back of the painting?"

Lucien's voice snapped Maggie back to reality. She'd forgotten about the other letter. Flipping the forged painting over, she saw a folded piece of paper with her name written on it. Her *given* name. Swallowing, she lifted it off the canvas, unfolded it, and spread it out on the table.

Dear Lady Hawkins—

Surprised? I wanted to send you this painting as proof of my own painter's abilities. He's quite good, wouldn't you say?

If you want the drawings to cease, I require two thousand pounds in two weeks' time. Otherwise, I'm afraid Lemarc may find himself (herself?) in a spot of trouble with the authorities. Instructions for delivery will be left with Mrs. McGinnis.

It was unsigned. Lucien, who had read over her shoulder, exclaimed, "Two thousand pounds! That is ridiculous. This scheme, who is behind it?"

Maggie shook her head. "I do not know. Anyone, I

suppose. Why target Lemarc? Many artists are more successful than me."

"This is meant to hurt you, *ma chère*. Someone wants to discredit you, to ruin your career. Who?" Lucien gave her a pointed look. "Perhaps—"

"*No.* Winchester would never do such a thing."

"Of course not." Lucien scowled at her. "The earl, he loves you. Passionately. He would never want to hurt you like this. I saw it myself, how much he cares for you."

"When? At the opera?"

He nodded. "He hardly took his eyes off you all evening. Staring at you like a girl at her very first *amour.*"

Though the information warmed her, she elbowed him in the arm. "Be serious. And do not make jests at his expense."

Lucien's brows shot up. "Is that so? While I am happy for you, I have now lost a great deal of money to Henri. I thought you would at least hold out until—"

"Lucien," she snapped, "you are not helping."

He straightened and regarded the painting once more. "Well, who then? Who else would do this?"

Though her mind reeled, Maggie tried to focus enough to come up with a name. Whoever had sent this note wanted more than just money; he or she wanted to tarnish Lemarc's name. And for all she knew, that plan may have already succeeded in London. Amongst artists, a fine line existed between noteworthy and dangerously improper. The former meant she could count on being hired by anyone wealthy and bored enough to want to rub elbows with a notorious artist. The latter meant she would never be hired by patrons who cared about soiling their precious reputations—in other words, just about everyone in the *ton*. If she didn't get to London and repair the damage already done to Lemarc's name, then all would be lost. Oh, and she'd still have to evade the authorities.

She really, truly did not wish to go to prison.

Pinching the bridge of her nose, she said, "I swear, I cannot imagine. I've kept a low profile in London, barely going out except for my own parties. There isn't anyone, other than Winchester, who is mocked enough in the cartoons for this sort of retribution— and I know he isn't responsible. What am I going to do?"

A knock on the door interrupted them. Tilda appeared. "My lady, the Earl of Winchester to see you."

"I beg your pardon for barging in like this." Simon stepped around Tilda and came forward. Dark blue trousers showed off his long, lean legs, while a tailored matching topcoat hugged his shoulders. His handsome face, ruddy from the cold, showed lines of concern. "Ah, I see you've received one as well," he said, gesturing to the table. "I came as soon as mine was delivered." Slipping a hand inside of his pocket, he retrieved a folded piece of paper.

"Yours? You mean you received a letter as well? But that makes no sense . . ." She looked at Lucien for answers, but her friend merely shrugged.

"Here. Read this." Simon thrust the paper into her hands. Maggie turned and spread it out on the table near the others, so she and Lucien could study it together. She motioned to her letters. "You might as well read mine, then."

Short and on point, Simon's missive informed him

of the seditious cartoons penned under Lemarc's name. It demanded money—three thousand pounds annually—in order to leave Maggie/Lemarc alone. In flipping it over, she noted the letter had been addressed to his hotel in Paris.

"Who knows you are in Paris, at Hôtel Meurice?" she asked him.

He glanced up from reading Mrs. McGinnis's note. "Anyone, really. I've made no secret of it."

"I must go back to London," she told both men.

"I shall go with you," Simon stated in a hard, determined voice she recognized well.

"No, that is—"

"Do not argue with me, Maggie." He slapped his hand on the scarred wooden table. "You have no idea what trouble you face. Do you know how serious sedition charges are? It is a common law offense. You could be imprisoned *indefinitely*. I can protect you from that. At the very least, allow me to use my position and name to shelter you from the worst of it."

He was quite worked up, and his concern warmed her. Nevertheless, she must prevent her troubles from dragging him down. "And what will it cost you to embroil yourself in this fiasco? More votes? Your political standing? I cannot allow you to align yourself with Lemarc against the Crown. What if you end up imprisoned?"

"That will not happen. I have known these men all my life, Maggie. They will not believe me of conspiring to overthrow the very system I have worked so hard to uphold. They will listen to me. And there is every chance I can keep your real identity a secret if I act as an agent for Lemarc."

Perfectly reasonable, of course, but it did not make accepting his help any easier to bear. The past decade, she'd only had herself to rely on. Any problem had been hers alone to solve. To allow someone else to shoulder those problems, even Simon, was a strange, unsettling notion. "I must do something. I cannot sit and wait for you to slay my dragons for me. I am coming with you."

Simon shook his head. "You must remain here. In Paris. It will keep you safe from—"

"I'm hardly safe here, with the forger aware of where I am. And remaining here is unthinkable. No, listen to me," she said when it appeared he would argue. "I will go mad waiting here for news of my fate. And I can be of assistance in tracking down the forger. No one knows my work better than me. There may be ways of discovering his identity through the forgeries."

His lips compressed to a thin, unhappy line.

"While this concern, it is touching," Lucien said into the tense silence, "it is better if you work together toward the same result, *non?*"

"Returning will only make it easier for the Crown to find you," Simon said, his jaw tight.

"Returning will make it easier for me to find the forger," she said.

When Simon did not argue, Lucien rose. "I will tell Tilda to pack your things," he said, and left the room.

Simon sighed as Barreau closed the door. He should have known it would prove bloody impossible to keep Maggie from the proceedings, as much as he did not want her involved. The maddening, stubborn female.

Did she not see the peril at hand? This needed to be handled with diplomacy and tact—not exactly two of Maggie's strengths. But they were his, and he would do all in his power to prevent her from losing everything she'd worked so hard to accomplish.

Without realizing it, he took a step toward her. She held up her hand. "Wait," she told him. Her eyes slid away and he noticed the color on her cheeks. "There is another matter we must resolve before London."

"And that would be?" He folded his arms across his chest. Could he convince her to move into Barrett House? He wanted her in his bed each night. But her bed would do just as—

"You and I. Us. We must stop seeing one another."

He felt his brows lower. Had he heard her correctly? "We must . . . stop seeing one another?" he repeated stupidly.

"Yes."

"Why in God's name would we do that?"

"I cannot allow my reputation, such as it is, to affect you or your standing. The gossip in London will be a hundredfold worse than Paris."

"Hang the gossip, Mags. I do not care what anyone says about us."

She thrust her chin up. "You say that now, but you have no idea of the damage that will befall you, damage that cannot be undone. It is best we end our association now. Then you may act on Lemarc's behalf in London with no one the wiser."

The sincerity and determination on her face caused a frisson of panic to slide down his spine. "Absolutely not. And my standing is not a concern at the moment."

"Not now, perhaps, but it will be. Soon. When Parliament reopens in a few months, you will care. However, by that time, it will be too late."

No, no. This was all wrong. He meant to have a much different conversation concerning their future, one that included her naked, day in and day out. One of love and laughter, of all the things he'd been missing over the last few years. And where the devil was this attitude coming from? She had never shrunk from Society a day in her life. She did as she bloody well pleased, and to the devil with the consequences.

So why was a relationship with him any different? Was he not worth the risk?

"What are you afraid of?" he asked. "That my invitations dry up? That I must work a bit harder in Lords? That I take some ribbing at our expense?"

"You make it sound so easy. Yes, I am afraid of everything you mentioned—and more. And there will be more, Simon. This will affect you in ways you cannot even begin to imagine. Markham is only the beginning. And have you thought of how it will impact your family?"

"My mother is the only concern, and I should like to see anyone try to snub her. Besides, she will be thrilled I have finally taken a bride."

"A bride?" Maggie screeched. Her eyes round, she gaped at him.

"Yes, a bride. How can you be surprised? Of course I want to marry you."

He assumed this information would reassure her, but if anything it made her appear even more anxious. "Are you mad? Look around you." She swept the bright, airy space with her hand. A converted library, the studio brimmed with canvases, cloths, brushes, easels, and other bric-a-brac. "You want to marry *this*?

Marry Lemarc? Because this shall never go away. My art, my work . . . this is who I am. I cannot give it up."

"I would never dream of asking you to give it up." He stepped closer, but she sidled away, out of his reach. He folded his arms. "Nevertheless, I want to be married. I want to wake up to you every morning. I want to travel with you, watch you paint, have you bear my children. . . ." He could go on; the list of what he wanted from her seemed endless.

"Children?" If possible, she turned paler. She covered her mouth with a hand, shook her head. "Now I know you are not thinking clearly," she whispered.

"What did you assume, that after all these years I'd be satisfied with a few weeks of you in my bed?" Before she could evade him, he moved to clasp her face in his hands. "I need you, Maggie, and nothing will keep me from having you. Not fear or threats, not even the disapproval of every Society matron in London. Even if I must give up my seat in Lords."

Moisture gathered in the corners of her eyes, pooling against the fringe of her lashes until two single tears streamed down her cheeks. He wiped at them with his thumbs. "Do not cry, darling. It will be fine. You shall see. Trust me."

She started to shake her head, so he bent to kiss her. He could taste the reticence and worry in the way she held back. Using his mouth, his hands, and his tongue, he poured all his determination and confidence into their connection. She might not believe the words, but surely she could *feel* how much he cared for her. How much he craved her. How he'd never, ever let anything or anyone hurt her. After a few seconds, she responded, her fingers digging painfully into his arms as she kissed him back with desperate hunger. Satisfaction roared through his blood, quickly followed by a lust so acute, so painful, it nearly knocked him to his knees.

"The door," he panted against her mouth.

"No need. They'll not disturb us." She nipped at his bottom lip, biting him, and then sucked the plump flesh inside her mouth. "Now, Simon."

He should refuse. After all, he would see her this evening. What was it about Maggie that drove him to absolute madness? Then her fingers found his trouser buttons . . . and any thoughts of waiting vanished. She freed him from his clothing and began stroking him hard, fast. He'd taught her too well, he realized, his head falling back in blissful surrender. Christ, she'd have him spilling in her hand in another minute.

Incapable of waiting any longer, he led her to the scarred wooden table. He pushed the letters and forged painting out of the way. "Up," he told her. "Lift your skirts."

Her hooded green gaze never left his face as she sat, reclined on an elbow, and slowly raised the hem of her faded morning dress, petticoats, and shift. Her mound, covered in soft, downy hair, lay bare to him in the midday light. So beautiful. He would never get tired of looking at her.

Her knees fell open in brazen invitation. Everything in him screamed to take her fast and hard, but he did not want to hurt her. He stepped between her legs and swiped a finger over the entrance to her body. Wet. Ready. He lined up and, with one thrust, buried himself as far as he could. The sheer exquisiteness of that motion ripped a groan from both of them. Hot and tight, her channel gripped his cock like a fist. She fell back against the table, his beautiful, wild Maggie spread before him like the most enticing banquet. As she watched him, her lips formed the one word guaranteed to raise his desire to a fever pitch. "Please," she whispered.

Oh, hell. Bending, he hooked her knees over the crooks of his arms and straightened. Her hips were up off the table, allowing him better leverage. He began slamming inside her, a rough, punishing rhythm they both craved. His hands wrapped around her thighs to pull her forward onto his cock with each thrust. She gasped, her lids fluttering closed. "Yes," she breathed.

Never had he been so out of control with a woman, not even in his youth. But Maggie twisted him up, turned him inside out—a fact she was well aware of and relished. Many nights she had teased and tortured him until he'd taken her like an animal in heat, delirious with a bestial craving for her. None of those evenings, however, had been quite as frenetic as this.

Pleasure built at the base of his spine. Each stroke brought him closer to release and he knew it would not be long. "Use your fingers," he gasped. "Come on, darling. Let me see you."

Unashamed and heart-stoppingly beautiful, she slid her hand down her belly and through the thatch of hair covering her mound. Clever fingers found the swollen bud at the apex of her crease, rolled it. The sight so erotic, Simon had to close his eyes. If he watched her, this would all be over too soon. She moaned and he doubled his efforts, hips pounding against her to drive his cock deep. Her muscles clenched, tightening as she reached the peak.

"God, yes. Come for me," he told her, lifting his lids to watch her body shudder and convulse as she pulsed around him. The feeling so exquisite, everything inside him coiled and then broke open. The orgasm tore through him without warning, and he emptied himself inside her body. He threw back his head and let out a shout as it went on and on, endless waves of ecstasy he was helpless to fight as she clutched him close.

When they both regained themselves, he slid out of her. "I apologize," he said, producing a scrap of linen from his pocket and holding it out to her. "I meant to withdraw—"

She accepted the cloth. "I know. We were both carried away, I fear."

He fastened his trousers, relieved she was not cross with his carelessness. He must've successfully convinced her of his plans to marry her. Without doubt, any child of theirs would not be born a bastard. "We should leave for London tomorrow morning. I'll secure us passage."

Maggie sat up and righted her clothing. "I have much to do before returning. Perhaps it would be best if we did not distract one another this evening."

He frowned, unhappy with the idea but unable to argue with the logic. "Fine. I'll collect you in the morning." Holding her hand, he helped her off the table. With hair askew and flushed skin, she looked like a woman who'd just been tumbled. His woman. He kissed her quickly. "Until tomorrow, then."

Chapter Nineteen

London
A week later

"I came as soon as I could," the Duke of Colton said as he strode into the drawing room.

Simon rose and went to the sideboard. "I am grateful, Colt. Sit down and I'll pour you a brandy." The London weather had turned frigid in these first few days of February. Though Simon had returned not even an hour ago, the wet cold had already seeped into his bones. He refilled his own glass, then splashed a healthy amount of brandy in a snifter for Colton.

As he sat, Mrs. Timmons knocked on the door. "My lords, Your Grace. I have a fresh pot of tea." Simon waved her in and the housekeeper set the tray down. A maid followed behind with a tray of sweets. "Would you care for Sally to pour the tea?" Mrs. Timmons asked.

"No, I think we gents can manage. Thank you."

The women both bobbed a curtsy and withdrew, closing the door.

"Why'd you say no? I like your maids." Quint selected a piece of cake, popped it in his mouth. "They're prettier than mine."

"You'd get prettier servants if you acted more like a viscount instead of a demented Bedlamite," Colton noted. "Now, Winchester, what's the hurry? When did you return from Paris?"

"Nearly an hour ago. Before we get onto other problems, tell me. How goes the search for Cranford?"

Colton shook his head. "Still cannot find him, I'm afraid. Fitz and I have turned the city on its head in our search."

"Damnation," Simon said and slapped the armrest.

"My thoughts exactly," Colton said. "We saw what he did to the girl at Hartley's. Another girl was beaten, raped, and killed in St. Giles not long after. Man fit Cranford's vague description and one of her friends noticed a signet ring."

"Not to mention what he did to Maggie," Simon added. "Where in Hades is he hiding?"

"Couldn't say. But O'Shea's men are keeping an eye out with the promise of a reward. He'll turn up eventually."

"Unless he's boarded a steamer for America," Quint finished, unhelpfully in Simon's opinion.

"Even a visit to that godforsaken country will not stop me from exacting retribution," Simon told them. "No matter where I must go, Cranford will pay for every second of suffering Maggie endured."

"Provided she isn't arrested for sedition first, I presume," Quint said.

"Sedition?" Colton's eyes widened. "What's this?"

Simon caught Colton up on the developments, from Maggie as Lemarc to the blackmail letters received in Paris.

The duke slumped back. "Staggering. The whole business. So let me see if I understand. You court Lady Hawkins during her debut until the scandal breaks, upon which time Cranford shows you a bunch of letters from her professing her undying love for another man. So she marries Hawkins instead of you, and when Hawkins dies she returns to London as Lemarc, sets McGinnis up with a shop, and Winejester is born."

Simon swallowed a mouthful of brandy. "Yes."

"Deuced clever, that woman. You have to admire her."

"Indeed," Quint agreed. "She's built a reputable name for herself. Lemarc is respected amongst artists. There was even talk of inviting him—er, *her*—to exhibit at Somerset House."

"I don't mean just the work," Colton clarified. "Though it is impressive. I mean her plan to make Winchester suffer. Not all ladies would turn a former paramour into a popular caricature. Think she'd sell me one of the cartoons now?"

"I'll allow that," Simon returned, "when Julia permits me to inform you of how she spent her time in London all those years you were away."

The duke's face darkened, his eyes narrowing to slits. "What do you mean by that? Spent her time, how?"

Simon didn't answer, merely smirked. When it looked as if Colton might work himself into a righteous fury, Quint put a hand up. "Children," he said,

"I believe we should return to the issue at hand. I've been thinking on the blackmailer since Paris. From the sound of the letters, I think it safe to assume he's someone close to you, Winchester."

"Me? Why me?"

"He's too smug. Rubbing your nose in it. This is personal for him. Or her. He's laughing at you, trying to bleed money out of both of you. But he asked you for more money. Makes me think it's someone out to hurt you, specifically, and hurting Lady Hawkins is a secondary motive."

Simon let that sink in while he reached for a small cake. Who would hate him so much? A political opponent, possibly.

"Do you plan to turn the blackmailer over to the Crown?" Colton asked.

"It's the only way. I won't give them Maggie. Or Mrs. McGinnis."

Quint reached for more tea. "I assume you'll arrange to pay and then watch to see who comes to retrieve the money."

"Yes, I daresay that is what Hollister will recommend," Simon said, referring to the investigator. "Whatever the plan, it should happen quickly. Once word travels that Maggie and I have returned, I suspect the blackmailer will contact us."

"I am surprised Lady Hawkins did not join us today, as this is a concern to her as well," Colton noted.

Simon did not immediately reply, so Quint said, "She left him in Paris. Snuck out in the middle of the night."

Colton chuckled. "Oh, extraordinary. I adore this woman. Verily, Winchester, you deserve everything she gives you."

A knock on the door offered Simon a blessed reprieve. "Enter," he called. His butler appeared. "A Mr. Hollister to see you, my lord."

"Excellent. Show him into the study, Stillman." He stood. "Come along, both of you, and do try to be helpful."

Four days later Mrs. McGinnis received succinct instructions:

> *Thursday, three o'clock in the afternoon, leave a book containing the bank drafts on the first stone bench along the footpath from Stanhope Gate to the Serpentine.*

The location worked to their advantage. Hyde Park allowed for a multitude of hiding places from which they could keep vigil over the parcel. It seemed doubtful the blackmailer would retrieve it himself, as it was too great a risk, but someone would surely come to collect such a large sum of money. All they needed to do was wait and then follow.

Simon refused to allow Maggie's involvement. She was kept abreast of the developments, of course, but Simon did not want her anywhere near the blackmailers. He could well imagine how angry this made her, especially when he had Hollister post a man to guard her house, but he couldn't risk her name attached to this operation in any manner. She needed to be far, far removed.

He hadn't seen her since Paris. He missed her. Terribly. Missed her stubbornness and her laugh. Her feisty temper and her wicked wit. And at night he ached for her soft, strong hands teasing him to madness. Nevertheless, he needed to stop this threat against her first. Once the forger and blackmailer were in the hands of the Crown, Simon could go to her and discuss their future, a future that very much included Maggie as the Countess of Winchester.

On the day of the delivery, Hollister stationed over twenty men in the park. Whoever came to collect the parcel would not get away, though that fact did little to lesson Simon's anxiety. The person responsible for this scheme stood between Simon and everything he'd ever wanted, and his entire future hinged on removing that obstacle.

As they expected, not even a minute after Simon placed the book on the bench, a young boy came to collect it. Simon and the other men followed him closely, staying far enough behind as to not draw his attention. They ended at Jermyn Street, where the boy knocked on a door, handed over the parcel, and collected a few coins before sprinting off. The partition closed quickly, the entire transaction happening in the blink of an eye.

"That's our man," Hollister murmured to Simon. They were positioned across the street. "He took the parcel."

"Let's go in, then." Simon eyed the door, then asked, "You have your lock-picking tools?"

"Indeed, I do. We'll sneak in and catch your blackmailer unaware. I'll put some men on the sides and back of the building in case he tries to run."

Hollister picked the locks with the efficiency of a seasoned dubber, then turned the handle carefully to noiselessly open the door. He gestured for Simon to lead the way.

Pistol in hand, Simon crept up the stairs, Hollister directly behind. The treads squeaked and groaned under their weight and they had to go slowly. When Simon reached the top, he checked the latch and found it unlocked. He threw open the door and rushed in, the investigator on his heels.

The large apartment was devoid of furniture, save a table and a few chairs scattered here and there. He saw well-used art supplies—canvases, easels, frames, paint, and brushes—which explained the heavy smell of turpentine in the air. A small, unfamiliar man sat at a table, paper and pencils in front of him. Wide-eyed, he carefully raised his hands in surrender.

Movement in the back caught Simon's eye. A head topped with thinning brown hair disappeared out the side window.

Simon rushed forward, determined to catch whoever was attempting an escape. Drawing nearer to the edge, he could see a rope attached to a hook in the sill. He leaned out the window in time to see a familiar face letting go of the rope and dropping into the alley below.

Sir James. His bloody brother-in-law. A furious growl rumbled in Simon's throat. "Stop him!" Simon shouted to Hollister's man at the entrance of the alley as Sir James ran toward the street.

The man raced into the alley, toward Sir James, and Simon spun away from the window and sprinted for the stairs. "Wait here," he told Hollister, who stood with his pistol trained on the unknown man at the table.

Simon thumped down the steps and wrenched

open the front door. Christ, now it all made sense. The money. The notes. That it had been a personal attack.

The damned idiot.

Once on the street, Simon found that Hollister's man had Sir James pinned in the back of the alley. James struggled to escape the larger man's grip, but Hollister's man held fast, leaning his larger body into James's girth to keep him still.

When James saw Simon approach, he stiffened. Fear flashed over his fleshy features before he thrust his chin up defiantly. "Here now, Winchester, what's—"

"Do not say one word, you miserable excuse for a man." Anger burned in Simon's throat. He'd never wanted to punch anyone so desperately in all his life. James had been a pustule on Simon's backside ever since the day he'd married Sybil. A blackmailer. Everlasting hell.

"Want me to send for the authorities, my lord?" Hollister's man stepped aside and produced a pistol from his coat. He pointed the weapon at Sir James.

Simon scrubbed a hand across his jaw, hating the position he'd been put in. It would be so much easier to turn everything over to the Crown. "No. Not yet, at least."

"You cannot have me . . . arrested!" Sir James sputtered indignantly. "Think of the scandal. Your mother and sister. Why, it would—"

"Enough! I can do whatever I damn well please, James, including having you sent to the hulks, if I bloody well choose."

He needed to speak with James alone. As much as he wished otherwise, this was family business and no one should overhear it. He turned to Hollister's man.

"Watch the entrance to the alley." The man nodded, took a few steps toward the street, and turned his back.

Simon narrowed his eyes on James. "Give me one good reason not to strangle you here and now."

James pushed away from the brick wall, straightened his clothing. "Sybil would never forgive you. And not even peers are able get away with murder."

"They can if they're smart about it. I daresay I'd be lauded as a hero in this case." Simon crossed his arms to keep from throttling James. "I cannot believe you thought this scheme would work. I should just put a ball in your bloody duplicitous heart."

"So do it!" the other man shot back, throwing up his hands. "I have nothing left to live for. We're completely done for. You've taken all our money, and I'm forced to depend on the kindness of relatives like a . . . a damned spinster aunt. You—"

"So the answer is to blackmail me? Hell, James, what else could I do? You spend every farthing you get your hands on. You're determined to drag my sister down with you, and I will not have it. You'll not bankrupt the estate. Not as long as I am the head of the family."

"As if we all need a reminder you are the mighty and powerful Earl of Winchester," James sneered.

Simon's jaw clenched tightly. Shouldn't his brother-in-law be begging for forgiveness right now? He took a calming breath. "Who put you up to this? I know this was not your idea."

"How do you know that? I am more clever than you give me credit for!"

"I give you precisely the credit you deserve, you

notorious nincompoop. Now tell me who you have been working with."

"Why should I tell you anything?"

Simon stalked forward, wrapped a fist around James's cravat, and shoved him against the rough brick. "Because if you do not, I will cut off your bollocks and feed them to the pigs. Start explaining, James."

James pressed his lips together, spite glittering in his eyes.

"Fine," Simon said, calmly. He released his hold—only to plow a fist in James's belly. The man doubled over, wheezing. Simon straightened his cuffs and waited for him to recover.

"Piss. Off," James rasped.

Simon wrapped his fingers around James's throat, yanking the man upright and slamming him into the brick. "Let's have some fun, shall we?"

James said nothing, his gaze openly hostile, so Simon leaned in to snarl, "I shall squeeze your throat until you tell me what I want to know. If you do not tell me, I'll cut off your supply of air."

"You would not dare," James returned, though his gaze darted over Simon's shoulder nervously, as if looking for assistance.

"Wouldn't I?" Simon tightened his fist across James's windpipe and James yelped. "It's the perfect place to kill you. They shall find your body in this alley and assume you were set upon by a thief or ruffian. No one will ever suspect me." James began to struggle, but Simon was considerably larger and stronger. His brother-in-law turned a nice shade of red.

"Let me go, you madman!"

"No chance," Simon bit out. "Not until you tell me who." To illustrate his point, he pressed even harder.

James's eyes bulged. "All right! Let me go and I'll tell you," he whispered.

"Now, you maggot. Or I'll strangle you where you stand."

"Cranford!" James shouted as best he could. "It was Cranford. Now let me go!"

Simon froze, unable to breathe. Cranford? Blackmailing Simon and Maggie? God above, *why*? He relaxed his grip on James, and James slumped against the wall to suck in air.

"Cranford?" Simon repeated and sorted what he knew of both men. "You and Cranford cooked up this scheme? How in hell did that come about?"

"We're friends." James stuck up his chin. "Have been for a long time. In fact, he's brokered many a deal for me over the past few years. He's got good ideas and always knows where the solid investments can be made."

"James, you've never made a solid investment in your life. Have you been . . . giving Cranford money?"

"Only when the opportunity arises. Can't get in every time, you see. And it ain't his fault when the business fails. He's a solid chap."

Everlasting hell. Cranford had been bilking James out of money for years, it seemed. No, make that *Winchester* money. "No, he's not. Cranford is a liar, a rapist, and possibly a murderer. Now we know he's a swindler and a blackmailer, too. Jesus, James." Simon pinched the bridge of his nose.

"A . . . rapist? A murderer? No, that can't be right."

"Tell me how you were to contact him after today's payment."

James shook his head. "I wasn't. Said he would contact me when he got back from Paris."

"Cranford was in Paris?" Simon's stomach clenched as the pieces began to fall into place. The man on Maggie's balcony. The carriage accident. The fact that the blackmailer knew how to contact them. He put a hand to the wall to steady himself. "So did you send the note to Mrs. McGinnis, asking for the money?"

"Cranford told me what to say." He scratched his head. "Now that I think on it, seems unlikely he's still in France. How would he know you both were here otherwise?"

Simon pondered James's surprisingly astute question. "Is the man in that room there the one who has been forging Lemarcs?"

"Yes. I found him. Good, isn't he?"

Simon's lip curled and he quashed the urge to strangle James once more. "Not a fact you should be proud of at this moment, James."

James instantly sobered. "So what do you plan to do, now that you know?"

Simon considered his options. He mostly wanted to finish what he'd started in this alley, but killing James would prove difficult to explain to the family. What he needed was to get rid of James for good without committing murder. "Fortunate for you that I maintain a house in Edinburgh. I see a lifetime of Scotland in your future, James."

Maggie stalked the floors of her studio, furious at being forced to remain home. The afternoon light had already started to fade. Surely the money had been turned over to the blackmailer by now, and she knew Simon and Mr. Hollister planned to follow whoever retrieved the parcel. Had they found the blackmailer? What was happening? She wanted to pull her hair out from the frustration.

She should be there. And she *would* be there, if it weren't for Simon's heavy-handedness.

He'd actually posted a man at her door to ensure she could not leave. Trapping her, as if she were a prisoner. The gall of that man . . .

He had no right to be making decisions for her or solving problems on her behalf. Nothing had changed between them since Paris. The threat of sedition still loomed, not to mention a madman was running amok in an attempt to ruin her life. Did Simon not realize the risk to his reputation if her identity was discovered? Or what about his political standing when his name became linked to hers?

Even if I must give up my seat in Lords.

That he would be willing to walk away from his family legacy both humbled and terrified her. She would not allow him to do it, of course, would never force him to choose. Though he'd brushed away her concerns, Maggie knew what would happen if they married. Eventually he would come to resent the ramifications of their association. Resent *her.*

Her chest constricted, making it painful to draw breath. The temptation to throw it all away, to run to Simon and ignore the consequences nearly overwhelmed her . . . but she resisted it. She knew what it was like to have Society turn its back on you, how ugly one's life could become when it was no longer in your control. Simon had been worshipped from the cradle, the golden heir to one of the wealthiest families in England. He had no idea of what awaited him should she give in.

So she would be the reasonable one. She would learn how to survive without him. She had no choice, really, because as soon as the blackmailer was dealt with Maggie planned to leave England for good.

"The Duchess of Colton to see you, milady," Tilda said at the door.

Maggie's chest fluttered as hope rose within her. She had not seen Julia since returning from Paris. Had the duchess brought news of the blackmailer? Maggie dashed past her servant and into the corridor. "No need to bring her up, Tilda. I shall go down!" she tossed over her shoulder.

She raced down two sets of stairs until she reached the front sitting room where Tilda always placed waiting guests. The duchess was examining a painting on the wall when Maggie entered. "Julia," Maggie panted. "Have you any news?"

Julia turned and shook her head. "No, I haven't. I was hoping you might have learned something. The wait, at home by myself, was interminable."

Maggie sagged and tried to catch her breath. "Well, at least we may wait together, then." She crossed and rang for tea.

"You are very talented." Julia once again stared at the landscape, the one with the plover Simon had used to identify Maggie as Lemarc. "And Winejester was a stroke of genius."

"Thank you, though part of me wishes I'd never thought of the name. None of this mess would have transpired in such a case."

"You cannot mean that," Julia exclaimed. "I was

told you and Simon worked out your differences in Paris."

"Allow me to guess," Maggie drawled. "Simon told you that."

Julia's brow creased with concern. "Yes, he did. Is it not true?"

Maggie sat and arranged her skirts, deciding how best to answer. If she were honest, would Julia keep her confidence or repeat everything to Simon? When she hedged, the duchess lowered into a nearby chair.

"Maggie, I must confess something to you. I'm afraid . . ." Julia sounded unusually grave, her blue eyes showing signs of both worry and guilt. "Well, it's time you knew, anyway."

"That sounds ominous."

Julia nodded. "Indeed, it is. And it's something I should have mentioned ages ago. You see, back during your debut, when the scandal broke . . ." She cleared her throat and folded her hands in her lap. "He wanted to challenge Cranford and I convinced him not to."

Maggie blinked. "Simon? Simon wanted to challenge Cranford?"

"Yes. He was furious. Convinced that Cranford had dishonored you. Of course, I did not know any of the particulars, else I would have let him issue the challenge. But I was selfish; I was sixteen, had just been married off to a stranger who immediately abandoned me. Simon had been my friend since childhood. At the time, I was petrified he'd either be killed or be forced to leave England as well. So I convinced him to speak with Cranford first, instead of meeting over pistols at dawn."

A duel. Simon had been willing to defend her. A wave of dizziness washed over her, one of amazement and gratitude. For so long, she'd assumed them all eager to shun her after the scandal, but Simon had cared enough to want to risk his life for her. Thank heavens Julia had talked him out of it. If he'd been killed . . . well, no sense dwelling on the past. Suffice it to say, she was grateful he hadn't died.

While Maggie struggled with this information, Julia shifted a bit in her seat. "I feel positively wretched over it, Maggie. If Simon had issued the challenge, your entire life would be different. Not only that, but the two of you would have ended up together much sooner."

"Perhaps . . . or perhaps not," Maggie allowed. "We shall never know what may have happened. Cranford may very well have killed him."

From the frown on her pale face, Julia did not appear reassured. So Maggie said, "Honestly, I am glad you stopped him. Challenging Cranford would have been monumentally idiotic."

"Maggie," Julia said gravely, "your reputation, your nickname. The cruelty you endured . . . none of that would have happened if I'd let him issue the challenge. You would be happily stowed away at Winchester Towers with four or five babies by now."

"Lord, I should hope not," Maggie snorted.

Julia cut her a glance. "Would it have been so terrible?"

Sobering, Maggie thought how best to express her thoughts. Not many women would understand, but perhaps Julia might. "My marriage to Hawkins was not a tragic one, and I had a great deal of freedom to

learn and practice my skills. I traveled to Paris. I met
Lucien. I gained insight into myself I never would
have achieved without the scandal. I do not regret one
minute of it. And while I might wish for others to
remain unblemished by it, my reputation allows me
certain liberties I'd never otherwise possess. I've led a
life most of the women of our world will never know.
It has not been perfect, but at least I can say I truly
lived."

She'd never put it all into words before, but Maggie
meant every single one. Tension she'd carried for far
too long disappeared off her frame, making her
lighter, happier. So what if some of them snickered
behind her back? Maggie could be more than the
proper Lady Margaret Hawkins; she was also Maggie,
the Half-Irish Harlot, as well as Lemarc. Pity the rest
of them only had one persona.

"It relieves my mind to hear you say so," Julia said.
"I would not blame you if you told me to go to the
devil. I would."

"No. I've grown too fond of you. Besides, you were
only concerned with Simon's welfare, and rightly so."

"Do you love him?" Julia cocked her perfectly
coiffed blond head. "I must say, I've never seen him
like this over a woman. If you break his heart, I do not
want to have to choose sides."

Love him? She'd thought she loved him once,
when she was a girl. Now she tried not to think on it,
tried to think of their relationship as fleeting. A
passing fancy they would both recover from when it
ended—and it *would* end. There was no choice,
considering the people they had both become.

She decided to be honest. "I plan on leaving

London once my affairs have been settled here, so do not worry over choosing sides."

"Leaving?" Julia's face clouded with confusion. "But I assumed. . . . Does he know?"

Maggie shook her head. "No. I've told no one."

"Why?"

Was it not obvious? Her tongue thick and uncooperative, Maggie gestured to the room. "Because of Lemarc. Because of the Half-Irish Harlot. Because of everything I am." Or rather, everything she was not. She gave a dry laugh. "Can you see me, a political hostess? It's laughable."

"Yes. I can," Julia snapped, straightening her shoulders. "Are you telling me you think you are not good enough to stand as Simon's wife? That you are unworthy?" She shot to her feet and began moving angrily about the room. "Has he in any way intimated—"

"No!" Maggie rushed out. "Absolutely not. He said he wants to marry me, though I expect him to change his mind once he's had time to consider the unfortunate ramifications of such a rash action."

"Rash? The two of you have waited nearly ten years for one another. How is that rash, exactly?"

Tilda entered with tea, and both women waited patiently for the servant to depart. Maggie busied herself with pouring while Julia resumed her seat. The duchess had clearly romanticized Simon and Maggie's relationship. Maggie, on the other hand, hadn't romanticized anything in quite a long time; she'd learned to be practical out of necessity, even when doing so proved difficult.

"You should know," Julia said, accepting her cup and saucer, "that while the Winchester men have all been brilliant statesmen, there's not a one without a scandal in his past. And while Simon may seem respectable now—"

"Men are forgiven their scandals," Maggie gently reminded. "You know that. It's much different for women. And he will come to resent me for it."

"Do not underestimate yourself or Simon. And I would throw Colton's considerable weight behind the two of you as well. We would be a formidable force, all of us together."

Not when the world discovers Lemarc's true identity, Maggie thought. That piece of news went way beyond an average scandal. If the blackmailer had his way, Lemarc would be unmasked and sent to prison for a long time. And even if this particular threat passed, there would forever be another one, someone else trying to ruin Lemarc. How could she allow Simon— as well as her friends—to be embroiled in her dramas time and time again? Better to leave while she still could.

Nevertheless, she did not want to argue with the duchess. "Let us speak of more interesting topics. You've never told me about meeting Colton in Venice. Tell me how you were able to get the Depraved Duke to fall in love with you."

Chapter Twenty

"No sign of him, my lord," Hollister said, striding into Simon's study after being announced.

Simon grit his teeth in frustration as Colton said, "It's as we expected. He's gone into hiding."

"Probably watched us chasing the delivery boy this afternoon and realized Sir James would be caught," Quint noted.

They had split up after dealing with Sir James in order to find Cranford. Hollister and Colton had taken the more disreputable locations Cranford had been known to frequent, while Quint and Simon had searched the clubs and West End haunts. It was after midnight, however, and failure hung over them like a dark cloud.

"Unless he's still in Paris," Colton said. "There's no way to know for sure. I've been hunting him for weeks. If he were in London, I would have smelled a whiff of him by now."

"Not necessarily," Quint said, lowering his cup and saucer to the table. "He could be languishing in an opium den for all we know."

"And still managing to pull Sir James's strings? No, I do not believe so." Simon stood up to stretch his legs, his mind turning over to find a solution. "What do we do now?" he asked no one in particular.

The room remained silent until Quint said, "Tell me again what Cranford said to Maggie in Paris?"

Simon rubbed his temples and tried to remember all Maggie had told him. It had taken some persuasion to get the full story from her several days after the fact. "She asked him to reveal himself and he refused, telling her he would do so in good time. He admitted he knew her to be Lemarc, and also told her that I would use her."

"I stand by my hypothesis that this is personal about you, Winchester," Quint said. "And those remarks only confirm it. What does Cranford have against you?"

Simon shrugged. He never had understood it himself.

"Nothing from school or university that I recall," Colton said. "Cranford was a few years older than us and I hardly remember him."

"That day, at Brooks's, you looked ready to throttle Cranford," Quint said to Simon. "What did he say to make you so angry?"

Simon had mostly forgotten that conversation. "He warned me away from Maggie—veiled as friendly concern, of course—and poked fun at Sir James." At the sideboard, he poured a fresh glass of claret.

"What doesn't fit is the attack on the girl at Madame Hartley's," Quint said. "Cranford is a thief and a liar. A swindler. He doesn't strike me as a murderer."

"He did attack Maggie during her debut," Simon pointed out. "Made advances and got rough when she rebuffed him."

"I want to talk to Maggie," Quint said, coming to his feet. "Perhaps she can recall something more about what Cranford said on the balcony."

Though the hour was late, Maggie found herself strangely awake when the duchess departed. The guard remained at the front door, and the idea that she was a prisoner in her own home made her edgy and restless. She decided to return to her studio.

After dismissing Tilda, she climbed the stairs to her haven, a lantern in hand to light her way. The studio dark, she took a moment to light several lamps around the room. When she finished, a shadow in the corner caught her eye. Maggie turned and strained to see if something lurked there.

Just as she took a step closer to investigate, a form emerged from the blackness. She froze in horror as the light slowly revealed Lord Cranford's face.

His expression was chilling, with dark eyes glittering in her direction. Maggie bit back a gasp. "Wh-what are you doing here?" she choked while edging away.

"Am I not invited? I thought this was one of your infamous parties."

"You are never invited here for any reason." She flicked a glance toward the only door. Unfortunately he stood closer to it.

"Thinking of running?" He shook his head. "You'll never make it in time. Though I would enjoy subduing you."

A shiver flew down her spine. She thought of Cora, the girl from Madame Hartley's that had nearly been killed. Was Cranford capable of such brutality? He had been rough that night in the Lockheed gardens, but he hadn't hit or injured her. Still, the possibility of violence kept her from lunging for the door.

She raised her chin. "Perhaps I'll scream. The entire house will come to my aid."

His arm shifted, materializing from behind his back. A small pistol now pointed at her. "You may try, but I cannot believe it worth your life. Especially since you shall want to hear what I have to say. Do have a seat, Maggie."

Maggie slowly lowered onto a small wooden stool, casting subtle glances for a weapon in the vicinity. Her studio was tidy, however, and nothing lay within reach but a lead pencil. When Cranford shifted to lock the door, she snatched the pencil and concealed it in her skirts before he spun around.

He moved toward her, his black trousers and ruby-red topcoat a strangely civilized contrast to the sneer he sported. She vowed silently to remain calm, not to allow him to frighten her. Drawing in deep breaths, she kept her gaze trained on his face. "You do not want to do this," she told him. "It's a mistake."

He stopped a few feet away, his right eye twitching slightly. "Do you toss your skirts up whenever he crooks his spoiled, privileged finger? Spread your legs and let him plow you to his heart's content, like a whore would? Is that what you are for him?"

God, he was talking about Simon. She forced down the revulsion at Cranford's crude words. "So this is about Winchester?"

"Why him? I've never understood it. You rebuffed me and yet jumped into his bed at the first opportunity."

"You were betrothed to my friend!" Not to mention

it had always been Simon for her, since the first time his brilliant blue eyes shined down at her.

"He cannot have everything! Why should they have it all?" Nostrils flared, he took a few deep breaths as if he were struggling to get back under control.

They? "Winchester's family, you mean?"

"He and every other privileged, spoiled man with a title. They do *nothing* but roll around in money they did not earn. Wagers, gaming hells, boxing matches . . . they throw it away like crumbs."

"But you are a viscount. You have—"

"Debt. I have a crumbling estate not worth the paper it's printed on. I've had to scrape and suffer, marry a woman I detested just for her dowry. But I will get mine." He gestured to her with the pistol. "That, my dear, is where you come in."

Mind reeling, she clenched her hands tightly in order to stay focused. "What do you mean to do?"

"My mistake was in trusting Sir James. The man is a buffoon. But you, however . . ." His mouth curved. "I should have used you right from the start. He'll do anything you ask, won't he?"

Sir James? What was he talking about? She gripped the pencil, praying it would be enough when the time came. "Not any longer. We are no longer . . . close."

He gave her a peevish look. "Please. Do not waste my time with lies. I've seen him with you, seen the way he watches you. God, you should have seen his face when I showed him those letters all those years ago! He truly believed you'd written them. I nearly pissed myself with joy."

"I thought this was about money," she blurted. "Or do you derive pleasure from ruining the lives of others?"

"Everything is about money—in this case the money I've worked damn hard to get. I've been forced to cozy up to Sir James for years just to bilk the Winchester estate of thousands of pounds." He grinned. "Ruining lives is merely an additional benefit."

She narrowed her eyes on him. "As you ruined Cora's?"

He blinked, confusion lining his forehead. "Cora?"

"The girl from Madame Hartley's."

"I know of no one named Cora," he said, taken aback, and Maggie believed him. "I've never cheated one of Hartley's girls."

So another man was responsible for the attack on Cora. Madame Hartley had been wrong. Maggie filed that away for later. "I will not help you steal money from Winchester."

"Oh, you will, madam. Or I will expose you as Lemarc to everyone in London."

Maggie froze as the pieces fell into place. Cranford was the blackmailer. God, would she never be rid of this man? "How did you learn I was Lemarc?"

"Followed you. And everyone else will find out if you do not help me."

"You wouldn't dare. It's your only hold over me."

"Wrong," he said with a sneer. "If you do not help me, I'll ruin you. Again. So before you say no, think of your sister's reputation. Think of your livelihood. Think of Winchester's family and his brilliant political career," he finished with a high drama Henri would envy.

She would never steal from Simon or abuse his trust in such a devious manner—even if it meant ruination once more. Besides, her sister had been the one to encourage Maggie to reveal herself as Lemarc; the likelihood of scandal had not concerned Becca in the least. And since Maggie and Simon were finished, any disgrace she endured would not affect him.

"Go ahead and do it, then. I'll not help you." She rose, still hiding the pencil in her skirts. "You're a coward and a thief, Cranford, and everyone in London will soon know it."

His face slackened, as if he couldn't believe she had refused. The hand holding the pistol wobbled. "You would not dare. You shall be imprisoned for those drawings."

She no longer cared. Without Simon, nothing else mattered. "I might, yes. At the very least, I hope they allow me a pencil."

He blinked and his gaze slid away as he tried to regroup. Sensing this was her moment, she lunged forward, pencil raised, and aimed for his shoulder or neck—any vulnerability at which she could strike to aid in her escape.

Her skirts rustled, betraying her movements, and his head snapped up in time to see her coming. He hadn't a chance to aim the pistol at her, however, and the force of her body knocked it from his hands, the weapon clattering to the floor. Her pencil hit the flesh of his shoulder and he yelped, shoving her hard with both hands to send her careening back into the wooden table. The impact knocked the breath from her lungs and she watched, helpless, as Cranford lifted a nearby burning lamp and hurled it into a stack of paintings and empty canvases.

"No!" she cried. With horror, she saw the lamp crash open, kerosene spilling, and the reaction was instantaneous. Flames erupted and engulfed the canvases, burning them at an alarming rate. Her heart raced. Fire was every painter's biggest fear, considering the mineral spirits and oil of turpentine so necessary in every studio.

Movement caught her eye. She turned to find that Cranford had retrieved his pistol and was leveling it at her once more. The flames leapt higher and the acrid smoke from the burning oily rags seared her eyes. Cranford pulled the trigger, but the pistol misfired, and the heat pushed him back. He turned to the door and she knew she had mere moments before the cleaning fluids succumbed to the blaze and all was lost. The resulting explosion was sure to level the room and leave her no hope for escape. Maggie sprinted for the door, but Cranford was faster. He slipped into the corridor, and slammed the door shut before Maggie could reach it.

Just as her hands touched the wood, she heard him lock it from the outside. "Let me out!" she screamed, pounding on the flat surface. "Let me out! I won't tell anyone, I promise. Just do not let me die in here!" She kept beating, her fists aching, yelling for him, Tilda, or anyone who might be within earshot. With all her strength, she threw her body against the partition—and met naught but resistance. "Damnation!" she cursed.

Looking around, Maggie realized with horror that more than half the room was already ablaze. The fire was mere inches from her solvents, and black smoke billowed toward the ceiling, burning her lungs with every breath. She knew she had a scant few minutes, if not seconds, to live.

She went to the row of windows and swallowed hard. Jumping down meant certain death. She looked up at the window in the ceiling but knew immediately it was of no help. Even if she could reach it, the sliver of an opening was too small to crawl through. She coughed, hardly able to breathe, and realized she had one choice. Quickly, she climbed out on the thin ledge that ran beneath the windows. It was no deeper than the length of her foot, so she flattened herself against the house as best she could, her nails digging into the stucco. *Do not look down. . . . Do not look down.*

Still worried about the imminent explosion, Maggie searched for a path to safety. Inching along the ledge carefully, she made her way to the side of the town house as quickly as possible. She'd never been happier that the town houses were so close together in London. Drawing in a deep breath, she leaped across the small divide to the adjacent building's corresponding ledge.

When she landed, her feet wobbled and, heart in her throat, she clutched the building to steady herself. After a harrowing few seconds, she gained her balance and exhaled in relief. She pressed her face to the surface, so grateful she could nearly kiss the building.

Her troubles were not over, however; if her studio exploded, this house could very well go up in flames as well. It was imperative to reach the ground as quickly as possible.

Chapter Twenty-One

The moment he alighted from the carriage, Simon knew something was wrong. There was an eerie stillness to the night and a strange odor—

"Do you smell smoke?" Quint asked, sniffing the air.

Simon's heart stopped. He had no idea of knowing which house was on fire, but painters frequently used flammable substances. If the fire was anywhere near Maggie's studio, the entire building could go up in a flash.

"Look there." Colton pointed. "Smoke in the back."

Sure enough, plumes of black-gray smoke wafted from the rear of Maggie's town house. "Oh, Christ," Simon said and took off at a run toward her front door. "Colton, rouse the fire brigade!"

He threw open the door and raced in, Quint on his heels. The acrid smell, now decidedly worse inside, hit his nose. Was the fire in one of the bedrooms? The kitchens? He had to find Maggie as quickly as possible.

Blood roaring in his ears, he flew to the stairs, taking

the steps two at a time. Just as he hit the landing, Quint yelled, "Watch out!"

Simon spun to see a disheveled Lord Cranford leap out from behind a corner and heard the unmistakable crack of a pistol. He ducked, covering his head. A body hit the ground, and Simon whirled to see Quint on the carpet, clutching his neck. Blood welled from beneath the viscount's fingertips.

Before Simon could help Quint, Cranford put a hand to the balustrade and vaulted over it, landing on the stairs below. Simon sprinted and gave chase, leaping over Quint's prone body to reach the steps. Acting on pure instinct, he sprung off the top step, catching Cranford's shoulders and knocking him off his feet. The two tumbled and slid down the staircase, Simon using his larger frame to advantage, directing most of the punishment of the fall at Cranford.

When they finally hit the bottom, Cranford didn't move. His eyes were open and he seemed to be gasping for breath. Simon shook him roughly. "Where is she?"

Colton appeared through the front door. "Flames are coming from the top floor in the back. Fitz is fetching the brigade. I'll handle this bastard. Go, Winchester!"

"Quint's been shot," Simon shouted. "He's on the landing. Get him to safety first and then send a groom for a doctor. Cranford is in no shape to do us any more harm."

Simon raced back up the stairs, now thinking only of Maggie. On the landing, he saw Maggie's servant hurrying down from the upper floors. "My lord! I cannot get in to her studio," the woman said. "The door's locked and the heat is something awful in there."

"Is there another way in?"

"The roof!" the woman said urgently. "There's a vent on the roof!"

Simon started toward her. "How do I get up there?"

"There's a door at the top of the servants' stairs. Follow me, my lord."

By the time Simon stood atop the studio, he was forced to hold the air in his lungs and squint through the thick clouds of smoke. His panic doubled when he realized neither of them could fit through the small opening. How in the hell would he get her out? He kicked at the window and screamed to be heard above the roar of the fire.

"Maggie! Can you hear me?" He heard no response and feared the worst. He ran to the edge of the roof and bent over to look for another way into the burning studio. Startled, he saw a figure clutching the front of the neighboring town house. His knees nearly buckled. *Oh, thank God.* "Maggie!"

He could see her lips moving, knew she was yelling, but couldn't hear a thing over the roar of the fire. She began waving her hands, indicating he should move away. All he cared about was getting to her.

He retreated a few steps, drove his legs full speed, and leapt across to the adjoining flat roof. Once he landed, he hurried to the edge and leaned down. She tilted her head to look at him. With her hair disheveled, and soot on her face and clothing, she'd never appeared more beautiful. His chest pulled tight, he called, "Are you hurt?"

She shook her head, panic etched into her delicate

features. "The window is locked. I cannot get inside! Hurry, Simon."

He straightened and quickly located the door to the inside—and kicked it with all his might. The wood splintered and another few heavy blows gained him entrance. He navigated the stairs and the top floor until he spotted Maggie through a bedchamber window.

Seconds later, he lifted the sash and was reaching for her. Once her feet hit the floor, Simon dragged her into his arms. "My God, woman. You gave me a—"

She pushed him away roughly. "No time for that. Fire. Solvents. Explosion. Move!" She shoved him toward the hall.

Simon grabbed her hand and raced out of the room. As they continued toward the ground, they yelled of a fire to alert anyone who may be within the town house. They were halfway down the main stairs when a crashing thunder echoed, shaking the building, and Simon tugged her more firmly to the street.

They flew out the front door and onto the walk. Chaos had ensued. It seemed all of Mayfair had lined up along Charles Street, not to mention that the fire brigade had arrived. Men were shouting and giving orders while others struggled to keep the throng of people at bay. The pump poured water toward Maggie's house—to little effect. The flames had engulfed the interior of every floor, and Simon cringed at each *snap* and *pop* of burning furniture or timber. Maggie might still be inside, if not for her quick thinking.

Maggie began striding toward her house, but Simon put a hand on her arm. Ignoring her surprise, he enveloped her into a tight embrace. He could feel her body trembling against his own. "You nearly scared the life out of me, Mags," he whispered into her soot-covered hair. "Try not to ever do that again."

She gave a weary chuckle and squeezed him. "I shall try, Simon. Now let me go see to my staff."

"And I need to look in on Quint," he said grimly.

"Quint? Why?"

"Cranford shot him."

She gasped, turned, and began pushing her way through the crowd on the street, leaving him to follow. When they found Tilda, he learned that Quint had been taken to a neighboring house, with the doctor having arrived moments earlier. He pulled Maggie aside before leaving to check on his friend.

"I fear your house may not make it." He wiped a black smudge off her cheek with his thumb.

"I fear you are correct." She raised a brow. "I wonder why you seem pleased by that information."

"First, everything lost can be replaced. That you are safe is what matters. And second"—he leaned to her ear—"I'm smiling because I happen to know where you'll be sleeping tonight."

The heat stung Maggie's eyes, the air so hot she could scarcely breathe. Panic and smoke filled her lungs. She fought her way up off the floor, struggling to avoid the flames—but they moved too fast. She couldn't get away—it was as if her legs were stuck in treacle.

She screamed for help.

"Maggie, wake up!"

Maggie awoke with a start, a gentle hand shaking her shoulder. Sweat trickled down her brow and she was gasping, every muscle clenched. *A dream,* she told herself. It had only been a dream. She was out of the fire, alive.

"Maggie, are you all right?"

She turned and found the Duchess of Colton at her shoulder. "Fine. Just a bad dream," she rasped. Her throat was still sore from the soot and smoke. Julia seemed to understand and helped Maggie take a sip from the glass of water on the table.

"I hated to wake you," Julia was saying, "but you were thrashing about and moaning. I grew worried."

Maggie swallowed and relaxed into the pillows. Bright sunlight peeked through the unfamiliar draperies. True to his word, Simon had insisted on bringing her to Barrett House early this morning. The fire had waned by dawn and there had been little left for her to do. Cranford, it turned out, had died from the fall down the stairs. So Simon had seen to both the constables and to Quint, who had been shot in the neck. The injury turned out to be a minor one, thank heaven. The ball had torn through the soft tissue and missed anything vital.

"Where is Simon?" she asked Julia.

"He went to see someone. He sent for me so that you would not be alone."

"How is Quint?"

"Recovering. He'll be as good as new in a few weeks, apparently."

"That is a relief. If anyone had died . . ."

"I know, my dear." She smoothed Maggie's hair off her forehead. "We were all terribly worried about you. Would you care for chocolate? Tea? Toast? I'll send down for whatever you'd like."

"Chocolate and toast, please."

Julia rose, went to the door, and spoke to someone in the corridor. When she returned, Maggie asked, "Did Simon tell you Cranford was not the one responsible for Cora's attack?"

"Yes. Which means whoever did it could still hurt someone else."

"Yes, precisely." Maggie stretched, the lingering effects of the nightmare waning. "I wonder who Simon needed to see so early. I should think he would still be abed as well."

Julia glanced down, not meeting Maggie's eyes, as she smoothed her skirts. "He went to see the Home Secretary."

"The Home Secretary? At this hour?"

"He wanted to clear up this business about Lemarc. Though I don't see how he can, without admitting the blackmail scheme or turning the artist over—both of which he already said he would not do."

Maggie sat up straighter, her stomach dropping. "So what will he say?"

"He's hoping his word will be enough. That once he promises the cartoons will stop and that Lemarc is not attempting to inflame the masses into revolt, the investigation will cease."

"How can he do so without drawing attention to his association with Lemarc?"

Julia pressed her lips together. "He cannot, obviously. He plans to admit knowledge of the artist's identity—without naming you, of course."

"What? But that is . . ." *Stupid* was the kindest word Maggie thought to use.

"Yes. I told him it was unwise," Julia said, reading her mind. "But he said better the suspicion rest on his own head than over yours."

Maggie closed her eyes. *Oh, no.* To align himself with an artist accused of seditious activity would destroy all of his standing in Parliament. Heavens, forget his political career; he'd be lucky not to be brought up on charges himself.

She had to do something. Her mind raced to come up with a solution, a way that Simon need not shoulder the blame. This was all Cranford's fault. If he were still alive, she'd kick him. She inhaled sharply, a thought striking her.

Cranford . . . Yes, that made sense. Perhaps there was a way to use him after all.

Struggling, she sat up and threw the bedclothes off. "Julia, help me dress. I need to get to Mrs. McGinnis quickly."

"We find ourselves in an awkward position, Winchester."

Henry Addington, Viscount Sidmouth, leaned back and steepled his fingers thoughtfully. In his early sixties, Sidmouth currently held the position of Home Secretary, leader of the Home Office—the group calling for Lemarc's head on a well-polished salver. "These cartoons are quite dangerous."

Simon had traveled to White Lodge, the viscount's residence in Richmond Park, where he'd waited for over an hour in the hopes of seeing Sidmouth. He'd rather be at home, in bed with Maggie, but the sedition situation was too critical to put off.

Earlier in the week, Home Office representatives had once again visited Mrs. McGinnis and frightened the shop owner in another attempt to learn Lemarc's identity. So he needed to convince the Crown that

Lemarc hadn't drawn the seditious cartoons as well as reassure them the person responsible had been dealt with. Perhaps then the investigation would be withdrawn.

"And as you know, we take threats of sedition seriously, especially after Peterloo. These cartoons demonstrate why the Six Acts are so instrumental in preserving peace in the realm," Sidmouth said, referring to the laws that prohibited perceived treasonous or seditious actions.

"Inciting seditious behavior was not the artist's intent," Simon said, smoothly. "Nevertheless, I have it on good authority the cartoons of this kind will cease." Simon did not want to go into too much detail, even though his brother-in-law hardly deserved protection. But his mother and sister would suffer if the blackmail and forging scheme were revealed, not to mention that any subsequent investigation might lead to Maggie's identity. Keeping the story vague would suit all involved, he reasoned.

"I find that interesting. Are you acquainted with the artist, perhaps?"

This was the slippery spot. "In a roundabout way. We have a mutual acquaintance."

Sidmouth stroked his chin. "Not the artist's intent, you say. So what was his intent?"

"What does any artist want? To gain notoriety. To increase sales."

"Are you prepared to tell me this artist's name?"

"No. I've given my word to keep his confidence. But he has promised to stick to more appropriate subject matter in the future."

Sidmouth did not care for that answer. His long face pulled into a frown and he stared out the window.

After a fashion, he said, "I quite liked your father, Winchester. He was a good man. I know you've had the responsibility from a young age, and by all accounts you've done a fine job with it, but this situation creates a bit of a dilemma for me. I've made promises, you see; that I would bring down Lemarc. Make an example of him. Can't very well do that if you won't tell me who the blackguard is." He pinned Simon with a hard stare. "Isn't you, is it?"

"No, indeed." He held the man's gaze. "I am not Lemarc."

"And there's no chance you'll turn him over, is there?"

"Absolutely none, I'm afraid."

"Are you prepared for the repercussions of withholding that information from me?"

"Yes, sir."

Sidmouth sighed. "I had such high hopes for you, Winchester. Your family has done much for shaping the laws—"

A knock on the door interrupted them. The butler entered, offered Sidmouth a note on a salver. "My lord, this was just delivered. I am told it is urgent."

"Excuse me, Winchester." Sidmouth tore open the correspondence, his eyes rounding at the contents. He looked up at Simon. "Well, this conversation appears unnecessary. They've found Lemarc."

Chapter Twenty-Two

The drawing room door burst open just as Maggie slid another canvas into a crate. She glanced up and watched as a windblown—but otherwise incredibly handsome—Earl of Winchester sailed into the room. Buff-colored breeches, tall boots, and a dark blue top-coat showed off his lean and powerful frame. Her heart stuttered then squeezed, her chest knotting with regret and grief.

Simon braced his booted feet and placed his hands on his hips. "I do not know whether to kiss you or take you over my knee, you foolish, foolish woman."

She couldn't stop herself from muttering, "Am I allowed to say which I'd prefer?"

He shook his head. "It is not amusing, Maggie. I nearly died of apoplexy when Sidmouth announced they'd found Lemarc. I swear, the news shaved ten years off my life."

"I can certainly relate, considering how I felt when I learned you'd gone to speak on Lemarc's behalf to the Crown. What were you thinking?"

"I was thinking of saving your terrifically appealing backside, madam."

"While throwing away your standing in Parliament? I could not allow you to do that. This way is preferable. Cranford loses and everyone else wins. Are you not always telling me how much you like to win?"

He did not answer, instead asking, "Tell me, how did you manage to turn Cranford into Lemarc?"

"I retrieved some of the Lemarc pieces from Mrs. McGinnis, which I took, along with various art supplies, to his residence. With his wife in the country and the servants dismissed, the place was a tomb. Julia and Lady Sophia helped me. Sophia's lock-picking skills are impressive, in case you were wondering."

Simon glanced heavenward. "I was not wondering, no. I vow, the three of you will be the death of me."

He exhaled and crossed to where she stood. A large hand rose to gently cup her cheek, tenderness shining in the blue depths of his eyes. "You've given away Lemarc after you worked so hard to achieve success. Cranford will be lauded as one of the great artists of the day."

"No." She stepped back, putting distance between them. "He will be considered a radical. Likely all his work will be confiscated and burned, no matter the subject."

"I cannot stand by and watch your work destroyed. How can you bear it?"

Because I love you more than I need to be Lemarc. She forced a shrug and continued to pack up her new canvases. "You can do nothing, Simon. Leave it be."

When she did not respond, he seemed to finally take notice of his surroundings. "Are these new supplies to replace what you lost in the fire?"

Maggie nodded. She'd had Simon's staff pick up a small number of things this afternoon while she was at Cranford's town house, just enough to get her by until she settled somewhere.

Simon scratched his neck thoughtfully. "Then why are you packing it up, including the supplies and blank canvases?"

"I cannot stay here." She had dreaded this part. Steeling herself, she faced him. "I am leaving London. It's past time, I think."

His jaw fell open. "Leaving? Are you . . . I'm afraid I don't understand." He drew closer, his skin growing visibly paler as realization dawned. "Tell me you do not mean to leave me as well."

Maggie cleared her throat in an attempt to ease the tightness there. "There will always be another Cranford, someone—"

"No," he barked. "Absolutely not."

"Simon, be reasonable. Someone will try to discover the identity of my sobriquet, whatever I choose to use. The threat will never truly go away."

"So do not use a sobriquet. Use your real name—or the Countess of Winchester, if you like." He crossed his arms over his chest, stern and unhappy. "Do not run from me, Maggie. I'll not let you go."

The Countess of Winchester? He couldn't possibly mean it. For a man of his position to be married to a sensational artist would bring nothing but embarrassment and shame. Not to mention she'd no longer have the freedom to paint and draw as she pleased . . . would she? No husband would allow raunchy political cartoons and half-naked mermaid chalk drawings.

"Whereby I must paint bowls of fruit and flowers?"

His brows lowered, lines etching his forehead. "Is that your concern, that I'll try to tame you into someone respectable?" When she didn't answer, he laughed softly. "Darling, if you want to paint nude frescos on the ceiling at St. Paul's, I'll go and speak with the archbishop. I could not be prouder of your talent. As long as it's not of me or our family, I'll never tell you what you can or cannot do."

She nibbled her lip, trying to decide if she believed him. Did he want her badly enough to lie? He admittedly hated to lose, the silver-tongued devil.

"If you like, I'll have it written into the marriage contract. 'The countess is allowed to paint and draw whatever she damn well pleases.'"

"You will?"

"Without hesitation, if that's what it takes."

She felt a burst of warm relief until she remembered all the rest of it. "My art is the least of our problems. My reputation—"

"I do not care a whit what the gossips say. Have your parties at Barrett House. And if you want to leave London, fine. We'll live at Winchester Towers—or in Paris. It matters not to me as long as we're together."

"But all your work in Parliament—I cannot ask you to give that up."

"Maggie, in case you've forgotten, I was ready to give it up a few hours ago when I went to see Sidmouth. I promise you, nothing is more important to me than you."

The strength of his conviction, unwavering and honest, seeped into her, an overwhelming feeling of happiness and love that brought tears to her

eyes. God, she hated to cry. But everything inside her
welled up, a joy so profound she could not bear it.
Before she knew it, he'd pulled her into his arms.

"I love you, you maddening, exquisite woman.
Whatever I must do to keep you happy, I'll do it.
Gladly." He buried his nose in her hair, inhaled. "Just
never leave me."

His warmth surrounded her, the security and acceptance she'd searched for her whole life in this one
embrace. She knew then she could never give it up,
never give him up. She sagged into him, melted into
his tall frame. Her arms wrapped around his waist,
and she felt him relax.

"I'll make you a terrible wife."

"You won't. You'll be exasperating, kind, loving,
and strong. The one thing you'll never be is boring,
which is more than fine with me. Does this mean you
agree to marry me?"

She almost said yes, but there were a few things still
to work out first. Leaning back, she attempted to
appear serious. "Will you build me a studio on the top
floor, as I had in my old house?"

"Yes. All that's there now is the nursery, which we
can move to another floor. What else?"

"Will you allow me to paint your portrait?" She
knew the ideal pose—one from the night where he'd
pleasured himself—and her cheeks turned hot.

He narrowed his eyes suspiciously as his lips curved.
"Is this a salacious sort of portrait, you minx?"

"If I am going to paint you, then it must be how I
see you."

He chuckled and glanced heavenward as if she

tried his patience. "You may only paint me fully clothed, Maggie."

"Why? It would only be for me, I promise. No one else would ever see it."

"You never know what will happen to such a picture. It could end up in the wrong hands. Besides, you may see a more realistic and intimate version of me in our chambers any time you fancy."

She tried to display the proper amount of disappointment. "You are already breaking your promise to keep me happy and we've not even married yet."

He clasped her hand and began tugging her toward the door. "Come to my chambers and I'll show you just how happy I can make you. Twice, if you ask nicely."

"Simon," she laughed. "There is still light outside."

He threw open the latch. "You are not the only one who can be scandalous, my lady."

Don't miss the first book in the Wicked Deceptions series, *The Courtesan Duchess*, available now!

And keep reading for a special sneak peek at *The Lady Hellion*, coming in June 2015 . . .

*Lady Sophia Barnes doesn't take **no** for an answer. Especially when she's roaming London's seedy underground . . . dressed as a man.*

A rabble-rouser for justice, Sophie's latest mission is to fight for the rights of the poor, the wretched— and the employees at Madame Hartley's brothel. She's not concerned about the criminals who will cross her path, for Sophie has mastered the art of deception—including the art of wearing trousers. Now her fate is in her own hands, along with a loaded gun. All she needs is instruction on how to shoot it. But only one person can help her: Lord Quint, the man who broke her heart years ago. The man she won't let destroy her again. . . .

The last thing Damien Beecham, Viscount Quint needs is an intrusion on his privacy, especially from the beautiful, exasperating woman he's never stopped wanting. A woman with a perilously absurd request, no less! For Damien is fighting a battle of his own, one he wishes to keep hidden—along with his feelings for Lady Sophia. Yet that fight is as hopeless as stopping her outlandish plan. Soon, all Quint knows for certain is that he will die trying to protect her. . . .

Chapter One

February 1820

Padding the crotch of one's trousers required a surprising amount of skill. Too big of a bulge drew attention. Too small and you risked the thing slipping down your leg.

Fortunately, Lady Sophia Barnes had enough experience to achieve the perfect balance. No one looking at her now would believe her a lady of twenty-seven, the daughter of a wealthy and powerful marquess—not dressed as she was, in gentleman's finery from head to toe.

Just as no one would believe her spare time was spent investigating matters for a class of women most Londoners did not even want to think about.

The evening, though chilly and unpleasant, had been moderately productive. As Sophie approached the hackney, the driver jumped down to open the door. Her maid, Alice, sat inside, huddled under blankets. Alice waited until the door closed before she spoke. "Well, my lady?"

Sophie knocked on the roof to signal the driver. Then she pulled a folded paper out of the pocket of her greatcoat. "No trace of Natalia, but I did find this." Beth, the girl who'd hired Sophie, was worried that ill had befallen her friend. Though Beth had now found herself a protector, Natalia still worked in a tavern near the docks, where extra coins meant taking a customer up the stairs. The two girls corresponded every week without fail, and Natalia hadn't sent word for almost a month.

Tonight, Sophie had gained access to Natalia's room and searched it. The only letter she found was in Russian.

Sophie stretched her unencumbered legs out in the small space as the carriage rumbled forth into the night. Breeches really were a spectacular invention. "I wish I knew what it said. Beth only speaks English."

"We'd need to find someone who can speak Russian, my lady."

A name came to mind. A name she tried not to think of more than five—or ten—times a day. She often failed even at that. "I do know someone who speaks Russian. Lord Quint. He gave a short lecture during a gathering at the Russian Embassy three years ago." Sophie had attended, standing in the rear of the room. She hadn't understood a word, but oh, he'd been glorious. Speaking on some recent scientific discovery, he'd commanded the attention of everyone present, even making the dour-faced Russians laugh at several points.

Alice clucked her tongue. "La, his lordship won't be speaking it for long, that's for certain."

"Whatever do you mean?"

Her sharp tone caught Alice's attention. "I thought

your ladyship knew. He's near death's door, that one. I saw one of his lordship's kitchen maids three—no, maybe four days ago. Fever's set in. His lordship won't let any of the staff tend to him and won't allow a physician in."

Sophie's stomach plummeted through the carriage floor and onto the dirty Southwark streets. No doubt Alice told the truth. The maid's network of servants would put any foreign spy service to shame. *Quint* . . . near death's door. Oh, God. She knew a bullet had grazed him that night at Maggie's house, right before the fire had swept in. But she assumed he'd recovered. Everyone had said the injury wasn't serious. Damn, if only she hadn't been so wrapped up in her own life—

Her fist banged the roof. The driver opened the small partition and Sophie barked in her low register, "Stop at the southwest corner of Berkeley Square instead." Quint lived just down the square from her father's town house so she would get out and let Alice continue on.

"What are you going to do, my lady?"

Was it not obvious? "I'm going to save him."

Alice gasped. "You cannot very well show up at his front door"—her hand waved at Sophie's attire—"dressed like that."

"Why not?"

"They'll not let a stranger inside to see him, even one dressed as a gent. And besides—"

"Do not even start lecturing me on propriety. We bid farewell to that ship eons ago, Alice. Not to worry, I'll manage a way into his house."

By the time she arrived at the servants' door of Quint's town house, Sophie had conjured a plausible story. A bleary-eyed older woman in a nightcap opened the door, a frown on her wrinkled face. "Yes?"

"I am here"—Sophie deepened her voice—"at the behest of His Grace the Duke of Colton to attend to his lordship, Viscount Quint."

The woman held up her light, looked Sophie up and down. "You're a surgeon?"

"A valet, though I do have extensive medical knowledge."

"From a duke, you say?"

Sophie lifted her chin. "Indeed. And I do not think His Grace would appreciate you leaving me on the stoop to freeze."

The woman stood aside to allow Sophie entrance. They went into the kitchens, where Sophie removed her hat and greatcoat. "Where may I find his lordship?"

"His chambers. Won't let anyone in, not even a doctor. Most the staff's already left. Figure we'll all be out on the street in a day or two."

Without another word, the woman turned and shuffled to the corridor. *Must be his cook,* Sophie thought, and followed. "Stairs," the woman mumbled, handed Sophie her lamp, and continued on.

A few wrong turns, but Sophie finally found the master apartments. Inside, the air was cold and stale, the fire left untended. Moonlight trickled in from the windows, enough to allow her to see a large shape, motionless, under the coverlet. Quint. *Please, God, let him be alive.*

She rushed over, and then nearly gasped. *Dear heavens.* His condition was worse than she'd feared. His skin was flushed, his lips cracked and swollen. His eyes were closed, blue-black smudges underneath them. Unable to breathe for the fear, she reached out to feel the side of his throat not covered with a bandage. Though his skin burned to the touch, she exhaled in relief. A pulse. Weak, but there.

She set her light on the table beside him. "Oh, Damien," she whispered, unable to resist gently smoothing the damp hair off his fevered brow. "This is what you get for eschewing a valet, you stupid man."

A strangled, pained sound came out of his throat when she checked the wound. Now red and ugly, the hole oozed when she gently poked it. He made another noise and weakly tried to shift away. At least he'd shown signs of life. Striding to the bell pull, she began a mental list of all the items she required.

Had she arrived in time, or was it too late? Ignoring the worry in her gut, she vowed not to fail. He would not die.

"Hear that, Quint?" she said loudly. "You. Will. Not. Die."

After ten minutes and many tugs on the bell, a weary, rumpled footman finally arrived. He'd clearly been asleep, but she felt absolutely no sympathy for the servants. They'd abandoned their master, which, whether he'd asked for it or not, was unacceptable as far as she was concerned. And Quint deserved better.

"Rouse every servant. Tell the cook to boil hot water. I need fresh bed linens and clean towels. Bring every medical supply in the house. And send for a physician."

"But—"

"No arguments. Your master is near death and I mean to save him, so do what I say. Now, go!"

Chapter Two

"You have a visitor, my lord."

Damien Beecham, Viscount Quint, did not bother looking up at his new butler, his attention instead focused on the rows of letters in front of him. He had to get this idea down. Now—before it was too late. "Pass on the usual response, Turner."

The butler cleared his throat. "I beg your lordship's pardon, but my name is Taylor."

Quint grimaced. He could hardly be faulted for forgetting the lad's name, could he? Taylor had only been on the job for a few days. Or was this further proof of Quint's worst fear becoming a reality?

Nearly three months since the shooting. Three months and he was no better. Oh, the wound had closed, the fever abated, yet everything else that followed had only worsened.

He exhaled and dipped his pen in the ink pot. The invocation he'd adopted these past weeks went through his head: *Remain occupied. Engage your mind while you can. Prepare for the worst.* He looked back down at his cipher. "Apologies, Taylor. No visitors. Ever. Until further notice, I am not receiving callers."

"She said your lordship might say no, and if so, I was to tell you her name—the Lady Sophia Barnes. I was also to mention she planned on coming in whether your lordship allowed it or not."

Quint felt himself frown. Sophie, here? Why? Displeasure was quickly replaced by an uncomfortable weight on his chest. He could not face anyone, most especially *her.* "No. Definitely not. Tell her—"

Before he finished his sentence, Sophie charged into the room. Smothering a curse, Quint threw down his pen, came to his feet, and snatched his topcoat off the chair back. He pulled on the garment as he bowed. "Lady Sophia."

He'd known her for years—five and three-quarters, to be precise—and each time he saw her he experienced a jolt of heady awareness. There'd never been a more remarkably remarkable woman. She had short, honey-brown hair that gleamed with hints of gold in the lamplight. Tall for a female, she had long, lean limbs that moved with purpose, with confidence. Her nose and upper cheeks were dusted with freckles that shifted when she laughed—which was often. People fell under the spell of that laugh, himself included.

"Lord Quint, thank you for seeing me." Holding her bonnet, she bobbed a curtsy in an attempt to give the impression of a proper young lady. No one who knew this particular daughter of a marquess would ever believe it, however. She and Julia Seaton, the Duchess of Colton, were close friends, and the two of them had landed in one absurd scrape after another over the years. Last he'd heard, the two had required rescuing from a gaming hell after a brawl erupted.

"As if I'd had a choice," he said dryly.

She laughed, not offended in the least, and Quint noticed Taylor, mouth agape, hovering near the threshold, eyes trained on Sophie. Good God. Not that Quint hadn't experienced the same reaction in Sophie's presence a time or two. "That'll be all, Taylor. Leave the door ajar, will you?"

The butler nodded and retreated, cracking the heavy door for propriety. Ridiculous, really, when the entire visit was already deuced improper. "I hope you at least brought a maid, Sophie."

"Of course I did. She's in the entryway, likely planning to flirt with that baby you call a butler." Her lips twisted into a familiar impish half-smile. Once, she had given him that smile, leaned into him, and parted her lips . . . right before he'd kissed her.

The memory nearly distracted him from the fact that he didn't want anyone in the house. Bad enough he had to keep the staff. "I am not receiving callers," he told her. "And this is not going to help your reputation."

She waved her hand. "No one worries over a spinster nearing thirty years of age. Now, shall we sit?"

He happened to know she was only twenty-seven, but no use quibbling with her. He glanced about. Books, papers, and various mechanical parts littered every surface. Not to mention there were the three heavy medical volumes on his desk—all on mental deficiencies. With rapid flicks of his wrist, he closed each one and moved the stack to the floor behind his desk. He then came around and cleared a chair for Sophie.

"Thank you." She lowered gracefully into the seat and arranged herself, bonnet in her lap. "I apologize for barging in. Your butler did try to turn me away, but I haven't been able to locate you elsewhere. You've become something of a recluse."

Better a recluse than a trip to an asylum. He sat in his desk chair and said, "I have been occupied."

A tawny eyebrow rose. "So occupied you missed the opening lecture at the Royal Society last Tuesday?"

"I had a conflict," he offered, lamely.

"A conflict? With what? You've never missed one of the opening lectures before. Not in recent memory, at least."

He tried not to react, though he wanted to grit his teeth. "I did not realize my schedule was your concern."

She sighed. "Oh, dear. I've upset you already—and I haven't even arrived at the purpose of my visit."

"Meaning that learning the purpose will only upset me further?"

"Yes, I daresay you shall not approve, but I've nowhere else to turn."

"Why do I feel a pressing need to close the door before you speak?"

She shot to her feet, so Quint started to rise as well. "No," she said. "Please, stay seated. I think more clearly when I am standing up."

Reluctantly, Quint lowered. He had no idea what she wanted, but with Sophie it could be nearly anything.

Whatever her troubles, Quint did not care. Could not care. A healthy distance between himself and others must be maintained, especially with anyone who'd known him before the accident. Therefore, he'd hear her out and then show her to the door.

He waited as she traveled the study floor, slapping her bonnet against her thigh. Nervous, clearly. Her dress was both expensive and flattering, yet her boots were worn. No jewels. A practical woman underneath the trappings of a lady.

Interesting.

And he hated that he still found her interesting, even after she'd so thoroughly rebuffed him more than three years ago.

"What in God's name is *that*?" She pointed to an abandoned teacup on the desk.

He shot up and grabbed the forgotten porcelain container, which held a greenish-brown gelatinous mixture comprised of various herbs and spices. It looked every bit as terrible as it had tasted. He set it inside his desk drawer.

"Why are you here, Sophie?"

She folded her arms over her chest, a motion that called attention to her small, enticing breasts. He forced his eyes away as she spoke. "I would normally approach Colton or Lord Winchester with this request, but as you know, they are both unavailable. You are the only person I can ask."

"Your flattery overwhelms, madam."

She stopped and pinned him with a hard stare. "I did not mean to offend you, as you well know. Stop being obdurate."

"Fine. I readily acknowledge I am to serve as the last resort. Pray, get it out, Sophie."

She straightened her shoulders, lifted her chin. "I need you to serve as my second."